SERVANT OF THE GODS SERIES
BOOK TWO

THE
LABYRINTHINE
JOURNEY

LUCIANA CAVALLARO

MYTHOS PUBLICATIONS
PERTH AUSTRALIA

ALSO BY LUCIANA CAVALLARO

Accursed Women: A Collection of Short Stories

Servant of the Gods Series
Search for the Golden Serpent

THE LABYRINTHINE JOURNEY

Mythos Publications
PO Box 7120
Karawara 6152 WA
Australia
www.luccav.com

Publisher's Note: This is a work of fiction. Names, characters, places, and incidents are a product of the author's imagination. Locales and public names are sometimes used for atmospheric purposes. Any re-semblance to actual people, living or dead, or to businesses, companies, events, institutions, or locales is completely coincidental.

Cover artwork, layout and interior design: Scarlett Rugers Design

Ordering Information:
Quantity sales. Special discounts are available on quantity purchases by corporations, associations, and others. For details, contact the "Special Sales Department" at the address above.

The Labyrinthine Journey/ Luciana Cavallaro. -- 1st ed.
ISBN 978-0-9874737-7-6

This book is dedicated to you, my wonderful and supportive reader

and

To my Yr 7 Humanities class of 2017 at PLC, Perth

'We are to study not only the origins of society,
but also society when it enjoys the luxuries of civilisation.
Not a bad idea, perhaps,
for in the process we may discover how justice and injustice
are bred in a community.'

PLATO, THE REPUBLIC

CHAPTER ONE

Evan checked the contents of the wagon. He was impressed with the king of Pylos, who true to his word, had loaded the cart with food, blankets and jugs of wine and water. Standing nearby, were four of the king's warriors, armed with swords, spears and embossed bronze shields, their gazes as steely and unyielding as a concrete wall.

Evan stepped back from the wagon, and indicated to Phameas, his swarthy Phoenician friend, and Dexion, a Sicilian boy thin in stature with a unique ability to foresee the future, to do the same. As they moved to the front of the cart, King Mentor emerged from the royal private residence flanked by two of his personal guards. The king bowed before the High Priestess, the expression on his face mixed with wonder and reverence when he looked up at her. Evan gritted his teeth and wondered how much more he had to endure of being stuck in the sixth century BCE before he could go home, back to the twenty-first century. Phameas elbowed him in the ribs, disrupting his dour musings, and Evan watched the king fawn over the High Priestess. She reminded Evan of the austere nuns who wore black habits, their heads covered with black and white-trimmed headdresses.

'My men will take you as far as Mount Ithomi, the border with Messene, where they will leave you to continue on your quest,' the king said in his deep baritone voice. 'The Messenians are wary of soldiers from other city-states entering their territory. Once you have crossed into Messene, head to Tegea, then proceed to Corinth, and from there, trek to Mount Parnassos, the home of Delphi.' He clicked his fingers. A hunched-over man and dressed in a brown khiton, scurried to the king's side, and with trembling, gnarled hands gave him a scroll. 'I had my scribe draw you a map with the roads to take.'

At Phameas' encouragement, Evan moved to take the proffered parchment from the king. 'Thank you, King Mentor, this will help a great deal.'

'We are grateful for your thoughtfulness and generosity,' said the High Priestess.

'It is I who am forever indebted for the gift from the Mother Goddess, and to you for showing me the true path,' the king said. He walked over to the cart. 'There is enough food and drink for the journey to Delphi. I am not sure where your search will take you afterwards, but if you happen to come this way, you are welcomed guests.'

The High Priestess gave a nod. 'We are honoured, King Mentor.'

Evan stowed the map in his bag and set about assisting the High Priestess when Hektor brushed past him and helped her onto the wagon.

'Master Evandros, may I sit on the back?' Dexion asked, tugging at his khiton. Evan drew in a deep breath and reined in his temper, resisting the urge to punch Hektor's gloating face as the barrel-chested Atlantean turned his back and stood with Leander.

'Of course you can.' Evan picked up the eleven-year-old boy and lifted him onto the wagon.

Evan glanced over at the kind-hearted Atlantean, Leander, who waited until the High Priestess and Dexion were settled in their seats, and then coaxed the mule into moving. Homer, at seven foot and broad-shouldered, stood in front of Evan, blocking his view of the cart. He wrote on his wax tablet.

I am proud of you.

'Thanks, Homer, but Hektor needs to change his behaviour towards me or I will not hold back,' Evan growled.

The king's guards assigned to Evan and his six companions led the way out of the palace grounds, and down the ramp. The road flanked the outskirts of the city and around the base of the palace. The guards veered right, away from the Akropolis and out onto a stretch of road that bisected the sandy plains. Scrub trees and tufts of grass sprouted from the ground, making the area resemble a chessboard.

Evan, Phameas, and Homer followed the wagon, while Hektor and Leander walked alongside the mule. No one spoke and Evan didn't feel the urge to talk. Instead he preferred the sound of sandaled feet slapping against the crude road and the squeak and groan of the heavy load of the cart to fill the void. Evan's mind drifted to his life in the twenty-first century and his profession as an architect. He tried to determine if there had been any telltale signs while he was growing up that indicated he was from this time period. There were pictures of him as a baby, held by his mother and father, and many subsequent photos from his childhood through to his teen and adult years. If he was from this century, how could there be evidence of his life in the future? And what of this existence? What proof was there to suggest he was even born in this period?

'See that line of trees a few stades ahead?' A warrior had dropped back and spoke to the High Priestess, disturbing his musings. 'We're going to stop there for a rest before continuing.'

Evan looked over his shoulder and was surprised by how far they had travelled. The Akropolis and the palace were mere specks on the horizon. What he'd give for a car or a motorcycle right now. And a pair of sneakers! He felt every rock, grain of sand and dip in the road under the thin leather soles of the sandals. No cushioning or comfort. In the summertime, as a child, he had gone barefoot everywhere: on the hot bitumen road, the sun-warmed footpath, and even to the beach, where he ran to the water's edge to cool his feet and escape the scorching sand. His father would often say one could cook an egg on the sand, that's how hot it got. The soles of his feet thickened and hardened during the Australian summer season, and thereafter, he was not bothered where he walked or ran. He longed for those innocent and carefree days, when the responsibilities of adulthood had been a mere speck in the mind of a youth.

The more Evan thought about home, the angrier he got. Here he was, trapped in world so different and alien, brought here by Zeus so that he, and not his useless supposed ancient other-self, could recover two powerful relics of the Mother Goddess in order to save the Olympian gods from extinction. He recalled the long period of entrapment by Zeus, showing images of how the birth of Christ changed the mindset of people and destroyed the supremacy of the gods. Zeus, his father, went on to explain how He sent Evan to the future, so that the knowledge of the past, comprehensive education and languages he learnt would be used, here and now, to restore the gods' sovereignty. How he was meant to do it, was still a mystery.

Evan plodded alongside the lumbering hulk of Homer, his newfound brother from the fabled land of Atlantis no less. Homer, Leander, Hektor and the High Priestess had been incarcerated by the king of Kyrene, where the three men had endured many beatings while being questioned as to their origins. The king did not believe they were from Atlantis and tortured them. Homer suffered the most, was beaten until he was unconscious and his throat almost ripped out. He could no longer speak and communicated by writing on his wax tablet.

Evan had been told by Zeus that the Atlanteans were isolated from the rest of the world, a punishment set by the gods for their iniquity, and in return, given a second chance at establishing a society. For Evan, it explained the extreme reactions by the king of Kyrene and Pylos, who remembered the legends of Atlantis and of their tyranny.

He scratched the back of his head, and then glanced over at Phameas, weather-beaten and skin like leather, walking with the rolling gait of a seasoned sailor. Evan looked to where Dexion sat in the wagon, and smiled at the memory of how they had met in Hippo Regius. The boy had intervened when he was propositioned by two street women. An unusual pairing of friends, people he would not have bothered to interact with in his own time. His mouth curved with a slight lilt to one side. He was reminded of an American television series where two men shared a flat, one meticulous and tidy, the other a cantankerous slob. The *Odd Couple*. He could relate to the characters and their many idiosyncrasies. He was living it.

They rested under the canopy of trees and ate some of the food prepared by King Mentor's kitchen slaves. The terrain became more mountainous the further inland they travelled, the craggy limestone outcrops punctured the skyline as if to emphasise their existence. Their smaller hilly siblings, verdant with cedar and cypress trees, lay alongside with pockets of valleys and plains. Rich, fertile land, with crops of wheat and barley, rows of chick peas and beans sown next to each other. Plantations of olive trees and grapevines cultivated on terraced slopes where the soil had been wrought by the hardship of the farmers.

The wagon juddered and pitched every second, the track rough and pockmarked. The High Priestess sat erect, her torso swinging with the shuddering movement of the cart, as if she were a pendulum.

'Not the smoothest of roads,' Evan said, grimacing as his toe caught the sharp edge of a rock. He stopped and checked his toe, brushing away the dirt. A thin film of blood oozed from the small cut.

'The roads in Aegyptos were much better,' said Phameas.

'And you didn't stub toes or roll ankles,' Evan grumbled.

The unyielding path skirted the base of a hill, and ahead, a herd of goats grazed on the meagre foliage on the hillside. The flock began bleating and the goats scattered as they neared. A young shepherd yelled and waved his arms at them before chasing his flock.

'Do you think we should help him?' Leander said slowing down and coming to a stop.

They watched the shepherd scramble up the hillside, going one way, then back the other way. He reminded Evan of a pinball, bouncing from one obstacle to the next.

'He appears to be an efficient herder,' Hektor said and moved on.

Leander watched the hapless shepherd try to round up his herd. 'How long did the king say it will take to get to Messene?'

'At least four days because of the circuitous route,' the High Priestess said, lurching forward as the mule was prodded.

'By the gods, I hope this Pythia, the Oracle, is helpful,' said Hektor.

'We were told Pythia had information for us,' said Evan, 'and Dexion confirmed the message was valid. Besides, Pythia is considered the most renowned seer throughout the Mediterranean. Kings, nobles and ordinary citizens consult her, wanting to hear what she knows.'

'I am certain Pythia will reveal information that is pertinent to our needs,' the High Priestess said. 'There is no point in discussing Pythia's virtues or the purpose of our visit.'

'I am concerned about Melaina and why she instructed us to go to Delphi,' said Hektor. 'Doesn't it trouble you not knowing who this lesser goddess is and her interest?'

'I have learnt the gods need not explain their actions or plans,' she said. 'If they require us to understand or be privy to their resolutions, they will tell us, as Divine Poseidon had when he came to Atlantis. We were chosen to prevent the downfall of the gods and the destruction of our people and home. We must concentrate our efforts on finding the final relic, returning home to unite the objects with Mother, and stopping the rise of this new god.'

'The success of our quest is why I question the motive of this Melaina,' said Hektor, his lip curling.

'Instead of trying to determine the negative aspect of the message, perhaps we should consider it as a way to get closer to finding the last relic,' Evan said.

'What do you mean, Evandros?' Leander said, glancing over his shoulder at Evan.

'Evandros, please come closer so you do not shout,' said the High Priestess.

Evan lengthened his stride until he was alongside the wagon and the High Priestess.

'Pythia is the mouthpiece of Apollo and may know more about the purpose of the relics and why the gods need them.' Evan paused. 'In any case, we're going to Delphi, to hear what Pythia has to say. However, I do think we need to protect ourselves and the golden serpent from visible and invisible enemies, even those who pretend to be on our side.'

'Ridiculous! Our gods would not harm us. They have brought us here to stop their demise, and ours as well.' Hektor bristled.

'Even allies can have an agenda,' said Evan.

'I agree with Evandros,' Leander said, cutting Hektor off from an outburst. 'Our people and home need us to safeguard them, and we must ensure they do not come to harm.'

'Is there a way to hide the relics somehow, so this old god of yours thinks we don't have it?' said Phameas, breaking the gloomy atmosphere. 'It's probable the god knows we have recovered the first relic, but He may not if it's concealed.'

'What did you say?' The High Priestess swivelled around in her seat, her ice-blue eyes piercing.

Phameas shrank. 'I… ah… I… just wondered if the relic could, you know, be made to disappear. You still possess it, but it can't be seen.' He moved closer to Evan. 'A silly thought, never mind.'

'No, Phameas, that is a clever idea,' she said, her eyes sparkling.

Evan scoffed. 'You need a cloaking device, or Harry Potter's invisibility cloak.'

'What?' The High Priestess squinted at him.

Evan felt Homer's warning glance. He cleared his throat. 'Well, it would be handy if there was a bag that disguised contents, and when you look inside, you didn't see the objects.'

'A disguise...' She tilted her head to the side. 'I wonder...' Her voice trailed off. The High Priestess reached for her rucksack and withdrew the bag with the relic. She undid the drawstring and took out the golden serpent. It remained inert in her hands. She turned it one way, then the other, the object sparkling under the sun's rays. Her blue khiton contrasted with the yellow hue of the relic. She stroked the head and gazed out over the ears of the mule.

'Ah... High Priestess... you may want to stop what you're doing,' said Evan, eyes bulging.

The High Priestess peeked down. The serpent's tongue flickered. Its once-inert body stretched and straightened in her now motionless hands. She began to murmur and lowered her head towards the relic. The serpent slithered from her hand, along the length of her arm and coiled around her bicep, then stilled and turned black. She raised her face to the sky and muttered a few more words.

The hair on Evan's arms stood on end and he shivered. Phameas paled, shades lighter than his natural olive complexion. Dexion reached to touch the serpent, but Evan snatched his hand away. He looked over at the others. Homer, Hektor and Leander seemed unperturbed by what had transpired.

'What did you do?' His mouth gaped.

'All have reunited.'

'Did you know that would happen?' Evan said, his mind still reeling from what he had seen.

'As acolyte to the High Priestess, I was privy to ceremonies that bound us to our Mother.'

'It's not what I asked,' he said. 'What force do the relics encompass?'

'Why, the power of Mother,' she said.

Evan gazed at the jewelled charcoal serpent coiled around her upper arm. He had seen what it had done to the Egyptian High Priest in the city of Thebes. The Egyptian had not managed a few steps before the relic had woken and sunk its fangs into his neck; death had been immediate. Evan shuddered and slowed until he fell back behind the wagon. If one relic could kill a man in an instant, what were the objects capable of when unified?

CHAPTER TWO

The soldiers drew to a halt. One turned to Evan and beckoned him over. 'This is where we leave you.' He pointed. 'Follow this road until you reach that mountain. The path will take you part way up the mountainside and into a narrow pass. It will lead you to the outer walls of Messene.'

Evan gazed at the whitewashed peak of the mountain. 'How long will it take to reach Messene?'

'Two to three days. I suggest you stop by the base of the hillside for the night,' the warrior said. 'The trees will provide cover and firewood.'

'Thank you,' said Evan.

They watched the warriors of Pylos trek back, their pace double time, no longer encumbered by the lurching wagon. Homer patted Evan's shoulder and resumed walking. Evan turned and trailed behind, with lagging steps. He stared at the unusual grouping of people, strangers and friends.

Right, Evan, one more item to find, then you get to go home, back to the twenty-first century, he told himself. He picked up the pace and soon caught up with Phameas, Dexion and Homer.

By day three, they reached the mountain pass, which was just wide enough for the wagon. The wheels skimmed the ledge. The High Priestess sat in the wagon, unperturbed by the precarious drop. Leander, reins in hand, came to a stop part way down and frowned.

Armed men blocked their path.

Evan looked over his shoulder and muttered, 'This is not good.'

A small group of warriors had moved in behind them.

Hektor stiffened and fingered the handle of the labrys.

Helmets covered most of their face, with the exception of their eyes and mouth. Their shields were round, brass adorning the outer edge, the surface covered in animal skin with an image of a gryphon lay at its centre.

'Who are you and why do you cross Ithomi?' one demanded.

'I am Evan...dros. We're on our way to Delphi.'

'From where have you come?'

'Pylos.'

'Have you seen any Spartans on your travels?'

Before Evan could answer, Leander asked, 'Who are Spartans?'

Evan saw the incredulity in the soldier's eyes and winced at the forthcoming questions.

'You don't know who the Spartans are?' the soldier said, his voice raised. Leander shook his head again. 'How can you not know? They're renowned throughout the world and beyond for their fighting prowess!'

'We are not familiar with the peoples of this land,' he said.

'From where do you hail?'

'No...' Evan started to speak.

'Atlantis,' cut in Hektor.

'Ah... crap.' Evan closed his eyes and dropped his chin to his collarbone, waiting for the laughter.

'Atlantis?'

'Yes,' Leander said with a nod.

'By the gods, Atlanteans! My humble apologies, Great Ones.'

'What the...?' Evan's head jerked back as if slapped.

The warrior pulled his helmet off, his face youthful and eyes shining. 'We will be honoured to escort you into our city and take you to meet with the Ekklesia, our city's leaders.' He beckoned a soldier. 'Hurry home and seek Neleos; tell him we bring esteemed guests.'

'High Priestess, as much as we are grateful for the generous invitation, I think we should continue on to Tegea,' said Evan, 'just as King Mentor directed.'

She nodded. 'Your offer is kind, but as Evandros stated, our destination is Tegea, and we must resume our journey.'

'You won't reach Tegea for at least a few days,' said the warrior, 'and it's not safe to cross the mountains so late in the day. There are brigands that prowl throughout the forested regions, waiting to accost unsuspecting travellers. It is best you come with us to our city, where you can eat and rest for the night. In the morning, you can recommence your journey to Tegea.' He turned to the soldier waiting at his side. The warrior nodded and sped down the mountainside as nimble and sure-footed as a mountain goat.

'Please come this way,' the leader instructed and indicated to the path ahead.

With a gentle tug on the reins, Leander urged the mule to move. Hektor, worked his jaw back and forth, yet did not hesitate to join Leander.

'Does anyone else think this is a bad idea?' said Evan as he, Phameas and Homer followed the wagon.

Homer's brow was knitted.

'The warrior's reaction at learning who you are appeared to be positive, one of surprise,' said Phameas. 'Nothing like the reception we received on arriving at Pylos.'

'That's true,' said Evan.

'However, we should remain watchful,' added Phameas.

'Agreed.' Evan nodded.

They were part way down the mountainside when Evan heard Hektor ask about the Spartans. He knew about this elite warrior class from books he'd read and various documentaries he'd watched. And despite that it was Hektor who had asked the question, Evan was curious and moved closer to listen.

The young warrior turned his attention from the path to the hulking presence that walked alongside.

'The Spartans are a race of warriors who subjugated my people for hundreds of years. They took our land, forced men and women to grow and harvest food and breed animals for them, while the Spartans trained to be skilled fighters. They learnt how to kill. They had a group of youths who would hide, stalk and slay helots who were identified as a threat to their city.'

'What are helots?' Leander asked.

'It's the name given to the Messenians, our ancestors. After years of servitude, they revolted and fought the Spartans. The great Epaminondas of Thebes founded our new city-state under the shelter of Mount Ithomi.'

'How do you mean the Spartans are a warrior race?' Leander said, head tilted to the side.

'From the age of seven, Spartan boys are taken from their homes and assigned to the care of an officer charged with their education,' the warrior said, eyes narrowing. 'This includes instruction in physical endurance, devotion to the city-state, and bearing hardship. They grow up learning how to fight. The Spartan hoplites are the most feared of all warriors because they do not fear death.'

'Why did you ask where we had come from?' Hektor said.

'They often send warriors to wage war against us. We patrol the region to stop them from entering our city. The Spartans have many allies and have used them to try and conquer us.'

'Why?' Hektor asked.

'Without helots to tend their lands, they cannot devote time to training. Without helots, their lands and animals will perish. Without helots, they are no longer feared or revered.'

How did this happen? Homer had moved alongside to listen. The warrior glanced down at his wax tablet and frowned.

'Homer wants to know how it happened,' Leander explained.

The warrior's face lightened. 'Of course. Sparta is surrounded by three mountains and doesn't have enough land for farming. Messene has vast fertile plains and this is what they covet. There were two wars in which the Spartans were victorious. They divided the land between their citizens, and the conquered Messenians became helots. Freed from toiling and farming, they developed techniques in fighting that made them formidable. No city wants to bear arms against elite warriors.'

'You know a lot about them,' Hektor said.

'If you know your enemy well, you live to fight and win,' he said, his brown eyes unblinking. He turned his attention to the pass. 'Watch your step for the next five stade. The road is uneven.'

The warrior's perspective on the Spartans fascinated Evan. Although the soldier admired them, it was evident he also despised them. Much of the contemporaneous information regarding the Spartans and their unusual political system and way of life had been written by outsiders, who had observed their uniqueness with derision and awe.

Apart from occasional questions Leander and Hektor directed at the warrior, the crossing was quiet, the squeaking wheels and clap of hooves filling the void. The light began to fade. Evan pulled out his cloak and covered his shoulders. The path ahead widened and levelled. In the city streets below, small figures moved with purpose, much as ants do when collecting food. Lazy filaments of smoke rose from many households, and hovered over the rooftops in dirty grey clouds.

'Welcome to Messene, Great Ones.'

Ahead there were fortification walls, running east and to the south, then west along the northern fringes of the mountain.

'They're not taking any chances of being invaded,' Evan murmured to Phameas.

The Phoenician shook his head and scratched his bearded chin. 'Not that anyone can blame them. I'd want to make sure my home was secure and protected.'

'Cities with the tallest and widest barricades can be conquered,' Evan said, 'much like the city of Troy, whose defences were supposed to be impregnable.'

'Troy? I am not familiar with that city,' said Phameas.

'I don't think there's much left of it now,' Evan said. 'It was once an influential and rich city. Many ships stopped there to and from the Hellespont. The Greeks call the city Ilios, but you may be familiar with the Hittites' name for it: Wilusa.'

'Ah yes.' He nodded. 'Wilusa I know. Stopped there a few times. It's not very big.'

The warrior pointed. 'The walls are fifty-two stades long. We have two main gates: the Laconian Gate on the east, and to the northwest, the Arkadian Gate.' He then beckoned two of his men. They hurried ahead and vanished down the slope. 'Come, not much further now.'

CHAPTER THREE

Evan noted how the flickering light in the dusk washed the entrance of the large double wooden doors to the city. He and his companions, escorted by the eager warrior and his men, were ushered past a line of soldiers positioned within the city's walls. They stared, and bowed their heads one by one. Five officious-looking men stood at the end of the procession of warriors.

'Not what I was expecting,' Evan muttered, brows raised.

'If you will wait here,' the young soldier said.

He hurried towards the waiting officials and bowed. While he spoke with the five men, Leander helped the High Priestess alight from the wagon. She ran her hands down the length of her khiton, ironing out the invisible creases. The Messenian soldiers watched her, mesmerised as she moved to stand at the head of the mule. Leander and Hektor stood on either side. Evan, Phameas, Dexion and Homer joined them. The soldier returned with one of the officials.

'Councilman Neleos, may I present the Atlanteans,' he said, chest puffed out.

The councillor was thin, his face angular, making his nose appear much larger, but his eyes were bright and appraising.

'You are from Atlantis,' he said in a deep voice.

'We are,' said the High Priestess, 'with the exception of our Phoenician friend, Phameas and the young boy, Dexion. I, Alexina, am High Priestess of Atlantis.'

'Welcome to Messene, Great Ones.' He bowed. 'Please come.' He stood aside, one arm stretched towards the road behind the four councillors. 'We're honoured to have such distinguished persons visit our humble city.'

The councillors led them through the streets, where people emerged from their homes and began to trail along. They moved deeper into the city and the crowd grew. A frail elderly man stumbled through the ever-growing throng, hands outstretched, and grasped Evan's arm.

'By the gods! It is true; the Great Ones live!' He tripped over the grimy edge of his khiton. Evan caught his elbow and helped him upright.

'Are you all right?'

The old man's eyes glistened and his hands trembled. 'Your return has been long awaited, and I'm grateful to witness this momentous occasion.'

'Return?' Evan frowned. He glanced over at Homer, who shrugged. 'What is your name?'

'Kallimachos.'

'Kallimachos, I'm Evan...dros. I am confused as to why you say our arrival was expected. How is that possible you knew we were coming?'

The old man's face lit up, and he was about to speak when Neleos touched Evan's arm.

'Is everything all right?'

Evan nodded. 'Kallimachos almost fell and I caught him. I am making sure he is fine.' He turned to the old man. 'Walk with us.'

Kallimachos drew himself tall and beamed. The councilman looked at him, screwed up his nose and pulled Evan aside.

'Great One, this man is notorious for his lies. He is not trustworthy.'

'Really?' Evan glanced over at Kallimachos, who stood with his lips pressed together and wrung his hands. Something in his eyes gave Evan his answer. 'I don't think he'll get into too much trouble with this many people around.'

Neleos pursed his lips. 'As you wish.' He bowed and moved away.

'Come along, Kallimachos.' Evan held his arm out. The old man took a few hesitant steps. Evan gave him an encouraging smile and put an arm about his bony shoulders. Kallimachos, dwarfed by Homer and Evan, walked between them with the broadest of smiles.

Men, women and children reached out, touched their arms and clasped their hands. Evan glanced at his companions, their expressions as bewildered as his. It was a slow march through the city as the crowd swelled.

'I wonder where they are taking us,' he said.

'The assembly hall. It's the only place big enough to seat the citizens,' Kallimachos said.

'Is that where the food is?' Phameas asked. He rubbed his stomach. 'I am looking forward to a meal, and it's been a while since we've eaten.'

The old man shook his head. 'The hall is a meeting place. I am not sure what will happen afterwards. Perhaps you will be guests of one of the councilmen.'

'Is everyone coming to the hall?' said Evan, gesturing at the crowd with a thumb.

'Just the citizens,' Kallimachos said.

Evan's attention was drawn to a grand structure nestled into the contours of the mountain slopes. At its centre was a propylaeum, the entrance into the hall with four imposing columns. Vibrant hues of red, cerulean blue, daffodil yellow and emerald green dressed the metopes and lifelike sculptures recessed within the tympanum. It was a brilliant and lurid spectacle in the waning daylight. Evan preferred the white marble of the ancient buildings in his time. Their majesty inspired reverence for the skill and workmanship involved in creating such works of art. Seeing them painted in garish colours negated their awe, he thought.

Neleos and the other councilmen led them into the gateway, past a row of pillars and through a stoa. Evan gawped as they cleared a row of columns. His eyes darted one way, then the other, digesting what he saw.

'Magnificent!' he said in a breathless voice.

The stoa they exited was one of three and formed a square that enclosed a courtyard. The enclosure was enormous, as big as the largest sporting stadium. The stoas were double colonnaded, with rooms behind the second row of columns. The first row of columns was Corinthian, and the capitals had a winged Nike emerging from the acanthus leaves. An Ionic architrave sat atop, decorated by a frieze with reliefs of bulls' heads that alternated with floral scrolls and bowls.

A Doric temple and altar dominated the space straight ahead. In the corners of the courtyard were exedrae, semicircular benches, places for people to sit and gather. Bronze statues, over one hundred of them, crowded the temple and altar, with many more positioned along the covered walkways. It was a perpetual gathering and a panoply of voiceless figures.

'We'll go into the assembly hall. The citizens are eager to hear you speak and learn of your return,' Neleos said.

'Of course,' said the High Priestess, 'we are happy to address the citizens of this fine city.'

Neleos moved to the left, walked to a door and led them into a compact theatre. He guided them to the row of marble seats nearest to the stage floor while the councillors sat on chairs on a raised platform. The people scurried to fill the seats, climbing stone stairways to the upper and lower sections of the cavea. Homer gazed behind him and scanned the faces. He then pulled out his wax tablet, wrote something and handed it to Kallimachos.

'Women and children are not permitted in council meetings,' the old man said in a bemused tone.

But aren't women and children Messenians? he scrawled.

'Yes, but it is only men, owners of land, who have political rights and can attend. Non-citizens and slaves also aren't allowed to participate. Though it is expected for women and children to take part in tributes to the gods,' Kallimachos said.

Hektor screwed up his nose, and Leander looked disappointed, but neither said anything. The High Priestess sat, hands resting in her lap, seeming unmoved by the conversation. Homer glanced at Evan, who shrugged, leaned over and said in a quiet voice, 'This is common practice throughout all cities in Greece.'

Homer did a double take. *Really?* he scribbled.

Evan straightened and nodded.

Neleos stepped to the centre of the stage and waited for the din to die down. He raised his hands, and the few still chatting stopped.

'Citizens, on this auspicious eve, the gods have graced and returned to us a legendary race of people whose existence was thought to have disappeared. Stories of their beauty, intelligence, virtue, architecture and technology have echoed through the ages. Their achievements were our inspiration, their downfall a gritty reminder of how hubris incurs the wrath of the gods.

'On one terrible day, the sky turned a blood red. A mass of black clouds surrounded an island and with it carried a sound so deafening it shook the earth. The land ripped asunder. People ran screaming, dodging falling debris. Thousands upon thousands of lives massacred. With an explosion heard across the sea and in faraway lands, the might of Hephaistos' mountain erupted, spewing forth tons of molten liquid and stone. When the one-eyed peak collapsed, it took with it that wondrous place and sank into the depths of the sea.

'An unnatural silence followed. The sky was blackened by hot ash, discharged from the mouth of the fiery innards of the mountain. The air so thick, no living creature could breathe. People from lands near and far looked to the skies, shook with fear and wondered what had angered the gods. Then great waves, taller than the highest mountain swelled and crashed against the shores, forever changing the shape of the land. Where familiar shorelines once existed, they now lay deep under the turquoise water. New valleys were formed and the raging sea created tributaries and rivers. Across the Mediterranean, people prayed and offered sacrifices, hoping the gods would hear them and spare their lives. The skies remained dark for days on end, a reminder of the immortals' vengeance.

'For many years, no human ventured near where the sea had swallowed a whole civilisation, for fear of retribution by the gods. Stories of the once flourishing and remarkable people and their fate were told and recited. We are fortunate this night to have here with us the Atlanteans, noble heirs of the gods.'

Evan knew the Greeks were famous for their rhetoric but had not expected to be sitting and listening to a live performance. He was impressed by the eloquence and passion of the recital. He looked at Homer, who seemed unmoved, then leaned forward and peeked at the others. Phameas and Dexion appeared to be more interested in the building and the people. Hektor had a disapproving expression, and Leander was startled by the speech. The High Priestess sat still, hands clasped on her lap, her gaze fixed on the councilman.

Neleos faced the visitors. The theatre resounded in muted reverence. The High Priestess turned to Evan and indicated he should speak. He shook his head, his brows puckered in deep furrows. Homer patted him on the back and gave him an encouraging nod. Evan pressed his lips together. It wasn't that he was nervous about public speaking; he had addressed large crowds before. He just didn't believe in misleading people, in particular lying about himself in this time. He wasn't who they regarded him to be. Evan stood and walked across to Neleos, who smiled and moved away to leave him standing alone. Evan felt the weight of curiosity as every person stared at him and waited for him to speak. He cleared his throat.

'Good evening, honourable citizens of Messene. My name is...' he hesitated, 'Evandros, and these are my companions.' Evan introduced them and then continued, 'We are grateful to be here in your fair city. I must first thank Councilman Neleos and congratulate him on his impeccable speech.' He acknowledged the Messenian with a slight bow. 'It was illuminating. Before I continue, and asking for some indulgence,' he said, looking at the councillors, 'perhaps the good citizens of Messene would like to ask questions so I can better address what you would like to know.' They agreed, and Evan swung back to face the crowd. There were rows and rows of faces, young and old, bearded and clean-shaven, all waiting with eager expressions. 'If you do wish to ask a question, please stand or raise your hand.'

'Greetings, Evandros, I'm Dymas and privileged to be in the company of such esteemed guests.'

'Thank you, Dymas.' Evan acknowledged him with a smile. 'Do you have a question?'

He nodded. 'How is it possible the noble blood of Atlantis is here with us today?'

'There were survivors who fled on ships, and tidal waves swept them across the sea. The Sea God rescued them, guided them to an island and helped to rebuild their home.'

'Why hasn't the world known of your existence until now?' another asked.

'That is a good question,' he said with slow, measured words. Evan glanced at Kallimachos. How had he known the Atltanteans were coming? 'With the councillors' permission, our High Priestess, who is also our city's elder, is the best person to address your question.'

No one in the audience dared to move or utter a word while Neleos and the councilmen conferred amongst themselves in low tones. Evan clasped his hands behind his back and resisted the urge to rock on his feet. The High Priestess sent him an enquiring look. He shrugged.

Neleos rose to his feet and addressed her. 'High Priestess, you grace us with your presence, and we would be privileged if you'd speak to the assembly.'

She acknowledged him with a smile, stood and joined Evan. She turned to the audience. 'Greetings, good citizens, and thank you, councillors, for allowing me to answer questions. In response to the earlier query, it took many centuries for our ancestors to resettle. They also made a pact with the gods not to interact with the rest of the world.'

There were rumblings from the auditorium.

'Why would the gods demand this?' someone called out.

'The Olympians decided the people of Atlantis should remain isolated so we would not influence others,' the High Priestess said.

'What did the Atlanteans do for the gods to impose such restrictions?'

'The ancient kings grew greedy and enjoyed the power they had. This angered the gods, and they punished our ancestors.'

'If you've lived in seclusion for all this time, why have you now returned?'

The High Priestess' gaze flickered at Evan as he took a step back, leaving her to stand alone. The flickering light of the torches bathed the stage in a soft yellow glow and centred on the High Priestess. Her beauty, highlighted by the ethereal light that illuminated her whole being, captivated the citizens. With a composed expression, she scanned the audience.

'The gods have summoned us to prevent the end of their immortal reign.'

The statement was made with finality and calmness, and the citizens' reaction was not one Evan anticipated. He looked from left to right at the expressions on the men's faces which varied. Some looked like a baby whose dummy's been taken away, and about to burst into tears, while many reminded him of wide-eyed owls, heads twitching one way then the other. There were those who bristled with fear and anger. Evan noticed Kallimachos, a diminutive figure as he sat next to Homer, the only one who did not appear to be surprised by the High Priestess' announcement.

There was a slight rumble, and the sound spread and grew louder.

'How is this even possible?' someone shouted. 'The gods cannot die!'

'Their demise is worse than death. They will no longer exist, and people will forget them.'

'What nonsense!'

'What you are saying is an affront to the gods!'

'They are gods! Nothing can destroy them!'

'We are here to ensure that does not happen,' the High Priestess said. She stood, unruffled by the growing furore.

Evan stepped over to her side and raised his hand. 'You have every right to be angry and afraid. The gods and your connection to them are important to you, as they are to my companions. It is the same as losing a loved one. You feel bereft and lost, a hollow shell.'

There were nods and mumbles of assent.

'If what you are saying is true, how are you going to stop this calamity from happening?'

'There are relics that once belonged to the Mother Goddess, and it is believed their power can avert the gods' downfall,' he said. 'We have recovered one and now seek a second item.'

'What if you are unable to find it?'

'We will,' the High Priestess said with confidence.

'But what if you don't?'

'Then our fate lies with that of the gods.'

***

The Dark Master sat back on his throne and pondered how he could manipulate the one called Evandros. He smiled. The Atlantean was an anomaly. He was nothing like the other Atlanteans. Whatever Zeus had done to the mortal, made him vulnerable and set him apart from the others.

Kronos drummed his long fingers on the armrest. Getting to the mortal would be difficult. He scowled, knowing Zeus and the other Olympian gods would be close by, watching every step their progeny took. He clutched the armrest, knuckles turning white, his head lowered and his eyes glittering. Then there was the Mother Goddess, who saw everything and was ready to protect her changeling. His body grew warm, and the blood in his veins bubbled, ready to erupt like the hapless volcano sitting in brewing silence on the foothills of southern Italy.

If only she had not yielded to Zeus and his siblings with such ease, he would not have had to resort to extreme action to set the world on the righteous path. The wretched younger gods with their insatiable desires and wanton behaviour jeopardised the welfare and longevity of the immortals.

He stood and began to pace. The cowl of his cloak kept his face obscured. It did not seem that long ago when he and his brothers had fought the Olympians. A war with neither side capitulating until the tenth year. He clenched his teeth, the cords in his neck stuck out, ropey and thick.

'If it weren't for the Cyclops and giants, Zeus and his pathetic siblings would not have won! He will pay for his iniquity! They all will!'

He glanced down at his scarred hands. His breathing came out in short bursts. He balled his hands, threw his head back and roared like an injured animal—a sound of deep-seated anger. The cowl had fallen away to reveal a disfigured face. The left cheekbone had been crushed by a missile thrown by one of the giants. When he had fallen, Apollo had struck him with a flaming arrow. The fire had come from the sun, the heat intense, and had consumed his body with alacrity. He had not known what had happened until the agonising pain had set in.

'The time to restore the true path has come, and my bloodline will become king of the human race.' Kronos smacked a fist into his palm. 'Nothing and no one will get in the way of my plan. Not even my daughter or Eris and her minions will prevent me from seeing the end of Zeus and the cavorting Olympians.'

He spun on his heel and walked back to the throne, the fringes of his gown whirling at his ankles.

'Eris! Your presence is required!' Kronos bellowed into the vast void. He sat. 'It is time to create havoc for Zeus' champion.'

CHAPTER FOUR

Neleos caught Evan's attention and waved him over, suggesting they should leave. 'It would be an honour to have you as my guests in my home.'

'Will they be all right?' Leander asked, glancing back at the audience, many of whom were standing, gesturing with excitement as they spoke.

'Oh, they will continue for some time,' the councilman said. He beckoned. 'Come, I am sure you are hungry and tired after your long journey.'

'It has been a while since I've last eaten,' Phameas said, rubbing his stomach.

Evan and the others followed Neleos through one of the three wooden doors on the stage into a short passage and exited via another door that led outside. The soldiers who had remained with the mule and wagon fell in step behind the group. Evan could not help but admire how the twilight bathed the buildings, the red and orange hues melting into the fading daylight. His awareness was brought back by the clip-clop of the mule's hooves and the slap of sandals on the cobbled path that broke the tranquillity of the city.

On Evan's left was an empty agora, the shadows of the buildings and columns filling the square. Evan stumbled when Neleos, who led the way, made a sudden left at the next street and guided them to the entrance of a modest house. The last to enter, Evan dawdled on the threshold. The entryway was a portal between the street and the inner sanctum. It was wide enough for a cart to fit and provided shelter from the weather for visitors or occupants returning home. On either side of the portico were shrines to the family's gods. Wreaths and food were placed on each altar.

Standing next to Phameas and Leander, Evan heard the double wooden doors pulled shut by the accompanying soldiers. He glanced around the neat and swept courtyard. A lemon tree was planted next to the staircase that led to the second floor. In the centre was a cistern filled with water, and beyond were rooms where dim light escaped through the doorways. From one, Evan watched a man as dark as midnight head towards them.

'Master, I am sorry. I didn't hear you arrive,' he said, hobbling forward dragging his right leg, tightening a belt around his waist. His face was wrinkled with age but his eyes were alert, as though nothing could surprise him.

'That's fine, Jengo. We've guests who will be staying. Bring food and wine to the andron, and see rooms are made ready.'

Jengo bowed. 'Yes, master.' He tottered away, withdrawing into one of the many entries facing the courtyard. From another opening, a small brown-haired child came running out. Neleos smiled, his expression transformed into delight and adoration as he stooped to embrace the girl and pick her up.

'Father, where have you been? I've been waiting for you for ages!'

'I had important council business to attend to, little one.' He kissed her on the forehead. 'This is my daughter, Chara. Chara, say hello to our guests.'

Evan muttered a hello, that was drowned out by Leander's cheerful greeting. The pretty girl stared and sniffed at Dexion, but when she caught sight of the High Priestess, she became coy. Evan was amused by the little girl's response to seeing Dexion and curious about her reaction when she saw the High Priestess. The High Priestess was an imposing figure.

Neleos placed his daughter on the ground. 'Tell your mother we have guests.' The little girl nodded and spun about, her long hair floating mid-air, running around the cistern and into one of the rooms. 'Please, come this way.'

Evan trailed after Homer as one by one they walked under the staircase and entered the anteroom. Neleos pulled the curtain aside and waved them in. Couches lined three walls, each adorned with colourful cushions. In the corners were backless stools. Evan shuddered inwardly at the walls, painted crimson, sea green and orange, and was grateful for the subdued lighting. He took Kallimachos by the elbow and walked across the room to the settee under the small window that faced the entry into the room. Phameas and Dexion followed. Homer took the stool in the corner close by. The others took up seats on one side of the room, and Neleos opposite.

'So the rumours are true,' said a voice from the doorway. Evan glanced up to see a dignified, yet handsome woman enter the room, her light brown hair arranged with meticulous care. The delicate curls framed her face and softened otherwise sharp lines. From the way her tawny eyes examined them, Evan felt as if they were species from another planet. In some way, he did feel like he came from another planet; his world and this one were so different. She stopped at the sight of the High Priestess. Though somewhat dishevelled, she radiated allure and power.

'My dear, let me introduce you to our noble guests,' said Neleos, rising from his seat. 'This is my wife, Hekabe.'

'You grace our humble home with your presence,' she said with a courteous nod. She sat next to her husband. The two then reclined lengthways and propped themselves on an elbow. The High Priestess and Leander imitated their hosts, while Evan and the others remained seated. They chatted, and sometime later, Jengo arrived with four young women in tow, each carrying a dish. The women placed the platters within reach on small tables.

'Everyone, please eat and drink, the food is best eaten when hot.' Neleos waved his hand and on cue, the young women handed out earthenware cups filled with wine and honey.

'Thank you,' Leander said, smiling. 'The food looks delicious and smells wonderful, Lady Hekabe. Could you tell us what's in these dishes?'

Neleos' wife could not help but respond to Leander's charm, and her face was radiant, which enhanced her features. 'We have soft-boiled quails' eggs, salted eel, baked pork, honey-flavoured beans and goat's cheese, honey cakes, baked yellowfin tuna, olives and mashed chickpeas, and afterwards figs, pomegranates and grilled chestnuts.'

'A feast fit for the gods,' he said and dug in without further prompting.

'I understand the sovereignty of the gods is jeopardised and your quest is of the utmost importance, but how could such a thing happen? They have been our gods for thousands of years. How could their power be extinguished?' Neleos asked, reaching for a piece of the succulent pork.

'Perhaps that's the reason why,' said Evan. He took a piece of the fish.

'What do you mean?'

Evan swallowed the spiced fish before responding. 'In the aeons they've reigned, they haven't changed. They make the same demands from their worshippers, expecting supplication and sacrifices in their names. I guess it is these expectations that people tire of. The general public are looking for something, a commitment from the gods, not just cursory acknowledgement of their human existence. They want a god who is willing to sacrifice himself, offer a new belief, one that comforts their needs and ills.'

Evan reached for an egg and popped it into his mouth. He happened to glance at the High Priestess whose light blue eyes flashed and deepened in colour. Hektor looked as if he would leap from his seat and strangle him.

'By Hestia's hearth, what are you saying? The gods may be forbidding, but they do reward those who follow their stead,' Hekabe said, affronted.

'When was the last time you received anything from the gods?' Evan said.

Hekabe opened and closed her mouth several times.

'I thought so.' Evan picked up another egg and ignored the daggers the High Priestess sent his way.

'What makes you believe the populace want new gods?' Neleos asked, his face drawn.

Evan wagged a finger. 'Not gods, a god. I saw it happen.' He turned to the High Priestess, his eyes boring into hers. 'Zeus showed me where and when it will happen and who leads the people to a new god.'

The High Priestess blinked and her face paled.

'Divine Zeus showed you?' Hekabe's voice came out a squeak, her eyes bulging. She shook her head with such vigour, her curls jiggled. 'Our gods are strong, and what you have said is improbable.'

'Nothing is improbable,' said Evan and reached for a piece of pork.

'When did Divine Zeus do this?' asked Hektor, eyes narrowing.

Leander was troubled. 'Why didn't Divine Poseidon share this with us when he told us of the errand?'

Homer leaned forward, turned to Evan and stared at him, unimpressed. Evan shrugged. He was tired of her superior attitude and wanted to show he too had inside knowledge she was not privy to.

'Zeus took me not long before we started our quest,' Evan said. 'As to why Poseidon didn't mention it, I don't know. Perhaps the gods didn't think it was essential to reveal this piece of news at the time.'

Evan looked back at Neleos. 'To answer your question as to why, people want answers. They need someone who sympathises with them, recognises their desires, and appreciates who they are for just themselves. Which of the gods puts their followers first?'

'The gods do not answer to us. We mortals are here to serve them,' Neleos said in a strangled voice. 'If it wasn't for their guidance, we'd have no purpose. We'd still be floundering and wandering the world, going from one place to the next, with little action, few ideals and principles.'

'I didn't say the gods haven't contributed. They have provided valuable strategies to teach people proper behaviour and expectations of a society,' Evan said. 'What has changed is there are masses of people who are no longer satisfied by the tenets set by the gods. They seek another who offers a different path and a new way of life.'

'You speak as if it has already happened,' Hekabe said, the pallor of her skin shades lighter than her olive complexion.

'The vision Zeus showed me indicates there is a strong shift in belief,' Evan replied.

'This is quite distressing,' Neleos said, shaking his head. 'You say you've found one of the relics.'

Evan nodded.

'Do you know where the remaining one is?'

'We're on our way to see Pythia to learn of the location,' Evan said.

Neleos sighed, pleased and relieved. 'If anyone would know, it would be the Oracle.'

'I am curious, though, about how Kallimachos knew of our return.' He swivelled to face the older man. 'Why did you say it was foretold?'

Kallimachos wrapped his hands around the cup he held and lifted his chin. 'The story begins with the eminent philosopher and teacher Plato.'

'Plato?' Evan repeated blinking.

The old man continued as if not interrupted. 'In his commentaries *Critias* and *Timaeus*, he describes the magnificence of Atlantis and how the Athenian statesman Solon learnt the tale while travelling in Aegyptos. Plato finished writing *Timaeus* but did not complete the dialogue of *Critias*.'

'Why not?' asked Leander.

'He said the plight of the Atlanteans wasn't over, so he could not write more until they return to stop a war.' The old man grasped Evan's hand and squeezed. 'If what you spoke of, and what Divine Zeus has shown you, is true, then the seeds of doubt in the gods and their reign have been planted.' The lines around Kallimachos' mouth and eyes deepened.

Evan stopped breathing for a second.

The old man stood, causing the tripod table to rock. 'I must go.' Without another word, he hobbled across the room. When he reached the door, he paused and turned back around. 'You must find the sacred relic,' he said in a grave tone. 'If you do not, a great war, one like no one has ever seen, will come to pass. It will change civilisation as we know it.' He scurried out the door and was gone.

'What in the name of the gods?' Hektor said, half-risen from his seat.

'A war? Not sure I like the sound of that,' Phameas said, staring at Evan.

'Me neither,' he said.

CHAPTER FIVE

While Evan itched to continue their search for the last relic, he and his companions remained Neleos' guests for a number of days and met family members, friends and associates. A youth by the name of Theodoros was a constant visitor, so enthralled by Evan, Homer and Leander, he peppered them about life in Atlantis, the quest, and of the gods. When Evan could escape from Theo's relentless presence, he had set off into the city and questioned a number of people regarding Kallimachos, but no one knew what had become of him after his abrupt departure from Neleos' house. He was nowhere to be found.

Chara took an instant liking to the High Priestess and followed her everywhere, except when the Atlanteans left the house. On the day they departed, the little girl, tears running down her face, gave her favourite doll to the High Priestess. Evan was impressed by the High Priestess, who was moved by the little girl's gesture and gave her a bracelet made from lapis lazuli.

On Neleos' suggestion, they left the city via the Laconian Gate and travelled eastwards on a well-used road towards Tegea. The fertile flat lands of Messene were verdant, a stark contrast to the dry, arid land of Egypt, and mountains instead of vast sand dunes dominated the landscape.

'What is it you do in this twenty-first century?' Phameas asked in a quiet voice, attention fixed on the backs of Hektor and Leander, who walked beside the wagon bearing the High Priestess.

'I am an architect. I design buildings,' he answered in an even lower tone.

'Do you earn good money from that?'

'You could say I live a comfortable life.'

'Do you have a wife and children?'

Evan gave a half grin. 'No, though my mother isn't too happy about my single status and would like grandchildren.'

'Your parents must be missing you,' Phameas said.

His heart pulled. He loathed to contemplate how his parents were feeling, first losing a daughter and then a son. They must be wretched. He despised the idea of them hurting and wanted to let them know he was alive and fine.

What aspect of that life do you miss the most? Homer wrote.

'Having regular baths and fresh clean water.'

'Bathing too often can't be good for you,' Phameas snorted.

'My friend, it is known that cleanliness is important for one's mental and physical health,' Evan said with a grin.

'Does everyone bathe often where you are from?'

'Most people wash once a day or twice a day.'

'Two times in a day? How dirty is it in your world you need to bathe twice in one day?' Phameas said, flabbergasted.

'It depends on the job a person has, the climate, and if one has exercised. Sometimes having two showers is part of the daily routine,' Evan said. 'We must pay for what we consume.'

'You have to pay for water?' Phameas' expression of incredulity was mirrored by Homer.

'Oh, yes. There are many expenses in my world and charging for the consumption of water is also due to scarcity.'

A city or place of province cannot survive without water, Homer wrote.

Evan nodded. 'And where I am from, every house has access to water. In my country, twenty-three million people consume over three hundred and sixty litres each. That's about eleven metretes of water every day.'

'Moloch! Did you say twenty-three million people?'

'That is small compared to other countries. The world population is over seven billion.'

'Great Baal! All those people... it must get very noisy.'

Evan laughed. 'I never thought of it that way. In big cities, the din is constant.'

Hektor turned and scowled at them. They all stared back without saying a word. When he looked back to the front, Evan restrained himself from poking his tongue out.

'Has he always been a miserable sod?' Evan asked Homer.

Homer shook his head. *He changed after our imprisonment and beatings by the king of Kyrene. He is angry, at himself for not being able to stop what happened and at anyone who threatens us. That includes you.*

'Me?' Evan pointed at himself in surprise. 'How am I a threat?'

You are not the same person who left Atlantis with us. He has no reason to trust you, and besides, you haven't made any conciliatory efforts to convince him to think otherwise, Homer added.

'I will concede to that, but in my defence, this is not the world I grew up in. How would you feel if you were ripped away from all you knew and find yourself in an alien place? Would you behave any different?'

Perhaps. I don't know. Homer shrugged. *We are not the same, the way we think, act and speak. Our experiences determine what we do and how we react. You've been given an opportunity no other has ever had. Embrace this unique situation and use it to your advantage.*

Evan glanced over Phameas' head and stared, oblivious to the undulating landscape. Homer's words kept reverberating in his mind, like a bell tolling on the hour, an incessant reminder of the shifting time. If he allowed himself to embrace his situation and apply his expertise, would this combination hasten his return home? The more he thought about it, the more the prospect of achieving his goal felt probable. First, complete the task, and then think how to get back to his time. If dreams had gotten him here, then dreams could send him home.

'Thank you, Homer,' he said, light-hearted and stepping with more bounce.

Homer's brows puckered and then smoothed on seeing Evan smile. He nodded and grunted an acknowledgement.

They travelled most of the day, stopping once to eat and drink before moving on. Hours passed as the group trekked along the road. When the temperature became cooler and the light began to wane, they pulled into a small clearing and a short distance from a river.

Leander helped the High Priestess descend from the wagon while Homer unharnessed the mule and tethered it to a tree. Dexion and Phameas went in search of kindling, leaving Evan and Hektor to organise the food and beverage. They worked in silence, neither feeling compelled to talk. Soon after, they sat around the campfire eating the provisions the Messenians had been generous in giving, ample supplies together with the goods from King Mentor, to see them through to Tegea.

'This Pythia we're off to see, do you believe her prophecy will be reliable?' Hektor asked.

'Oracles are the mouthpiece of the gods. I have no reason to expect otherwise,' said the High Priestess.

'The Oracle of Delphi is the most powerful of all prophets,' said Dexion. 'My father told me people voyaged from faraway places to hear her predictions. My homeland was settled by Greeks who sought Pythia's advice. She described the location, how far it was, how to get there and what they would find once they arrived.'

'Is your ability the same as hers?' Leander asked.

'No.' Dexion shook his head. 'My ability only allows me to see a person's future, whereas the Oracle's gift sees all.'

'It must be difficult to shut out the visions and chatter,' Evan said. 'It would make me crazy having all that noise in my head.'

'Some days it is difficult to ignore,' Dexion conceded.

'What do you do to try to block the stream of natter?' Evan leaned back on an elbow and stretched out his legs.

'I have gotten used to their presence and forget they're with me. When they get boisterous and annoying, then I tell them to leave,' he said.

'I wonder if that is where the concept of imaginary friends came from,' Evan mused.

'Imaginary friends? Who are they?' asked Leander.

'Little children playing games pretend they have companions with them. They give them names and often explain in detail what their friend likes and dislikes, even the clothes they are wearing,' said Evan. 'Perhaps these imaginary friends are real, spectral beings only seen by small children and those gifted like Dexion. Their minds are open to psychic phenomena.'

I've seen my daughter do that many times. I thought she was playacting, Homer scribbled.

'You have a daughter?' Evan said, staring at him in wonder.

Homer nodded and raised a hand.

'You have three children?'

Homer beamed.

'I did not realise.' Evan paused. 'You must miss them, and your wife.'

Homer's face clouded, his jaw tightening. He then placed his hand over his heart. A few moments of silence passed, and Homer pointed to Hektor.

'How old are your children?' Evan asked Hektor.

'Four, seven, two and ten annuals,' Hektor said stiffening.

'Then we must recover the relic as soon as possible so you can return home to your families,' he said.

'And fulfil the gods' quest and save Atlantis from destruction,' the High Priestess restated.

'Yes, that's what brought us here in the first place.'

Evan pulled out the black book from his backpack and began to write. The last entry, written while in Messene, was short, but he had drawn many of the buildings that captured his interest. He yawned and shook his head, the words blurring.

'That's it for tonight.'

He closed the book and shoved it into his bag. Evan lay back, folded his arms under his head and looked up at the night sky. The purple hues melded with the blackness. A smattering of stars began to emerge, small beacons of light in a sea of obscurity. Were these stars the same as the ones he'd observed on his last visit to Greece? Or in the following three thousand years, had they burnt out into oblivion and gone for eternity? His eyes fluttered, and the chatter faded into a gentle murmur. The fire crackled and its warmth lured him into sleep.

***

Zeus crossed the marble floor of the great hall in quick strides. The golden doors swung open as he neared. Perched on the black marble throne was the god's tawny eagle. The bird's black eyes blinked and it spread its wings, their span twice the height of the tallest man. With the slightest of thrusts, the eagle flew after Zeus.

The King of the Gods charged down the stairs, taking two steps at a time, and leapt into the waiting chariot. The sun's rays struck the golden basket and illuminated his strong features. Sensing his impatience, the celestial steeds stomped at the ground. Zeus flicked the reins, and the horses soared into the air and raced to the Gate of the Clouds. The Four Seasons, the gatekeepers, mouths gaping and eyes wide, sprang into action as Zeus hurtled towards them. They shrank back as the chariot careered through the narrow opening.

'I am telling you, Zeus flew out through the gates on his chariot as if the winds of Boreas were chasing him,' said Ares. 'Something is wrong.'

The Olympian gods gathered in the throne room after the Four Seasons had hurried to the gods' home and told the God of War of Zeus' inexplicable departure. Hera sat next her husband's empty throne, her fingers tapping on the armrest.

'There could be any number of reasons why Zeus left with urgency,' Hephaistos said in a mild tone. 'Odds are he's making sure Evandros and his companions are safe and on their way to the location of the next sacred object.'

'A plausible reason, but doubtful,' said Ares with a grunt. 'Has anyone ever seen Zeus leave the palace grounds in such haste unless there is trouble afoot?' He eyeballed his fellow Olympians and smiled in triumph when no-one responded. 'No, I did not think so.' He whirled back to face Hera. 'I wager my sword and shield a terrible event is happening or stirring.'

'If that is so, why didn't he tell us and ask myself or Poseidon to assist?' said Hades, his pupils dark and fathomless.

'He is the King of the Gods and Men,' said Hephaistos. 'He doesn't need to inform us of every detail.'

'Such as the Atlantean Evandros,' Apollo said, lip curled. 'Zeus has not told us where he has been? Why is that so? Don't you find it curious that, following the sacrificial death of his wife, the Atlantean disappears? Where did he go to?'

'Zeus doesn't need to explain his actions or decisions,' said Athene, scowling. 'Does it matter if we know or don't know where Evandros may have been? What is important is his ability to recover the relics and prevent the rising of this new god.'

Hephaistos nodded. 'Athene is right. It's imperative Evandros fulfil his tasks rather than that we concern ourselves as to his prior whereabouts.'

'Of course you would agree,' Ares said, sneering. 'You and Zeus have been in each other's company quite a bit of late. Are you his herald now?'

Hephaistos' eyes narrowed and he clasped the head of the hard black stone of his hammer.

'Where's your gossamer net now?' Ares taunted.

The blacksmith's knuckles turned white, the muscles in his upper arms bulging.

'Enough, Ares,' said Hestia, placing a hand on Hephaistos' forearm. 'I daresay Zeus has Hephaistos creating a range of objects which may aid the Atlanteans. Isn't that so?' she added, turning to Hephaistos.

'The weapons the Atlanteans carry were forged by my hands,' he said through clenched teeth.

'Fine weapons too, from what I have seen,' Athene said in an approving tone.

'They cannot be broken or wielded by another besides the rightful owner,' he said, his gaze never leaving Ares'.

'Interesting. Why make the arms that way?' said Hades, his dark eyes intense.

'So people with malevolent intentions cannot attain and use the armaments.' As an afterthought, Hephaistos then added, 'And as they are divine offspring, it was fitting they be provided with the finest and best weaponry.'

'I am troubled by Evandros.' The gods turned to the queen. Hera stood and joined them at the foot of the dais. 'He doesn't appear to have any of the traits the other Atlanteans display. Nor is he comfortable in their presence, with the exception of Homer. Why is he different?'

'He is who he needs to be,' said a deep voice.

Hera blanched. Ares took a step back. Athene smiled. The gods stepped aside for Zeus as he walked into their midst.

'He defies you,' said Hera, lifting her chin at him.

'He does, which makes him the one who will defeat the new uprising,' said Zeus. 'His unique abilities and unconventional way of thinking are an advantage to him and us. His knowledge is unsurpassed by any mortal, and that is the reason he was chosen.'

'He was chosen because he is your son,' said Hera, crossing her arms against her breasts.

Zeus' lips thinned. 'Yes.' He walked to his throne and lingered on the first step. He turned. 'We have greater concerns than my son. The protective seal surrounding Tartaros was ruptured.'

'What...?'

'How can that be possible?'

'It can't be!'

The gods gathered closer, standing shoulder to shoulder as they kept peppering the King of the Gods with questions. Zeus held up his hand and waited until they quietened.

'I've mended the seal.' He hesitated.

'And?' Poseidon prompted.

'Eris has escaped.'

Athene's face paled, Aphrodite clasped her hands over her heart and Hera clenched her hands.

'The fissure had weakened, but the gap from which she fled was widened by another.'

The Olympians were stunned. Hestia pressed her hands to her cheeks.

'So it is a Titan,' said Hades in an abrupt tone.

Zeus nodded, expression grim.

'Do you know which one?' Poseidon said.

'Kronos.'

⚜

Evan twitched and brushed away the annoyance buzzing in his ear. He turned on his side and tried to get comfortable on the hard ground. He opened his eyes, bolted upright and scanned the forest. The darkness shrouded it like a cloak beyond the ring of light cast by the fire. He heard the faintest rustling of leaves, then twigs breaking, as though something or someone stepped on the dry tinder. The fine hairs on his nape tingled. He got onto a knee, pulled his sword from the scabbard and stood. He bent and shook Phameas awake. Evan put a finger on his lips and pointed to the forest with the sword. Phameas got up and grabbed his sword.

They woke the others, careful to minimise sound. Evan scanned the interminable blackness of the trees, hand clenching and unclenching on the hilt of the sword. The others stood alongside, while the High Priestess and Dexion remained behind them. Evan could feel the heat radiating from Homer's body. He looked down at Phameas who gave him a tight smile. The hilt bit into Evan's palm. Loud rustling and branches snapping splintered the eerie silence.

'Help!'

The resonance of feet pounding on the earth came closer.

'Help me! Someone!'

A body stumbled through the last barrier of the forest and into their campsite. A juvenile sped towards them. His eyes were wild, fine lines of scratches covering his face, arms and legs. His dishevelled hair sported green fronds, and his khiton was torn.

'Mountain thieves!' He wheezed and pointed to the woods.

Hektor grabbed the boy's arm and flung him behind. A group of rough-looking men in tattered clothing burst into the clearing, waving swords and spears. The group skidded to a halt. One grinned, showing his few remaining decayed teeth when he spotted the High Priestess.

'Well, well... this has indeed turned out to be a profitable evening,' one said, leering. With a shout, he charged, his motley brigands rushing headlong with him.

Evan's mouth went dry and his heart banged against his ribcage as he gripped the sword and shield. His body went cold, then hot. He stared at the faces of the outlaws. Their mouths opened in grimaces, spittle flying everywhere and eyes feverish. They reminded him of rabid dogs. He held the shield closer and stiffened, ready for impact, much as a boxer did when facing an opponent.

Two came at him, the white of their eyes red. Their swords clanged against his shield. His arm vibrated, sending shockwaves from his fingertips to his shoulder. He swung his shield into one, knocking him onto the ground, and thrust his sword at the other. Sparks flew as Evan deflected the next attack. He slashed at his attacker in one swift motion, breaking the other man's sword. Evan's blood surged and thundered in his ears, the adrenaline soaring as he ran his sword through the disarmed man. The brigand screamed, clutched at his stomach and fell to his knees.

Evan felt a sharp burning sting beneath his ribcage. He looked down and saw a blood-tipped sword at his waist. His nostrils flared. With a roar, he kicked the man in the chest, leapt forward and swung his sword. The severed head flew backwards. Blood spewed from his neck. The body crumpled at his feet. He pivoted, beat off another attack and lunged. Evan fought with blind fury, striking and cutting down the bandits.

When there was a moment's reprieve, he noted the loudness of the clash of metal in the small clearing. The scent of iron was strong. In a daze he took in the scene. It was if he watched the skirmish in slow motion.

Leander let fly arrows, each one hitting their target. He retreated to defend the High Priestess, Dexion and the boy as they crouched by the fire. Hektor swung his axe, severing limbs of those who came too close. Their screams pierced the night. Homer wielded his sword with ease; the blade dripped with blood. Phameas thrust and parried those that swarmed towards him, and as a moth to a flame, he drew them in and maimed many.

Evan was brought out of his stupor by horrible shrieks. Sounds of death permeated the air as the fight went on. Bodies of the dead lay strewn, their limbs littering the area like discarded waste. Gore and blood, dark as the night, soaked the ground. The last surviving thieves began to falter, and one by one, they turned and fled. Leander aimed his bow into the sky and released a volley of arrows. The slender projectiles disappeared into the darkness. Sharp, dreadful squeals echoed.

Then there was silence.

They looked at each other. Splatters of crimson stained their bare skin and clothes.

'You've been injured,' Phameas said, pointing at the gash on Evan's side.

He looked down. His blood soaked the linen. He sucked in a breath as the adrenaline began to wear off and agony set in.

'Damn.' He clutched his side and winced.

The High Priestess stepped over the bodies. 'Let me see.'

Evan lifted the hem up. She leaned closer and touched his side with light fingers. He flinched.

'Evandros, I need to attend to your wound right away,' she said. A flicker of concern crossed her features, then was replaced by her usual stoic one.

'It's bad, isn't it?' he said between clenched teeth.

She did not respond.

'I thought so.'

'We must act now.' The High Priestess took him by the elbow and turned to Phameas. 'Help me with Evandros.' She then looked to Homer. 'Take his weapons.'

Homer nodded and reached to take the sword. The tip hit the ground. Homer grunted, hefted the sword, his neck muscles protruding and placed it by Evan's bag. He returned to take the shield.

'Watch your toes,' Evan joked in a weak voice.

Homer gave him a lopsided grin and beckoned Hektor. Between the two men, they carted the shield away. With the help of the High Priestess and Phameas, Evan lay down by the fire.

'Look!' Dexion pointed.

They turned to see an elongated blue-white shape speed towards them from the sky. It stopped beside the fallen bodies. The blinding light faded to reveal the Messenger of the Gods, holding a staff in his hand, his winged sandals glowing. He scanned the carnage before giving them his attention. Hermes frowned, seeing Evan wounded.

'Evandros, my brother, I will guide these soulless individuals to Hades. I also bring tidings from Father Zeus. Eris, the Goddess of Discord, has been freed from the realm of Tartaros and beseeches you to remain vigilant.' Hermes gazed at him a while longer and then turned to the High Priestess and bowed with flourish. 'Your beauty rivals that of the Spartan Queen Helen.'

'You honour me, Divine Messenger.' She acknowledged him with a slight nod.

He smiled, giving Evan another lingering look before vanishing, and with him, the bodies of the dead thieves.

'Who was that, and where are the bodies?' Theodoros asked, mystified.

'How many brothers do I have?' Evan rasped, fighting hard not to pass out. 'Gods, that hurts.'

CHAPTER SIX

The High Priestess instructed Dexion and Theodoros to collect water and heat it over the fire while she administered to a semiconscious Evan. She rummaged through the medicine bag acquired from the doctor in Kyrene. It had various vials and powders she'd used on Homer, who was injured by the tyrant king of Kyrene's guards during their imprisonment. She removed a vial and some green leaves from a pouch. The latter she mixed with the hot water in an earthenware bowl.

She murmured words as she applied a poultice. She placed her hands over the wound and lifted her face to the sky. Eyes closed, she continued to recite. At the end of the chant, she wrapped a bandage around his middle.

'Young Theodoros has been following since we left Messene,' she said, sitting back on her haunches. Evan moved to sit up. She pushed him back down with a firm, gentle hand. 'The dressing needs to set, and I fear you have lost a lot of blood. You will lose consciousness if you get up too soon.' She glanced at the Messenian. 'He's the brother of Neleos' wife.'

'I... remember. He... asked a lot... of questions... about... Atlantis,' Evan said, breathless. 'Does... Councilman Neleos... know... where you are?'

Theodoros shook his head, fiddling with the hem of his khiton. Evan closed his eyes and flinched at the High Priestess' feathery touch.

'Why did you follow?' asked Phameas.

'Messene is so boring. Nothing ever happens. When you came, it was exciting and the places you've seen and the adventure you're on! I want to be a part of that,' Theodoros said, his eyes sparkling.

'You seek adventure?' Hektor's nose wrinkled.

'I don't suppose you let your family know what you were doing,' Leander said.

'Of course not! They wouldn't let me go,' Theodoros said with a snort.

'He must go back. He cannot come with us.' Hektor crossed his arms against his chest, stance wide.

Theodoros shrank back and stepped closer to Dexion.

'We can't send him back alone,' the High Priestess said. 'He was almost killed by those marauders, and there could be more hiding in these lands. He accompanies us to Tegea, and someone there can take him back home.'

'I will not go back!'

'You don't have a choice,' said Hektor, glaring.

'I won't go,' Theodoros repeated and stuck his chin out.

'You will return to Messene,' the High Priestess said. 'Now let's retire and try to get some sleep.'

✳

Evan woke with a start. He tried to stretch his legs, but the shooting pain sent sickening waves through his body. Beads of sweat dotted his brow. He touched his side and saw blood on his fingers. The wound had reopened. He tried to sit up but could not. His head flopped to the right.

'Dexion...' His voice was a low rasp. 'Dex...ion.' The boy's eyelids fluttered. 'Dex...'

Dexion's eyes opened. 'Master Evandros!' He scrambled to Evan's side, his lower lip trembling. 'High Priestess! Come quick!'

Evan heard the flurry of movement, and within seconds she was kneeling at his side, her face colourless. 'Leander! The medical bag. Now!' His stomach contracted at the expression on her face. 'Evandros, the dressings are saturated. Your wound is much more extensive than I expected.'

Leander placed the bag down next to her and squatted close. Homer and Phameas hovered and watched with anxious expressions. Dexion held his hand, face glum. Hektor clasped a hand over his mouth and dragged it down over his chin. The High Priestess' hand had a slight tremor as she cut away the blood-soaked bandages. She peeled back the layers and drew in a sharp breath.

'Baaaad?' Evan said. His voice sounded tinny and thin to his ears.

Leander and Hektor looked away. Dexion's eyes watered. Homer's face was bleak but he did not turn his head. Phameas bit his lip and wiped away the tears with a balled hand.

'The cut may have... compromised the internal organs,' the High Priestess said, biting her lip.

Evan smacked his lips. 'Water... pleeassse...'

'Theodoros, water! Quick!' she ordered.

The boy darted away. Evan could hear him rummaging for a cup. He licked his lips and gazed up at the High Priestess. Despite her outward appearance of strength, he saw for the first time her vulnerability.

'It's... f...f... fine, High Priestess.'

'No,' she whispered, swallowing hard, 'it isn't. I will ask Mother for her help.'

Evan smiled. 'I don't... think the... gods... can... fix... thisss.' He looked at Phameas. 'Now... you seeee... I am... mortal.'

'Shut up, you idiot. Let the High Priestess do her thing.'

Evan laughed, then grimaced in agony as the shock waves of pain jolted every part of his body.

'I need hot water to clean his wound.'

'I will do that,' said Hektor, and he was gone before anyone else moved.

Theodoros had returned with water and handed it to the High Priestess. Phameas hurried to kneel behind Evan. He lifted Evan's head, and the High Priestess place a hand under his neck as she gave him water. He drank a few mouthfuls.

'Thank you.'

His eyes closed as they laid his head back. He could hear them talking, their voices growing fainter as he slipped in and out of consciousness. A good long sleep was what he needed, and then he would feel better.

'Evandros!' he heard someone shout. 'Evandros! Stay awake!' A hand grasped his shoulder and shook it. He blinked. The light was bright and hurt his eyes. 'Evandros, you must remain conscious. It's the only way to survive your injuries.' His head lolled to the side. 'Do you understand?' The High Priestess' hand felt heavy on his arm.

'Yyyyyyyyessssssss.'

'The Mother Goddess is on her way.'

Leander's face swam into view. 'You'll be well soon, Evandros.' He crouched down. 'The gods will watch over you.'

Evan gave him a wry smile. 'Perhaps… perrrrhaaaaps not.' And he closed his eyes, unable to keep them open any longer.

✳

'Evandros.' The voice was tender and musical. 'Evandros, I know you can hear me. Open your eyes.'

Evan did as commanded. He gazed at the stunning woman, her blonde hair cascading over her shoulders. Her age was difficult to guess, her face free of the usual passage of time that humans cannot escape. Her eyes, on the other hand, spoke of eternal wisdom and existence.

'Who are you?'

'I am Mother.'

Evan hesitated. 'As in Mother Goddess?'

She smiled, her face brightening. 'Yes.'

'Forgive me for staring, it's just that I am…'

'Overwhelmed,' she finished for him. He nodded. 'That is to be expected given the turmoil you have been through. My son Zeus can be quite overzealous when he gets excitable, as in what he did with you.'

'You know about that?'

'Of course.'

'Why didn't you stop him?'

'A parent allows their children to be independent, to learn and experiment in order to understand life.'

'Even if it's at the expense of other people's lives?'

'Immortals are not governed by the same principles as mortals,' she said.

'They should be. They don't have the right to do as they wish with the lives of humans.'

'In this case, it is well justified.'

Evan grumbled. 'Uprooting someone's life whenever you please is not justifiable in any situation.'

'Zeus' actions are well-founded, although he did not account for the effects the transitioning would have on his chosen advocate. It was impossible to predict how time-shift affects individuals.' She tilted her head to the side. 'He made the right choice in selecting you, for no other would have survived the slips through time, nor accepted living in a futurist world.'

'For the record, I don't accept this one.' Evan jabbed his finger at the ground.

The Mother Goddess smiled. 'Yet you have promised Homer and Hektor to find the relic so they can return home to their families.'

Evan nodded. 'I keep my promises, and they will see their families again.'

'What of you? What do you want?'

'I want to go back to the twenty-first century,' he said without hesitation.

'What if you are compelled to stay by someone you meet or by something that changes your mind?'

Evan stared at her. 'That's what Dexion said the first time we met. I will not be staying.'

The Mother Goddess shrugged, an elegant gesture. 'When the time comes, and if you still want to leave, I will make certain Zeus honours your wish.'

'Thank you. I am most grateful to you, Mother Goddess.'

'Come here so I may hug you,' she commanded.

Evan took a step, closing the gap, and the Mother Goddess wrapped her arms around him. She pressed her cheek against his. A white light enveloped them; it was neither warm nor cold. Evan closed his eyes against the blinding luminescence. Black dots peppered his eyelids. He melted into her arms, at once feeling comforted and protected. Never before had he felt such unconditional love and warmth, other than from his parents.

The light changed to green. Evan gasped. The Mother Goddess held him to her as his knees buckled. When he clutched at her, a piercing pain ripped through his body. The Mother Goddess gathered him closer. His breathing was ragged and harsh.

'My dear son, my dear, brave son, you are my greatest creation.' He could feel the softness of her lips and her gentle, warm breath against his ear. 'Use your wealth of knowledge and talents to do as you must. Do not be influenced by the machinations of others, and listen to your instincts. The strength of your intuition is a gift. Use it well and you will succeed.'

Evan's breathing returned to normal, though he swayed a little and felt light-headed. She took his face in her hands, her eyes hypnotic as he gazed back.

'I am so proud of you, Evandros, but in future, please refrain from being injured,' she said lifting a brow.

He gave her a lopsided grin. 'That may be difficult given where I am and the expedition. Besides, I'm not a swordsman.'

She tapped his forehead with a finger. 'It's all in here. Your skills are all there. It is a matter of you accepting the here and now. Treat it as a challenge to yourself and prove to the others you are worthy of leading them.'

'I thought I was in charge.'

'You are guiding them. However, you need to earn their trust. Show them respect, and in turn they will respect you as well.'

'The High Priestess and Hektor aren't too happy about who I am now. I can't change, nor do I want to. I like the person I am.'

'You are who you're meant to be, and in time they will accept that. However, you must be open-minded and considerate of their point of view. You are not the same person they knew, and that has upset them. Give them time to accept who you are now.' She stepped back. 'Awaken, Evan!'

Evan woke with a start. He heard the crackling of fire, the yellow orange glow spreading light around the camp. On his right, Phameas sat cross-legged, and head nodded forward as he slept. Dexion lay not far from him, and Homer sat vigil at his feet. Evan propped himself on his elbows. Homer's eyes widened, and a broad smile crept across his face. He leaned and shook Dexion's leg and reached across to wake Phameas.

'Great Moloch!' Phameas stared at Evan, mouth falling open. 'We thought the gods had taken you!'

The others were roused, hearing the commotion.

'Thank the gods!' said Leander. He crouched by Homer and beamed at Evan. 'We were worried you were lost to us.'

'I thought the same,' Evan said. He glanced at the bindings around his waist. He touched his side. 'Incredible.'

Evan looked at the High Priestess in wonder as she knelt next to him. She touched his forehead with the back of her hand and peered into his eyes.

'I feel great,' he said when she finished.

'Let me look at the wound.' She undid the knot and proceeded to unwrap the bandage. The last layer was removed; the lesion was gone. Evan laid a hand where the laceration should have been. It was smooth, not even the ripple of scar tissue.

'Unbelievable.' He said as he stared in amazement.

'By Almighty Baal! You are a god!'

'No, I am not, but I was healed by one.' He looked up at the High Priestess. 'The Mother Goddess heard you. I thought it was a dream, but it appears it wasn't.'

'The Mother Goddess came to you?' Hektor said, affronted.

Evan nodded. 'That's who she told me she was. She is… extraordinary.'

'Did she say anything to you?' the High Priestess asked. She tilted her head and looked at him as though he was an exotic specimen.

'She told me off.'

The High Priestess' brows arched. 'What did she say?'

'Not to get hurt again.'

'That's good advice. I suggest you listen.' Leander chortled.

Homer grinned, Phameas and Dexion laughed. Hektor stood back, arms crossed against his chest, a sullen expression marring his handsome features.

CHAPTER SEVEN

Evan rose early the following morning, unable to sleep, his mind in a turmoil over his extraordinary experience. He placed his hand over where he had been stabbed. If this was a dream, albeit an elaborate one, would he have felt the sharpness of the blade as it pierced his side, the burning sensation and the excruciating pain that crippled had him and his ability to think? The Mother Goddess was not what he had expected. Evan had no doubt that if she was crossed, no person or immortal could bear her wrath.

He poked at the small fire, the embers igniting and placed twigs atop. Evan felt the Mother Goddess would prove to be a strong foil to the rise of the Messiah, if she sought to reign. The others began to stir. Evan decided not to voice his views, as the idea was more theoretical than a realisation.

'You're up early,' said Phameas with a yawn.

'I couldn't sleep,' replied Evan.

'Are you in pain?' asked the High Priestess, rising, her brows crinkled.

Evan shook his head. 'I'm feeling great. Let's have a quick breakfast and be on our way.'

Evan led them out of the confines of the clearing. He shivered and drew his cloak closer. There was a chill in the air, a hint of cooler weather on the way. They continued along the road to Tegea until they came to a fork in the road. One went south-east and the other northwards. Evan checked the map and veered north. The path straightened and cut through the plain.

After a few hours, they pulled to the side to stop and rest. On the right, some metres away on a hilltop, Evan noticed a temple. It was not as big as the Temple of Concord he had seen in Sicily, but it was not small either. The colours were not as vibrant as the day the building was painted, but still showed vestiges of what it might have looked like.

'We mustn't be too far from Tegea.' Evan pointed to the sanctuary. 'Do we want to stay overnight or keep going after we find someone to take Theodoros back to Messene?'

'I will not go back!' Theodoros crossed his arms against his chest and pouted. 'And if you do leave me here, I will run away!'

'You may think this is all very exciting, but believe me, it isn't,' Evan said. 'It's no fun trekking from place to place, getting attacked by monsters and brigands and imprisoned by crazy kings. Not to mention being injured, and that, I can tell you, is most unpleasant.' He waved a hand at the others. 'Do they look as if they are enjoying themselves?'

Hektor's face was hard and unflinching. Leander raised a brow but did not smile. Homer remained deadpan, while Phameas crossed his arms, unsmiling. Dexion seemed unperturbed as he reached for an orange and began to peel the rind.

'Evandros is right,' the High Priestess said. 'Our journey is one of necessity and not of adventure. We are here because the gods have decreed it so.'

'What of Dexion and Phameas? Aren't they here of their own choice?' Theodoros said, lifting his chin. 'How are their lives less important than mine?'

'They're not. Both Dexion and Phameas are integral to our search,' the High Priestess said in a cool voice. 'They helped Evandros while we were separated and are valuable members of our group. You, on the other hand, are here to seek excitement, and that could imperil your life and ours.'

'As it already has done,' Hektor said, eyes narrowing.

Theodoros' arms fell to his side. 'I didn't mean to cause anyone harm.' He turned to Evan. 'I am sorry you were injured.' Then his face brightened. 'But the Mother Goddess healed you! Isn't that good? If anyone is wounded, the gods will restore our health.'

The High Priestess stared at him. No one spoke.

'Won't they?' He looked at each of them.

'Homer's inability to speak is due to the physical abuse ordered by the king of Kyrene,' Evan said, tight-lipped.

'He was unconscious for a few months,' added Leander.

Theodoros looked at Homer. 'The gods didn't come to your aid?'

The big man shook his head.

'The actions of the gods are not for us to question; we are their servants.' The High Priestess reached over and took Homer's hand. He smiled and gave her hand an affectionate squeeze. 'Now, let us resume our journey to Tegea.'

An hour later they arrived at the fortified city, a large territory, the heart of the metropolis built in the middle of the plain. Evan, Phameas and Dexion escorted Theodoros into the city while the others waited on the outskirts under the shelter of trees.

Evan left his weapons with Homer, not wanting to draw too much attention or spend too much time locating a suitable individual to chaperone Theodoros home. The youth pleaded with Evan, and when that didn't work, he turned to Phameas.

'If you accompany us, you will not see Delphi or your family again,' said Dexion, interrupting his incessant whining.

Theodoros stopped. 'What?'

'You will not become a man.'

Theodoros blinked. 'I… er… what?'

'Dexion is saying you need to return home,' Evan interjected.

'I still don't understand.'

'Take it as a piece of advice, one worth listening to,' Evan suggested.

'Or a warning,' Phameas added under his breath.

Theodoros gazed at them for a few seconds. 'Am I going to…' He paused, unable to finish the sentence.

'It is worth heeding Dexion's words,' Evan said. 'Come on, we'll go to the agora and ask around.'

It took time to find someone willing to escort Theodoros. After much haggling, they left the youth in the care of his beaming benefactor. Evan glanced over his shoulder and sighed, seeing how crestfallen Theodoros looked.

'I feel sorry for him,' he said to Phameas and Dexion. 'I can understand how he feels, wanting to explore new places and experience different things.'

'Me too. That's why I became a sailor,' said Phameas.

'He would have been killed,' Dexion said.

'Did you see where and how?' asked Evan.

Dexion's face clouded and nodded. 'We were on a ship and he was taken by a harpy.'

'Harpies again!' Evan juddered. 'Now there's a group of monsters I'd rather not see again. Now that he's safe and no longer with us, your vision should change.'

CHAPTER EIGHT

Evan was intrigued by the varied shapes and styles of shrines that dotted the roadside, a sign of a well-travelled region. When he toured the Peloponnese, which seemed in the too far distance, or rather, too far in the future, the stone epitaphs were non-existent. Vineyards, orchards and grazing lands dominated the scenery in the twenty-first century, but here in this time, farmlands and the houses were set away from the main thoroughfare. Olive trees, barley and wheat crops flourished in the pastures. Further afield, in the mountains, Evan heard the faint bleating of sheep and goats.

Evan bid a good morning to a small group of travellers heading towards Tegea, who acknowledged them with a nod and continued on their way. As the day came to a close, Evan pointed to a small cluster of trees. Leander nodded and pulled off onto the shoulder of the road, where the group wasted no time setting up camp.

'How long will it take to get to Corinth?' the High Priestess asked, the flickering flames giving her face an ethereal appearance.

'Let me check the map King Mentor prepared for us.' Evan rummaged through his bag, pulling out the other maps before locating the one he wanted. He unrolled it and held out an end to Phameas. 'Could you hold that side, please?' He calculated the distance in his head. 'We should arrive in Corinth tomorrow early evening, give or take a few hours, depending on the terrain.'

The High Priestess nodded with approval. 'Good. We'll stay the night before setting out for Delphi.'

'That won't be possible,' said Evan.

'Why not?' The High Priestess bristled at his response.

'There is a gulf in between, and to cross it we need to hire a boat.'

'King Mentor did not mention it,' she said, displeased.

'No, but it is here on the map.' He showed her the body of water, where Corinth was located and the site of Delphi.

'Is there another way we can go to Delphi?'

'Not unless you want to spend a week to two weeks trekking.'

'It appears as if we don't have any other choice,' Leander said in a conciliatory tone. 'Besides, staying an extra night or two in Corinth will allow us to rest,' he added in a cheerful tone and patted the High Priestess' hand.

She gave him a tight smile and nodded. 'Of course, a sound idea, Leander.' She held his gaze for a while longer before turning to Evan. 'By boat we shall go.'

Evan roused everyone early, eager to arrive in Corinth before nightfall. Around midday, he spied something speeding towards them, kicking up clouds of dust in its wake.

'Dexion, jump in the back of the wagon,' Evan said, cupping a hand behind the boy's head. He waited until Dexion was seated before setting out at a quick pace ahead of the mule. Homer and Phameas were not far behind.

The sound of laughter drew closer, and over it a frantic voice shouted to slow down. Evan tensed and eased to a stop.

'Move to the side,' Evan said, waving a hand at the others.

Seconds later, a black chariot emerged from a grey-plumed haze and careered at them, as if the hounds of Kerberos were in hot pursuit. The driver whipped the reins, spurring the horses on, the pounding of hooves thundered on the road.

Evan could see the whites of the horses' eyes and flare of their nostrils. He was about to shout out a warning when he saw the driver was a young woman, who whooped in wild abandonment. The youth standing next to her, clung to the sides, his eyes and mouth as wide open as the stallions'.

'Look out!' the youth screamed.

The woman yanked on the reins and the four horses skidded. Dirt curled and dust ballooned behind the chariot. Her companion was flung forward and hit his head on the rim of the chariot. Leander soothed their mule as it tried to back away from the impending crash. They came to a stop within fifty paces of where Evan and the others had halted. The woman brushed her windswept hair from her face.

'What is wrong with you?' Evan bellowed. 'You could have killed us!'

Her eyes flashed and her brows drew into angry line. 'How dare you speak to me in that manner. I am Princess Adrasteia!'

'I don't care who you are,' Evan said, growling. 'Your reckless driving has injured your handler and upset our mule. And look at the condition of your horses.'

The horses' coats glistened with sweat, their legs shook, and they were foaming at the mouth.

'Homer, come and take a look at them,' Evan called over his shoulder.

'What do you think you are doing?' the princess demanded. 'Get away from my horses. I am a princess of Mykenae! Wait until my father hears of this.'

'I don't really care, princess or not. You do not treat animals in this way.'

Homer moved from one horse to the next, running a hand over their flanks and legs. He placed a hand over the muzzle and shook his head. He patted them on the forehead and they rubbed against him. He scowled at the princess and headed to the wagon. He grabbed a water container and walked back to the horses. Leander joined him and helped give the horses water. Satisfied they had enough, Homer took out his tablet, wrote with quick strokes and passed it to Evan.

'Homer suggests you walk the horses' home, and make sure they are rubbed down, given water and oats.'

'What nonsense, they are fine,' she sniffed. 'Besides, what would commoners know about horses?'

'More than you. Otherwise these horses would not be overwrought. Move aside so we may pass.' Evan turned to Leander, who gathered the reins of their mule and began to move. Evan glared at the princess. 'Get on with it, we haven't all day.'

The youth at her side reached for the reins. A flicker of annoyance flashed across her face and she slapped his hand. Her attention shifted from Evan to Leander, Hektor, Homer and Phameas, and a slow smile transformed her face.

'Let's begin again. I am Princess Adrasteia of Mykenae.' She thrust the reins at the shaking youth and alighted from the chariot. She sidled over with practiced coquetry and gazed up at Evan, batting her eyelids. Wavy brown hair framed her heart-shaped face, but her golden-brown eyes belied cunning and trouble. 'What is your name?'

'Evandros.' He stood rigid, eyes hard as granite. She ignored his frosty reply and poked her head around him, her glance sweeping over Dexion and the High Priestess, who sat in the wagon.

'What is the hurry? We should get acquainted. After all, you did say the horses should not run.' She smiled. 'Where are you heading?'

'I don't see how that concerns you.' Evan scowled.

'If we're heading in the same direction, we can travel together. Also I'd feel safer. These roads are notorious for wayward thieves accosting travellers.'

'You should have thought of that beforehand,' Hektor bit back.

'I did not expect to come this far from home.' She shrugged.

'We do not have time to babysit a spoilt brat,' Evan said. 'Now get back on your chariot and move out of the way or I will shift it for you.'

Princess Adrasteia's face turned red and her eyes glittered. She spun on her heel and stomped back to the chariot. She snatched the reins from her handler and pointed a finger at Evan. 'May you rot in Hades.'

She snapped the reins. The horses started. The princess yanked the reins to the left and hollered. With another hard smack on their rumps, the horses bolted, the chariot snaking in the wake. Clouds of dust shrouded the road as the princess raced away.

'I don't believe we've seen the last of Princess Adrasteia,' the High Priestess said.

'You think she'll return?' Leander asked.

'She doesn't appear to be accustomed to being told what to do or having her demands denied. She was also humiliated.'

Homer pulled out his sword from the wagon and strapped on the scabbard. Leander reached for his bow and arrow, and Hektor picked up his axe.

'What is the likelihood she won't return with reinforcements?' Evan asked, fixing his shield and sword on his back. They all looked at him. 'That's what I thought too.' He sighed. 'Right, let's get on with it.'

CHAPTER NINE

Evan clutched the hilt of his sword, scanning the road ahead for the telltale signs of a sizeable force heading in their direction. So far the line of sight was clear, yet he could not shake the niggling feeling that something was about to happen.

'The calm before the storm,' Evan muttered to himself. He then said to the others, 'What is the plan if the princess does return with soldiers?'

'We reason with her,' said the High Priestess.

'And if that doesn't work?' Evan asked. The sceptical expression on his face was echoed by Phameas and Homer.

'I doubt the princess is a rational person,' Leander added in a mild tone.

'That is an understatement,' said Evan with a snort.

'If she is unwilling to be sensible, I will provide a more fitting response,' the High Priestess said.

'What if the soldiers attack?' asked Evan.

'I will also deal with them.' The High Priestess brushed at unseen dirt on her lap.

Evan stared at the High Priestess and wondered at her meaning. He then turned to the lush and full cornfields, the slender crops laden with fruit, swaying back and forth in the wind.

The next few hours on the road were uneventful, and Evan began to relax. In some pastures, farmers ploughed the land, guiding a team of oxen, ready to sow for the next seasonal produce. They stopped for a quick drink by a river that ran parallel to the road, refilling their urns and containers. When they set off, the High Priestess half stood from her seat on the wagon and shielded her eyes.

'Something is coming our way, and it looks to be sizeable.'

'Dammit,' Evan murmured. His stomach churned and fine perspiration covered his forehead. He hadn't emerge from the last confrontation with great success, and didn't want to repeat the near-death experience.

A large column of grey haze on the horizon moved at a brisk pace. Evan pulled out his sword and held it by his side. Phameas looked over at Evan, his face grim, clutching his curved short sword. They forged ahead, their attention fixed on the fast-approaching dust storm. The ground trembled under the thunder of horses' hooves.

Over the din, a solitary voice yelled a command and the rumbling eased. The dust settled, and leading the retinue of hoplites and cavalry were two chariots: one black with images adorned in gold, and the other was driven by Princess Adrasteia. She watched Evan with a smug smile.

Evan and the others were forced to stop. From the rear of the cavalry, a line of horsemen rode out and surrounded them. The soldiers were armed with swords and spears, their body armour and shields glittered under the sun.

'Which of you is Evandros?' shouted the black-bearded man in the chariot. His eyebrows were drawn into an angry line, and his face distorted in fury. 'The one who defiled my daughter!'

Evan blinked, his mind recoiled. He did not know what to think or say.

The riders closed in. The hot breaths and snorts of the horses filled the tense atmosphere, the possibility of escape squelched by the nearness of the animals and their riders. Then Evan's mouth twitched and he burst out laughing. Phameas turned to him, incredulous. Homer looked at him as if he'd lost his sanity; Hektor, Leander and the High Priestess stared at him, nonplussed. Dexion was the only one who seemed unperturbed by Evan's reaction.

The king glowered as Evan clutched his stomach, the tears running down his face. He caught sight of the princess' inflamed face and doubled over in hysteria.

'How dare you find the desecration of my daughter amusing!' the king roared, his face as scarlet as his daughter's.

Evan's laughter subsided and he wiped the tears with the back of his hand. Composed, he said, 'I don't find the violation of any woman at all funny. What I do not appreciate is being accused of a heinous act that I did not commit!' He pointed at the princess. 'I would not go near your daughter if she were the last female on this planet!' He took a step. A rider flicked out his sword. Evan glared at him but did not advance further. 'How can I possibly be in contact with your daughter when I have been with my companions the whole time? I've never seen or known of her until she lambasted her way into our path. Ask her poor heckled handler, if he hasn't been threatened to lie.' Evan clenched his hands, and his eyes glowered. 'Now, get out of our way!'

'You dare to speak to me in this manner!' the king sputtered. 'You are a nothing more than a commoner. It is your word against my daughter's!'

'Your daughter is a liar. And I have witnesses, six of them who can vouch for my version of events.' Evan threw the princess a murderous look. Her face contorted, ugly and venomous.

Homer stood behind Evan, drawing the king's attention. The king then glanced at the others in the group and settled on the High Priestess. She did not flinch or look away. He leered at her.

'It appears you have much to lose.'

Evan stepped into the king's line of sight. Leander and Hektor butted against the wagon, and Phameas and Homer closed in on either side of Evan.

'It would be wise for you to step aside and let us through,' Evan said through gritted teeth.

The king laughed and flung an arm at his warriors. 'You are outnumbered. Besides, did you really think I was going to let you go?'

Evan's skin prickled.

'What in the name of the gods!' The king's head jerked back.

From the periphery of his vision, Evan saw a red luminescent glow emanate and grow until it encompassed their small group. He turned. The High Priestess was standing, the whites of her eyes and pupils had changed to the colour of ebony. Her long black curly tresses spread around her head like snakes. The golden serpent curled about her upper arm moved. Its mouth had opened, projecting the coloured light, and its eyes were red like the sphere that protected them.

'This can't be good,' Evan said. The last time the golden serpent had sensed a threat was when the High Priest of Re had tried to steal it from the High Priestess. It hadn't ended well for the High Priest. Evan had found the golden serpent in the Karnak Temple in Egypt, the location given to them by

Poseidon and confirmed by a visit from Zeus. Evan shuddered as a chill ran down his spine.

'You have made a grave error in judgement.' Her voice was disembodied. 'Let us pass.'

'Kill them!' the king yelled.

A volley of lances arced into the sky. Evan flung his shield up to deflect the whistling missiles. The spears disintegrated as the bronze tips touched the red light. The protective shield fluttered and then stilled. The expressions on the faces of the warriors and their king would have been laughable if the situation weren't dire.

The king ordered his hoplites to attack. The first line advanced holding their swords out. The weapons crumbled on impact. The soldiers faltered, weaponless except for their shields. They looked at each other and at the people enclosed within the red dome.

'Keep moving!' the king commanded.

The men took a tentative step and raised their shields. With small steps, they inched forward. There was a horrific scream, followed by another, and soon joined by a cacophony of shrieks. The discordant sound chilled Evan's blood. The colour drained from his face. The gruesome vision of men rendered helpless and mortally wounded by the red light.

'Dear God.' Bile rose and Evan threw up.

'Moloch!' Phameas dry-retched a few times, and then vomited.

The wails increased as dismembered hoplites tried to back away from the protective sphere. Some had their arms, which held shields, shorn to their elbows. Others weren't as fortunate. Many lost an entire arm; a few were missing a foot or a leg. There was no blood, the wounds cauterised by the light. The soldiers positioned behind the maimed, spun on their heels and pushed against the tight formation, yelling and screaming.

The horses reared, their eyes wild as the squeals of terror reverberated, and unseated their riders. Confused and frightened, the animals collided in their attempt to escape. One unfortunate horse rammed into another and its rump made contact with the fatal glow. Evan threw up again until nothing was left. He wiped his mouth with a shaking hand.

'Move back!' he cried.

The king stood in his chariot, paralysed. His daughter was nowhere to be seen. Evan guessed she had fled during the chaos. His blood bubbled and his anger smouldered like hot embers of a fire, thinking how her lie had caused the loss of innocent lives.

The red light faded, and strewn around them were the bodies of the slain and wounded men, moaning. Evan strode out to the king and pulled him from the chariot. He seized the king's neck.

'You stupid fool! This is all on you!' He flung his other arm out at the carnage. 'You and your daughter are responsible for what has happened here. You are not fit to be a king.'

Evan's grip tightened around his neck. The king's face turned a mottled red-blue and his tongue stuck out. Not one of his remaining and abled warriors stepped forth.

'Your ancestor, King Agamemnon, in spite of his faults and supersized ego, would be shamed by your actions here today.' Evan tossed the king to the ground like a rag doll. The king's fingers clawed the dirt as his chest heaved, trying to draw breath.

'If you are smart,' Evan said to the king's retinue, 'you will leave this pile of shit and find a more judicious leader. Now get out of our way!' He whirled on his heel, took a few steps and stopped with a thumb thrust over his shoulder. 'And get rid of that rubbish that's blocking the road.'

The way was cleared without any further prompting. The High Priestess sat, her hands clenched in her lap, her face white and drawn tight. The hoplites, faces gaunt, stiffened as she passed by in the wagon. They did not move, nor did they whisper. When they reached the bend in the road, Evan looked back and nodded with grim satisfaction. The warriors were meting out punishment to their king.

CHAPTER TEN

Evan and his companions arrived in the bustling city of Corinth a day later, though Evan couldn't appreciate the vibrancy of the city. The noise and laughter were surreal in the wake of the recent atrocity. Evan's mind still reeled from the horrors inflicted on the Mykenaean soldiers. He'd never seen anything so sickening or frightening. Not even the scariest movie he had watched came close. It gave him pause. Could a person's mind conjure vivid scenes of butchery while dreaming?

No one had spoken since their departure from the scene of slaughter. The tragic events had left an indelible impression on everyone; from the High Priestess reticence, it was difficult to determine whether she was affected by what happened. Evan glanced at Phameas. The usual bounce in his step and merry sparkle in his eyes were absent. Evan needed a distraction, and focussed his attention on the largest city other than Athens.

He had visited the ruins of Corinth and been impressed by the size of the site. The remnants of the buildings were Roman in his time. Only the foundation and a few columns of the Temple of Apollo had withstood the destruction when the Romans invaded. The Akrocorinth, which he hadn't gotten to see, overlooked the city and was the location of the Temple of Aphrodite. He remembered reading that the temple had housed over one thousand prostitutes and was a popular destination for ancient travellers. He'd also read that the prostitutes would walk along the shores of the gulf and leave an imprint in the sand from their sandals, with the words "follow me". Whether that was true or not, it made the story memorable as well as exemplifying the city's ignoble reputation.

The road leading into Corinth was wide and busy. There were numerous carts laden with goods headed in and out of the city. Evan caught sight of the majestic temple sitting atop the hill, remote from the main populace, yet offering the tantalising promise of intimacy.

Houses, big and small, seem to sprout like wildflowers as they entered the gates. Narrow staircases cut into the incline led to houses built on the slopes of the hill. The streets ran in straight lines, intersecting at right angles. They followed the road into the heart of the city and towards the sound of hawkers.

'Shall we split up?' Evan said. He came to a stop. 'One group goes to purchase supplies, and the other group seeks out where we can stay the night.'

'I'm happy to go and restock our provisions,' said Leander.

'Great, thanks Leander. Anyone else would like to go with Leander?'

'I'll go,' Hektor said.

The High Priestess nodded. 'I'll accompany Leander and Hektor.'

Evan reached into his bag and pulled out a small pouch. He checked it and handed it to Leander. 'That should be more than enough.'

Leander nodded and secreted the money within the folds of his khiton.

Evan studied the High Priestess. 'You need to cover your head with a scarf. We don't want to draw attention if we can help it.'

'That's right, I remember the reaction of the men when we were escorted through Pylos,' Leander said. 'They were not very pleased at seeing the High Priestess.'

'Yes, women cannot venture in public without a male escort nor without their heads covered.'

The High Priestess pulled out an elegant almost see through wrap of sky blue and placed it over her head.

'We'll meet back here,' Evan said.

Dexion jumped down from the wagon and joined Evan, Phameas and Homer. They entered the noisy marketplace, then Leander and the other Atlanteans veered to the right and headed for the food stalls. To their left were shops where craftsmen worked and displayed their wares. A few stalls along, signage outside a couple of shops advertised a bank and money exchange facilities. On the right, where Leander, Hektor and the High Priestess had blended with the throng, was the stoa, a covered walkway where merchants sold food and unique goods from various countries.

Evan spotted a gathering of older men, who sat on the steps of the stoa, watching the busy market like overseers.

'Come on,' he said to the others.

He led the way, zigzagging through the crowd. A few locals stopped and stared at Evan and Homer.

'Excuse me, honoured elders.' The men turned, a few blinking as they looked from Evan to Homer. They continued to stare, their eyes growing wider. 'We're travellers and are looking for a hostel suitable for a high priestess and with a stable?'

'Almighty Zeus, you are tall!'

Inquisitive eyes grew brighter as they gawked at the newcomers.

'Yes. Are you able to help us?'

'Where have you come from?' one asked, his greying hair cropped, as was his beard. He wore a long khiton and a yellow himation, a mantle that draped over his left shoulder and wrapped around his body.

'Pylos.'

'You've travelled far,' the old man said, raising a brow.

'You could say we've covered some distance.' Homer tapped Evan on the shoulder. Evan glanced at what was written on the tablet and nodded. 'Sorry we have bothered you. Thank you for your time.'

Evan and his companions swung away.

'Wait, young man! No need to be so hasty!' the old man called out, getting to his feet. Evan shared a look with Homer. The grey-haired Corinthian added with haste, 'Many strangers come to Corinth from as far as Aegyptos, and we,'—he swept a hand at the men sitting behind him—'like to know where people come from, hear their stories.'

'I am sure you do, but all we need is directions to a good hostel,' Evan said. 'Again, thank you for your time.'

'It's just that I'm not sure whether any of the hostels will accommodate you!' the old man said, raising his voice as Evan stepped away.

'What do you mean?' Evan looked at him.

'Men who come to Corinth don't usually bring a woman with them.'

'You're referring to the Temple of Aphrodite.' Evan's jaw tightened in annoyance. 'We're not here to seek pleasure, only to stay the night before moving on.'

'Of course. There's a reputable hostel next to the gymnasium. It has a stable and the proprietor is discreet.' He gave directions and added, 'Tell Kleitos, the owner, Mydon sent you.'

Evan nodded and said thank you again. He then added under his breath, 'Quick, let's get away.'

They returned to the location to wait for the others by the wall of the shop.

'Can't stand nosy people,' Evan said. 'Always wanting to know what you're doing and where you're going, especially those who don't like to share anything of themselves.'

'Are there people like that in the twenty-first century?' Phameas asked. He leaned against the wall and looked up at Evan.

'There's a saying by a man called Alphonse Karr: "The more things change, the more they are same". The same could be said of people. I've met and know of individuals who interfere and pry. It's a personality trait I don't admire.'

'What else can you tell us about where you're from?' Phameas gave him an eager look.

Evan scratched his stubbled chin. 'There is so much. The world is vast and small at the same time.'

'How is that possible?'

Dexion and Homer shuffled closer to listen.

'We can travel from one continent to another by flying. In a day you could be across the world and in a different country.'

Phameas gasped. Homer and Dexion's mouths fell open.

'Fly? Like a bird?'

'In a way,' Evan nodded. 'We have flying machines that soar eleven thousand metres into the sky. That is approximately twenty-four thousand cubits.'

'Moloch!'

'Have you flown in the sky?' Dexion asked.

'I've been in a plane many times,' he said.

'Do you fly...?' Dexion frowned.

'The plane?' The boy nodded. 'No, pilots are trained to navigate and steer the aeroplane.' Evan looked at Phameas. 'Much like a captain of a ship.'

'Except you're in the sky with the birds and gods!' Phameas hugged himself. 'The sky should be left to the gods and birds.'

Is it safe to travel in the air? Homer asked.

Evan shrugged. 'As much as it is to sail.'

'Wouldn't you fall from the sky?' Dexion tilted his face at the sky.

'No, the design of the aircraft stops it from dropping to the earth.' He squatted and with a finger drew an image of a plane in the sand. Homer, Dexion and Phameas crouched with him. 'Planes can fly with or without an engine. The ones I'm speaking of have powerful engines. They lift the craft into the air and the speed moves it forward. The wings, like a bird's, allows the wind to glide over and thrusts the air downwards.'

'And this prevents it from falling to the ground?' Phameas pulled at his ear and frowned at the picture Evan drew.

'Yes. There are other forces that help and I'm not doing justice to the inventors of the plane with my explanation. As a bird uses the air and the pull of the earth to keep aloft, the design of the aircraft is based on the same principle.'

Homer rubbed out the image and stood, stamping his foot on it. Evan looked up at him, noted the change in his posture and stood up as well. He brushed his hands on his khiton and turned. Leander gave them a wave and a smile. Evan lifted his hand. As he moved to meet the others, from the corner of his eye, he saw Homer take a heavy step, leaving a deep depression in the sand. Phameas followed in his stead, obliterating any further evidence of the etching.

CHAPTER ELEVEN

Evan's mind whirled in awe as he and his companions trundled past the shops, each occupied by merchants or craftsmen. He had not expected such diversity and quantity of shops, or such a thriving commerce. Although he had read Corinth and Athens were renowned for trading, he had not imagined the impressive scale he saw here. This city would rival the likes of any busy twenty-first century metropolis. Evan saw an artist painting a vase with angular geometric patterns in red and black. Displayed opposite along the wall were various jugs with flora and fauna designs. The artisan did not use templates to trace the picture onto the ceramic surface; he drew it freeform. The complexities of the geometric shapes were repeated around the neck of the vase, and the precision of size and consistency astounded Evan. Such craftsmanship had died out with the introduction of technology and mass production. Those items that were handcrafted had a hefty price tag.

On the right-hand side of the road was a large temple dedicated to Apollo, a landmark the old man had told Evan to keep watch for. Facing the temple across the road were smaller buildings, their function concealed behind the double-wooden doors. They made a sharp right turn and a quick left. Ahead on the left, separated by parkland and trees, was an open-air theatre, and a part of the wall of the semicircular structure faced the road. Inside, citizens who sat to watch plays, had magnificent views of the valley below.

They skirted past a large building, and Evan slowed to take in the structure. He recognised it as the palestra, an ancient gymnasium. The lower precinct was surrounded by lush grass, cypress and laurel trees. There were single and two-storey homes, the layout similar to those they had seen in Messene.

The façade of the hostel was nondescript and looked like any other house except for the small plaque stuck on the wall with the name inscribed. The wooden doors were open and Evan entered first. Inside, a cistern filled to the brim with water, dominated a swept courtyard. A clean-shaven man with curly red hair and green eyes emerged from a room. He wore a short pale green khiton and approached them, wiping his hands on a cloth.

'Good evening,' Evan said with a slight bow.

'And a good eve to you.'

'Are you Kleitos?'

The proprietor looked from Evan to the others, and then nodded, standing still.

'Mydon recommended your establishment to us. We are hoping you have rooms available for the night and a place for our mule and wagon.'

'How do you know Mydon?' Kleitos asked, his head cocked to the side.

'I don't. He was with a group of men I queried in regard to a hostel appropriate for our High Priestess. He was the one who suggested coming here,' Evan said.

The expression on Kleitos' face lightened and he looped the soiled cloth on his belt. 'We've enough room for you all. It's one drachma per night, and two drachmas for the mule.'

Evan turned to the High Priestess, who nodded. He faced the innkeeper. 'Thank you, we'll take it.'

'Leave your mule and wagon here. I'll have the stable boy take care of them. Would you like to bathe, and perhaps have something to eat?'

'That's the best idea I've heard today.' Evan beamed at him.

'I will arrange it for you. In the meantime, I will take you to your rooms and later show you to the andron, where you'll eat your meals.'

Evan was woken by the sunlight streaming through the window. He turned on his side and shut his eyes, but the bright morning sun made it impossible to go back to sleep. He lay listening to the birds twittering. A familiar comforting sound, yet given where he was, and when, it seemed alien. He wondered how long he'd been dreaming. The previous experiences had lasted a few hours, with the longest topping four hours. Either he was in a coma, or this was one heck of a delusion.

He glanced out the window and noted the flawless blue sky. *Are all dreams as vivid as mine? Do people eat, sleep and get injured as I've done? Or feel the heat of the sun, the dirt between toes or getting rained on?* Evan ran a hand below his ribcage where he'd been stabbed. He recalled meeting the Mother Goddess, and their discussion. If this was a dream, why had he created such an elaborate world, and why this time period?

Evan thrust off the blanket, sat up and swung his legs over the side of the small cot. He got out of bed, donned a khiton and padded out of the room he shared with Phameas and Dexion. He gazed up at the sky through the opening in the roof, clasped his bristly chin and pressed his fingers into the flesh.

'Now if I am dreaming, would my hair and beard grow?' he said to himself. He glanced around taking in the painted walls, the rank scent of body odour and the smooth, dark discoloured wood under his bare feet. 'Real or not, I'm stuck here until I find the remaining relic and Zeus lets me go home.'

He took the steps down to the ground floor, the cobblestones smooth under his feet as he crossed the courtyard. The heavy scent of orange blossoms and the sound of bees buzzing added to his disquiet about the elaborate illusion.

'Good morning, Evandros,' Kleitos greeted him. 'You're up early. Did you sleep well?'

'Morning, Kleitos.' Evan joined him by the entrance to the andron. 'Well enough.'

'Is there anything I can do for you?'

'Indeed, would you know where we could go to hire a boat to cross the Isthmus?'

'Yes, if you go to Lechaion, there's a small harbour. Ask for Jason. Tell him I recommended him.'

'Brilliant, thank you. How long does it take to walk to Lechaion?'

'Oh, it's less than two hours.'

'Many thanks, Kleitos.'

The innkeeper nodded. 'Will you be staying another night?'

'That is a good question. Can I let you know once I've spoken with the others?'

'Of course.' Kleitos bowed and went on his way.

Evan wandered over to a stone bench under the orange tree and sat. He leaned his head against the stone wall and closed his eyes. The morning sun filtered through the white buds of the leafy fruit tree, the rays of sunlight speckling his torso. He drank in the heady perfume of the blossoms, and the quietness of the inn. The warmth of the sun soon lulled him to sleep.

Evan awoke with a start, rubbed his eyes and stared. He swung his head from one side to the other, a slow robotic motion. His head and neck were cushioned by a soft pillow. The scent of a crisp, clean bed linens was a sharp contrast to the coarse woollen blankets imbued with body sweat. Evan propped himself on his elbows.

'How can this be?'

He took in the familiar surroundings of his bedroom, the Tasmanian blackwood dresser against the wall with his wallet and watch placed on the surface. He glanced at the digital clock, the red numbers glowing against the backdrop of the LED screen.

'Am I really home?'

He flung off the cotton sheet and got out of bed, the bamboo timber flooring smooth under his feet. He ran a hand over the bedside table and padded along to touch the white-painted wall. He walked around the bed, touching everything until he stopped outside a doorway. Evan whooped, did a little dance and flicked on the light switch.

'Now this is a bathroom.'

Evan stepped across the cold white tiles to the large recessed shower. It had tiny aquamarine tiles on three walls, with a floor-to-ceiling double glass door. Evan removed his boxers, opened the door and walked in. He turned on the hot water, placed a hand underneath until it warmed and then added cold water. He stood under the square shower head, face turned towards the water spray. Seconds later, spurts of water jettisoned from the opposing sides of the walls. He stayed under the water, enjoying the experience.

On a ledge, next to the taps, were bottles of shampoo and conditioner. He grabbed the shampoo and squeezed a liberal amount into the palm of his hand. He washed his hair, and drew in a deep breath, drinking in the sweet blend of papaya, tea tree and sage. Evan revelled in the shower, taking longer than he normally would.

Afterwards, with a fluffy cream towel wrapped around his waist, he grabbed another. He buried his face in the soft, thickness of the towel and drank in the lemony smell of the washing detergent. Evan towel-dried his hair and threw the towel over his shoulder. He walked to the vanity and peered at his reflection in the mirror. He pulled at the ends of his hair. It was longer than he liked. He leaned in and stared into his eyes. He didn't look any different, though within himself, he was not the same. Somehow he felt older, and world-weary. Could a dream change a person?

Evan spent the next hour shaving and clipping his hair. He returned to the bedroom refreshed and invigorated, and entered his walk-in wardrobe. He stood in front of his clothes, which hung on coat hangers and lined the length of the wall. He laughed and jumped, thrusting a fist into the air.

'Now, that's what I'm talking about!' With the broadest of grins, Evan discarded the towel and like an excited child in a toy shop and dove straight into selecting his clothes.

He spent the next ten minutes wandering from room to room, touching walls, light switches, doors, door frames and knickknacks. He walked into the kitchen. The clean lines, tiled walls behind the stovetop and floor, the shiny marble benchtop and stainless-steel sink gleamed as the morning sunlight flooded through the huge glass window. His greedy eyes drank in the furnishings and the flat-screen television. He took in a deep breath and slowly exhaled. The air was uncontaminated and free of the stench of unwashed bodies, animals, and sewerage.

He stepped around the kitchen bench and opened the fridge door. The light came on and bathed the floor and the front of his body.

'I've missed cold clean water, but I've missed this the most.' He reached in and grabbed a glass bottle. 'And I don't care what time it is.' He twisted the bottle cap, releasing the effervescent air. Froth grew and rose in the neck of the bottle. Evan raised the bottle to his mouth and took a large swig. 'Ahhh… now that's how beer should taste like, nice and cold.'

He placed the bottle on the bench and pulled out bacon, eggs, butter and a few fresh Roma tomatoes out of the fridge. He carried the ingredients and put them on the bench by the sink. Evan opened a cupboard and took out a frying pan. Using a spoon, he scooped some butter out and dropped it into the pan. Fifteen minutes later, Evan carried a plate of fried bacon, eggs, tomato and toast over to the table with a large cup of coffee made with the machine. He sat down and closed his eyes, savouring the aroma of the food and coffee. He then tucked into his breakfast, relishing every morsel.

Evan was on his second cup of coffee when he began to think about what day of the week it was. He turned the TV on with the remote control. Music, colours and voices swamped the room. He lowered the volume and gazed at the familiar faces of the weekend morning news presenters. Nothing had changed with the doom and gloom of world events or the banal chatter that proliferated on commercial morning news.

Evan tuned out as his mind drifted. *Am I dreaming this or am I actually home?* The chair he sat on was solid; so was the table he sat at. The cup in his hand was warm, as was the food he had eaten and could still taste. This was real. He glanced down at his clothes, clean jeans and a black t-shirt. He could smell the washing detergent on them and the aftershave he'd splashed on when he'd finished shaving.

'How can the dream be as tangible as this?' he mused out loud.

Even in his dreams, the smells, the gritty sand of the deserts of Egypt, and the mountains of Greece were as tangible as his home. He gazed at his hands, the skin bronzed from the sun. Not unusual during the hot Australian summers, but the colour was darker than normal. It was if he spent most of his days in the sun, which he did while in his dream state. He hadn't noticed it as he'd showered. He turned his hands, palms up. Thick, coarse calluses covered the mounds. Though he designed buildings, he didn't hesitate to pick up a shovel or trowel to work on the sites. He ran his fingers over the hard skin. Perhaps he was doing more physical work at the building sites than he'd realised.

The light in the room changed. It grew brighter. He smelt orange blossoms. A shadow of a tree plunged him in the shade and covered the table. He blinked. The air shimmered. The room warmed, as if someone had turned on the heating. Evan set the coffee cup on the table, next to the empty plate. Voices filtered in, a language other than English. He felt a featherlike touch on his shoulder. He heard footsteps but knew there was no one else in the house.

A white light flooded the room. A hand clasped his shoulder. Evan jumped. His heart raced as fast as a jack rabbit's. He whirled his head from side to side in quick succession but did not see anyone. The blinding radiance forced him to close his eyes. Even behind his eyelids the brightness grew. He covered them with his hands. The temporary shield helped to reduce the glare.

Two hands, one on each of his shoulders, shook him. His head bobbed back and forth like a bobblehead toy. When he opened his eyes, he saw three concerned faces. He shrugged off the hands and stood, twisting one way, then the other.

'What the…!' He rubbed his eyes. 'This cannot be happening!' Evan ran from the courtyard and out onto the street and stumbled to a stop. He sank to his knees. The smooth, worn cobblestones pressed against his flesh. All around him were the buildings of Corinth, vibrant with colour and life.

Dexion, Homer and Phameas had followed and stood in a semicircle in front of him. He looked up at them, heart heavy and face haggard.

'I'm never going to escape this place.' He rubbed his brow. They kept staring at him. 'What is it?' He stood.

'You look different,' Dexion said.

'Huh? What do you mean?'

Phameas wrinkled his nose. 'And you smell funny.'

Evan scrunched up his face. 'What on earth are you talking about?' Then he smelt it. He lifted his arm to his nose and sniffed. His eyes widened. 'Fantastic! I was home! It actually happened.' He laughed and did a bit of a dance. He stopped when the others continued to stare at him. 'What?'

Homer pointed.

Evan touched his face and then his hair. 'Incredible! What I did transferred to here and now!' He beamed. 'Do you know what that means?'

They shook their heads at the same time.

'That there is a way home! I've just got to find a way to make it permanent.'

They returned to the courtyard and sat on the bench where Hektor and Leander arrived to join them under the tree. The High Priestess had yet to emerge from her room.

'What happened to you?' Hektor asked.

Leander's head tilted to side as he took in Evan's new appearance.

'Oh, I had my hair cut and a shave.'

'I don't think I've ever seen hair that short,' Leander said.

Evan ran a hand over his head. The clippers he'd used had left him with a buzz cut. 'It's convenient and invigorating.'

Phameas grunted. 'It's an affront to the gods. A man's hair is a show of strength and manhood.'

Evan grinned. 'I will apologise to your gods, Phameas. Although I don't think they'd mind much.'

The Phoenician sniffed and crossed his arms. 'You looked more handsome with long hair and a beard. I don't know why you keep cutting them.'

'I like it this way. Besides I don't have to worry about it.'

'You know, I'm inclined to agree with Evandros,' said Leander, face pensive. He ran his fingers through his golden locks. 'Short hair would be easier to maintain. I may do the same.'

Hektor's jaw worked back and forth, eyes narrowed.

'What will you do?'

Leander and Hektor turned as the others stood.

'Good morning, High Priestess,' they said.

She acknowledged them with a nod. The High Priestess took a step back when she saw Evan.

'Evandros did the same thing while we were in Carthage,' Phameas said.

'It does take a little getting used to, but I like it,' Leander said.

'The important thing is that Evandros likes it,' she said, her tone neutral. 'What is the plan for today?' she added, businesslike.

'A bit of breakfast for those of you who are hungry,' said Evan, 'then we seek transport to Delphi.'

Leander rubbed his stomach. 'Good. I am hungry.'

Evan went in search of Kleitos, and ten minutes later, the group was sitting in the andron. The serving girls brought out bread, wine, figs and olives. Kleitos hovered by the doorway as his guests ate.

'Kleitos, would you give us directions to Lechaion?' Evan asked.

'Of course.' Kleitos nodded. 'The road will take you onto the main thoroughfare for Lechaion. At the crossroads, you will see the gate of Helios on your right, where you must turn left. It should not take more than two hours to get to the port.'

'Many thanks, Kleitos,' said Evan.

Kleitos bowed and ambled away. They finished eating and returned to their rooms to pack. They later assembled in the courtyard, where Kleitos waited by the entrance.

'If you pass through this way again, you will be welcomed guests,' he said.

Evan grasped his hand and shook it. 'You are a gracious host, Kleitos. Goodbye.'

The stable boy was waiting outside the hostel with their mule and cart. Leander assisted the High Priestess aboard and took the reins. They passed a number of buildings and before long came to the intersection. Evan saw the gate Kleitos had mentioned: two gilded chariots erected on top of the architrave, one carrying the sun god and the other his son, Phaethon. The chariots glinted, as if set on fire and reinforcing Helios' power. Their magnificence held Evan spellbound. He blinked. White spots filled his vision and he had to turn away.

A little further along, was a bronze statue, the face framed by long wavy hair. Though the expression was stoic, it had an aura of sadness. A leopard skin draped the broad shoulders and a hand clasped a massive club. Evan recognised who it was straight away before he scanned the inscription on the base of the statue: Herakles. He thought about the deeds the doomed hero had performed and wondered if he was fated to meet the same end.

More statues adorned the roadside. One of Hermes sitting, and alongside him was a ram. Next was a statue of Poseidon, Leukothea and Palaemon, who sat on dolphins. Evan was thankful to see the impressive monuments yet saddened at the same time. The skill and artistry of these objects had been lost over time, either to destruction by narrow-thinking Christians or by natural disasters.

'Evandros, what are you thinking about?' asked Phameas.

'I was considering the correlation between Herakles and my situation. They are too close for my liking,' he answered.

'Who is Herakles?'

'He, my friend, was a hero cursed from the day he was born.' Evan went on to give a brief overview of the legend of the man and how he died. When he finished, Phameas had a wry smile on his face.

'You think you're destined to die as this Herakles?'

Evan shrugged. 'There are similarities; the most significant is we have the same father.'

Phameas shook his head and guffawed. 'What nonsense! From what you've said, he was not the most noble of men and was punished for his pride. You are nothing like him, so stop feeling sorry for yourself. Concentrate on finding the last relic and getting home.'

Evan gave him a sheepish grin. 'You are, as always, right. No more wallowing in self-pity.'

'Good.' Phameas gave a sharp nod. 'Now let me tell you about a hero from my home, called Gilgamesh.'

Evan found the journey to Lechaion uneventful. The parallel walls protected the road and its travellers all the way to the port town. They shielded against possible attacks, but they created a vacuum. The air was still. The odd bird that flew overhead cast long silhouettes on the road. The sun's rays beat down on the road, and the heat radiated back with a vengeance. Beads of sweat ran down Evan's face and torso, making the tunic cling to his damp back with an uncomfortableness he hadn't felt in a long time. His nose twitched. The scent of soap and aftershave was overcome by the rising stink of body odour. He glanced at the others and noted they weren't faring any better, with the exception of the High Priestess. She did not appear to be suffering from the humidity and looked cool and composed.

Evan grabbed the water container from his backpack, took a swig and handed it to Phameas.

'Going to need a refill soon,' he said, wiping the perspiration from his brow with the back of his clammy hand.

'We're getting closer.' Leander pointed. Evan looked over and saw the sprinkle of roofs on the horizon.

They headed for the well as soon as they entered the gates. The mule slurped, its tongue flicking back and forth in quick succession from a trough fed from the well. Evan plunged his hands into the cold water, relishing the relief it gave, and splashed his face before taking a drink. He refilled his container and waited for the others in the shade of a building. Closing his eyes, he drew in a deep breath, filling his nostrils with the briny air.

They resumed walking through the narrow streets, the air cooler and fresher as they neared the gulf. Ships, big and small, filled the odd-shaped harbour. It was a hub of activity with local merchandise loaded onto ships and crews unloading wares. Leander led the mule and cart with the High Priestess to rest under the shade of laurel trees.

'I'll go and find this Jason while you wait here,' Evan suggested.

The High Priestess nodded. 'A sound idea.'

'I'll come with you,' Phameas jumped in.

'Me too,' Dexion added.

'All right.' Evan looked over at Homer, who shook his head.

They approached a small group of men working near a ship. Some were fixing nets, others mending the sail while a few were checking the hull, removing barnacles and patching gaps with tar.

'It is so good to be close to the sea again,' Phameas said with a blissful sigh. 'The sea air, the splash of waves, and even the squawks of seagulls are warming my heart.' He squatted and lifted the net. 'That is fine work.'

The sailors stopped working. Although not hostile, they weren't happy at the interruption.

'Good day, noble sailors, we're after a man called Jason,' Evan said.

'What do you want with him?' one said in a raspy voice.

'We'd like to cross the gulf and are told he's a fair man to deal with.'

'Ahoy, Jason! There's someone here who wants to sail on the *Argo*!'

Evan blinked. 'No way...'

A younger man appeared on the stern of the ship and peered at them. He was dressed in a loincloth, and though slight in build, he had a muscular frame. The sea breeze ruffled his long, wavy light brown hair.

'I'm Jason. Who gave you my name?'

Evan stood mute, staring, his mind whirling.

Jason frowned. 'Well, who was it?'

Phameas glanced up at Evan and elbowed him in the ribs.

'Oh... ah... sorry. Um... Kleitos of Corinth gave us your name. We stayed at his hostel.'

Jason jumped down, bending his knees as he landed. The ease of movement reminded Evan of cats leaping from their lofty positions to the ground. Jason strode over, youth and vigour evident in each step. His green eyes sparkled against his tanned skin.

'Kleitos is a good man. He must like you if he mentioned me to you,' he said. 'Where is it you wish to go?'

'To Delphi.'

'You're seeking the wisdom of the Oracle?'

'I guess we are.'

'Just the three of you?' Jason glanced at Phameas and Dexion.

'No, there are seven of us.' Evan pointed to the group waiting under the trees. 'One of our companions is a High Priestess.' Jason shielded his eyes and looked.

'A woman!' said one of the sailors. Jason held up his hand, stopping further outbursts.

'Will that be a problem?' Evan asked.

Jason stared at the others a while longer before turning back to study his ship, his expression thoughtful. 'I'll grant you passage on the *Argo* only because Kleitos is a good friend. Before we negotiate a price, what is your name?'

'Evandros. This is Phameas and Dexion.'

'Evandros, the price will be higher as you have a woman in your midst and I must appease my men.'

They haggled for a bit before settling on a fare.

'Will it take long to cross the gulf?' Evan knew it took thirty minutes, forty at most in his time.

'No more than a few hours.' Jason ran his hand through his hair. 'It'll depend on the wind and currents.'

'What was that all about?' Phameas asked as they walked back to where the others waited. 'You were acting strange.'

'There are stories of Jason and the Argonauts and their legendary journey,' Evan said in an excited whisper, lowering his head towards Phameas. 'I read them as a young boy, the adventures and obstacles they faced. I never thought he was a real person.'

Dexion tutted. 'After all you've seen, you still have doubts?'

Evan pursed his lips. 'Yes, until proven otherwise.'

'Don't allow disbelief to cloud your thoughts. It may cause consequences you won't be able to fix.'

'I swear, sometimes you're much older than you say you are,' Evan said to Dexion.

The young boy smiled but did not answer.

CHAPTER TWELVE

Evan had to pinch himself as he stood alongside Jason, who manned the two steering oars of the ship. The story of Jason and the Argonauts was one of his favourites in Greek mythology, and here he was on the deck of the *Argo*. He took out the booklet from his bag and began to sketch, noting a few differences from the *Argo* to a Phoenician ship and those he had seen while in Carthage and Egypt. The stern curved and rose high over Evan's head, the tail shaped like a fin.

He took in the crew of fifty men as they sat on either side of the gangway, just wide enough for one person to walk from the stern to the prow. The single large mast billowed. It was positioned a third way up from the stern, the heavy sail rigged with four ropes on each side of the post and secured to the railing on opposite sides of the stern. A central heavy rope that controlled the rise and fall of the mast, was tethered to the mast-crutch next to the stern, and its counterpart fastened to the forestay on the prow. The hull was painted black and had bright blue eyes painted on either side of the prow, where a beak jutted in defiance as it skimmed the surface of the sea. Wooden boarding steps were built into the beak. Evan shook his head at this ingenious concept. *Better than scaling up the sides*, he thought, drawing in the foot-sized supports.

Jason glanced at what he was doing. 'You have the gift of the gods.'

Evan scowled. 'The gods have nothing to do with it.'

Jason stared at him incredulous. 'You don't…'

'What in the name of the gods?' a crew member blurted, stunned.

'Who's standing in my light?' Evan asked, still focussed on his picture.

Jason tapped him on the shoulder.

'What is it?' asked Evan, swatting Jason's hand away.

'Look.' Jason pointed.

Evan sighed and turned to see what had caught Jason's attention. 'What on earth?'

A flock of birds, small and big, flooded the sky, blocking the sunlight. Their frenzied squawks got louder as they drew closer. Feathers and excrement dropped from the sky as the birds dashed overhead, the bigger avians soon outdistancing their smaller cousins.

A sailor shouted out an alarm.

'Captain, there in the sky, what in the name of Zeus are they?' He pointed to two creatures flying towards the ship at great speed.

Evan's stomach fluttered. 'Not again.'

'It's those same monsters that attacked us in the desert of Aegyptos!' Hektor growled, hands clenching.

'Dear Mother!' The High Priestess paled.

'Arm yourselves!' Jason shouted, grasping his sword.

Evan reached over his shoulder and grabbed the hilt of his own sword, pulling it from its sheath. He held it out and squinted, the sun's rays shimmering off the blade. Men hollered and cursed as they scrambled over each other, clutching swords. The harpies swooped over the deck and screeched, their human faces contorted in fury. Evan's ears rang. Then he gagged. The stench of rotting meat washed over the ship, an airborne slaughterhouse. Evan spun on his heels to see the soul-eaters turn and come back.

A number of the crew covered their ears with their hands, holding their weapons in a loose clasp. The two harpies continued their deafening onslaught. One veered, its beak open, baring razor-sharp teeth, and then snapped it shut, skimming the head of a sailor. He screamed and fell backwards. The harpy reached out with its talons, stabbed a man and tossed him overboard. Blood splattered the deck and sprinkled the harpy's breasts. They came about again, flying lower, their wingspan close to four metres, casting a shadow over the ship.

Evan's heart pounded against his ribcage. His ears roared, his blood pumping as fast as a racehorse pounding the 3,600-metre race course. He tried to swallow, but his mouth was dry. Leander, steady as ever, shot a volley of arrows, all finding their mark in the chest of one harpy. It flew at him, shrieking. Homer pushed Leander out of the way, swung his sword and slashed its torso.

'Dear God!' Evan winced as the harpy's screech reached another octave higher.

Black, hot blood splashed onto the deck as it flew over. It did a quick about-turn, blood dripping from its wound. Evan took a step to check on the other harpy. He slipped on the blood and bumped into Hektor, and they both fell.

'Watch out!' Phameas yelled, running towards them, his sword held aloft. The creature swerved and swept over Evan and Hektor.

'*No!*' The High Priestess screamed.

'Phameas!' In his haste to get up, Evan slipped again, the blade of his sword missing his face by millimetres. Strong hands pulled him upright. 'Phameas!'

A terrifying shriek echoed over the water. Evan closed his eyes, not wanting to see. He could not bear to watch his friend die in such a manner. But as much as he didn't want to, he knew he owed his friend more. He opened his eyes, looked up, and caught his breath. His body went cold.

A young crew member dangled lifeless in the clutches of the injured harpy. The talons bit deep into his flesh and punctured his tender, young body. A wet ripping and breaking of bones resounded. Evan clenched his jaw. His mouth watered and bile rose. He swallowed back the rising nausea that threatened to erupt from his gut. He wiped his face with a shaking hand, hoping it would erase what he saw.

It was then he became aware of raised voices, cries of disbelief and anger. They watched as the two halves of the body were dumped into the sea. As it sank, a small pool of water turned pink as it mixed with the water. The High Priestess turned away and sought solace in Leander's arms. Evan stared at the ruddy water and clenched the hilt of his sword, knuckles taut and white. The harpy came into view.

Evan strode to the prow of the ship and stepped onto the rail. The monster squealed, beak open wide, its hideous face twisted in fury.

'Evandros!'

He jumped and thrust the sword into its belly. It howled. Evan's ears rang. The harpy wrapped its talons vice-like around his waist and they descended at a rapid pace plunging into the water with a splash. Evan tried to wrench free, tearing his skin on the sharp edges of the iron claws. They sank deeper and deeper, the weight of the monster heavy and unmoving. Evan's lungs felt like they were about to rupture. He tugged at the sword to free it from the harpy's body. Black spots appeared in his vision. The sword would not budge.

This is it, he thought as he felt the edges of unconsciousness beckon. *Maybe I'll wake up in bed.*

'Come, Evandros,' a voice sang. His head flopped back. 'We have come to help.' Evan felt a soft mouth close over his and exhale air into his lungs. He felt hands grasp his arms and touch his face. His head fell forward, as lifeless as a marionette. The tender touch of a second mouth covered his. The retinue of soft lips continued until Evan's mind cleared and he realised he was still alive. He opened his eyes and stared. He gaped and water rushed in. Choking, Evan could not draw air until one of his rescuers placed her mouth over his.

She smiled at him when she drew away from him. He looked from her to the other beautiful women. They smiled, teeth glowing against the dark blue water. They held him close, their bodies warm and soft. Against his legs, he felt a strong surge of movement and… he glanced down… scales! Shiny, iridescent colours.

Mermaids!

'We are the children of Triton,' they sang.

You heard me? His words came out as a shrill.

'Of course. We don't need to hear the words be spoken.' Their long hair floated in the water and caressed their faces. 'We are nearing the surface.'

Evan glanced up and saw the faint light of sun penetrate the wine dark sea. He then noted they had slowed their ascent.

'Goodbye, venerable Evandros, keep well.' They each gave him a last kiss and propelled him upwards.

Wait!

Evan's head broke the surface, the sun blinding after the depths of the sea.

'Mermaids! Oh my God, mermaids! They're real!' Evan made to dive back into the water when he caught sight of the *Argo*.

'There! Port side!'

Evan raised a hand and watched the crew manoeuvre the *Argo* and head in his direction. He felt a tap against his leg and saw the hilt of his sword emerge from the water. He glanced down to the see the mermaids' radiant faces as they descended deeper into the sea.

'I really wish I had a camera to record this,' he said to himself.

'Ahoy, Evandros!' Jason threw over a heavy rope. 'Take this and we'll pull you up.'

Evan swam the short distance to the ship and grabbed the thick rope. Within moments he was back on deck.

'Evandros, what were you thinking?' The High Priestess' cheeks were flushed and her nostrils flared. 'You could have been killed.'

'I wasn't, and besides, someone had to get justice for that poor boy,' he said.

'That was an extraordinary act of bravery, Evandros,' said Jason. 'My men and I are very grateful for what you did.'

'If it wasn't for us, he'd still be alive.' Evan lowered his head and clasped the back of his neck. No one said a word.

'Regardless, what you did proves you are an honourable man,' Jason said after a while.

'You were down there a long time,' Phameas commented. 'I thought you had gone to meet the god Melqart in the Underworld.'

'At one stage, I thought I may have. I was brought to life by beautiful mermaids.' Evan paused and watched bemused as the crew ran to the side of the ship and peered into the water.

'Mermaids! Where?'

'Let me see!'

'Can you see them?'

'Stop shoving!'

'Move over! I can't see with your big fat arm in the way!'

Jason shook his head and muttered. Before moving away, he clasped Evan's shoulder and gave him a grim smile of thanks.

'Right, you lot! Get back to your oars! We want to reach the shores of Itea before dusk!'

CHAPTER THIRTEEN

The remainder of the voyage was quiet and subdued, except for the continual splashing of water against the hull. It was the hollow expressions on the faces of the crew members as they rowed with mechanical strokes that left a lasting impression on Evan. Their loss hung in the air, a mournful fog. He could not erase the vision of the poor youth's last moments, and the sound of his dreadful screams reverberated in his mind. Dexion gazed up at him.

'Master Evandros, no one could have stopped it from happening. If it wasn't him, it would've been someone else.'

'That was Theodoros' fate, wasn't it? That's why you said he would die if he came with us. One youth's life for another's.' He paused and then added, 'Will he now live a long life?'

Dexion's eyes glazed over and pupils dilated. 'If he chooses to be good and respectable, he'll prosper and live to an old age.'

Evan grunted and shook his head. 'From my own experiences, making intelligent and moral decisions isn't always certain. It was the here and now that influenced what I did.'

'Each of us have to make choices. It's what happens afterwards that will determine future actions.'

'There you go again, spouting words of wisdom.' Evan squatted and peered into the boy's dark brown eyes. Dexion stared at him. 'You know, I am good at keeping secrets.'

Dexion face lit up, eyes sparkling with mischief. 'As am I.' He then gave Evan a hug. Evan almost lost his balance, startled by Dexion's sudden show of affection. His arms hung at his sides for a few minutes, not sure what to do. He wasn't quite comfortable around children. He'd never interacted with young children let alone spoken with them, until he'd met Dexion. Hesitant, he put an arm around the young boy. A few minutes later, Dexion let go.

'My father used to hug me all the time,' he said. 'You remind me of him.' He moved away to join Homer, leaving Evan still squatting.

'Evandros! We're about to make landfall. You'd better hold on to the rail,' Phameas called out, ambling over.

For as far as the eye could see, rocky peaks of varying heights occupied the skyline of the countryside. Speckled with trees and bushes, they appeared unforgiving and impervious to those who inhabited the region. Evan pulled out the map King Mentor had given them from his bag and checked the directions marked out by the scribe. He looked up to see Jason walk towards him and lowered the map. Sadness was etched deep on the seafarer's face.

'We are going to pay tribute to young Leon's death. The men have built a bier, and we'd like you and your companions to join us.'

'It would be our honour to attend,' Evan said.

'When Helios settles on the steep apexes of the mountains, we will begin.' Jason pointed to the craggy crests which the sun still had a few hours to reach.

Evan nodded. 'We'll be there.'

Hours later, everyone gathered on one side of the tall wooden platform filled with long branches and sticks.

'While there is no body to cleanse and lay, we are here to say farewell to Leon. He was a good sailor and warrior. A fine young man who would've grown into a reliable and honest man. Though naïve as to the way of the world, his valour and steadfast nature won the hearts of all who stand here, and he'll be missed. Young Leon, may your psyche take heart to wander the fair fields of Elysian, for you have earned a place in the Isle of the Blest.'

Jason stepped over to the bier, climbed an unseen wooden ladder and placed a sword on top. Back on the ground, Jason turned to his men and gave a nod. Against the backdrop of lapping water on the shoreline, the soft, haunting strings of a lyre were strummed. Two members of the crew came forth with burning torches and set the bier alight. The dry wood and tinder crackled and burst into fiery life.

> "Hear me, O Death, whose empire unconfin'd, extends to
>   mortal tribes of ev'ry kind.
> "On thee, the portion of our time depends, whose absence
>   lengthens life, whose presence ends.

*"Thy sleep perpetual bursts the vivid folds, by which the
soul, attracting body holds:*
*"Common to all of ev'ry sex and age, for nought escapes thy
all-destructive rage;*
*"Not youth itself thy clemency can gain, vig'rous and strong,
by thee untimely slain.*
*"In thee, the end of nature's works is known, in thee, all
judgement is absolv'd alone:*
*"No suppliant arts thy dreadful rage control, no vows revoke
the purpose of thy soul;*
*"O blessed pow'r regard my ardent pray'r, and human life to
age abundant spare."*

Evan's throat ached and tears trickled down the sides of his face. He wasn't sure if it was the words or the music that affected him. He'd never heard such beautiful lyrics before, and the soulful tune of the lyre pulled at his heart. Raising a hand, he wiped the tears away and focussed on the pyre. The yellow-orange glow of the fire enveloped the wooden stand, smoke billowing into the air, masking the sky. Wood snapped, cracked and popped, singing its own dirge as the flames consumed its food.

Homer laid a hand on Evan's shoulder and indicated they should move away to leave Jason and his crew on their own. They settled on the beach some distance away and pulled out rations to eat. Evan retrieved the map and placed it on the sand for the others to see the path to Delphi.

'Quite the rugged terrain,' Leander observed.

'It may take us a week to get to Delphi,' Hektor said. 'This is the time we should spend on finding the last sacred relic.'

'That's why we're going to see the Oracle,' said Evan in an even tone. 'She can tell us where it is.'

'We only have your word, and that of a lesser goddess. No one was there to witness this encounter of yours. This could be a trap to kill us. There is a Titan who wants the relics and it's possible she is acting on his directives.' Hektor sat back and crossed his arm against his chest.

Evan's eyes narrowed.

The High Priestess intervened. 'That is possible, and whatever the goddess' motives are, we do not know. We know the message is genuine.

Dexion has confirmed the Oracle wants to meet and tell us the location of the relic. We agreed this was our next destination and our best option. There will be no further discussion.'

Hektor's jaw worked back and forth as he glared at Evan. He stood and stalked away, his back and shoulders rigid.

'I'm growing tired of his attitude. If he doesn't find a way to deal with it, I'll do it for him,' said Evan through clenched teeth.

'You will refrain from any physical encounter,' the High Priestess ordered.

Evan bristled, the colour of his irises changing. The High Priestess sucked in her cheeks and clasped her hands tight.

'He hasn't forgiven himself for our imprisonment by the king of Kyrene,' added Leander trying to calm the situation.

'What the king did was wrong, but it doesn't excuse Hektor's behaviour. People make bad decisions all the time. You learn from it and move on,' Evan said in a clipped tone. Leander shrank back, sucking in a breath at Evan's inky eyes. 'I will not stand for it anymore.'

'And what of you? You are different.' The High Priestess baulked when Evan turned to her.

'Yes. My transformation is essential to ensuring the successful retrieval of the objects. Zeus saw to that. If not, we'd all be dead.' He stood, his gaze holding hers. 'Keep Hektor away from me or I will mete out punishment suitable for a spoilt brat.'

He strode away his body shaking with anger. Behind him, he could hear the quick scrunch of heavy footfalls on the sand. Within moments, Phameas and Dexion pulled up alongside and walked with him.

'What are the ships like in this twenty-first century of yours?' Phameas said after a lengthy period of silence. 'I am assuming you do have ships.'

Evan glanced at the Phoenician, who was looking at him and waiting for a reply. He drew in a deep steadying breath, and then gave Phameas a crooked smile. 'There are many different types of ships, ranging from small dinghies to huge transport vessels. Including luxury liners for the holidaymakers and speedboats for the racing enthusiasts.' He slowed to a stop and sat on the cool, grey sand. Phameas and Dexion did the same. He went on to describe the various ships, how they worked and their different uses.

'People have their own boats?' Phameas asked, staring at Evan wide-eyed.

'Those who can afford to buy one. There are cheaper types for those who like to do a bit of fishing on the rivers or estuaries.'

'What is a holiday?' asked Dexion.

'Ah... yes... it's when people, families or couples go away for a break. They take time off work.'

'How extraordinary,' said Phameas, slack-jawed. 'This time of yours must be a special and wondrous place.'

'It has many benefits, but there are people who do terrible things. The technological and scientific advances have improved lifestyle; however, they have also allowed for groups of people to abuse them and harm the innocent.'

'Why would they do that?' Dexion asked.

'For the same reason as the man who bought and enslaved you and your parents. It's about power over others. In extreme cases, it corrupts and perverts impressionable individuals into committing heinous acts of violence.'

'The people of your world don't seem very pleasant,' said Phameas.

'The history of the world is riddled with atrocities, terrible things people do to others. I don't mean to be gloomy. There are a lot of good people too, who help others without expecting anything in return. Talented and intelligent individuals who create and develop marvellous tools to enhance the way things are done.'

'Like what?' asked Phameas.

'Schools, colleges and universities, places of education for everyone, not just for the rich or the males. Both boys and girls learn to read, write and undertake subjects to study the world. They are educated in history, mathematics, astronomy, biology, human anatomy, art, mechanics—the list is endless. Unfortunately, there are still countries where education isn't available, but for the majority it is.'

'I'd like to go to school,' Dexion said.

'You'd do very well. You are a bright boy.'

'Perhaps I can come back with you to the twenty-first century,' he said, looking hopeful. 'And I can go to school there.'

'I, too, would like to see the planes you've spoken about and the different ships,' Phameas said, stretching out his legs and reclining back on his elbows.

'I need to work out how to get back there,' said Evan, gazing at the fading daylight on the horizon. 'But it won't happen until we find the relic. Zeus promised me I'd get to go home when all the items are found.'

'We'll find them,' said Dexion.

CHAPTER FOURTEEN

Evan rose early the next morning and enjoyed the solitude of swimming in the gulf. If he did get back home, he wasn't sure Phameas and Dexion would be able to join him. He must find a way to include them as part of the deal he made with Zeus. He swam a few extra laps before turning back to the shore. He picked up his drab and threadbare khiton and wiped himself.

'Morning, Evandros!'

'Morning, Jason.'

'I've never seen someone swim like that before or as fast.'

'It's something I like to do when I can. It helps clear my head.'

'Oh…' Jason scratched his jaw. 'We're going to return to Corinth and make our way to the southern Italic shores. If you ever need anything, seek me out.'

'That's very generous of you, Jason. Not sure how I would reach you but thank you for your kind offer.'

Jason grinned. 'The gods will provide, you'll see.' He stuck out his arm. Evan grabbed his hand and nodded.

'Safe journey.'

'May Hermes watch over you and your companions.' Jason smiled and sauntered to his ship.

Evan led the way to the mountainous region that dominated their intended destination. The path they followed was well trodden from locals and foreigners who trekked to the sacred centre seeking Apollo's wisdom. Small communities had sprouted along the main road, eager mushrooms ready to take in passers-by. They spent the night in a hostel and set off at first light.

'According to the map, that is Mount Parnassos, where the city of Delphi is situated.' Evan gestured at the snowy-capped mountain, the peak hidden in the clouds. Thick, verdant foliage gave way to craggy outcrops speckled with an array of colourful flowers. Lilac, canary yellow and apple-red blooms covered the hard grey surface like precious jewels on a bracelet.

'Zeus!' Leander's eyes widened. 'How tall is it?'

Evan did a quick calculation. 'It's almost 2,500 metres high. That's over five thousand cubits.'

Phameas whistled.

'And we have to climb that?' Leander asked, shoulders sagging.

Evan glanced at the route on the map. 'To get to Delphi we do, though the path zigzags up the side. The track can't be too arduous, not with the large volume of people who frequent the city every year.'

After hours of navigating the circuitous landscape, they came to the foothill of Mount Parnassos. The slope of the wide pathway followed the gentle incline of the mountain. Evan noticed the high defensive walls that surrounded the sanctuary and the lower city. He had visited the site before and had been impressed by the sheer size. The vista of the ruins from both the sanctuary and township had been exquisite. To see it living and breathing and still intact would be stupendous.

'With so many twists and turns, it's a wonder people bother coming.' Leander remarked. 'It is making my head spin.' He then fell silent.

'Great Mother!' The High Priestess stopped, her hand covering her mouth.

High on the slopes, commanding a superior position, was a temple, the festooned colours on the columns and tympanum, ablaze under the sun. A path meandered through the sanctuary and beckoned them onwards.

'Now this is a fitting home for a god,' Hektor said, the first words he'd voiced since his outburst on the beach.

'Oh yes. My father would be most pleased by this honour,' agreed Leander.

'This is much bigger than I expected,' Evan said, his skin tingling.

Evan's attention was drawn to the tholos of Athene and the gymnasium as they neared the city's precinct. Houses and a two-storey stoa surrounded the two structures. People wandered through the open colonnade of the stoa and between the row of columns and the wall, the roof providing cover from the sun. Towards the rear were rooms, and on the second floor there were more shops and offices.

'What now?' Phameas asked, his head swinging from side to side, taking in the views.

'We go to the temple and speak with one of the pythioi, the priests of Apollo, to request a meeting with Pythia. If we do get to see the Oracle, we must bring an offering, a gift to the god, or we won't be permitted to see her,' said Evan.

'Will they allow us to petition the Oracle today?' asked the High Priestess. Evan shrugged. 'I don't know. We can only ask.'

The main entrance to the sacred precinct was on the eastern escarpment, and delineated the intersection between the city and the defensive walls. The sanctuary was built on a series of terraces, a gradual incline that steepened as it went higher. Despite the large crowd within the grounds, a reverent peace enveloped the area. Some walked along the sacred path, and a few deposited items of value in the treasuries, while others seemed content to wander and take in the atmosphere.

'What are all these buildings?' Phameas asked.

'The smaller ones are monuments commissioned by various city-states and dedicated to Apollo for deeds of triumph, either against an enemy or for good fortune,' Evan said. 'They were constructed following the Oracle's prediction and favourable outcome.'

'Which one is the Temple of Apollo?'

'That large rectangular one.'

'How do you know if that is the temple of Divine Apollo?' Hektor said. Evan bristled.

'Not now and not here,' the High Priestess jumped in, and placed a hand on his chest. 'This is a sacred site.'

'You're not doing a good job at keeping him away from me,' he hissed into her ear. She shivered.

'Of course it's Divine Apollo's temple. It's the largest one here and commands the best position,' Leander said interceded, glancing at Evan and the High Priestess with concern.

Homer placed a hand on Evan's shoulder and propelled him forward. Evan turned to him. Homer indicated with his head to move.

'This is the last warning,' Evan whispered at her. As he was about to walk away, he saw Leander put an arm around her. Homer prodded him again.

The Temple of Apollo, like the others Evan saw, had a propylaeum, an entryway to the sacred grounds. The altar still smouldered with the latest offerings, the pungent scent of burnt offal lingering in the air. Opposite was the votive column with the winged sphinx sitting atop. The tympanum, a triangular pediment, had life-sized sculpted images of creatures and gods, with Apollo as the centrepiece. A few priests loitered by the altar. On seeing the group nearing, they ventured over.

Evan's ears prickled and he looked up at the temple.

'What is it, Evandros?' Phameas asked when Evan did not move.

'Not sure,' he said. 'Maybe I'm tired, or just fed up with Hektor's bullshit.'

'I'd wager you've given the High Priestess good reason to keep him away from you,' Phameas said with a wry grin.

'She didn't listen very well the first time,' Evan grumbled.

'I think she heard you on this occasion.'

'I hope she has.'

'Master Evandros!' Dexion ran to where Evan and Phameas stood. 'The priest said the Oracle is not available to listen to further petitions and to come back tomorrow morning.'

'Then we shall find a hostel for the night.'

'He is finally here,' she said with bated breath. 'I can feel his presence.'

'I don't think this is smart or wise.' Her companion scratched the back of his ear. 'If Zeus and the other immortals learn of your interference, or yet your presence, you will bear their wrath. I have witnessed their fury and borne their punishment.'

'How is it, my dear Prometheus, that you are no longer chained to a rock and Zeus' divine eagle does not feast on your liver?' came the quick response.

'Kronos released me from my endless suffering and in recompense charged me with guarding you.'

'He fears for my safety?' Melaina sneered. 'I doubt it. He wants you to watch what I do and where I go.'

'He wants to be sure your plan to garner favour with the mortal works.'

'I bet,' she muttered, her face darkening.

'The Olympians have done well since my incarceration,' Prometheus said, observing the site of Delphi. 'I remember Mother was worshipped here for many thousands of years. Whatever happened to Python?'

'Apollo killed him and claimed ownership of the area,' Melaina said.

'They did that to Mother even though she and the other Titanesses did not participate in the war?' Prometheus glowered.

'Zeus wanted to establish dominion over all elements the Titans once ruled and obtain the complete adoration and obeisance of the mortals,' she explained. 'The names of the Old Gods are now uttered in contempt.'

'If you are the daughter of Kronos, what do you hope to gain after he overcomes the Olympians?'

'To be worshipped and glorified by the mortals, just as they do the Olympians,' she said without hesitation.

Prometheus did not comment and kept his face as expressionless as possible. He did not want to give her false hope. The odds Kronos would grant any immortal who sided with him recognition or rewards was slim to naught. Prometheus did not expect anything from the old Titan and knew when his usefulness came to an end, Kronos would cast him aside. At least he was free to come and go as he pleased, as long as he fulfilled his obligation. And he intended to do so for as long as possible, no matter what he must do.

CHAPTER FIFTEEN

Evan tiptoed out of the room, not wanting to disturb Phameas and Dexion, who were asleep. He exited the hostel and strolled down the street. Under his arm, he held the writing pad. He climbed a series of steps between a cluster of houses until he was clear of the town. He turned, and his mouth fell open. The pad slipped from his hands. Evan fumbled, juggling with the pad until he caught it and clutched it with a firm grip. The black-covered booklet now secure in his hands, Evan fixed his attention on the panorama below.

He sat on a nearby rock, flipped open the pad and began to draw. His hand flew over the blank paper, as if guided by the muses. When creating and designing new structures, Evan often felt as if he were watching himself as he drew. How long he sat there, he did not know. He grimaced, and shifted. The hard, uneven surface of the rock pressed into his backside.

'Nope, that's not helping.'

He stood and rubbed his bottom. When the ache subsided, he sketched in the last few trees and buildings. He took a deep breath, drawing in the fresh crisp air, and exhaled through his mouth.

'Better head back before the others begin to panic.'

He followed the path he'd taken earlier. As he neared the olive grove, he glimpsed a white flash. He looked up at the sky. It was cloud-free and a pristine blue. He resumed walking. A few paces along, the hair on Evan's skin stood on end. The shadows of the trees made it difficult to see beyond the first row. He wished he had brought his sword. He glanced at the booklet in his hand, fingers and knuckles white. It wasn't much of a weapon, but he could inflict some damage if he got close enough. At least give someone a headache.

'Come on out, you coward! Stop hiding behind the trees!'

Silence.

Evan took a step towards the trees, head sweeping left to right and back again. Then he smelt perfume. His heart quickened and his breathing came out in short bursts. He blinked and stared. Standing two metres away in the shade of the trees was a figure. Evan stood immobilised. The silhouette moved with slow, deliberate steps, wending its way between the shady confines of the trees. The person stopped at the perimeter, screened by the trunk of a tree and its shadow.

Minutes passed, and then she stepped into the sunlight. Evan's mind went blank. The woman tilted her head to the side, a hint of amusement playing across her face. Her khiton accentuated her every curve as she sashayed towards him.

'Hail, Evandros,' she said, coming to a halt a mere foot from him.

'Hail nothing! I was about to clobber you over the head with this!' Evan said in an outburst, his face flushed. 'And what were you doing sneaking about in the olive grove?'

Melaina arched an eyebrow. 'Are you not pleased to see me?'

'That's beside the point! Didn't anyone ever teach you etiquette about making an appearance? And you don't snoop on people, that's bad manners,' Evan continued his rant. He ran a hand over his stubbled hair and took a breath. 'What brings you here?' he asked after his ire had cooled.

She leaned forward, the heat of her body and perfume clouding Evan's mind. 'I told you to come here, remember?'

Evan cleared his throat and took a step back. 'I haven't forgotten. You said the Oracle would give us the information we require. So why have you come?'

'I am here to provide further assistance.'

'I didn't think the gods were allowed to help us in any way.'

'I am not restricted by the same doctrines as the others,' she said.

Evan digested the information. 'Does that mean you don't belong to the same Family?'

'More of a distant relative.' Melaina's eyes twinkled.

'Huh.' Evan pondered her last answer. 'They don't know you exist, do they?'

Melaina beamed. 'You are very astute.'

'If you've kept yourself hidden from them, why risk being found out?'

'Their knowing of me is of little consequence. Besides they should be grateful someone with my capabilities is able to assist you, Evandros.'

'Not just me,' Evan said, frowning. 'There are others involved.'

'Of course,' she said with a careless shrug.

'We've done quite well on our own,' he added. 'Why do you think we need any help?'

'There will be times when you'll be confronted by obstacles that cannot be dealt with by mortal means,' she said.

'Not sure about that. The High Priestess has unique gifts that I didn't think a human possessed.'

'Ah yes, her power is impressive. However, it cannot match that of an immortal or prevent someone from falling to their death.'

Evan blinked. 'It was you? You were the one who rescued me from the harpy in Egypt?'

She nodded.

'Why? Why would you do that?'

She looked away and shrugged. 'No reason. I felt it would be a shame if you died so early into your journey.'

'Oh, then thank you for saving my life.' He tapped the booklet against his leg. 'I should head back. My friends will be wondering where I am.' Evan hesitated before asking, 'Will you be popping in more often from here on, or at random? I'd like to know in advance what to expect.'

'You can expect more appearances,' she said.

'Right… okay.' Evan nodded. 'I'll be seeing you around. Bye.' He lowered his head, shuffled his feet and then walked around her. He reached the path, stopped and turned. 'One final question.'

'Yes?'

'Why did you kiss me?'

'To see what you tasted like.' She smiled, her eyes glinting with laughter.

Evan felt his ears go warm. 'I hope I passed the test.'

Her smile broadened. 'Quite. It exceeded my expectations. I look forward to further experimentations.'

Evan's cheeks grew hot. 'Till next time.' He coughed and left. He darted down the path, not sure who he was running from—himself, or the attractive and very seductive goddess. His step faltered and he tripped.

'Listen to yourself, man. She's playing you. It's what they do. Now get a grip and figure out a way to get back home!' Evan slapped a hand against his thigh.

Phameas and Homer were loitering in the entranceway when he entered the street of the hostel. Phameas nudged Homer, and the two met Evan part way down the street.

'You were gone a long time,' Phameas said.

We thought you had ventured back to your twenty-first century, Homer wrote.

'I needed some alone time,' he said. 'And I had another visitation from our mystery goddess.'

Homer's brows arched.

'She is a goddess, then?' Phameas whistled.

'She confirmed she is.'

Did she say what her purpose is?

'Not in so many words, except she's here to help.'

You best let the High Priestess know.

Evan sighed. 'Lead the way.'

Leander was leaning against the wall and when Evan finished explaining the visitation, he straightened.

'She's not one of the Olympians but somehow connected to them?' said Leander, forehead wrinkling.

'That's what she told me.'

'What is concerning is how she's been able to move around without the gods knowing of her existence,' the High Priestess said.

'I did wonder about that,' Evan said, 'and the one plausible conclusion I can draw is that she has been sequestered until now.'

'Like the Titans?' Leander said.

'I don't think she was sealed in Tartaros with them. I have a feeling her mother or someone close to her may have kept her hidden.'

To what end?

'I don't know.'

'Did she reveal why she wants to help us?' asked the High Priestess.

'No. She wasn't very forthcoming, except to say we may encounter trouble of a nature that will require her assistance.'

'Having a goddess on our side is a good omen,' said Phameas.

'Where was she when the soul-eaters attacked us on the ship?' said Hektor, arms crossed against his chest. 'Why didn't she come to our aid then?'

'A fair question. However, the gods do not need to assist us each time we encounter a threat,' the High Priestess said. 'There's no point in the gods assisting if we can manage the encounter. I'd surmise, however, they'd intervene where they consider it essential.'

'The fact she can act beyond the constrictions of the other gods and the Titan, is a concern,' Leander said.

'I agree,' the High Priestess said. 'This is worrisome, and it goes back to her true intentions.'

'Are you able to find out more about Melaina from the Mother Goddess?' Evan asked her.

'If Mother wants to inform us of this goddess, she will in her own time.' The High Priestess pressed her lips together.

'What is the harm in asking?'

'One does not question Mother.'

'Then how do you learn anything if you don't ask?' Evan raised a brow. 'If you won't, I will. She was quite forthcoming when she healed me.'

'You will get your answer from Pythia.'

Everyone turned startled. Dexion gazed up at them with a serene expression. He hadn't uttered a word during their discussion, standing by as they went back and forth.

'Pythia?' repeated Evan.

Dexion nodded. 'She's waiting for you. I suggest you go while she's in good humour.'

CHAPTER SIXTEEN

Evan led the group back to the sanctuary, retracing their steps from the previous day and traversing the sacred way to the Temple of Apollo. Nearing the temple, Dexion tugged at Evan's khiton.

'What is it, Dexion?'

'You must give this to the priest. It is a gift for the god Apollo.'

Evan took the object Dexion held out. Carved from green marble was a statuette of Apollo playing the lyre. The attention to detail was exceptional, from the elegant folds on the clothing and the fine strings on the musical instrument to the melancholic expression on the face.

'It is magnificent. Where did you get it?'

'I purchased it from a sculptor in the town,' Dexion said. He lowered his voice. 'It's to appease the god.'

They entered the temenos, the sacred grounds of the temple. The embers and remains of offerings smouldered in the sacrificial altar. It was quiet except for the sound of their sandals slapping against the cobblestoned ground.

'Where are the priests?' asked Phameas, scanning the area. 'They were out here yesterday.'

Hektor headed for the steps of the temple.

'Wait!' Dexion called out. Hektor swivelled, his jaw tightening. 'Pythia wishes to speak to Master Evandros alone.'

'Just me?'

Dexion nodded.

'Are you sure?'

'She only wants to talk to you.'

Evan stared up at the open doors of the temple and the preternatural obscurity beyond, and proceeded up the steps alone. At the threshold, he came to a halt blinded by the dimness. Evan waited for his eyesight to adjust and shivered. He did not expect the sudden drop in temperature. He entered the temple. Small oil lamps recessed at intervals in the wall on either side of the interior cast a yellow glow. A long line of Doric columns stretched the entire length on each side. Placed on top were big blocks of marble that supported smaller Doric columns. He looked up at the ceiling. Planks of wood ran lengthways and then across to form a series of inverted cubes. By the massive statue's pedestal, were two free-standing lamps, the golden light spreading its warm arms.

'You have entered the house of Apollo without permission,' a voice said from the depths of the shadowy temple.

'My apologies, I meant no offence. I did wait outside, but no one came.' Evan peered into the darkness, searching for the owner of the voice.

'Then you are to remain outside until a priest takes your pledge.'

'Wait! I am here now. May I please ask my question of the Oracle?'

'It is not proper to enter without first meeting with a priest,' came the curt reply.

'How can I put forth my request if there's no priest outside?'

'Then you remain outside until one becomes available.'

Evan rubbed his brow. In his business as an architect, he encountered difficult clients who were intent on including features in the building regardless of how it might affect the structural integrity.

'I realise you have protocols to abide by so that petitioners cannot take advantage. I, too, am a stickler for following procedure, but I also know when to make allowances for unexpected circumstances.' Evan took a step in the direction where he thought the priest stood hidden. 'I was guided here by Pythia herself. She communicated her wishes via a goddess and by a boy who has the gift of foresight.' Evan stretched out his hand and held out the statuette. 'This is for your god as thanks for hearing my request.'

Evan kept his hand extended. Five minutes passed. He lowered his head, disappointed.

'Place your offering at the feet of the god and ask your question,' the priest said.

Evan leapt forward before the priest changed his mind and placed the icon on the pediment. 'I, Evandros, am here to ask Pythia for the location of the final sacred relic of the Mother Goddess.'

The priest, a man nearing his fifties, walked into the fluttering light, and picked up the figurine. He studied it, the front and back, then looked at Evan, his face innocuous as still water.

'Wait here while I put forth your request.' He slipped behind the statue of Apollo, the patter of his feet receding into the gloominess.

A weird quietness descended on the cella. Evan rubbed his arms, the chill in the air seeping into his bones. The hair on the back of his neck stood on end. He did a slow turn, scrutinising the interior from top to bottom. Facing the statue again, he stared up at the marble features. His heart jumped, his breath caught in his throat and Evan stumbled backwards. The statue's brows drew into an angry scowl, its lips curled and its blue-painted eyes flashed with loathing. A hand came at Evan, fingers as thick as his thighs. Evan shrank back as the tips of the fingers came within a hair's breadth of his head. Then there was the sound of footfalls. The statue shifted back into place and was lifeless, as it had been just moments earlier.

Evan shook, unable to keep from gawping at the statue. 'What the ff... f.., was... was that about!' Evan's heart galloped. He stepped away from the statue and pointed. 'That was effing uncalled for!' A vein stuck out on Evan's temple and he stopped shaking. His nostrils flared. 'What a spoilt brat!' He caught sight of the priest and clamped his mouth shut.

The priest paused by the base of the statue and gazed at Evan with a quizzical expression. Evan had moved some distance from the statue and standing half hidden behind a pillar. The priest walked over.

'The Oracle's answer is thus: "Seek the Temple of the Serpentine Goddess buried within the city of the dead. Though shrouded, she holds the power of the gods. There you shall find a double-headed tool, one crafted from metal and wood."'

'Great, another riddle,' said Evan, nose crinkling. 'I don't suppose you know what it means?'

'The answer lies within.' The priest turned and walked away.

'Of course it does.' Evan shook his head and muttered as he headed for the entrance. A low rumble came from behind. He slowed to a stop and turned.

'But this is not how it is done!' the priest protested.

'Oh, shush, and bring me that boy,' ordered an imperious voice.

'I will not! This is not how we operate!'

'If it were not for priests, there would be no need for such practice. The ancient oracles did not have priests to speak for them, and there is no need for them now. Bring me that boy, *this instant!*'

The priest stomped out from behind the statue. '*You!* Come back! The Oracle wishes to see you.'

Evan glanced over at the statue.

'Come along!'

One foot dragging after the other, Evan returned to the depths of the temple.

'This is highly irregular...' the priest grumbled, hands twisting over each other. 'She is *not* supposed to meet the patron...' He beckoned at Evan. 'Get a move on!'

Evan remained as close as possible to the columns. When he reached the priest, he was led to the rear of statue. The priest pointed to a nondescript door.

'She is waiting for you.'

Evan pushed the door open. At first glance, he noticed how sparse the room was, and then he spied a smaller door to his left. Sitting opposite, on a wooden seat was the Oracle.

'Come and sit,' she said, waving a hand. She chuckled at his expression. 'Were you expecting someone... a little different, perhaps older?' The aura around Pythia was serene and eternal, which belied her youthful appearance. Thick russet tresses framed her heart-shaped face and her warm grey eyes. Her gown, made from golden silk, was fitted, the folds emphasising her body and allure.

'I, ah... please excuse me for staring. I was... um surprised by your invitation.' Evan bit his lip. 'It was my understanding a more mature woman held the position of the Oracle.'

She grinned, eyes twinkling. 'Intelligent, respectful and handsome, a quality women find desirable. I can see why she's taken with you.' Evan's face reddened. 'She will reveal herself in time, but this is not why I wanted to see you.' She patted the space next to her. He sat and waited. 'What you seek to restore will not prevent the Dark Master from succeeding until you have also located the sacred statue to which it belongs.'

'What?' Evan straightened in surprise. 'Isn't the icon on Atlantis?'

'It is a copy of the original. You must recover the true figurine to ensure victory.'

He fixed his eyes on the wall, digesting this new morsel of information. 'Do you know where it is hidden?'

Her lily-white hand covered his, all lightness gone. 'Evandros, beware, for the labyrinthine bull rages and seeks retribution from the children of Minos. The bull's entrapment has engendered hatred and murderous longing within. It harbours the icon, but it is the blood of the true heir who will find it.'

Evan paled. 'The Minotaur is real?'

She nodded.

'We need to find two objects instead of one?' He wanted to reconfirm what he'd heard.

'Yes. You cannot defeat the Dark Master without them.' She squeezed his hand. 'You must be careful, Evandros. There are those who wish to prevent you from finding the relics and will do anything to ensure you do not.' She stood.

Evan clasped her small hand in both of his calloused ones and looked up at her. 'What of Melaina? Can she be trusted?'

She bent down, embraced him and whispered into his ear, 'The wrath of a goddess is unquenchable.' Evan gulped. She placed a hand over his thudding heart. 'The one you give this to awaits your arrival. Do not cast her aside when she comes to you. Her revelation will bring you clarity.' She kissed him, her lips soft and sweet, and then she was gone.

Evan sat dazed. His head spun, and he was confused by what the Oracle told him. He leaned his head back against the marble wall and tried to order his thoughts. He needed to compartmentalise what he'd heard and clear his mind so he could recall the various myths and legends of King Minos and the Minotaur and determine the location of the next object.

CHAPTER SEVENTEEN

When Evan emerged from the temple, his companions were loitering near the votive column. Phameas was the first to see him. They converged at the base of the steps and watched him descend.

'Something happened. What did she tell you?' Phameas said as Evan came within earshot.

'I think it may be best if we return to the hostel,' he said, looking over his shoulder at the temple.

'Not sure I like the sound of that,' Phameas said.

'What have you learnt that troubles you, Evandros?' asked Leander.

'Let's leave,' he said and hastened away from the temple, forcing the others to follow.

His companions threw surreptitious glances Evan's way. He kept an even pace, steady yet purposeful. He remained silent, unable to shake the feeling that they, or rather he was being watched. It felt as if someone or something was boring a hole between his shoulders. They arrived back at their hostel and Evan paused by the water cistern. He looked to the High Priestess.

'While we were in Egypt, Leander used white light to commune with his father. Can that same white light stop people and the gods from eavesdropping?'

She studied his face before giving a nod.

'Good. Let's go to one of the rooms.'

Without saying more, he pivoted and headed for the stairs. They crowded into a room. The High Priestess, Dexion and Leander sat on the small bed. Homer and Hektor leaned against the wall nearby, while Evan and Phameas stood opposite those who sat.

'Can you please white-light this room?' he said to the High Priestess.

She closed her eyes. Evan waited and saw an almost imperceptible white light descend in the doorway and fade into almost nothingness. A faint blurry shimmer filled the room, but it was so minimal, and the longer he stared, the more difficult it became to detect.

'Why the need for the secrecy?' she said, her ice-blue eyes holding his.

'The location of the second relic is hidden somewhere, in a place where the remains of the dead lie. Some double-headed object made from metal and wood.'

'The labrys,' the High Priestess said without hesitation.

'Any clues as to the location of the labrys?' Leander asked.

Evan shook his head. 'Although, I do have a good idea of where we need to go next. But that's not all. Pythia said the icon that resides on Atlantis is not the original, and to prevent the rise of the new religion, we must find the true one.'

'What? That cannot be true!' The colour drained from the High Priestess' face.

'That is impossible. The ancestors would have known if the icon they carried was a copy.' Hektor's brow knitted.

'Perhaps not,' said Evan. 'You said back in Egypt that the last High Priestess had split up the sacred relics. What if she gave the icon of the Mother Goddess to another to hide so all three pieces would be as far away as possible from each other? The replica may be one of many intended to prevent the objects from being found and used.'

The High Priestess cupped her cheek with a shaky hand.

'The Oracle could be telling us a falsehood,' said Hektor.

'Pythia has no reason to lie,' said Dexion.

'I agree,' the High Priestess said in a strangled voice. 'Given the turmoil and how frightening the last days were before the cataclysm, the last High Priestess would have made sure the sacred relics were secured with priestesses she trusted.' She stood to look Evan in the eyes. 'Did the Oracle tell you where the icon is secreted?'

Evan nodded. 'It's with the Minotaur.'

The High Priestess wavered and sat back on the bed with heavy jolt. 'Mother Goddess!'

'Zeus! There's no possible way to recover the icon,' said Leander, running a hand through his hair.

'No one who has entered the lair of the beast has ever come out,' said Hektor.

'Without the three objects, we cannot defeat the Titan,' Evan said.

'We must recover them all,' the High Priestess said, clasping her hands. 'Did the Oracle say more?'

'She said we must be careful, for those who wish to stop us will be relentless in their pursuit of the relics.'

'Well, we've faced the harpies, what more could they do?' Leander asked.

'It's more of a matter of what they won't try to get the relics,' said Evan.

'Does that include this goddess Melaina?' Hektor asked.

'It would,' Evan acknowledged with a slight nod.

'Is this why you asked for the white light? So this goddess cannot overhear us?' the High Priestess asked.

'Not just her,' Evan said. 'From here on, whenever we need to discuss anything in relation to our search, the white light should be applied. Also, we should use some code when talking outside the confines of the shield. I realise we cannot hide where we are going, but we can control what we say. There's more to this retrieval expedition than we've been told.'

Homer nodded.

'I agree,' said Leander, standing. 'We must save the gods from extinction and our home from annihilation.'

'And what of the Minotaur?' said Hektor. 'It cannot be defeated.'

'First we get the labrys, and then we'll worry about the Minotaur,' said Evan.

'And where shall we go to find the labrys?' Hektor asked sneering.

'To the one place where the catastrophe and exodus began: the island of Thira.'

'Umm… excuse me?' Everyone looked at Phameas. 'What is a Minotaur? And why are you all frightened of it?'

'It is a creature, part human and part animal. It has the body of a man and the head and tail of a bull,' Evan said.

'A vicious beast that feeds on the flesh of humans,' added Hektor with a hard edge to his voice.

'In the time of our ancestors, King Minos of Krete and King Aegeos of Athens signed a treaty for retribution over the wrongful death of King Minos' eldest son. Under the agreement, King Aegeos had to send eighteen Athenian maidens and youths to Krete every nine years. They were imprisoned in the labyrinth along with the Minotaur, who hunted and fed on them,' the High Priestess said.

'I heard stories of such a beast in my years as a sailor but did not think one existed!' Phameas shuddered.

'Would it still be alive? After all, the destruction happened a thousand years ago,' said Evan.

'It is of the gods' making, and to kill it would take a unique weapon,' the High Priestess said.

'The labrys,' said Dexion.

'Pardon?' Evan said.

'The labrys of the Mother Goddess is the only weapon that can harm it,' he said.

'Then we're off to Thira. Time to pack and leave.'

CHAPTER EIGHTEEN

*Z*eus sat hunched forward, elbows on knees and hands cupping his face. Since his announcement of Eris' and Kronos' escape, he'd been scouring the earth looking for them. He had begun the search in the locations where they once had roamed and frequented the most, but they had not gone there. Poseidon and Hades checked the outer regions of the world and as yet have not had reported back.

He saw a flash of gold and looked up to see his wife Hera march towards him. 'Still no trace of them?' she asked.

He shook his head, sighed and straightened. 'They cannot stay hidden forever. It's not in their nature to remain out of sight.'

'Will you inform your son of this news?'

'I will communicate in a such way that it does not breach the ties we are bound by or bring harm to him and the others.'

She sat on her throne. 'I don't think that matters, not in this instance.'

'I will not endanger Evandros any more than necessary.' He glowered at her.

Hera regarded him for a moment. 'Your attachment to a mortal will jeopardise us all. Kronos is no fool and will use him. What we have done and achieved will be for naught.'

Zeus slammed his fist on the armrest of the throne. 'I have risked much to ensure Evandros is capable of fulfilling his duty. You have no idea as to the lengths I have gone to, to create a person such as him so that we'—he jabbed his finger at her and then himself—'can be revered for eternity.'

Solitary clapping resounded in the throne room.

'What a splendid performance.'

'Eris!' Zeus stood, his eyes turning black. 'You offend us with your presence.'

She tut-tutted. 'No need to be so rude, dear Zeus.' The Goddess of Discord walked to the centre of the room and smiled.

'What is she doing here?'

'How did she get past the gates?'

She twirled as the remaining Olympian Gods entered the room. Her gaze settled on Athene and Aphrodite, who glared at her. 'Ah… sisters, it has been such a long time.'

'How did you get out of Tartaros? No immortal can escape the depths of the underworld,' Athene said, lips curled and teeth bared.

'That is true, until an extraordinary thing happened.' She stepped over to Ares, running her eyes over his ebony armour. 'A fracture appeared in the seam, a small one.' She held out her thumb and forefinger. 'I wondered what could cause a fissure in such an impenetrable place. There was only one possible conclusion: an immortal so strong and powerful that he could rupture the wall.' She sidled over to Demeter and beamed.

'Do you know what happened next? A most splendid event. I had a visitation.' She wandered to where Apollo stood and ran a finger down his chest. 'He said, and this was quite surprising, that he would help me escape Tartaros if I did one thing for him.'

Eris turned her fathomless eyes to Zeus. 'How could I resist such an evocative offer? And so, here I am, bringing a message to my brothers and sisters.' Eris paused and tilted her head to the side. '"The Messiah comes and his blood will inherit the earth."'

Eris snickered as the gods shouted and raged; only Zeus did not react. She backed away, her eyes never leaving those of King of the Gods. 'I do love it when a plan comes together.'

Zeus stood and Eris fled.

Feeling pleased with the outcome and revelling in her newfound freedom, Eris longed to reacquaint herself with the mortal world, but thought it best to visit the lands of Judea first. She wanted to see for herself what the fuss was about.

CHAPTER NINETEEN

A frail old Messenian man, covered in road dust, dragged one foot after the other and led his donkey to the water trough. While the donkey drank, he cupped a handful of water and splashed it on his face. He wiped his face with the edge of his grimy khiton, feeling a little refreshed, then reached in for another handful and raised it to his mouth.

Wiping his mouth on the sleeve, he straightened and examined his surroundings. Houses lined the streets, big and small, like mushrooms sprouting in a field. Overlooking the city was the Akropolis, the stoic protector and home to sacred old buildings. The wooden temples dominated the vista; the tendrils of smoke spiralled into the sky. The priestesses of Athene started the morning with an offering to the goddess and to the first king of Athens, Erechtheus.

His eyes were drawn to the larger temple. Its colourful friezes and sculptures leapt from the pediment. In one section of a relief, a charioteer mounted a chariot. On a corner of the pediment, there was a three-bodied monster, painted in red, green and blue. The upper bodies were of bearded men who shared a snake-like tail. One of the figures held an urn with wine, another corn and the third a bird. On the opposite side, there was a sculpture of Herakles fighting a sea daemon, in the same hues of its counterpart. In the centre was the Gigantomachy, the battle between the gods and the giants, and garbed in vibrant yellow was the figure of the goddess Athene, who stood over a fallen giant.

'Come along, Echo just a little bit further,' the old man said. 'I must see Plato and tell him about the Atlanteans. He'd want to know they are here.' He tugged on the rope harnessed around the donkey's head. The animal brayed. 'Oh, stop your complaining. I'm going to walk... gods!' The donkey bared its teeth and moved, its hooves clattering on the cobblestones. 'The time is coming when you will be sent out to pasture,' he said, 'to fertilise the grounds!' The donkey shook its head and brayed again, loud and long, drawing startled looks from passers-by. 'The time is coming,' the old man swore under his breath.

They crossed the bridge over the River Eridanos and headed into the centre of the city. The agora bustled with people, the shopfronts busy and filled with merchants hawking their produce, an assortment of tradesmen shouting their services—fish-sellers, butchers, vendors of pottery, bronzes and slaves—all competing for the attention of the prospective buyer.

A wide road bisected the spacious marketplace and led to the Akropolis. Myrtle, elm, olive and laurel trees lined the pathways where houses had once stood. The donkey plodded behind his master as they wandered past the Royal Stoa, a small covered walkway with eight limestone columns. Sitting on the thrones in front of the stoa were the archon, chief magistrate, and his two assistants.

'The tyrant Peisistratos did one good thing during his reign by moving people from here,' the old man said. The donkey snorted. The pair headed for the council hall, where they would find the philosopher.

'Citizens, the time for a decision has come,' announced a statesman standing at the altar. 'No longer will we be dictated to. Ours is a democracy where all Athenian citizens vote on issues for the good of our city.'

People in the back rows began to stir as the sound of raised voices from outside the hall became disruptive, making it difficult to hear the speaker.

'I propose we gather an army to protect our city. The time has come to stand and fight.'

'You cannot go in there!' bellowed a voice from outside. 'The councillors are in session. You are forbidden to enter!'

'Plato!' called out a tremulous voice. 'Plato! I must talk to you... Take your hands off me!' The commotion continued until the old man stumbled into the hall, his hair dishevelled and his dirty khiton torn. 'Plato! It is I, Kallimachos. The Atlanteans! They are here!'

The assembled men stared at him in stunned silence. His face went slack, his eyes rolled. The old man collapsed and hit the floor with a resounding thud.

Kallimachos moaned, his eyelids fluttered.

'Citizens, please stand back and give the man some room,' said a cultured voice. 'Kallimachos, can you hear me? It is I, Plato.'

Kallimachos blinked and tried to focus on the face hovering over him. He blinked again, his vision clearing. A bearded man with a kind round face and shoulder length brown hair stared at him. His blue eyes gazed at Kallimachos under a heavy frown. The old man tried to sit up, but the room swam and his stomach convulsed, bile rising.

'Steady there, Kallimachos, you may have hit your head harder than expected,' Plato said and with a gentle touch pressed him back down. 'Bring me water,' he barked at an attendant who loitered by his shoulder.

'What happened?' Kallimachos asked, clutching his head.

'You fell unconscious after you forced your way in.' Plato leaned closer and said in a whisper, 'You were shouting that the Atlanteans are here.'

'Yes!' Kallimachos bolted upright, the pain in his head forgotten. 'The legends are true, Plato! They are here. I have seen them with my own eyes, and talked to them. Taller than any man I've seen, and they possess such magnificence equal only to that of the gods.' He clutched at Plato's sleeve. 'They survived the great flood of Deukalion and have returned to complete the task as foretold by the Oracle.'

'What did he say?' someone asked.

'He said he saw Atlanteans,' another answered.

'What? I'd say the fall addled his brains.'

'Ridiculous, they were all killed like the Trojans.'

The room buzzed as the details were passed from one to another. Voices rose in contempt, denouncing the claim as preposterous, while others contemplated the possibility of the return of mythical beings.

'Where are they?' Plato asked. His heart thumped against his ribcage, as if he had just run the first length of the stade. He wanted to believe his old friend, but it did not seem probable that the Atlanteans had survived the devastation as described by the Egyptians to Solon.

'I left not long after they arrived in Messene. I had to come and see you. I knew you'd want to know.'

'When did you leave Messene?'

'About four days ago. I am not as young as I once was.'

'They'll have moved on. Did they say anything to you about where they were going?'

Kallimachos looked down and shook his head. 'I have failed you. I am sorry.'

Plato patted him on the shoulder and gave him a sympathetic, reassuring hug. 'You came to see me, which is more than enough. Let us leave and get you cleaned up. We'll talk some more.' The philosopher helped Kallimachos to his feet and with the aid of another man they exited the council hall, leaving behind heated discussions.

Both men and Echo left the precinct of the agora and set out towards the Academy, located on the outskirts of Athens. They passed through the Dipylon Gates, west of the city, and kept going until they came to a fork in the road. Plato veered to the right. Kallimachos saw the high defensive walls built by Hippias, once tyrant and leader of Athens, as they neared the school. The Academy grounds were vast and green, and had a gymnasium nearby. When Plato was a boy, his father had turned a section of the grounds into a small garden, and after his death, Plato had inherited the land. Not long after, he had set up the Academy and conducted classes on politics, life and eugenics.

Plato moved off the road and headed for a cluster of trees that concealed a path. It was a steady and gradual climb up the small hill, and before long, Plato's home came into view, secreted behind a variety of fruit and shady trees.

'Master, you are home early.' A tall, agile man with skin the colour of sable emerged from the house and took the reins of the donkey.

'Jelani, see that the donkey is fed and given water, and have Eshe bring food and wine to the andron.'

'Of course, master.' Jelani bowed and led the donkey away.

'Gods, Plato where did you find him?' Kallimachos said, watching the slave lope away, his long stride forcing the pack animal into a trot.

'I was travelling through Aegyptos when I came across Jelani and his wife Eshe. They were slaves of a wealthy trader of spices, but Jelani was to be stoned to death for breaking a jar. I felt it was unjustified for the man to die. Punished, yes, but not by death. So I spoke to the trader and we came to an agreement.'

Kallimachos eyes glimmered with admiration. 'I expect you were eloquent and persuasive.'

Plato shrugged. 'A wise and virtuous man knows temperance, and when justice, courage, and wisdom are governed, then a good life can be realised.'

'What happened afterwards?'

'I paid the man.'

Kallimachos did not know what to say and was startled by his friend's sudden burst of laughter.

'It would seem the trader is yet to acquire the ability to be virtuous, but canny he was.' Plato grinned. 'Let's go inside and have some food and wine.'

Cool air embraced them as they stepped into the covered entryway. A temporary bliss until they crossed the courtyard. The sun's rays radiated off the cobblestoned surface and the stone walls, trapping in the heat. Plato paused at the household shrine, mumbled a few words, and headed towards the dining room.

'Please sit, Kallimachos.' He waved at a couch.

The Messsenian sat on the nearest one, closed his eyes for a brief moment and sighed. The soft cushion was a blessed respite from the constant jostling of riding the donkey. Light filtered through the window, brightening the room and making the painted walls vibrant. Thick red, white and yellow stripes adorned the lower third of the wall. A striking sky blue filled the upper section, enhanced by a simple frieze of geometrical shapes.

A statue of Academos— benefactor of the garden and grove, after whom the academy was named—was recessed into an alcove in the wall opposite the doorway. In a corner, flanking the two long couches were vases, one from Megara and the other from Sicily. A black-painted Egyptian figurine of Anubis stood under the window.

Strange people, those Aegyptians, thought Kallimachos as he stretched out on the couch.

He caught a glimpse of movement by the door and gawked. Eshe entered the room, attired in a yellow sleeveless khiton that contrasted with her blue black skin, her jet-black hair tied back with a yellow ribbon in the style of the woman of the house. She set the platter of food on the table between the two men, bowed and left the room.

'Astonishing,' he said in a hushed tone.

'Indeed, and she is a very good cook.' Plato reached across, took a stuffed sardine and popped it into his mouth. 'Now, Kallimachos, tell me about these Atlanteans,' he said after he had swallowed. 'What are they like?'

'I have never met anyone like them,' Kallimachos gushed. 'There is an eternal quality about them. They are everything we have heard about them. Godlike in appearance, and they possess a wealth of knowledge we'd find hard to fathom. To be in their presence was akin to being with your first love, breathless and exciting.' Reverence and adulation shone in the old man's face. 'They are like no other peoples: tall, standing at six and seven cubits; as strong as Herakles, with dark golden skin and features so fair and handsome.' He leaned forward. 'There is a female amongst them, a High Priestess, an absolute vision, and four men plus a Phoenician and a boy. I spoke with one called Evandros.' He frowned.

'What is it?' Plato asked.

'He appeared different from the others. Not sure what it is, but it's as if he set himself apart from the others.'

'He's Atlantean, yes?'

Kallimachos nodded. 'Indeed, he had the same stature and appearance. But there was something more. I cannot quite work out what was different about him.' He picked up his cup of wine and drank, swallowing the contents in one gulp.

'I'm sure it's nothing,' said Plato. 'Did they say why they are here?'

'It's as you said many moons ago: the gods have sent them to find the sacred relics of the Mother Goddess to prevent their downfall.'

'It has begun? So soon? It wasn't to happen for another few hundred years.' Plato put a hand to his forehead. 'Why now? Something has changed.'

'I do not know what that may be, but this Evandros mentioned that Divine Zeus took him to witness the emergence of this new god, one god for all people.'

'Gods…' Plato's hand trembled. 'It is as Socrates believed. He alone was the one who thought and spoke of one god.'

Kallimachos nodded. 'I remember when he spoke of it. We did not believe him. Our gods are too powerful.'

'If the gods have set their champions in play, they have discovered there is more to happen.' Plato's face was grave. 'We must help.' His friend opened his mouth, but Plato held up a hand. 'I don't know how or what we can do, but when the time comes, we will do it.'

CHAPTER TWENTY

'Do we head back to Itea, to return to Corinth?' asked Leander, looking to Evan.

'I'm not convinced that's our best option,' Evan said. 'To get to Thira we need a bigger port city where a lot of ships set anchor.'

'Where would that be?' the High Priestess asked.

Evan pulled out the maps from his bag and selected the largest one. He laid it out on the floor, Phameas holding the corners down on one side. Evan pointed. 'We need to go there.'

'And we are?'

'Here.' He tapped the outline of Mount Parnassos.

'That is a long way,' said Phameas.

'Which way do you propose we go?' asked the High Priestess, her attention on the map.

'This way.' Evan traced an imaginary path leading from Delphi to Piraeus, a harbour city south of Athens.

'Won't it be quicker to return to Itea in order to gain passage on a ship?' asked Hektor.

'Sailing from Piraeus to Thira is shorter than going from Itea.' Evan leaned back on his haunches.

How long will it take us to reach Piraeus? Homer scrawled.

Evan tapped his fingers against his lips. 'If we keep a steady pace, we should arrive in Athens in two days, three at most, and another few hours' walk to Piraeus.'

Best we stay another night and leave at first light, suggested Homer.

Evan rolled up the map and nodded. 'We should also check our rations. Make sure we have enough for the trek and extra for contingencies.'

Evan stood and admired the dawn sky when he exited the hostel, the dark purple hues giving way to lilac and pink shades. He drew his cloak tighter about his body and pulled the cowl over his head. Not for the first time since his arrival to this time, he wished for the comfortable clothes and footwear back home. He led the others onto the well-used road and steered them away from the sanctuary that snaked down the slopes of the mountain. An hour or so later, Evan discarded the cloak and shoved it into his bag. They skirted hills and mountains, and as the land levelled, farm lots appeared.

Fields of wheat, barley and legumes abundant in lentils, peas, beans and chickpea flourished. The surrounding mountains and water fed the fertile soil and enabled farmers to grow cereals and maintain healthy livestock. In the distance, Evan could hear dogs barking and cows lowing. By mid-afternoon, they reached the outskirts of the city-state of Plataea. The township lay nestled at the base of Mount Kithaeron. Evan wanted to tell Phameas, Homer and Dexion about the famous battle between the Greeks and Persians, a defining historic achievement for the former, but refrained from saying anything. He had so much to share, yet he must be cautious. It wasn't that he didn't trust his friends; he did. But too many ears were listening, those that could not be seen, and those of the Atlanteans.

They turned westward and followed the river that ran alongside the mountain and into a valley. On either side, trees and shrubs covered the hillside. They stopped by the river to refill their containers, rest and eat.

Evan pulled off his sandals, sat on the edge of the riverbank and put his feet into the water. He closed his eyes and exhaled.

'Going to need orthotics after walking in these things.'

Phameas and Dexion joined him.

'With all the walking people did, I'm surprised no one invented better footwear.' He groaned.

Phameas swung his legs back and forth, his feet immersed in the water. 'I must admit, our thicker-soled boots are much suited for walking.'

'Next time we're in Carthage or one of your countryman's cities, I'm buying a pair of boots.'

Phameas chuckled. He scratched his bearded chin. 'What sort of sandals do you wear in your time?'

'My friend, you would not believe the range of shoes that are available,' Evan said. 'There are thousands of types: from casual footwear to formal, as well as for those who play sport. Then there are specialty ranges for those people who have feet problems.'

'Moloch! Thousands? How can there be so many?'

'There are factories that produce products in mass, where items are made with machines and by humans. Hundreds and thousands manufactured to be sold in shops.'

'Such abundance!'

'Yes, and it has created materialism.'

'What is that?'

Evan looked over his shoulder, hearing the crunch of dried leaves and twigs. Homer beckoned.

'It's for people who are more interested in acquiring comfort, and having the latest and flashiest objects.'

'Isn't that what rich people do?' Phameas commented, getting to his feet.

Evan laced up his sandals. 'It's not just the wealthy who are materialistic in my time.'

They trekked along the meandering river leaving the valley and venturing into further cultivated land. Four mountains dominated the region, and was connected by three plains: one branching out to the west, another to the south, stretching to the sea and the last to the east, where the ground rose and fell in gentle waves.

The scent of rich toiled earth filling the air reminded Evan of the days when he'd accompanied his grandfather to the family farm. Ahead was a plantation of olive trees, grapevines heavy with fruit and lush fig trees. Laurel, fir and oak trees stood alongside pine and plane trees by the foot of the mountains and along the fringes of the plateau. A road cut through the flatlands and deviated west, skirting the base of a mountain.

'We have been walking for a while and passed a few towns,' said Leander, glancing over at Evan. 'I'm wondering if we are going in the right direction.'

'We are.'

'I don't mean to question your navigation skills. It's just, there are mountains everywhere! It would be easy to get disorientated.'

Evan pulled out the map. 'Here, take a look.' He unrolled a part and pointed. 'See this valley?' Leander nodded. 'We just came through there. We're now crossing this section and heading west around this mountain to arrive at Eleusis. We spend the night there and in the morning leave for Athens, which we should reach by mid-afternoon.'

'My apologies, Evandros. I did not mean to doubt your ability.'

'Your apology is accepted.' Evan rolled up the map. 'Let's keep moving.'

Halfway across the plateau, Evan paused, his legs vibrating.

'Whoa… what was that?'

'What is the matter?' the High Priestess asked, stopping alongside.

'Did you feel that? The ground trembled.' He looked at her and she shook her head.

He turned to Phameas who shrugged. 'I didn't feel anything.'

Evan glanced at Homer and Dexion, who shook their heads.

'Perhaps we should stop for a rest,' suggested Leander.

'No need, we'll keep—'

The ground juddered, pebbles jumping. The jolts increased. Evan spread his feet apart. His body wobbled from head to toe; it took him back to his childhood, when he'd gone on a shaking machine at the agricultural show. He turned at the sound of a low rumble that emanated from behind. The others stood next to him. Rocks had loosened from the summit of the mountains. Clouds of sand gathered, blanketing the green foliage. Small and bigger pieces of rock fell away and crashed down the sides, colliding into each other and smashing into small trees. A thunderous crack echoed.

'Run!' Evan bellowed.

Boulders broke away and tumbled in a slow, deliberate rotation and gathered speed as they rolled downhill, dust and debris billowing in their wake. The land swelled. The trees swayed back and forth, then plummeted to the ground, uprooted. Evan stumbled, the earth surging in a violent ripple. He tripped and fell, scraping his hands and knees. He tried to stand but kept losing his balance. His teeth rattled and it felt as if every bone his body would fly apart.

'What in the name of the gods is happening?' Hektor cried out.

There was a loud crack. The earth shuddered and groaned. A jagged line marred the landscape. It widened as a fissure tore the plain apart. The High Priestess screamed. Leander and Hektor shouted. Phameas and Dexion's voices were drowned out by the ensuing sound of earth's painful rupture. Evan felt the ground give way beneath him. Blood pounded in his ears. He rolled to his side as the soil crumbled and disappeared from under his legs.

'Sssshi…!'

Dirt, rocks and sod showered him as Evan plunged into the chasm. He grappled at the collapsing walls with claw-like fingers. Then he stopped. His shoulder jolted at the sudden impact as he clutched at the ledge. He latched on with his other hand. Gritting his teeth, he looked down into the abyss.

He closed his eyes. 'Jesus, Mary and Joseph.' Evan's heart galloped so fast he thought it would burst. His mind flashed with memories of his parents, his sister, mates from school and university. Images flitted of the girls he dated, the holidays he'd been on, his home, and the beaches he'd frequented. It was a montage of his life in super-fast forward. His nostrils filled with the scent of the earth, particles rained over him. He could taste the grit in his mouth. His arms began to shake. The weight of the shield and sword pulled at him. He bit his bottom lip.

'How effed up is this!'

He coughed, the dirt clogging his air passages.

'Evandros!'

'Down here!' It came out as a hoarse yelp. Evan cleared his throat and spat out the dirt. *'Down here!'*

Evan looked up, and blinked, the soil drifting into his eyes. He saw a shadow prior to closing his eyes against the continual drizzle of sand.

'Evandros!'

'He's over here!'

'Evandros! Can you hear me? It's Phameas! We're going to get you out!'

Evan nodded, head bowed between his shoulders. The tips of his fingers were numb.

'Evandros! Answer me!'

'You'd better hurry, I don't think I can hold on much longer!' he shouted. Silence followed. His shoulders began to burn.

I wonder what would happen if I let go. Would I wake up back home, or would I die?

'Evandros, grab the rope!'

Evan looked up. 'We have rope?' He tried to lever himself upwards. 'Can't... reach...'

'Hang on, Evandros!'

Evan began to laugh and then couldn't stop, the tears running down his face. 'Hanging on... is all... I'm... doing.'

Fresh dirt sprinkled over him. He looked up and saw a body clamber over the edge.

'Homer! No... it's too... dangerous!' Evan's head drooped. 'So tired.'

Evan couldn't feel his hands or arms anymore. An arm dropped to his side. He glanced at it and saw it was his, fingers and hand a mottled blue.

'That's not good,' he murmured.

He then caught sight of another hand.

'That's not mine.'

The hand beckoned him. Evan reached up, his fingertips brushing the other hand. After minutes of a finger dance, the hand grasped Evan's wrist and the weight of the weapons wasn't as heavy. With each tug, he was levered away from the precipitous ledge. Sunlight touched his hand and then his arm. Evan looked up and saw a grim Homer, who held his wrist in a vice-like grip. At the top he could see the worried faces of Dexion and the High Priestess.

Hektor's face loomed over the side. He reached down and grabbed Evan's free hand and helped to lift him out. With Phameas' assistance, Homer scrambled out from the ravine. Evan sat on the ground, slumped over, chest heaving. Homer collapsed next to him.

'Thank you,' Evan said in breathless spurts and grabbed Homer's hand. Dexion flung himself at him. Evan embraced the boy with one arm. 'I'm fine, thanks to everyone.' He gazed up at the others. He frowned, seeing the bruise on Leander's face, and noted how close the High Priestess stood next to him. 'What happened to you?'

'When I fell, my face hit the ground first.' He grimaced and then gave a sheepish grin.

'He had lost consciousness but came to a few minutes later,' she said, her hand brushing Leander's.

Phameas knelt by Evan, his brown eyes solemn. 'No more falling into the earth, promise me.'

Evan swallowed back the lump in his throat. 'I'll do my best.'

Phameas pursed his lips and nodded. 'Good.'

Are you able to walk? Homer asked.

'One way to find out,' Evan said. He got onto a knee and moved to stand. He pitched forward. Homer and Phameas leapt forward and grabbed hold of his arms.

'Perhaps not.' The High Priestess laid a hand on his forehead and then closed her eyes. His head tingled and the sensation progressed into his neck, to his torso, along his arms to his fingertips then to his pelvis, legs and toes. When she removed her hand, it stopped. 'How do you feel?' she asked.

'A little light-headed.' He shook out the tiredness from his legs. 'What was it you did?'

'I revitalised your energy by bringing forth your strength and restoring your depleted power.'

'Impressive. Thank you.'

'If the Titan caused the earth to shake, where was this goddess you speak of? Why didn't she come to save you?' Hektor said to Evan.

Homer shook his head at Evan and glowered at Hektor. He scribbled on his tablet and thrust it under Hektor's nose. The big man stiffened, clenched his jaw and angled his body away from the others.

Evan raised his brow at Homer, who still bristled with anger, and decided to ask later. 'I don't think he triggered the earthquake. From his perspective, it would be more logical to allow us to find the relics and then take them from us. That's what I'd do,' he said.

'That makes sense,' said Leander.

Phameas nodded. 'Smarter too. Why do the hard work when others are already doing it for you?'

Homer pulled at Evan's khiton, indicating they should continue. Evan nodded and picked up his gear. Also, he wanted to get as far away from the precipice that almost took his life. If Homer hadn't reached him when he had, Evan knew he would have plunged to his death. Though Hektor's question rankled, he did not want to dwell on it. Both the goddess and his father had rescued him in previous incidents when his life was in peril. However, the

Greek gods were infamous for their fickleness, and he wasn't prepared to test them with his life too many more times. Not if he could help it. However, as the gods had not come to his aid, was it because they had not known? Evan scowled. Something was amiss.

They reached the other side of the plateau, where the trees stood untouched by the earthquake. Faint sounds of water rushing grew louder as they approached the forest. Evan did a quick check of the map—not that he needed to, the image was imprinted in his mind. To reach Eleusis, they needed to bypass Mount Kithaeron and cross the Eleusinian plain.

'This place is riddled with mountains,' said Hektor, echoing Leander's words before the earthquake. 'Everywhere you look there is another one.'

The mountains provide a natural defence against enemies, Homer wrote.

'Yes, of course, but did the gods have to create so many?' he griped.

'I am grateful we don't have to climb them,' said Leander, arms swinging as he picked up the pace.

Hektor responded with a grunt.

A few hours later, the defensive walls surrounding the site of Eleusis came into view. Outside the walls were houses, huddled close together and not far from the main entrance. The flat-top hill protected the rear of the city, unoccupied save for trees and shrubs and a glimpse of the roof of a large temple.

South of the defensive wall was a hostel, where they were able to secure rooms for the night. From the second floor, the fascia of the temple was visible outside the window. Evan itched to explore the city, sacred to the goddesses Demeter and her daughter Persephone. He turned to Phameas and Dexion.

'I recognise that look,' said his friend who was reclining on the small bed. He sat up. 'Where are we going?'

Evan beamed. 'For a little walk.'

'I hope you haven't taken your sandals off, Dexion,' Phameas said, getting to his feet.

A shadow loomed in the doorway of their room.

'We're about to head into the city. Would you like to join us, Homer?' Evan said.

Homer grinned and nodded.

'Which way shall we go?' Phameas asked once they were outside, standing in a small group on the street.

'Let's take a look at the temple and whatever is inside the walls,' said Evan, 'then afterwards we can wander around the city.'

What do you know about this place?

They crossed onto the main road that led towards the entrance of the temple grounds.

'Did the gods ever explain what was happening in the world during your people's confinement?' Evan asked Homer.

The big man shook his head.

'Why am I not surprised,' he said. 'How did they expect you to interact with everyone, and know what to do?'

Homer jabbed a finger in Evan's chest.

'True, that is why Zeus brought me here, but how were you to complete the task if you had the other Evandros and not me?'

Homer scratched his head, and shrugged.

'Your father brought you here as your other self does not have the skills or knowledge you have,' said Dexion. 'Divine Zeus had told you this, but still you refuse to accept your fate.'

Evan digested Dexion's words, and then said, 'Dexion, you continue to amaze me by what you say, and I do believe you are much older than you claim. In any case, I will answer Homer's question: the city is home to the Eleusinian mysteries, which are still unknown.'

'And why is that?' Phameas asked.

'Initiates into the mysteries were forbidden to speak of what happened during the ceremonies.'

'What is the purpose of these mysteries?'

'It's about a mother and daughter. Demeter, the goddess of fertility, and her daughter Persephone. Hades had kidnapped Persephone and kept her in his realm. Demeter was so upset she roamed from place to place, mourning the loss of her daughter. During this period of her grieving, crops stopped growing, and the animals went without food. The days were short and the nights long, and it was cold. Demeter came to Eleusis searching for her daughter, and the queen was sympathetic and took her in. She then revealed her true self when she began to transform the young prince from a mortal into an immortal. To show she meant no harm, she asked the queen to build a sanctuary for her, and in return, she'd teach the citizens of Eleusis the sacred rituals of renewal.'

'What of Persephone? Were mother and daughter reunited?' Dexion asked.

'They were, but not before Hades tricked Persephone into eating a few seeds from the pomegranate. Hades didn't want to let her go, but Zeus forced him. So for three months of the year, Persephone returns to Hades' dominion. Twice a year, the people of this region come together and the initiates prepare for the safe passage of Persephone to the underworld and for her return at the beginning of spring.'

No one knows what happens during these rituals?

Evan shook his head. 'If anyone spoke of the mysteries, they would be sentenced to death.'

'Moloch! As I said before, your gods are harsh masters!'

'I don't think you'd find too many benevolent ones,' said Evan.

'Even our gods punish those who do not follow the tenets,' Phameas admitted.

'It's a good system to instil fear in people,' Evan said. 'Enough talk of the gods, let's explore this town.'

CHAPTER TWENTY-ONE

Plato wound his way through the large and excitable assembly of Athenian citizens. In all his years attending meetings on the Pnyx, he'd never seen the place full so early. People were jostling for a better view of the platform, where the speaker stood biding his time. Plato shook his head. He did not think such showmanship was necessary in a well-prepared speech; it was what was said that mattered. He settled in and waited as the convener gave the orator a nod and released the cork from the water clock.

'Citizens of Athens, have we not suffered enough at the hands of tyrants!' Aristagoras said with a hand on his chest and the other pointing at the throng. 'We have battled and beaten the Persians not once but twice, and were they not a mighty foe? I say if the Atlanteans come, let them, and we will show them we are not afraid to fight for our homes, our people, our democracy!'

A forest of fists stabbed the sky as the crowd roared their approval. Aristagoras beamed, pleased with himself and the response of his countrymen. He gazed at the sea of faces, young and old, as he stood on the stone podium, the sun warming his back. A few kilometres behind him were the impressive defensive walls with guard posts overlooking the city and the outlying terrain. The council had called all Athenians to meet on the Pynx, a low flat-topped hill a short distance from the agora and with a view of the Akropolis.

Aristagoras laced his fingers over his ample girth and waited for the din to lessen before he continued. The herald tried to restore order, but the mercurial crowd did not heed his warnings. He ordered the Scythian archers into a shooting stance, with an arrow nocked and ready to release. The mob began to quieten and grumbled at the overreaction by the herald.

'Citizens, please listen,' Aristagoras said, palms facing out as he beseeched the six thousand men for their attention. He put on his best sincere face. He needed to convince them the danger was real and imminent.

The last time such a large number of members had attended the assembly was when Persia had invaded their country. Members included young men from the age of eighteen to those in their most senior years, and from a wide range of occupations: farmers to artisans, senators to generals. All must attend. Failure to do so incurred criminal charges.

'We are gathered to discuss a serious threat, one our ancestors thought we would never confront again. Over nine millennia ago, a great seafaring nation sought to conquer and rule those they invaded, subjugating lands from as far afield as the Pillars of Herakles and to the farthest reaches of the eastern provinces. These people came from the Isle of Atlantis. But'—he paused and pointed a quavering finger—'one ancient nation, forgotten by its new inhabitants and descendants, resisted the might of Atlantis. The war was long and bloody, many lives lost, but Atlantis was defeated.' Aristagoras drew in a deep breath and waited a few seconds. 'And it was this one state, this solitary land with its people, who crushed the Atlanteans. They were the men of Attika, citizens of this great city.' He examined the eager faces before him, their eyes shining with anticipation. 'It was the power of Athens that brought Atlantis to their knees!'

Aristagoras threw his head back and arms up. His heart thumped so loud in his ears, it muted the uproar of the crowd. Their collective voices thundered, the sound washing over him in waves as the momentum of excitement grew. Adrenaline surged through his body like a powerful drug, drinking in the exhilaration of his performance. He kept his face neutral. He knew even the most apathetic listener would be stirred and hungry to act.

The herald shouted for calm, his voice drowned out by the ongoing clamour of the mob. It took the archers longer to quell the more overzealous members. The herald scowled at Aristagoras and stomped over to the bema, the stone platform. The orator shrugged and stepped down to make way for the convener.

'I cannot help if the power of my speech has stirred the blood of the good citizens of Attika,' he said with a small smile.

'Of course not, Councilman, we are fortunate your oratorical presentations arouse such fervour,' the herald said, sarcasm dripping from every word. He then waited while the archers restored order. 'Is there anyone who would like to counter the words of Councilman Aristagoras?'

When there was no immediate reply, Aristagoras stuck his chest out, clasped his hands behind his back and rocked on his heels.

'I would like to respond to Councilman Aristagoras' provocative speech,' a voice called out.

The herald squinted, raised a hand against the glare and sought out the volunteer. He grinned and turned to Aristagoras, whose face paled. 'You may take your place with the rest of the councillors.' Then he dropped his voice to a harsh whisper. 'Do you now feel the power of your speech?' He turned back to the assembly and announced, 'The ecclesia recognises the Academician Plato, and he is invited to speak.'

Plato made his way to the speaker's platform and acknowledged the herald with a nod as they moved past each other. He ascended the steps onto the bema and faced the assembly. He scanned the bevy of faces and hoped to be eloquent and persuasive in his oratory.

'Councilman Aristagoras has regaled us with his passionate account of the events our forebears withstood, but negated to include in the story the Age of Deukalion. Following the war between Athens and Atlantis, Divine Zeus and the Olympians caused the great deluge that enveloped the earth and destroyed humanity. The King of the Gods sought to cleanse the world, such was his wrath at the impiety of man. In doing so, he destroyed the island of Atlantis in a single day and night, the people swallowed by the greatest of floods.' He raised and wagged a finger. 'But Atlantis was not the only place destroyed. The ground shook, echoing the god's rage, and the earth tore apart, consuming the ancient city of Athens. In time, what happened was forgotten and the records of the past lost.'

Plato paused to catch a breath when someone called out, 'If these stories were forgotten how is it we know of them today?'

A few citizens snickered and jeered.

'A good question,' Plato said, ignoring the taunts.

The man was patted on the back and congratulated.

'The reason we know the legend is due to the esteemed statesman Solon. During his travels searching for laws and doctrines for governance, an Aegyptian priest told him the story of Atlantis, the war with Athens and the great deluge. If not for the diligent record keeping of the Aegyptians, we would know nothing of the achievements of Atlantis and what happened.'

'Was it not their transgressions that caused their demise? What if they have returned to reconquer?' shouted another. There were rumblings of agreement.

Plato gave a small smile. 'If that was their intent, would they not have invaded some time ago?' The crowd shuffled and grumbled, some agreeing and others not. 'If they did survive the Age of Deukalion, their days would be consumed with building a new home, wherever that may be. However, their return is a sign that a fateful event is about to happen, one that will affect everyone.'

The philosopher cast his gaze over the gathered assembly and to the Akropolis, where the Temple of Athene stood, its bright colours a beacon to all people who visit the city. 'It has been foretold that in the Age of Iron, man will reject the mysteries of the gods. As this Age draws to a close, the people will favour only one divinity, and the Pantheon of the Gods, as well as their offspring, will no longer exist.'

The crowd gasped, but Plato continued, relentless. 'It is said those who carry the blood of the gods can stop this new divinity from succession, for they have the skills and gifts of the gods. But these children of the gods were eradicated for their wrongdoing. If the people succumb to this new god, our gods will be forever forgotten. If by chance the children of the gods come into being, they will seek objects of the Mother, for She alone can restore the way of the gods.'

His last words drifted to the rear of the assembled citizens, then there was silence, dumbfounded expressions mirrored on the men's faces, both young and old. The distant chattering of birds encroached on the heavy stillness. Then, like a clap of thunder shattering the peace, there was an outcry of questions. They surged forward, a heaving mass of writhing bodies. Fear, anger and disbelief bubbled like a hot spring. The Scythian archers moved and formed a line between the frothing horde and the speaker's platform.

'When is this happening?'

'What becomes of us? We cannot live without our gods!'

'What is your source of information?'

'That I can answer,' Plato said, looking at the man who had asked the last question and pushed his way to the front. 'The source is the Delphic Oracle, whom I visited many years ago.'

People muttered to one another.

'What about the Atlanteans?' a man called out.

'What of them?' another shouted back.

'Could it be they are the children of the gods?'

Plato pursed his lips and breathed through his nose. The citizens jostled against each other, many shouting for the others to be quiet and listen. Voices hushed and they waited for an answer.

'I believe the words of Pythia do refer to the Atlanteans, who alone can avert this tragedy.'

The commotion from the assembly was tremendous, like waves crashing against the rocky cliffs during a storm. Pleased by the reaction of his fellowmen, Plato remained stoic while the herald and the guards called for order. When the men calmed down, the herald turned to Plato.

'Is there anything more you'd like to add?'

He nodded. 'I would like to put to a vote that we, the citizens of Attika, will help the Atlanteans in their quest to ensure the gods survive.'

The crowd roared. The throng swelled to the fore, each person pressing against each other from the rear and the sides, eager to cast their vote. The guards fought to hold them back, their arms straining against the weight of bodies that threatened to overcome them.

'*Wait!*' the herald bellowed. Those in close range of the bema flinched and took a backward step.

'Ouch! That was my toe!'

Disgruntled mutters rolled along the front line as does a low tide laps at the shore.

'Before anyone votes, we will hear from those who oppose Plato's speech.'

'I believe Plato! He would not lie to us,' a member yelled. 'I don't need to hear any more.'

Shouts and cries rang out to a fever-pitch crescendo. Plato raised his hands and waited until he had their attention.

'My fellow citizens, the herald is following tenets set down by our lawmakers so each person may have an opportunity to speak. It is our right as a democratic state to express our opinions, and it is only fair that anyone who wishes to dispute them may do so.' He bowed to the herald and stepped aside.

The herald faced the throng, grasped the folds of his khiton and drew in a deep breath. 'Who would like to address the claims of Plato?'

Aristagoras thrust his way forward. 'I would.'

The herald bade him to approach.

Aristagoras waddled over and puffed up the few steps. He clasped the folds of his tunic, hands resting against his collarbone. 'First, I would like to congratulate Plato on his engrossing and enlightening speech. I, for one, was enthralled by what he spoke of, but I wonder whether the goal of the Atlanteans is to restore the way of the gods.' His brow knitted, deep lines furrowing his forehead. 'We do not know if their intention is pure or whether they will use this opportunity to invade our homeland. We do know from evidence of the past what they are capable of and we must consider all possible actions. We do not want and should not make decisions based on unfounded information. How can you'—he pointed at Plato, his voice rising—'know the true intentions of these Atlanteans? What proof do you have to support what you have stated so exaltedly before this assembly? I do not want to see our way of life and freedom vanquished because of the words of one man.'

His rebuttal was met with cheers and boos, the crowd baying. Plato stepped back onto the bema.

'Councillor Aristagoras, you are either very brave or a fool to question the words of the Oracle.' Plato shook his head, mouth downturned at the corners. 'Would you question the wisdom of Divine Apollo? For that is what you do by calling into doubt the prophecy given by the vessel of the god.'

Aristagoras' eyebrows lowered and he squinted at the philosopher. He stormed onto the platform and thrust his girth at Plato, forcing him out of the way.

'I do not question the prediction but do wonder at the interpretation of it. We all know the explanation of such divinations can be ambiguous, and it is this I have reservations about. Can the Priests of Apollo be certain that is what the Oracle meant, or was there perhaps an exchange of monies to appropriate the desired message?'

'That is an affront to the god!' someone called out.

'Did he call Plato a liar?'

'Perhaps the councilman should seek the Oracle for his future and see how favourable it would be now!'

Laughter and raucous comments continued until Plato stood with the councilman.

'Perhaps some may resort to such underhanded dealings to ensure a prophecy of their choice. But know this.' He turned to face the assembly. 'The forecast given to me is true, and I believe the Atlanteans are here to stop the downfall of the gods. I will be voting to help them if they require it.'

The herald cut off Aristagoras, forestalling any further discussion, and reminded the ecclesia of the issue they were about to vote on. He called on two of his assistants to bring out the earthenware jars, one with white pebbles and the other with black. Next he ordered four archers to take positions around the large urn in which the voters would place their pebbles. Once satisfied, he instructed the citizens to form a queue and commanded the remaining archers to form a protective line on either side of the line of citizens.

Plato placed his pebble in the jar and sat back on the grass. It was going to be a long afternoon, with six thousand voters to register their choice, after which followed the counting.

CHAPTER TWENTY-TWO

Evan was impressed by the city of Eleusis and the buildings. He was considering setting up a new business dedicated to designing and constructing houses based on what he'd seen. Distracted by his musings and formulating a business plan for when he got back home, he stumbled into Homer.

'What's happened? Is there something wrong?' He reached for his sword.

Homer shook his head, staring in amazement. He then grabbed Evan's arm, pulled him alongside and pointed. Evan blinked, his lips parting. From where they stood on the crest of a hill, they saw the sprawl of the city, multitude of houses cocooned within the circumference of protective walls. He looked for the familiar landmarks, ones he'd visited on a trip to Greece.

'Oh… that's not what I expected.' He stared at the Akropolis. 'A pity they painted the Parthenon. It detracts from its innate beauty.'

Homer nudged Evan and resumed walking. Shrugging off his disappointment, Evan followed, and the city vanished from sight. A snaking path took them through a cluster of firs. Beyond the woodlands was a river that meandered in a southerly direction. Scattered across the land and on the slopes of the hills were homes and farms. The sky was streaked with lazy low-hanging smoke eddying from chimneys.

The bleating of goats and braying of donkeys greeted them as they walked past. On one farmstead, olive trees planted in neat rows were full of plump black fruit. The number of homesteads increased as they neared the city. Like their compatriots on the farms, the occupants were preparing meals, the aromatic scent of cooking wafting into the air, whetting their appetite.

Closer to the city, on the east side of the road, were stele and marble sarcophagi, inscribed with lettering and images of the deceased. The bright colours painted on the stone imbued life into the stoic sentries as reminders of the living.

A group of warriors stood beside an open door of a double-gated entrance, their faces concealed by their burnished helmets. Evan saw more soldiers standing on the ramparts. Inside the gates there was movement, and he noted extra armed men had arrived.

'This doesn't look reassuring,' said Phameas in a low voice.

'Hmm…' Evan slowed his pace and reassessed the practised stance of the soldiers.

'Perhaps there is trouble afoot,' Leander said.

'We'll soon find out,' said Evan. 'Keep walking and don't stop.' He glanced over his shoulder at the High Priestess. 'You should cover your head.'

She pulled the silky sky-blue scarf from her shoulders and draped it over her head. The warriors stepped aside as they approached the gates and let them pass. Hard, cold eyes followed their progress through the gates. The men clutched their spears, the butts on the ground, yet ready to launch on command.

'Halt!'

Oh, crap. Evan groaned inward and turned. 'Yes?'

'Are you here for the Panathênaia Festival?'

Evan gave him a blank look. 'Panathênaia Festival?' Then his face brightened. 'Oh, the celebration and worship of the Goddess Athene and Erechtheus. We are not from Attika and are unable to participate in the procession or festival.'

The warrior nodded. 'On your way, then.'

'Can you recommend a respectable hostel suitable for our High Priestess?' he asked.

The soldier turned his attention to her, his eyes widening as she gazed back at him. 'Follow this main junction until you come to the crossroads. Turn right, and a little way along there is a place called Hermes. There is a plaque over the doorway with a picture of the messenger.'

'Thank you.'

The High Priestess acknowledged him with a slight tilt of her head. 'May the Mother Goddess protect you, your family and your men.'

The soldier's mouth opened and closed a few times. 'Th… thank y… you, High Priestess.'

The group were halfway down the road when the commander barked instructions to close the gate.

'We made it just in time,' Leander said, glancing back.

The road narrowed as they walked from the outer reaches of the defensive perimeter and into the residential area. Small, humble homes were in greater numbers on the outskirts of the city. They were built from stone and mud-brick, the roofs tiled or made from timber and the entrance faced the streets.

Crooked, narrow streets veered off the main road like a series of veins, only to disappear around corners and venture in another direction. Smoke escaped from cooking hearths, the smell acrid and low in the air like pendulous clouds of smog. They encountered a few locals heading in the opposite direction, who quickened their pace on seeing their weapons. Hektor raised a brow but did not comment. They came to the junction the warrior had told them and turned right. Further along, Evan spotted the hostel. The sign squeaked as it moved to and fro in the slight breeze.

The next morning, feeling rested and refreshed, they gathered outside the High Priestess' room. Leander leaned against the door frame; Hektor stood opposite while Homer, Phameas, and Evan rested against the wooden railing. Dexion sat cross-legged on the floor in front of Evan. The sun streamed through the opening in the roof and warmed their backs. Fragrant perfume of orange blossoms wafted from below, the familiar scent reminding Evan of the many times he'd sat under the tree at his grandparents' place and eaten the fruit.

'How far is it to Piraeus?' asked the High Priestess. She was sitting on the bed, hands clasped on her lap.

'It's about a two-hour walk,' said Evan.

'We should pack our belongings and leave for the port,' said Hektor.

'I'd agree, but we've been travelling non-stop since we left Pylos. I think we need to rest for a few days.'

'We don't need any further delays,' Hektor said, stiffening. 'We must continue. Your inability to endure the journey cannot hinder our duty.'

Evan glowered, stepped around Dexion and stood toe to toe with Hektor. 'You self-centred megalomaniac, I was considering the welfare of the High Priestess and young Dexion. If you stopped thinking about yourself for one minute, you'd see how demanding this trek has been of them.'

Hektor's hot breath fanned Evan's cheek, his eyes glinting and pupils dilated. Evan clenched and unclenched his hands but did not back away.

'Enough!' The High Priestess stood, nostrils flaring. 'This constant bickering is wearing and absurd. We are here to complete a task for the gods. Both of you need to stop behaving like children and act like adults.' She swayed. Leander, the quickest to react, leapt forward to catch hold of her hand and put an arm about her waist. Her face greyed and the lines at her mouth and around her eyes became more pronounced. She fixed her gaze on Hektor. 'We will remain here as Evandros suggested. Now leave me in peace, all of you.' She pulled her hand out of Leander's and shut the door.

'I'm going for a walk,' Evan said, staring at Hektor. 'Anyone want to come along?'

'I'll come.' Phameas levered himself away from the railing.

'Me too.' Dexion stood.

Evan stepped to the side.

'Evandros!'

From the corner of his eye, Evan caught a blur. He raised his hand and caught Hektor's fist. With his other hand, he grabbed Hektor's throat and squeezed until he could feel the bones and the blood pulsing through his veins at a rapid clip. Evan tightened his grip. Hektor began to gasp and choke, hitting at Evan's arm with weak punches. Hektor's face turned red, then blue.

'Evandros! Let him go!' Leander said, trying to pry his fingers from Hektor's neck.

'Evandros, stop! You will kill him.'

Hektor's eyes rolled and his tongue stuck out.

'*Evandros!* You will let Hektor go!'

'Divine Zeus!' Evan heard Leander's surprised voice. It was if his ears were stuffed full of cotton wool.

Zeus grabbed Evan's hands and pulled him away from Hektor.

'*No!*' Evan growled, eyes black. He lunged at Hektor, who had collapsed at his feet, gasping for air.

Zeus wrapped his arms around Evan and both were gone.

Evan hit the water with a loud splash. He jackknifed to the surface, spluttering and coughing, vomiting water. The veins in his neck grew thick and red as he tried to regain his breath. Heaving, he glared at Zeus, who stood on the embankment watching.

'You should have let me deal with him,' he said through spurts of breath. 'His negative attitude is not helping.'

'Hektor's behaviour is not what you need to be concerned with,' Zeus said, tone grim.

Evan stood in the river, water chest high, and studied the god's face. Took a few deep breaths before asking, 'Has it got something to do with what Pythia told me? She called the old god "Dark Master". It's your father, Kronos, isn't it?'

Zeus blinked. 'Is that who she said it was?'

'No, you just did.' Evan waded out of the water. 'You should have told me from the outset who wants to see you and your Family destroyed.'

'Perhaps,' Zeus conceded with a nod. 'Has he reached out to you?'

'No.'

'He will. You must resist any attempts he may use to coerce you.'

'Like how you captured and manipulated me into being here?' Evan grumbled. He pulled off his khiton and wrung it out.

'As I told you many times before—'

'Yeah, yeah, you sent me to the future to become a better and smarter person so I can use my newfound skills and knowledge to find the relics and defeat Kronos,' Evan finished. He hung the tunic on limb of a tree. 'You know, it still doesn't make sense as to how or why you and your Family can't prevent the rise of Christianity. It's not like you don't know when it's going to happen.'

'It's not that simple…'

'Never is. Enlighten me.' Evan stepped into the sun and shivered, his body covered in goosebumps.

Zeus lowered his head, his long golden hair glimmering under the sun. When he lifted his face, his ice-blue eyes had a glare which reminded Evan of the starkness of headlights in the blackest of nights. 'The birth of the leader of this new religion is known to me, as is where he will be born. When he arrives, our power will be diminished and we won't be strong enough to eliminate him or his followers.'

'He was killed and it didn't stop the religion from becoming a major world faith.' Evan rubbed his arms and hugged himself.

Zeus waved a hand over him.

'Thanks.' Evan glanced at the midnight-blue khiton that covered his body. 'If you know when and where Jesus will be born, why can't you fly in before it all happens—' he lifted his hand and swept it across his torso, right to left—'and be done with it.'

Zeus' eyes bored into Evan's. 'No mortal realises our power lies with their belief in us.' Evan opened his mouth to speak when Zeus lifted a finger. 'As long as people continue to offer sacrifices, pour libations, ask for our assistance, pay tribute to us during festivals and the events where they compete against each other for glory, we remain strong. We draw strength from their worship. When word of this new demigod spreads, people will shift their allegiance, and in time, our power will wane. We will no longer be held in esteem and venerated, thus cannot prevail nor counter our demise.'

'Let's see if I understand... your existence and sovereignty are based on your followers' devotion. When they stop believing in you and your Family, you become redundant and powerless, relegated to mere fictional characters in a story.'

Zeus crossed his arms against his chest and scowled. 'We are not fictitious. My heart beats and blood runs through my veins just as it does in yours.'

'So your connection to humans is symbiotic. You are dependent on their worship, a psychological dependency that once gone, is detrimental to your welfare. Fascinating.' Evan tilted his head to the side. 'Your emotional and physical reliance on humans is your Akhilles heel, so to speak. In fact, you need them more than they need you. It's their fear of the repercussions of not revering you and your Family that spurs rituals.' He scratched the back of his head. 'Huh. That is some legacy you left behind. Religious leaders and fanatics have since used fear to manipulate people to act contrary against each other all in the name of God.' Evan shook his head.

'What mortals do to each other is not of our doing,' Zeus said, and pressed his lips into a thin line.

'No, humans are their own worst enemy, and don't need external influences to create adversity,' Evan said. 'History can attest to that.'

'If mortals were to learn of their extraordinary ability, it would be the catalyst for our downfall, and a catastrophic ending.'

'It could.' Nodded Evan. 'That is certain. I must be stupid. I still don't understand why you can't retrieve these objects with the influence you have now.' He plucked at the new clothing. 'You created this for me, and can move from place to place in an instant, start storms and stop them. So why do you need me and the others to find the relics? And, yes, I realise the High Priestess is the one person who can handle the objects.' Evan shivered again, and not from being cold. 'She is a frightening woman. I've seen what she can do.'

'Her power is one of the oldest, and attuned with Mother. She is formidable, and an important part of the plan to locate the relics. If we were to seek Mother's icons, we'd alert Kronos and a war would ensue, one that would affect both immortals and mortals. Having our offspring search and locate the relics will prevent conflict.'

'What of Eris, the Goddess of Discord? Should I be worried about her?' Evan asked. 'And what of Melaina, this other goddess? What do you know about her?'

'Kronos will let Eris do as she wishes as long it doesn't interfere with his plans.' Zeus placed a hand on Evan's shoulder. 'She is crafty, and dangerous. Be watchful and wary of those who are willing to give and yet will not hesitate to spurn you when they do not receive what they believe they're entitled to.'

'Such as Hektor.'

'No, nothing like Hektor. You know what to expect from him. I am speaking of those who give the appearance of friendship and are artful in their benevolence. They may ply you with gifts with the expectation of being compensated rather than giving through selflessness.'

'Isn't that what you get from your worshippers?'

'No. We listen to our petitioners and reward them where suitable.'

'Sounds the same to me. You still haven't said anything about Melaina.'

'Don't worry about Melaina, I have plans for her,' Zeus said.

'Right. Anyway, why did you intervene and bring me here? Hektor's constant pettiness and obstinate behaviour is causing friction.' Evan folded his arms across his chest.

'Hektor is essential to finding the relics, and you will need him to be an ally. Besides, I don't need Ares baying for your blood if you do kill him, along with Hera's constant complaints about you.' Zeus leaned forward and poked Evan in the chest. 'We have a common foe and task to contend with. You and your fellow Atlanteans find the relics and restore order, and I will send you back home.'

'I will hold you to that,' said Evan in a grim tone.

CHAPTER TWENTY-THREE

Evan blinked. 'Damn it! I wish Zeus would stop doing that!' He took in his new surroundings. He was in the courtyard of the hostel. On the wooden bench by the wall appeared his dry khiton. He walked over and picked it up.

'Evandros! You're back.'

He looked around to see Dexion and Phameas scamper down the staircase, Homer a step behind them.

'What happened? Where did you get to?' Phameas asked.

'Had a chat with Zeus. He said it's probable that Eris may interfere with our recovery of the relics.'

Homer blanched.

'Who is Eris?' Phameas said, looking from Homer to Evan.

'She is an old goddess who causes chaos and mayhem,' said the High Priestess. Phameas glanced over at her as she joined them.

'Yes, and she has joined forces with Kronos.'

'Kronos? He's the one we're to defeat? Gods,' said Leander, eyes wide. 'Two Titans. How are we to win against two old gods?'

'I don't think you can. That's why we need the relics,' Evan said.

'What else did Divine Zeus tell you?' the High Priestess asked.

'He explained why the immortals couldn't look for the relics. If they did, a war like none the world has ever seen would happen.'

'Worse than when the younger gods fought the old ones?' Leander asked.

'It sounded that way,' Evan acknowledged with a nod. 'Zeus was concerned with the impact it would have on the people and the likelihood it could change the way individuals worship.'

'Is he suggesting people will seek veneration in another god and turn away from the divine gods?' The High Priestess' brows arched.

'Yes.'

'And if this new god is allowed to be born, many will follow?'

'It will spread across the whole world,' Evan said.

'Then finding the relics will be the only way to prevent either outcome from occurring,' said Leander.

'This is much direr than I expected,' the High Priestess said, sitting on the bench. She looked up at Evan, troubled. 'Both propositions have bleak conclusions. That is why the gods sought our assistance.'

'Yes, and to prevent one or the other consequence from eventuating.' Evan glanced at Phameas and Dexion.

'I thought the gods needed us and that's why we were chosen,' the High Priestess said, her hands clenched.

'They do, and only you can handle the objects. Remember what happened to the Egyptian High Priest.' Evan's memory of the charred remains of the Egyptian after he'd snatched the golden serpent from the High Priestess was still vivid. That and the High Priestess' use of the red light. 'Using us serves their purpose.'

'The reason does not matter. What is important is that the gods have prevailed upon us to recover the sacred relics to maintain their power,' said Hektor. 'We alone can forestall change.'

'Change and progress are inevitable,' said Evan. 'It's in our human nature to want to learn about the world around us and discover new ways of living. We cannot be stagnant. Otherwise we become redundant and worthless.'

'Your knowledge of our ancestors' writings gives you greater insight into their achievements but also their folly,' said the High Priestess. 'However, the gods' plight and that of our home is intertwined. Our people will die if we are unsuccessful.' She stood. 'Our purpose is to save the gods and our home. And we shall.'

'I also asked Zeus about Melaina,' said Evan.

The High Priestess looked at him with renewed interest. 'And did he know of her?'

Evan nodded and turned to Hektor, his gaze hardening. 'He is aware of her and said not to worry about her.'

'I thought her appearance would not go undetected,' said the High Priestess. 'I am going back to my room to rest for a while longer.' She left and returned to her room.

Hektor took a step, his hands balled, his heated gaze on Evan. Leander intervened and put a hand on his chest.

'Enough, Hektor. Do you think you'd be standing here if Divine Zeus had not interceded?' Hektor began to shake, the veins in his arms and neck protruding. His face turned red. 'This is the last time I will stand up for you. I have grown weary of your complaints and vitriolic tirades. You keep saying Evandros is different. It is you that has changed. We all have. Not one of us is the same person who left Atlantis. If anyone should be angry, it should be Homer.'

Hektor uncurled his hands and the tension drained from his face. His shoulders slumped. He bit his lip and searched Leander's hard expression for redemption. Leander did not relent. Hektor lowered his head and shuffled away.

'It had to be said. Hektor's continued antagonism would cause more damage to our tenuous relationship, and we cannot be divided as a group in our hunt for the relics,' Leander told Evan.

'Agreed,' Evan said. They stood in awkward silence. 'I suggest we go find a bar and have a drink or two.'

'Now that is the best idea I've heard since leaving Carthage!' said Phameas, rubbing his hands.

Evan grinned. 'It has been a while, hasn't it?'

They left the hostel after asking the proprietor the whereabouts of a local tavern. He advised they leave their weapons behind, believing that carrying arms might provoke those who were already full of drink and false bravado. The directions he gave had them weaving in and out of the maze of streets.

'The town planners didn't like wide thoroughfares. This whole area is a rabbit warren,' commented Evan. 'Let me try something.' He stood in the middle of the street and stretched his arms, his fingertips mere centimetres away from the walls of the houses. 'I bet you can touch the houses, Homer.'

Homer moved to the centre and lifted his arms. Evan grinned.

'You couldn't even drive a cart through here,' said Phameas in disapproval. 'Back home, the streets are double the width, and both people and carts share the roads. It doesn't make sense to build houses so close together.'

'The homes may have been built before any planning was done,' said Evan as they recommenced walking, 'which is why the streets are narrow and haphazard.'

'Even our narrow streets are wider than this,' Phameas muttered.

'I think we're not too far from our destination,' Leander piped in and pointed.

A man stumbled out of a doorway and lurched towards them, emitting a loud belch. They slowed to a stop as he wobbled, regained his balance and criss-crossed his way towards them. They stepped aside, backs to the wall as he neared. He glanced up at them with bloodshot eyes, and burped again, the stench of fermented wine billowing over them. Dexion screwed up his nose. The drunkard continued his uncoordinated gait down the street. They watched as he navigated his way along the laneway until he turned the corner and disappeared from sight.

'Yep, we're in the right place,' said Evan with a crooked lilt of the mouth.

The hum of voices and laughter filtered through the doorway of the tavern. Evan ducked, then straightened. He looked around for a spare table. The boisterous chatter mellowed, followed by a cagy silence. Phameas and Dexion stood on either side of Evan, while Leander and Homer halted behind them.

'Greetings,' said Leander in a cheerful voice.

'Gods!'

'By Zeus, he's big!'

'Poseidon's beard, they're huge!'

Evan ignored the astonished looks and moved towards an empty table. He sat and waited for the others to do the same. He swivelled in his seat and searched the room. He saw a short, squat bearded man head their way, a grubby towel in hand.

'What can I get you?' the man asked in a hoarse voice.

'A jug of wine, five cups and extra water,' said Evan.

The man gave a nod and walked to a darkened corner of the room.

'At least there aren't any ill-mannered captains here,' Evan said to Phameas.

The Phoenician grinned. 'That is a day I will not forget.'

'What happened?' asked Leander.

'We had disembarked at Hippo Regius and been given shore-time. We went to a tavern popular with sailors, and three captains happened to be there. One of them demanded to know who Evandros was and where he came from. Well, Evandros told him to mind his own business and said that he did not answer to anyone but his captain and then walked away,' Phameas said, eyes shining. 'No sailor has ever stood up to a captain before. That was the day I knew I'd follow Evandros anywhere he went.'

'I did not know that!' said Evan. 'I thought you decided on the ship, when Dexion stole aboard.'

'At the time, I assumed you'd remain on the ship, when you and the captain came to an agreement. I didn't think about it afterwards until Dexion came along,' Phameas said.

Evan looked to Dexion, who nodded. 'And you knew?'

'Not at first. It wasn't until we talked about the purpose of your journey that his intentions were clear,' said Dexion.

Evan clasped Phameas' shoulder. 'You are a good friend and an honourable man.'

Phameas' face glowed as he beamed. The barman returned with their order. Evan paid him and he left to serve another customer. Evan poured wine into the cups and added water, tipping extra into Dexion's cup.

Evan raised his cup. 'To Phameas, the best man I know.'

'To Phameas!'

'We're almost at the end of our search,' said Leander, placing his cup on the table. 'Once we find the relics, we can go home.'

I suggest caution. We do not have the protection of the white light and there are many ears here, Homer scrawled.

'Of course, wise words.' Leander nodded, his cheeks reddening.

'Hang on,' said Evan, pointing at Leander with his cup, 'you used the white light back in Memphis when you contacted your father. Can't you use it here?'

'No, my use of the white light isn't as strong as the High Priestess',' Leander said.

'Did you know what she could do? Either of you?' he said.

Leander and Homer looked at each other.

'We aren't privy to the teachings of those who serve the Mother Goddess,' said Leander.

'That is not an answer, Leander.'

It is known is that the High Priestesses are transformed when they are chosen, but not of what happens to them.

'What of Sibyl, did she have the same ability?'

She would have gone through a transition at the time of her initiation, though her abilities were not as powerful as the High Priestess'.

'Sibyl? Who is Sibyl?' asked Phameas.

'Evandros' wife,' said Leander.

'You have a wife? You never mentioned her.' Phameas stared at Evan.

'She's dead.'

'Oh... I am sorry, Evandros. I did not mean to offend.'

'You haven't, Phameas. Let's not discuss it.'

'As you wish.' Phameas clasped his cup and tilted his head to the side. 'Then we shall drink to surviving the shaking earth and Evandros' ability not to die.'

'I'll drink to that.' Evan nodded, raising his cup to Phameas.

'Yes, indeed,' said Leander, lifting his cup.

Homer nodded and joined them.

'Me too,' piped in Dexion. Evan grinned at him and ruffled his hair.

'Excuse me,' someone said, disrupting their conversation.

They looked at the newcomer.

'I do not mean to disturb you.' They stared at the young man. He swallowed and wrung his hands. 'I... er... I mean... we, my friends and I... um... were wondering if you are Atlanteans?'

'No.' Evan's eyes hardened.

'Oh...' The youth blanched. 'My apologies. I will leave you to enjoy your drink.' He scurried back to his table. Evan watched as his friends questioned him. From the expressions on their faces, they seemed disappointed by what he told them.

Evan tossed back the wine from his cup. 'Shall we return to the hostel?'

'That is probably wise,' said Leander. He drank the rest of his wine.

Homer stood, drawing the attention of the patrons, and walked towards the exit, the others not far behind. They retraced the route they had used earlier and continued along the narrow streets.

'Master Evandros, there are people following us,' said Dexion after they turned into a street. 'It's that same man who came to our table, and his friends are with him.'

'Here I was hoping there'd be no trouble.'

'What shall we do?' asked Leander.

'We don't want to draw attention, and it won't do us any good if we get into a fight. That would stir up a whole lot of problems we don't need,' Evan said.

'I am not fond of being pursued; it generally means whoever it is is up to no good,' said Phameas. 'I suggest at the next street, we hide and wait for them, and then ask what they want.'

'A good idea, Phameas.' Evan led them into a quick trot and rounded the next corner. They flattened themselves against the wall of a house, keeping to the shadows. The sound of footfalls drew nearer to where Evan and his fellow companions waited.

'I am sure they came this way,' said a voice.

'We've lost them,' said another. 'They could be anywhere by now.'

'Not the most salubrious area to be residing,' one said with a sniff. 'The air reeks with despair.'

'You are such a snob, Agrias,' said a familiar voice. 'Not all people are as fortunate as us. You know Plato would not be impressed with your words.'

'What does it matter. He's not here,' came the retort. 'These so-called citizens of Athens need to find work, even if they have to shovel shit out of the latrines and stop burdening the good citizens with pleas of money.'

'As if you'd know what work is, Agrias. Your father is the richest man in Athens and pays everything for you.'

'I'll have you know, Phoinix, my father has entrusted me with an estate of which I need to watch over the slaves and ensure they do their work.'

'More like your head slave, Balor, oversees the labour while you lie under a tree and sleep the day away.'

There was laughter.

'At least I don't have to traipse after my father while he negotiates with tight-fisted traders,' Agrias bit back.

'Oh, I don't mind. It has been an education, and I've learnt a great deal about trading,' said Phoinix. 'One day, I will take over the business, and my father is making sure I understand every aspect of being a mercantile trader.'

'Humph. I wouldn't do it,' Agrias said.

'No, you wouldn't. You'd have to get up early every morning, which we all know you are incapable of doing.'

More laughter.

'We should turn back, we're not going to find them now,' said another youth.

'Just a few minutes more, and if we can't see them, then we'll leave,' said Phoinix.

Evan pressed into the wall as the first of the youths stepped into the street. As the four moved away from the corner, still bantering, Evan moved on light feet behind the four youths, and with a tilt of his head, the others surrounded them.

'By the gods!' said one of the youths, mouth falling open.

'Ug, ug, ug,' said the one called Agrias. His eyes rolled and he crumpled to the ground.

'By Zeus!'

The three remaining youths drew closer, clutching each other, gazes flicking from Evan to his companions. Homer crossed his arms against his chest, and another of the young men fainted.

'Why are you tailing us?' Evan asked, his face as hard as stone.

'I... ah... er... thought... if...' Phoinix trembled as the three tall men and the shorter man and boy moved closer.

'Spit it out, boy!' Phameas barked.

Phoinix swallowed and tightened his hold on his friend. 'We... we... wanted to... to... pass on inf... information, that is if... if... you hailed fr... from Atlantis.'

'What information would that be?' Evan said.

Phoinix licked his lips. 'Some months ago there was a... an assembly discussing what the citizens would do if... if Atlanteans ever came to Athens.'

'And?' Evan pressed, brow furrowed.

Phoinix lifted a shaking hand and wiped the sweat from his forehead. 'The citizens voted in favour of assisting the Atlanteans.'

'But?' Evan urged.

'There are factions who believe the Atlanteans have returned to finish what your ancestors failed to accomplish.'

'What is he talking about, Evandros?' Phameas said, looking at him.

'Atlantis was a great sea power and ruled throughout the Mediterranean and beyond the Stra...' He caught himself and rushed on. 'The Pillars of Herakles. They conquered those who attempted to usurp their dominance. The Athenians had enough of the tyranny and waged war.'

'And then what happened?' Phameas asked.

'The kings of Atlantis found out what the Athenians were planning and attacked, which was a bad strategy. The Athenians defeated them, and soon afterwards Atlantis was destroyed, eradicated from existence. Or so it was believed, until now.'

'This is concerning,' said Leander. 'What are we going to do?'

Evan rubbed his brow. 'We leave in the morning for Piraeus.'

'What of the High Priestess? She needs to rest,' Leander said with concern.

'Excuse me, may I make a suggestion?' Phoinix offered. His pulse quickened as three pairs of ice blue eyes speared him. 'I... I know someone who would open his house to you.'

'And who might that be?' Evan said.

'Our t... teacher P... Plato.'

Evan started. 'Did you say Plato?'

Phoinix nodded. 'You have heard of him?'

'You could say I have.'

CHAPTER TWENTY-FOUR

Evan and his companions stood aside while Phoinix and his friend roused the two who had fainted and returned to the hostel with the four youths. The courtyard was filled with other guests and the innkeeper's slaves, who were staring up at the second floor.

'What's going on?' Evan asked, threading his way through the crowd. He wondered what had caught their attention when blue light flashed from one of the rooms. 'The High Priestess!'

He shoved people aside, bolted up the stairs and dashed for the room. He skidded to a halt.

'What the hell is that?'

'Great Mother!' Leander slammed into his shoulder and tried to get into the room.

'Wait, Leander!' Evan held him back. 'We may endanger them if we charge in.'

'But…'

'Go get your bow and quiver of arrows. Homer, get your sword. Don't enter the room until we figure out what to do.'

Evan took in the scene. Hektor was standing in front of the High Priestess, his gaze locked on a two-headed snake. It was on the bed. No one could enter or leave the room. He hurried to collect his sword.

'The room is too small. We'll hurt each other if we all go in,' he said as they stood outside. Phameas clasped his chin. His dark olive complexion had an unhealthy grey sheen. The snake swung its heads at them and hissed.

'We have to do something,' Leander said, pacing.

'We will,' Evan said. 'We need a strategy to kill it.'

'This was sent to stop us from leaving.' Evan glanced at Dexion, who seemed to be in a trance.

'I know you thought the earthquake wasn't sent by the gods, Evandros, but now I am not so sure. This creature, here in a room occupied by the High Priestess, can't be a coincidence.' Leander clutched the bow, his knuckles stretched taut.

The boy blinked, did a little head shake and looked up at Evan. 'It was intended for you.'

Evan's heart flipped. 'It's either Kronos or Eris who sent it.'

'It's personal.' Dexion bit his lip, eyes wide and fear-struck. 'The Dark Master wants you because you're Zeus' son.'

Evan's mouth went dry and a cold chill travelled down his spine. He had never seen Dexion frightened before. 'Good to know I'm popular,' he said with a humourless guffaw. 'I might as well paint a red target on my back and be done with it.'

'That's not funny, Evandros.' Phameas' face was strained.

'I'm not laughing. We need to work out how to rescue the High Priestess and Hektor.'

The snake's two heads swayed, its black eyes watchful and its tongues flickering out, licking the air. Then it swung and coiled its long serpentine body tighter. The High Priestess pressed herself against the wall, her face peering over Hektor's shoulder. The pallor of her face was as white as a sheet of paper. She looked from the serpent to Evan, her gaze lingering on Leander.

'Can't you—' Evan waved his hand at her—'get that red light and kill it?'

'It… it doesn't work… on immortal creatures,' she said, voice quavering.

'Fan-bloody-tastic.' Evan gritted his teeth. Homer patted his arm, pointed at himself and made a running motion into the room with his fingers. 'No. That crazy-arse reptile is here for me. I'll draw its attention, and you and Leander attack it.' Homer shook his head so hard, his jowls quivered. 'It's the only way.' Evan edged closer to the door. 'Whatever the outcome, make sure it dies.'

Before he lost his nerve, Evan slipped into the room, on the opposite side to where the High Priestess and Hektor stood. He kept his back to the wall and held out his sword.

'I'm over here, you double-headed brainless snake!'

The heads rotated in unison, and the necks flattened like those of a cobra when ready to strike. From the corner of his eye, Evan saw Hektor and the

High Priestess take a step towards the door. Homer sidled into the room and moved in Evan's direction. Leander hovered inside the doorway.

Evan's eyes widened. 'Oh crap!'

The snake grew bigger and bigger until the heads skimmed the ceiling. The bed creaked and bowed under its weight. It hissed.

Evan flinched.

'By Zeus!' Hektor paled. He thrust the High Priestess at Leander, who shoved her outside with Phameas and Dexion.

Quick as lightning, the serpent's heads swung in the direction of the doorway and it opened its mouths. Large fangs dripped with venom. Leander launched arrow after arrow, the long black serpentine body soon studded with projectiles. The snake struck at him. Leander dove through the doorway. The serpent's head whistled and smashed into the stone floor with its maw. Homer leapt forward and swung his sword. A head tumbled to the ground. Evan covered his eyes. Sparks flew from the head and crumbled into dust.

'Great Mother!'

Evan lowered his arm and gawked. 'That is not good.'

Another head replaced the severed one.

Evan took a swing and cut off a head. A new one sprouted. Leander sent a barrage of arrows, until a head exploded. Evan faltered as the blinding light rendered him sightless. He blinked, luminous spots filling his vision until he could see the faint form of Homer lashing out with his sword. Evan sucked in a breath as a large head, with fangs as long as a sword blades, attacked. He ducked, the air swept over him like a gale-force wind, and followed by a loud thud. Plaster crumbled, the debris raining over him. Evan hastened upright, and hacked at the reptile's coiled body. Flashes of light, brighter than a solar flare, burst through the dismembered parts. The serpent hissed and shrieked at the same time.

Evan doubled over, dropped his sword and pressed his hands over his ears. The snake emitted a long shrill and soared over Evan, heads poised to strike. A strong wind buffeted the room. Homer and Hektor were slammed against the wall, arms spread out and hair billowing in all directions. Leander was flung into a corner next to the door, feet dangling off the floor. Evan was pressed to the floor. He tried to push himself upright but couldn't move. It reminded him of the time when he was ten years old, and he and his friend were playing around with high jump mats. His mate had dared him to get underneath while his friend lay on top. Just like back then, it felt like the two hundred and fifty kilograms sat on his chest now, and he struggled to breathe.

The serpent's heads flattened, the tongues flickering and fangs gleaming. Then the oppressive weight and noise disappeared. Homer, Hektor and Leander crashed to the floor. Evan drew in a ragged breath. He dared not move, fearing the snake might strike.

'Where did it go?' he heard Leander say.

Evan poked his head over the bed and stared. The reptile was gone. He got onto his knees. Dexion flew into the room and flung himself at Evan, wrapping his arms tight about Evan's neck. The boy trembled in his arms.

'I'm okay, Dexion.' He patted the boy's back. Dexion tightened his grip. Evan looked up as Phameas squatted beside them. Deep worry lines around his mouth and eyes spoke volumes.

'Let's get out of here.' He thrust his hand at his friend. Phameas helped him up. Dexion did not let go. Evan had no choice but to carry him.

'Mother is going to be very upset by this,' the boy whispered into his neck.

Leander had his arm about the High Priestess' waist as she clung to him. Homer and Hektor stood next to them. Phameas and Evan exited the room. The High Priestess laid a trembling hand on Dexion's arm. He turned to her.

'Mother is not going to be pleased.'

'No, she is not.' The High Priestess' voice wavered. Leander pulled her closer to his side.

A crowd had gathered on the landing.

'What happened?'

'Is it true there was a monster in the room?'

'Did anyone die?'

'Was anyone injured?'

'Let us through,' Hektor growled and pushed his way through the people. Progress was slow as the mob swarmed, eager for answers.

'There is someone still in the room!'

The throng jostled past them, trying to get to the chamber. Evan spotted Phoinix, who beckoned them with an eager look on his face.

'Quick... let's go before they realise it's a ruse,' said Phoinix.

They collected their belongings and raced for the stairs. They huddled together outside the hostel. Evan put Dexion down, slipped the shield onto his back and slid the sword into its sheath. With the bag over his shoulder, Dexion grabbed his hand.

'Come this way! We'll take you to a safe place.' Phoinix pointed away from the city centre.

CHAPTER TWENTY-FIVE

'*How much longer must we wait?*' Eris demanded. '*The Atlanteans are getting closer to finding the second relic.*'

The Goddess of Discord paced in front the Dark Master, who watched her in amusement as he sat on his lustrous white marble throne. His golden eyes were the only feature visible behind the black cowl he wore.

'*Well? When are we going to terminate the Atlanteans?*' She put her hands on her hips and glared at him.

'*Patience, dear Goddess.*' He leaned back and rested his hands on the armrests. '*One of the greatest virtues is to learn patience, for without it, mistakes occur. I have learnt over the aeons to restrain myself from doing the unthinkable, to wait for events to unfold and then act. When I do, it will be a lesson no mortal or immortal will ever forget.*'

He waved a hand and a blurry image appeared; with another quick flick of his hand, it cleared. They watched the Atlanteans follow a group of young men through the back streets of the city and head westwards.

'*Then why send Hydra, then take it away? It could have killed them all.*'

'*It is important to learn how one's foe reacts when faced with adversity,*' Kronos said. '*And in spite of your haste to eliminate the Atlanteans, we require them to locate the last relic.*'

'*Have you found a way to harness the objects without being impaired in the process?*'

'*There are one or two possibilities I am considering.*' He studied the procession and his eyes darkened. '*If you wish to send your creatures to impede their progress, you may. But,*' he added in a cold and menacing tone, '*if any of your bestial monsters slays Evandros or the High Priestess, I will send you back to Tartaros.*'

Eris sniffed and her lip curled. She did not like his almighty and imperious ways, but he had promised her the realm of Mount Olympos. All she needed to do was bide her time and wait for her opportunity to exact revenge.

'What do you want with the High Priestess?' she asked, changing to a more conciliatory tone. 'She is nothing but the mouthpiece of the Mother Goddess.'

'She will prove to be the most valuable... once Evandros is dead. Mother will do anything to protect her daughter, and it is the Earth Mother I want.'

CHAPTER TWENTY-SIX

Jelani tied a belt around his waist and hurried to answer the door, wondering who would be calling so late in the evening. Whoever it was at the door was impatient, and they knocked again, the rapid staccato loud in the quiet household. He had gone to bed, leaving the philosopher and his guest talking. He straightened his shoulders, yawned, shook his head, and opened the door. He recognised the youths and was about to bow when he froze, mouth hanging open.

'Go and tell your master, his students request an audience with him, and we have brought friends.'

Jelani kept staring.

Phoinix clicked his fingers in front of Jelani's face. 'Move along, man! Go and get your master!'

Jelani blinked and stuttered. 'Mm… mm… my apologies, Master Phoinix. Come this way.'

He escorted them to the andron, his heart pounding as they filed in. He had never seen such people. They were glorious to look at, such was their stature, and the aura they exuded. The fair-headed man smiled at him. Jelani's scalp tingled.

'I hope we have not disturbed your evening,' the man said, his voice as smooth as honey.

'N… no…' He backed out of the room. 'I will go and get the master of the house.'

He spun on his heel, half walking and running. The small flame in the oil burner sputtered and fluttered on the way to his master's bedroom. He knocked on the door, shifting his weight from one foot to the other while he waited. He glanced back down the dim passage, his mind reeling. When there was no answer, he rapped on the door louder.

'Master!' he called in a loud whisper, leaning in, head brushing the door. He jumped as it was yanked open.

'By the gods, Jelani, this had better be important! I'd just gone to sleep!' Plato pulled a khiton over his naked body.

'You have visitors.'

'I know, and he is asleep,' Plato groused.

'No, master, it is your student, Phoinix. He is here... he has brought... others with him.' Jelani words came out in a flurry.

Plato did not notice his slave's nervousness and instead grumbled. 'What in the name of the gods does he want? The youth of today have no respect. It's all about me, me, me.'

He bustled down the passageway in the wake of the flickering oil burner held aloft by Jelani. Plato smoothed down his dishevelled hair, but the stubborn flyaway strands refused to stay down. He muttered to himself, annoyed at being wakened and irritated by his wayward hair.

'Now, Phoinix, what is...' He stopped, seeing the crowded room. They all turned. Plato stared, his mouth opening and closing, no words forthcoming. His legs shook.

'Looks as if he may pass out,' said one man with short dark hair.

Plato's knees buckled. The man who had spoken and the fair headed man were quick to catch him and guide him to a seat.

'Put your head between your knees and take deep breaths,' the dark-headed man instructed.

Minutes passed, and when Plato straightened, he stared at his visitors in confusion. 'He said you were in Messene, but you are here... and in my home. How did... from where have you come?'

'Are you speaking of Kallimachos, the older gentleman we met in Messene?' the dark-headed man asked. Plato nodded. 'I wondered where he had gone.' The man stood. Plato had to crane his head back to look at him. 'We've come via Delphi.'

'You went to Delphi?' Plato blinked.

'Hmm... yes. Are you Plato?'

He nodded.

'Phoinix thought it would be best if we came here.'

Plato looked at his students, registering their presence. 'Phoinix?'

'We were having a drink in the tavern when five of them came in. I recognised them straight away and went over to ask if they were Atlanteans. Evandros'—Phoinix pointed to the dark-headed man—'said no. They left soon after and we followed them. I then told them of the meeting by all citizens and offered to bring them here. When we got to the hostel where they were staying, a terrible and incredible incident transpired, much like the deeds Herakles faced!' He went on to describe the fight with the two-headed serpent, waving his arms about, brandishing an imaginary weapon. His fellow students piped in when he paused, adding extra details.

'Gods! How did you destroy it?' Plato asked, his head whipping from the one called Evandros to the other tall men.

'It did not happen the way Phoinix or his friends have explained,' said the fair-headed one.

'And with much less excitement. It was over in a matter of minutes,' added Evan.

'The serpent vanished before we could slay it,' the fair-headed man concluded.

'How is that possible?' Plato asked, glancing around at the people standing in his andron.

'By the hand of an old god,' said the High Priestess, speaking for the first time since leaving the hostel.

'High Priestess.' Plato bowed. 'What makes you believe it was an old god?'

She and Evan shared a look, to which he nodded.

'Divine Zeus told Evandros earlier today Kronos or Eris may impede our search and that we are to be watchful.'

'Zeus? The King of the Gods spoke to you?' Plato said in surprise. His students bunched together in excited whispers.

'Divine Zeus is Evandros' father,' she said.

Plato clutched at the edge of the couch to stop from reeling backwards. 'Does each of you have divine parentage?'

'We do.'

'Gods.' Plato clamped a hand over his mouth and dragged it down. 'Do you hail from the Age of Heroes?'

'Age of Heroes?' the High Priestess repeated with a frown.

'Hesiod, a great poet who walked this earth some three hundred years ago, told of the birth of our gods, the war with the Titans, the creation of our world and of demigods. Men, women, who were a noble and righteous godlike race of hero-men.'

Evan was amused. 'I don't think Akhilleus was very noble or righteous.'

'He was a demigod, possessed greatness and was a hero,' Agrias retorted. 'No man could match his skills as a warrior or best him in a fight. The filthy Trojan Hektor, called the man-slayer, had no chance against the mightiest of Greek warriors.'

'I am sure his ability to fight was unsurpassed, but abusing Hektor's body the way he did was dishonourable and immoral.' Evan's ice-blue eyes hardened. Agrias shrank back and cowered behind Phoinix, who swallowed. 'His behaviour demonstrated a lack of empathy and he was too full of pride. Godlike my ar—'

'Evandros.' The High Priestess warned.

He acknowledged her with a slight nod and stepped away to stand with the boy and Phoenician. Plato watched him with interest.

'Our connection with the gods is old, although we do not consider ourselves to be demigods.' The High Priestess looked from Plato to the four youths. 'It is by the grace of the gods we exist and our bloodline binds us to them. Nothing more.'

Plato stood, eyes shining. 'My dear High Priestess, it is your connection to the gods that makes you unique. There has been no one else since the Heroic Age who was the offspring of the gods.'

'And when was the period of heroes?' she asked.

'Several thousand years ago or so.'

'And there have been no other liaisons with the gods since?'

'No direct relationship with the exception of worship. The gods left this world not long after the war between our people and the Trojans. We do not know why, nor did they give instructions on how to live after their departure.'

'The gods do not need to explain themselves,' the High Priestess said. 'We honour them with our devotion and acts of subservience.'

'Indeed.' Plato nodded. 'However, the prophecy of their end has come, and you have been summoned to ensure it does not occur.'

'What do you know of the prophecy?' she asked.

'The people will no longer revere the gods, and only one shall reign. It will cause a war that is horrific and devastating, and will change our lives.'

'How did you learn of the gods' plight?'

'I was writing a discourse between Socrates and Critias on the history of your people and mine. There wasn't a great deal of oratorical evidence or information on what happened after the war between our nations and the destruction of your home. I sought the guidance of Pythia, who told me the prophecy.'

'So did we. That is, we went to ask for her help,' said the fair-headed man.

'You required her counsel?' Plato asked, his eyes widening.

'Yes, a goddess had instructed us to visit Pythia.' The High Priestess looked over at Evan.

'A goddess? Which one?'

'She is not known to us. When we landed in Pylos, she revealed herself to Evandros and communicates only with him.'

Plato turned to Evan.

'Her name is Melaina. She claims to be here to help us, which so far she has. Other than that, I know nothing else about her.'

'Do the other gods know of her?'

'Zeus is aware of her. However, she has been careful to keep her presence from them.'

'That is odd. If she is an immortal, why avoid the gods? Unless she doesn't want them to know about her.'

'We aren't sure why she does, but she is mindful of the repercussions if the gods do learn about her existence.'

'Plato, what is going on?' a tremulous voice called out. 'What is with all the noise?'

They turned to see a figure standing in the doorway.

'Good evening, Kallimachos,' said Evan.

The older man stared, mouth ajar. 'What are... how? Gods...' He collapsed to the floor, like a piece of material descending from mid-air. Plato hurried to his side and patted his cheeks.

'Up you get, old friend.'

'Here, let us help him onto the couch,' said Evan. He and the fair-headed male took Kallimachos by the arms and placed him on the cushion-covered wooden bench.

'Perhaps we should continue our conversation in the morning,' Evan said.

'Of course! It is late, and the ordeal you have been through must be taking a toll. I'm afraid my home doesn't have many bedrooms. High Priestess, you take my room and I will share with Kallimachos.'

'I cannot allow you to give me your room, good Plato.'

'Nonsense. It is decided! As for the rest of you, you'll have to sleep here. I'll have Jelani bring extra blankets.' Plato stepped to the doorway, where his slave emerged from the darkness. Minutes later, he disappeared into the depths of the house, as silent as a mouse. 'Now my young pupils, you have done well. It is time you head home, and be sure to keep out of sight of the patrols.'

'Yes, Master Plato.' Phoinix bowed. 'May we return tomorrow?'

Plato beckoned them and ushered them out of the andron. 'The day after may be better.'

CHAPTER TWENTY-SEVEN

Evan scanned the long wooden table set under the orange trees in the courtyard, and thought a number of the dishes would not be out of place in a cafe or restaurant. The table was laden with a platter of barley cakes and boiled eggs and a large bowl with barley porridge; another bowl had fresh grapes and myrtle berries, and a plate of sun-dried grapes and figs. The earthenware jugs contained wine and goat's milk, of which Evan reached for the latter and poured into a cup. Evan sighed in content, as the morning sun lit up the yard and took the chill out of the thick stone blocks. First he had met Jason, and now Plato. As dreams went, this was stupendous.

'What did Pythia tell you?' Plato asked as he reached for a myrtle berry.

'The information Pythia gave will aid us in our search, and serve as a warning,' Evan said. He helped himself to the porridge and added the berries.

'Could you be more specific?'

'I could.'

Plato scratched his bearded jaw as he gazed at Evan. 'I see. What can I do to help?'

'You already are by allowing us to stay here in your home,' said the High Priestess.

Plato shrugged. 'It is my honour, dear High Priestess, but I am sure there's more I can do. If you were to tell me what the Oracle said, I may be able to help.'

'You must understand our caution, good Plato. It's not that we do not want to disclose to you what she said; it's that others may overhear.'

'My slaves are trustworthy, and I am sure Kallimachos will not speak of what he hears.'

'I am sure that is true, but they are not the ones we are concerned about.'

'And if we do tell you, we may put your life and that of those living in this house in danger. We don't want to put you in harm's way,' Evan said.

Plato sat for a few minutes, looking at Evan and the High Priestess. 'Are you able to tell me how you intend to prevent the fall of the gods?'

'That bit of information I can reveal.' The High Priestess set aside the wooden spoon. 'We must find sacred objects that belong to the Mother Goddess and unify them with the icon of Mother. Their unification will prevent the decline of the gods.'

'The Mother Goddess? Is she the one who birthed the gods?'

'She is the Mother of all.'

'And these objects are powerful enough to restore order?'

'The power of Mother is far greater than all the gods can wield.'

Plato shivered. 'Gods! If they were to be possessed by one with ill intentions, it would be devastating.'

'Quite,' agreed the High Priestess. 'It would be the end of our world.'

'As I said, I'd like to help in any way I can.'

'We do need to stock up on rations before we set out for Piraeus,' Phameas said.

'Good, good.' Plato clapped his hands together and called for Jelani. The tall, dark man loped over, his gait reminding Evan of a giraffe walking.

'Yes, Master?'

'Get my stylus and pad from my room.' Plato picked up a barley cake. 'I'll write what you need for your journey and have Jelani go to the market to buy the goods.'

'No need, we can go ourselves,' said Evan.

'It may be prudent to stay away from the city.'

'Why so?' asked the High Priestess.

'There may be rumours of your arrival, and if that is so, a contingent of citizens wants to see you imprisoned.'

'It appears the memory of the Athenians is long,' said Leander.

'And unforgiving,' Hektor said.

'Not all believe as these individuals do, and many want to help, such as Phoinix, Agrias and all my students. Nevertheless, better to be cautious than provoke a slumbering beast.'

'We will heed your advice, good Plato, and accept the offer of your help.'

After breakfast, Evan wandered outside, leaving Phameas and Dexion to slumber away in the sun-warm courtyard. Six bodies packed in the tight confines of the andron did not allow for a fruitful night of sleep. Besides, he wanted to see the famous Academy where the renowned philosopher spent his time teaching. Plato was not what he had expected. Evan could not determine his age, as his youthful demeanour and agility gave the impression of a person in his forties. His thick brown hair, kept a little long, and his trimmed beard also made it difficult. The images he was familiar with were of a man in his mid- to late sixties with long greying hair and a flowing beard. Something else modern scholars had gotten wrong.

He walked past the olive and fig trees and followed the dirt path until he came to a grove of oak trees. The large trunks obscured the way ahead. Evan entered the copse and was plunged into the obscure confines. His skin prickled and he rubbed his forearms. He weaved in and out of the clustered trees, his pace quickening as he spied the welcoming beacon of sunshine. He came to the edge of the clearing and stood in the sun, basking in its warmth, glad to be out of the cool shade of the forest.

Evan strolled onto the vast area, the soft grass cushioning his feet. To his left was a gymnasium, and opposite was a peripatos—a covered walkway. He walked over to the building, sat on the stone step and leaned against the Doric column.

'I bet there's been a lot of interesting discussions held here,' he said, glancing around.

Evan relaxed, the surroundings comforting and serene. A first, since being brought to this time by Zeus. He propped an arm on his knee, rested his head against the column and closed his eyes. He must have dozed off, for when he woke, the sun was higher in the sky. He stood, winced and rubbed his cold, numb backside.

'How long was I asleep for?' He walked around, trying to shake off the numbness, and stopped. Evan cocked his head. His ears and nape prickled. He did a slow turn, hands clenched at his side. He then relaxed, the tension draining.

'Peace, Evandros,' said Plato, lifting his hands and smiling. 'You'd been gone for a long time, so I thought I'd come and see what caught your attention.'

'How did you know I'd be here?'

'Logic brought me here.' Plato clasped his hands behind his back and walked away from the building.

Evan stood for a few minutes before joining him. 'I am curious, Plato. Why didn't you finish writing *Critias*? You stopped mid-sentence. It was if you didn't want to complete the dialogue.'

Plato stopped and looked at him, surprised. 'You've read my works?'

Evan nodded. 'Both *Critias* and *Timaeus*.'

'How is that possible? You couldn't have read my dialogues.'

Evan averted his face and took a keen interest in the verdant grounds. 'Um... er... when Kallimachos disappeared back in Messene, we went to his house, and it was there I read your expositions.'

'Ahhh... yes, of course.' Plato nodded and resumed walking. They continued in silence, the lush grass softening their footfalls. 'So, you are the man who is displaced by time.'

Evan's step faltered. 'Huh? What?'

Plato turned to study the younger man.

Evan lowered his gaze and stepped around the philosopher. 'I don't know what you're talking about.'

'The Oracle said one of the Atlanteans was taken from his world not once but twice and his return is a catalyst for transformation.'

Evan hesitated, lifted his head to the sky and said, 'Who told you this strange tale?'

'Pythia. It was one of the many prophecies she divulged.'

Evan kept staring at the sky, his back to Plato.

'She explained this man, the one who is out of step with time, carries two burdens: one of the past, which he denies, and another that is tied to the far-distant future. That he will come to a juncture and must decide between the two lives.'

'Every person has problems and must make difficult decisions,' Evan said.

'Yes, indeed that is so, but their choices do not impede the right, desirable result.'

'Meaning what?' Evan looked at Plato.

'The actions and judgement of one individual will affect the lives of many.'

'So now I am responsible for everyone's lives, is that it?' Evan retorted. 'Whatever I do or say will cause a chain reaction, whether intentional or not? What bullshit! People are responsible for their own actions and decisions, not me.'

'Is that why you are protective of Dexion and Phameas, even of Homer?'

'They look out for me, and I watch over them.'

'What happens to them when you leave?' Plato raised a brow. 'That's what you intend to do, when this task is over.'

'I'm sure Homer will take care of them.'

'No doubt he will, if he is able.'

'Phameas is a smart man and wise of the world. He'll be fine, and as sure as my heart beats, he'll look after Dexion.'

'He's a virtuous man and will be a good father to Dexion,' Plato acknowledged. He then added, 'You have been given a unique opportunity, Evandros, which most men would like to possess—knowledge of the future.'

'And that is why I'm here.'

'I presumed as much.' Plato recommended walking. Evan moved with him. 'From whence have you come?'

'As much as I'd like to answer your question, it is better I don't. It's not that I don't trust you, I do. There are too many ears, and it is preferable certain individuals do not know.'

'Of course. Then tell me, do you know how Kronos and the Goddess of Discord escaped Tartaros?'

'There was a small opening in the shield.'

'I wonder why he released the goddess and not his fellow brothers,' Plato pondered.

Evan shrugged. 'Odds are Zeus repaired the damage before the others could be freed. As to why Eris, perhaps he has plans for her?'

Plato bit his lip and then said, 'Either way, it isn't good when an old god wants revenge.'

'It would appear that is his purpose.'

'And these sacred relics will prevent the rise of a new god?'

'That is the assumption.'

'You don't sound convinced.'

'I've no doubt the objects once joined will do something. It's a matter of what.'

'Do you know much about who this god Kronos wants to supplant the Olympian gods with?'

'He's semi-divine, his mother a mortal and his father, an immortal, which I am assuming is going to be Kronos. This man is a carpenter, teacher, preacher and healer. His purpose is to spread goodness, morality and faith under a single religion. He protects the weak, is a defender of the good and forgiver of those who are corrupt. His influence is one of unification and instilling a righteous belief where all people are equal, no matter the colour of their skin, their gender, or whether they're poor or rich.'

'Socrates always believed in one god.'

'He was a man ahead of his time. Jesus had good intentions, and his teachings demonstrated his purpose. However, his words and instructions became distorted and abused by individuals hungry for riches and domination. The people who follow in his stead, despising the worship of the gods, instilled fear in their believers, which led to the death of innocent people. All in the name of God and religion.'

They ambled in quiet repose and then Plato spoke. 'Perhaps this is Kronos' machination—to promise what cannot be attained. To create confusion, terror and eventual supplication via threats.'

'That was achieved. Let me give a small example of the faithful exacting righteousness. Women who were gifted with healing or prophecy were called witches, a demeaning and demoralising term. These women were rounded up and herded into law courts and denounced as devil worshippers. Their punishment was twofold—they were bound and thrown into a river. If they floated, they were found guilty and burned at the stake for being a witch; if they drowned, they were considered innocent, but it's too late, they're dead.'

'How barbaric!'

'Quite, yet the same could be said of the Olympian gods and what they expected from their followers. They are ruthless and unforgiving. There are many stories of what the gods and goddesses did to people who opposed or challenged them. Like what happened to Marsyas. He was a talented musician who challenged Apollo to a musical competition with the lyre. Marsyas lost and was flayed.'

'There is a significant difference in what you've said. The gods have the right to mete out punishment when justified. Humans cannot presume to punish those in the name of a god. Only the gods may do so.'

Evan shook his head and gave a wry smile. 'I disagree. Both acts of retribution are horrific and do not encourage loyalty or belief. What it does is spread terror and hatred and provoke eventual retaliation—war.'

'Are you suggesting not restoring the gods and allowing Kronos to win?'

'Neither scenario is appealing. What if there was another way?'

'What do you mean?'

'Kronos can't initiate his plan to introduce a new god, and the mighty Olympian gods aren't reinstated. What if there's another choice?'

Plato stared at him. 'Impossible. There are no other gods.'

Evan smiled. 'Of course there is: the Mother Goddess.'

CHAPTER TWENTY-EIGHT

No amount of arguments and reasoning, could change Plato's mind, and he insisted on guiding them to Piraeus, the port city of Athens. Evan went along with Plato's advice, and he and his companions left Plato's home mid-morning. It was Plato's assertion that by the time they got to Piraeus, the port would be filled with ships loaded with supplies, some that had come from nearby locales and some from as far away as Egypt.

'You may be fortunate in finding a captain willing to take you on as passengers as they will be much happier and content from the deals they've made,' Plato said with a spring in his step. 'And when people are in a good mood, they are more obliging.'

'I have found people are more open to suggestions and genial in the mornings,' Evan said. 'By the afternoon, they are tired and temperaments are short.'

'Indeed,' said Plato, beaming and tapping his head. 'That is why the best thinking and ideas are created in the morning. Our minds are not as cluttered and we are refreshed from a good night's sleep. By the end of the day, our judgement is clouded and errors can occur. Perhaps not in every situation, but more probable to happen.'

'Do you hold classes in the afternoon?' Evan asked.

Plato shook his head. 'I find students are more receptive to learning in the morning. However, symposiums are wonderful for stirring speeches and discussions that have been induced by wine and food.' He chuckled. 'I have found the practice interesting and it has generated various concepts for me to explore and ruminate on.'

'Like your rhetoric on what makes a good republic?' asked Evan.

Plato came to a halt and stared at Evan. 'I've only begun writing on the concept of a republic. How could you…?' His gaze flickered to the others. 'I'd like your view on a few of the elements I am considering.'

'What's a republic?' asked Leander, who had overheard their conversation.

'It's a political system I am exploring, one of which I believe, under the right and fair leadership, will see a city grow from strength to strength,' Plato answered in haste, casting a sidelong glance at Evan.

'How would your republic work?' Leander asked.

'The political body must be structured where justice for all classes of people creates a harmonious society. Let's say there are three classes of people, which is what we have in Athens, such as the producer: men of the land, craftsmen and so on; then the warriors, the protectors; and finally guardians of the land, the leaders. For society to work, each of the three groups must execute their purpose, for this is proper. Each person fulfils their societal role as nature intended and does not interfere in the other groups' responsibilities.'

Plato turned to Evan with an eager expression. Evan declined to comment. He wasn't sure whether if it was wise to participate in the conversation, given the knowledge he possessed and the fact he had read Plato's *Republic*. It would be difficult to refrain from divulging information from the twenty-first century, as the real Evandros would not know what a republic was or who Plato was, so he allowed the others to continue to ask the philosopher questions.

'A sound proposal,' the High Priestess said. 'Can a person move from one class to another, if they desire to be more than they've been born to?'

'If justice is maintained and a person does not seek to better themselves through iniquitous means, then yes,' Plato answered.

'What of these fortification walls? Do they fulfil the requirements you propose?' Hektor pointed to a distinct line that vanished and reappeared across the sweeping and undulating landscape at various intervals.

'A government must have in place the means to protect their citizens. These walls were built so the people of Athens can move to and from Piraeus without fear of being accosted by brigands and the city's enemies.' Plato paused for a minute. 'Unfortunately, the walls weren't constructed before the invasion by Xerxes, the king of Persia. He destroyed the Temple of Athene and all the buildings atop the Akropolis.'

'A tragedy when sacred temples are ruined,' said the High Priestess.

'A new and bigger one has been built, as well as other structures.' He drew their attention to the high walls. 'When we reach Piraeus, we will go to the

Port of Zea, where merchants from Aegyptos, Rhodes, Tyre and many other places come to sell their wares.'

Evan let their discussion wash over him until he could feel the change in the air and a familiar scent of the briny breeze. His step quickened.

Twenty minutes later, they entered the gates and traversed the maze of streets. Evan heard Phameas draw in a deep, long breath, and looked at his friend, who had closed his eyes and then exhaled with equal slowness.

'What a joyous smell, the freshness of the sea.' He sighed, giving Evan a lopsided smile.

'We'll be back on the water soon enough, my friend,' said Evan, grinning and patting him on the shoulder.

Evan and his companions followed Plato past the busy agora where people spilled out onto the surrounding paths and organised chaos reigned. Over the din was the resonance of different languages that doused them like a jug of water. They shouldered their way into the large stoa and weaved through the throng.

'Great Mother!' said Leander.

That is a lot of ships, Homer wrote.

Phameas snorted. 'The port at Carthage holds three times more vessels.'

Homer looked to Evan, who nodded. 'It is huge.'

He took in the colourful scene of a flotilla of merchant ships, moored within the protective bay, bobbing up and down. Ships of various shapes and sizes sat side by side, their crews bustling to and from the pier with purpose.

'Traders seeking to purchase exotic goods come here as Piraeus is the gateway between the east and the west,' Plato said, 'much like Atlantis a thousand years ago.' He turned to the High Priestess. 'Now that your people have returned, will your leaders re-establish mercantile interests with other cities? The benefits to all would exceed expectations.'

'It is a noble suggestion, though we would need to proceed with caution,' she said. 'We do not wish to be the cause of disharmony or ill feeling with those with whom we share the world.'

'It is wise to consider a strategy before announcing your arrival,' Plato acknowledged with a nod. 'When the time comes and you're ready to be reintroduced to the world, please allow me to be your representative.'

'You honour us with your generous offer. We shall accept your wisdom and counsel.' The High Priestess took his hand and gave him a peck on the cheek.

Plato's face reddened. 'Ahem... yes... the honour is mine.'

Evan was about to thank Plato when Phameas nudged his side.

'Isn't that...' Phameas started to say.

Evan turned and caught sight of a slender bronzed man with long, wavy light brown hair standing some metres away with his back to them. Evan grinned.

'Ahoy, Jason!'

The man twisted from the waist with a suspicious look, and then his face lit up.

'Evandros!'

Evan walked over, grinning like a schoolboy at Jason.

'What in the name of the gods are you doing here? Weren't you meant to be in Delphi?' Jason asked, moving to greet Evan.

'We were, and now we're in need of a willing captain to take us to Thira,' Evan said.

'The gods of fortune have smiled upon you, my friend,' Jason said with a grin and clapped Evan on the shoulder. 'I, Jason, captain of the *Argo*, am happy to assist, as are the Argonauts.'

'We are very fortunate.' The High Priestess smiled at Jason.

Jason bowed with flourish. 'High Priestess, it is an honour to be in the company of your extraordinary beauty and illustrious presence once again.'

Her face shone. 'It is good to see you too, Captain.' She introduced him to Plato and the two men were soon chatting away, with the High Priestess in their midst.

Evan was surprised and amused by the High Priestess' warm response to Jason's charm, until he saw the grim look on Leander's face. He sidled up to him. Leander gave him a quick nod.

'Evandros.'

'Leander, Jason is one of those men who like to compliment women. He has no romantic interest in the High Priestess,' Evan said.

'How do you know he doesn't?' Leander asked, the pupils in his eyes darkening.

'If he was, his attention would be focussed on her and no one else. Like how you watch her every movement.'

Leander stared at Evan and bit his lip. 'You've noticed?'

Evan grinned. 'Not hard to miss.'

'What about the others? Do they know?'

'It's possible.'

Leander groaned.

'It's no one's business but yours. But I can tell you, the High Priestess feels the same way about you,' Evan said.

'Really? How do you know? Did she mention it to you?'

'She hasn't. I can see it in her actions.'

'But…' began Leander.

'Leander, one thing I do know is women, and believe me when I say she holds the same affection for you as you do for her.' Evan nodded at Leander and smiled.

Leander's expression became soft and flushed.

CHAPTER TWENTY-NINE

Evan and Phameas stood with Jason, who piloted the ship through the bay's entrance and out into the sea. They had thanked the philosopher for his hospitality, with the High Priestess promising to return to Athens before going back to Atlantis. The ship cleared the breakwater, and a handful of the crew moved quick to hoist the sail.

'There's nothing at Thira but ruins,' he said, glancing at Evan. 'It was destroyed some thousand years ago. Only the city is inhabited, and the few settlements that were there are gone. What is the interest in the place?'

'Pythia told me we must go there.'

'Why?'

'We've got something to do before we head for Krete.'

Jason checked the sun and horizon and adjusted the rudders the smallest fraction. His face was serious when he faced Evan and Phameas. 'Will my crew be in danger?'

Evan and Phameas exchanged a look. Evan exhaled through his nose and said, 'They may be.'

Jason's eyes narrowed. 'Then you need to tell me what it is you are doing.'

'Fair enough. I need to get the High Priestess.'

'Why? Can't you tell me?'

'I can, but not with so many ears listening.'

'My men can be trusted.' Jason glowered.

'It's not them I am worried about.'

'What in the name of the gods are you talking about?'

'That's who I am referring to. I'll be back in a minute.'

Evan returned with the High Priestess and Dexion.

'It may be prudent to have one of your men take over during our conversation,' said the High Priestess.

For thirty minutes, Jason listened. His expression did not change as Evan and the High Priestess took turns explaining.

'I understand the need for secrecy, though isn't it counterproductive considering the immortals know where we are going?' he said when they finished.

'We cannot hide what we are doing. The gods see and hear all, which is why there is a need to be as circumspect as possible,' the High Priestess said.

'It's not foolproof, but it gives us the best chance to retrieve the objects and keep one step ahead,' said Evan.

'And the serpent back in Delphi, was it a warning?' Jason asked.

'Kronos may be showing how easy it is to find us and what he can do. He has more in his arsenal than a lethal double-headed snake.' Evan gazed at the water, the colour the bluest of blues he'd ever seen. Not for the first time, he wondered if he'd die in this world and what would become of him in the twenty-first century.

'Sailing is a treacherous job, and we have faced our fair share of monsters and survived to tell the story,' Jason said. 'This journey will inspire Orpheus to sing of the great deeds and encounters that come our way.'

'What will you say to your men?' the High Priestess asked.

'That you are on an important and perilous mission and require our skills to help accomplish it.'

'Shrewd. Enough information to let them know they need to be prepared, and appeal to their pride so they won't ask what the mission is about.' Evan nodded in approval.

Jason tapped the side of his nose. 'A wise old centaur once told me a man's folly lies in the lack of understanding. However, one's honour can be stoked with the minimum of plaudits, as long as they are true.'

'That's if they don't learn the truth,' piped in Phameas. 'If it were me, I'd want to know more.'

'I know my men,' said Jason. 'Knowing they are getting paid is enough. They are secure in the knowledge they can feed their families. And if there are any treasures to be found...' He turned to the High Priestess with an expectant look.

'The treasure is theirs.'

'The men will be most pleased with idea of going to Krete. Legend has it King Minos secreted his riches in the labyrinth.'

'With the Minotaur?' The High Priestess' face blanched.

Jason nodded. 'That is if the creature is still alive. What I do know is King Minos had Daedalus build the labyrinth for the beast and set traps inside. As far as I know, anyone who went in never came out.'

'Do you believe the Minotaur is dead?' asked Evan. He sensed Phameas and Dexion's eyes on him.

'It has to be. King Minos has been dead for over two thousand years. No animal can live that long.'

'Unless it's immortal,' the High Priestess said in a tight voice.

'According to Pythia, the Minotaur is very much alive,' said Evan. 'It's got the statue of the Mother Goddess in its lair, and if King Minos stored his wealth in the labyrinth, I don't think the Minotaur will give it away.'

'One creature against fifty men plus five of you; it cannot attack us all while preoccupied with defending its treasure.'

'Let's deal with one obstacle at a time. First, we get to Thira, then go to Krete,' Evan said. His stomach clenched. It felt like something clawed at his insides.

'Be careful with the words you use after the protection of the white light is gone. If it is a matter of urgency, seek me out. Understood?' The High Priestess' icy gaze bored into Jason's. He quivered and nodded. 'Good.' She then walked away.

'Is that it? We can move now?' he asked, looking around.

'It seems so.'

'What happens if you walk into the protective shield?'

'I don't think the white light would hurt, but it's safer not to test it. Besides it's the red one you need to steer clear of,' said Evan, eyes clouding.

Phameas baulked. 'You don't want to know. I've never seen men die in such a manner.'

Jason stared at him. He watched the High Priestess as she sat with Leander and Hektor. 'She killed them?'

'I don't think it was intentional. She was screening us against attacking warriors. When they ran into the sphere, it...' Evan rubbed his brow. 'As Phameas said, it's a horrible way to die.'

Jason gulped. 'Gods. Next time we meet under her shield, remind me not to move until she does.'

CHAPTER THIRTY

*E*ris arrived at the rocky outcrop between the island of Sicilia and the tip of
Italia. The narrow body of water that separated the two lands appeared
calm on the surface. She stood on the ledge of the cliff, where the strong sea breeze
whipped her hair about her face and moulded her clothes to her voluptuous body.
The crash of the waves pounded against the cliffs like two rams butting heads.
She closed her eyes and let the sound wash over her until it diminished. She then
stamped her foot on the ground.

'Where are you, you exasperating leviathan?' Eris sat on the ground with a
huff. 'Return from whatever ship you're devouring; I've come with good news for
you.'

The clouds strayed across the path of the sun and the temperature dropped
a few degrees. Eris smiled, oblivious to the change. Her thoughts drifted to the
Atlanteans, in particular the one called Evandros. He was different from the
others. As to why, she was not sure. She must have one of her pets keep watch to
learn more about him. Her face darkened.

'And he killed two of my beloved harpies, for which he will pay.'

Her blood thundered with the anticipation of the game, like a predator
stalking its prey. Her musings were disrupted by the strange mewling of a beast
whose contentment echoed across the water. Eris peered over and glimpsed one of
its six heads on a gangling neck snaking back into its hiding place.

'Skylla, come on out. I am here to offer you a worthwhile treat.' Eris stood.

There was a bark.

Eris put her hands on her hips. 'Skylla, it is I, Eris, and I need you to do
something for me.'

Skylla yelped back, irritated at being disturbed.

'I know where you can find food aplenty.'

Eris listened to Skylla's answer, shook her head and raised her eyes to the sky.

'I know you don't venture far from your home, but I can guarantee you, you will be feasting on tender morsels until you've had your fill,' Eris said in dulcet tones. 'All you need to do is go to the Aegean Sea and to the island of Thira. There is a volcano in which you can nest while you wait for a ship called the Argo.'

Skylla barked a response, not convinced of Eris' honesty.

Eris' eyes narrowed, but she replied without rancour. 'If you do this, I will ensure you will never go hungry.'

Skylla did not answer. Eris began to fidget and her breathing quickened, her ire growing. Getting angry would not help; she took a deep breath and another.

'My dear, Skylla, do you think I would seek you out if I thought this opportunity would not benefit you? The crew on the Argo is not the only prize. There are many ships that sail those waters, far more than what pass through this strait.'

Skylla grumbled a response.

'Of course, there are ships coming from the east, west and south. Just today on my way to see you, I must have seen a hundred ships sailing to and from the many ports. A veritable feast waiting for you.'

There was a sharp bark, then the ground trembled, followed by a heavy splash. A slow smile crept across Eris' face.

'Enjoy your meals!'

Eris rubbed her hands together. 'Now that plan is in place, I think I may take a peek around here.' She clapped her hands. 'This is going to be so much fun. I am sure the inferior mortals can do with a little catastrophe or two.'

CHAPTER THIRTY-ONE

The island of Thira came into view by the third day. Evan stood at the prow with Homer, Phameas and Dexion. He stared at the crescent-shaped land with the blackened volcano at the centre and smaller isles nearby. The cliffs were bare, with the exception of a scattering of structures. The famous whitewashed buildings and blue domes of the Greek Orthodox churches that first welcomed visitors to the island in Evan's time were a faint glimmer of its future.

'This is so weird,' he said to himself.

Homer scribbled something on his palette and showed it to him.

'I don't feel a sense of belonging, but the place is familiar. I've been here a few times as a tourist.'

'Tourist? What is that?' Phameas asked.

'A person who travels for pleasure and visits cultural sites. This island is a popular destination in the summer for holiday makers and weddings.'

'Holiday makers?' Phameas raised a brow. 'What are those?'

'People who take time off work and go someplace.'

Does everyone do this?

'Those who can afford to go away on a holiday do.'

'I can see why you want to go back to this world of yours,' said Phameas.

Leander and the High Priestess joined them and they went quiet. 'Do either of you feel a connection to the place? I know it's an odd thing to say, but I feel a kinship; so do the High Priestess and Hektor.'

Homer nodded and wrote, *Is it possible our ancestors came from here?*

'We were instructed to come here to find an object of Mother's, which would suggest the people here revered her and indicate possible associations with our ancestors,' the High Priestess said.

'Could this be our ancestral home?' Leander asked. He looked at Evan. 'Do the historic entries of our ancestors mention Thira or Krete?'

Evan looked at the island, his mind going through the countless books, documents and documentaries he read and viewed.

'These locations were mentioned as reference points. I don't think the ancestors considered it essential, nor did they imagine any Atlantean would one day leave the island. It wouldn't have been foremost in their minds.'

'According to the ancient High Priestess' texts, our ancestors were careful in what they included in the annals as they did not want to repeat the actions that precipitated their downfall,' said the High Priestess.

'It appears the ancestors did replicate some features,' said Hektor. He indicated to the outline of the island. 'There, see the two land masses encircled by rings of water? Our home has been fashioned in the same manner. We have returned to our ancestral home.'

'Evandros, as the scholar and scribe, you should make a record of our visit to this island for the Elders and citizens of Atlantis.' The High Priestess said without turning, her attention fixed on the ever-growing vista of the island.

'Of course.' Evan took in the charred remains of the three islands, the tips poking out of the azure sea. The largest of the three was half the size of the future version he was familiar with. Volcanologists predicted there would be another eruption, more volatile than the original explosion that had blown it apart. And this time, a lot of people would be affected, thousands more.

The red, white and black striations of the cliffs were denser and deeper in colour. Plato's detailed description of the island and hues had given rise to the speculation by historians and archaeologists that Thira was the fabled land of Atlantis. Evan remembered his visit to Akrotiri and understood why: the buildings, the layout of the city and the sophistication of objects found there mirrored Plato's words. He pulled out the book out from the bag at his feet and began to draw, adding notations as he completed each section.

'Drop the sails!' Jason shouted, the muscles in his arms and torso straining as the water currents pushed against the rudders.

The crew jumped into action, their skills honed over many years of sailing evident as the men secured the masts. The others manned the oars and rowed into the caldera. They coasted past the smallest of isles and soon came abreast with the larger smouldering island, oozing yellow sludge. Phameas and Dexion covered their noses and mouths. Evan screwed up his nose.

'Phew! That reeks. Didn't expect the sulphur to be so strong.'

'Sulphur?' Leander gave him a blank look.

Evan pointed. 'See that yellow substance in the water and on the edge of the shoreline?' Leander nodded. 'That is sulphur.'

'It does have a peculiar smell.'

'Like rotten eggs.'

Leander hooted. 'So it does!' As the ship drew closer to the slumbering volcano, he grew sombre. 'Seeing the bleak and forbidding remains, one may believe this to be Tartaros.'

'Yes, I see why one would.' Evan was soon distracted by the approaching crescent-shaped main island. The long concrete boardwalk and the sheer staircase that zigzagged its way up to the city of Thira were yet to be built. What he saw was a jagged ridge left behind when the terrain was ripped apart. He shook his head, unable to comprehend how different it looked compared to the last time he had visited the island.

Homer nudged him. Evan glanced at him, and his half-brother signalled he turn around. Evan saw Jason beckoning and walked over.

'I was thinking about what Pythia had mentioned,' he said as Evan came within earshot. 'On the southern-most tip, there was a city. It's now long gone, but it might be a good spot to start your search. I will pilot the ship as close as possible and find a safe place to land, and where my men and I will set up camp.'

'I wonder...' Evan stared at the island.

'Yes... what?'

Evan's heart beat faster as he bit his bottom lip. He could be the first person in recorded history to find Akrotiri. 'What do you know about the city?'

'Not much, except it was one of the oldest occupied settlements, older than Athens.'

'It has to be...'

Jason frowned. 'Has to be what?'

Evan's eyes shone. 'It is possible the city was the original home of Atlantis.'

'Your people?' Jason scratched his head. 'I don't know, Evandros. The inhabitants who once lived here were consumed by the suffocating debris expelled by the black island, and no one survived.' The two men half twisted towards the menacing volcano, observing the fine filigrees of vapours that rose into the sky.

'You may be right.' Evan pulled a face and then brightened. 'Although, we may still find the ruins of the city.'

Jason shook his head. 'Treasure seekers have scoured the island when the waters cleared and were safe for ships to sail. The city was buried, and no one knows where its exact location was.'

But I do. Evan kept the thought to himself. If he did reveal where the city was situated, it would further complicate his uneasy alliance with the High Priestess and Leander. No, best he said nothing.

'Go secure your belongings, Evandros. We'll be landing soon,' said Jason watching the coastline.

CHAPTER THIRTY-TWO

'Oars up!'

The men raised their oars, pulled them in and stowed them away. The currents and impetus propelled the ship towards the shore.

'Brace for impact landing!' bellowed Jason.

The High Priestess and Dexion had their wrists bound and secured to the wooden rail with leather straps. Evan checked over the knots. Satisfied, he then wrapped his leg around the post and clutched at the rail. He watched, heart pounding as the grey beach loomed. Though he knew what to expect, he was still unprepared for the abrupt jolt as the keel hit the granulated shore. He hit the railing with his stomach and pitched forward, his head grazing the horizontal beam. Winded, he drew in a ragged breath and rubbed his abdomen.

'How is everyone?' he asked. He undid the straps holding Dexion. Leander helped the High Priestess from her bonds.

'All good,' he said to Evan.

'A well-executed landing.' Phameas nodded in approval.

Evan gave him a crooked smile and turned to Homer, who indicated he was all right.

'Hektor?'

'Fine,' he said, stiffening.

Evan ignored his taciturn behaviour. 'Time to go ashore and start looking for a way to the top.'

'I hope there is a track or a route,' Leander said. 'It would take us a long time to scale those cliffs.'

They studied the sheer landscape. The cloudless, brilliant blue sky was a sharp contrast to the dazzling white cliffs, relentless in their efforts to reflect the sun's rays. Evan averted his face and closed his eyes, scrunching them tight. Black spots appeared behind his eyelids.

'Almost as bad as looking into the sun,' he said, opening his eyes.

'I guess it's too much to hope for a path.' Phameas crossed his arms against his chest.

'We'll explore the coastline. There has to be a footpath or some conduit to the hilltop.' Evan strapped on his sword and shield and picked up his bag. He and Phameas threw ropes over the side of the ship near the prow and scaled down. The others followed. Jason and his crew carried food supplies and shelter for the High Priestess.

'We must begin our search for the object.' The High Priestess' body cast a shadow over Evan as he munched on dried fruit and hard bread.

He looked up and saw the determined expression on her face. He swallowed, took a swig from his water container and got to his feet.

'All right. We'll split into two groups.'

Evan, Phameas, Dexion and Homer set off eastwards along the coastline, while Leander, Hektor and the High Priestess went in the opposite direction. After some time, Evan looked back. He lifted his hand and measured the height of Jason and his men, who were setting up camp, between his thumb and pointer finger: two centimetres. The three others were mere specks, dark dots on the beach.

'Ahoy, Evandros! Come and look at this!'

Evan spun and saw the excited expression on Phameas' face. Homer reached out with a hand and pulled at the thick verdant bushes.

'It might be a tunnel,' said Phameas, bouncing on his heels.

The lush vine-like plant ran from the base of the cliff-face to the top. Evan leaned into the wall and felt a slight breeze. Homer grabbed a fistful of the tendrils and yanked them out. He threw the green foliage aside and grabbed another handful. Evan grabbed and pulled back his wrist. Homer raised a quizzical brow at him.

'There could be snakes or other nasty creatures nesting in the bush. We should use our swords to cut it away.'

Homer nodded. He pulled out his sword and began to hack the vine. The three men took turns, while Dexion removed the debris. The green mound grew and the depth of the fissure was revealed.

'Sweet Mary!' Evan dropped his sword. His fingers tingled and his ears rang at the loud clang. He shook his hands.

'Are you all right?' Phameas asked, face red, rivulets of perspiration running down his hairline and his tunic drenched.

'I think we've reached the wall.' He stepped back into the sunlight and Homer took his place.

Evan stooped, collected the cuttings and throwing them on the pile.

'Great Moloch!'

'What is it?' Evan dashed back. 'Oh my God.'

They gaped at the steps cut into the cliff, which continued upwards until they disappeared into the skyline.

'Dexion…'

'Yes, Master Evandros?'

Evan kept gawking at the staircase.

'Master Evandros?'

'Oh… um… yes, Dexion. Go and get the others. Tell them what we have found.'

'Yes, Master Evandros.'

Dexion sped away, kicking up the grainy sand in his wake.

'We should clear away as much of the vine we can.' Evan picked up his sword.

'There's no need,' said Phameas.

'Huh? Why not?'

The Phoenician pointed. 'The plant has grown across the crevice and the way to the top is clear.'

Evan peered upwards and tilted his head to the side. 'Would you look at that!' He moved a few steps up and pivoted one way, then the other. 'Clever engineers.' His face shone and couldn't contain the excitement in his voice. 'They cut into the rock at an angle.' He craned his head back further. 'It appears to be at forty-five degrees.' He smiled at Phameas and Homer. 'From this angle, it gives the impression of a vertical climb and would deter any person from scaling the stairs.' Evan grinned. 'Ingenious.'

Evan, Phameas and Homer were sitting not far from the fissure when the others arrived. Dexion knelt next to Evan, who smiled and ruffled his hair. They waited in companionable silence while the High Priestess, Leander and Hektor examined the imperceptible staircase.

'Remarkable!' said Leander. 'Even standing a few paces away makes it difficult to see the stairs.'

Evan nodded and stood, brushing the grit from his backside. 'The builders knew about perspective and depth, complex concepts to create with a dense surface.' He looked to the High Priestess. 'Shall we go up?'

She wore a half smile, a rare expression. 'Let's.'

'After you.' Evan held out an arm.

The High Priestess inclined her head and went up the first few steps, Leander right on her heels. Hektor moved next, then Homer, followed by Dexion, Phameas and Evan. From the ground, the staircase seemed to go straight, but the pattern was serpentine. They didn't notice the subtle and imperceptible change until they moved to the next level.

Evan wiped his brow and pulled at the tunic that clung to his skin. The others were faring no better, with the exception of the High Priestess and Dexion, who seemed unaffected by the arduous climb. Evan's calf muscles burned and his quads felt stretched, as taut as the strings on a tennis racquet. He thought he had peaked with his fitness with the rowing and walking and had never felt better, not even with all the workouts he'd done at the gym. Climbing the long stretch of steps proved he needed to improve his stamina.

When he reached the top, his hair was drenched, and trickles of sweat ran down his face. He grabbed the water container from his bag and drank a mouthful. He pulled at the edge of his tunic and wiped his face.

'Eww! I'm going for a swim when we get back to the beach.' Evan trudged a few steps to where Phameas and Dexion stood under a tree.

'Phameas, you look as I feel.'

'Bah… you look as bad as I do!'

Evan laughed. 'I am in good company, then.'

'We should look for a path,' Hektor said in a loud voice, arms folded across his chest.

Evan's good mood evaporated. 'Go ahead, but I intend to use that one.' He pointed to a row of trees where, in between, overgrown shrubs obscured a track. He stared at Hektor, jaw clenched. Hektor's eyes narrowed and his lip curled. Homer clamped a hand on Evan's shoulder and shoved him towards the pathway. Phameas and Dexion moved in step with the two men.

Homer pulled out his sword and began to chop through the bushes. Evan worked a few feet away from him, slashing and hewing at the low-growing scrub. The two kept cutting away until they came to a clearing. The others fanned out on either side. The High Priestess took a step, but Hektor moved to front, preventing her from going any further.

'Allow me to check the stability of the structure first.'

He started out for the gateway.

'We could go around it,' said Evan with derision.

'That would be more practical,' said Phameas.

Hektor ignored them, continuing to approach the entrance, slowing as he neared. Rows of large stone blocks, each identical and symmetrical in shape and size, were reinforced with thick horizontal lengths of wood. The interior of the entrance and architrave were reinforced by a wooden frame. Hektor paused, head moving left to right and then up. He took a step and stood beneath the entrance. He pushed against the framework. Then he shoved his shoulder against the timber, his feet skidding in the dirt the harder he pushed. He straightened and turned to Evan with a smirk on his face.

'It is safe.'

'Well done on working that out. It still would have been quicker if we had gone around.' He marched towards the entrance, where Hektor stood glowering.

'Hektor.' His gaze flickered to the High Priestess. 'Continue onwards.'

His jaw worked back and forth. He then pivoted and stomped his way to the other side of the entrance.

'Evandros, please refrain from provoking Hektor.'

'Me?' Evan stared at her, incredulous. 'You've got to be kidding. He's the one causing the problem.' His eyes became pitch-black. 'I'd be more than happy to settle our differences.'

The High Priestess drew in a sharp breath at the change in Evan's eyes. She looked away and started walking. Leander moved with her, his arm brushing hers. Her hand skimmed his, lingering for a moment before dropping to her side.

CHAPTER THIRTY-THREE

The path continued for a considerable distance before disappearing into a tree-line ridge.

'Any thoughts as to where we will find the Temple of the Serpent Goddess?' Phameas asked.

'Our ancestors did not build temples as such,' the High Priestess replied. 'They used caves and sacred trees where initiates and priestesses would gather to offer gifts to the goddess.'

'What of Sibyl? Didn't you sacrifice her in a temple?' Evan said, his voice tight and more hostile than he intended.

The High Priestess was taken aback. 'Yes. However, her sacrifice took place in the Temple of Poseidon as decreed by the gods.'

'Still, didn't it...' Evan stopped as Homer clasped his hand on his neck and squeezed. He looked over at the big man, who mouthed, *Not now*.

Evan glared. 'Then when? It'll be too late if I'm dead.'

Homer's face became melancholy and his grip lightened. *This is not the right time*. He patted the back of Evan's head and dropped his hand to his side.

Evan heard Phameas' voice and used it as a beacon to bring him back from the ire boring in his gut.

'That's not what Pythia said. She told Evandros the temple is buried in the city of the dead.'

'We must not take what the Oracle says as a literal statement,' the High Priestess said. 'Prophecies are obscure. We need to interpret her words to seek the message within.'

'I think she was quite clear in her prophecy,' said Evan. 'Why else would we be here?'

'The city of the dead could refer to a necropolis,' Leander said, cutting in. 'Or it could mean where people had died.'

'The Serpent Goddess personifies life and death, but we will not find the sacred relic in a necropolis,' the High Priestess said.

'Then the city is dead,' said Hektor.

'So, we really don't have any idea of what we're looking for or where to start?' Phameas looked from Evan to the High Priestess.

We do; we're looking for a temple that is not a temple and a city with no citizens, Homer said.

'Let us hope the souls of the past do not mind us traipsing over their place of rest,' Leander said. 'Mother Goddess, protect us.'

'I have a question that's been churning in my mind for a while now,' said Phameas. They waited for him to continue. 'If these relics help your gods retain their power, then the objects must grant the Dark Master the same ability. Why else does he seek them? And if the relics are restored and all is well again, does that mean my gods will cease to exist?'

'No. Although, if the Dark Master succeeds in obtaining the relics, your gods will no longer prevail. The rule of one god will spread across all nations,' Evan said.

'Great Moloch! We need to find the relic!' Phameas quickened his pace. He glanced over his shoulders at the others and beckoned. 'Come along!'

An hour later they came to the end of the path, the way blocked by encroaching thickets and mounds of rubble. Hektor, with axe in hand, hewed his way through the thick bush. It was as silent as a graveyard, with the exception of the Hektor's heavy breathing and his continual chopping. After a lengthy period, he stopped; it was still, no birds chirping nor even the slight brush of air. Ahead were knolls of black earth rich with vegetation in various states of growth, from saplings to young trees on the verge of adulthood.

'There's nothing here,' said Hektor, the anger in his tone evident. 'No sign of buildings or inhabitation.'

'Jason said the city was buried following the eruption of the central island and no one survived,' said Evan.

'When did he tell you this?' the High Priestess asked.

'Before we landed.'

'Didn't you think it was important to share that information?'

'I was hoping he was wrong and we'd find something, evidence of a town,' Evan said.

'It is a good thing we're looking for a cave and not a temple,' Leander said in a light tone. 'We don't need to search for a lost city.'

'How right you are. We'll go in that direction—' Evan pointed to the left—'and you go that way.' He indicated to the right. 'Let's meet back here in a few hours, when the sun reaches midday.'

Leander nodded. 'And if we find something before we are to meet?'

'A way to communicate,' Evan said and clasped his chin with a hand, finger tapping against his lips. His eyes brightened. 'I have an idea.' He ran back from where they had come, scrounging through the chopped debris until he found what he needed. 'Hektor, can you chop this into two strips about this thick?' Evan held out his fingers one centimetre apart.

A few minutes later, Hektor passed the pieces to Evan. Everyone gathered around Evan as he bored a hole into each flat piece of wood. He cut two strips from an old tunic, a metre long and threaded them into the two pieces. He stood.

'I hope this works.'

He moved away from the others, wrapped an end of the strip around his hand, let the flat wood fall to the earth and began to whirl it around. Evan increased the speed until the wood blurred followed by a strange low throbbing sound. He rotated his arm faster until it grew louder, similar to a lion roaring.

'Mother Goddess!' Leander said, striding over to Evan and eyeing the contraption. 'That was frightening.' He reached for the device. 'That noise came from a piece of wood and a length of cloth. Remarkable and ingenious.'

'That's yours. If either group finds a cave before we're supposed to meet, use this and we'll return here.'

'How did you know about this instrument?' the High Priestess asked.

Evan shrugged. 'I must have read about it somewhere.' He bent and picked up his bag. 'See you in a few hours.'

'What if we don't find any caves?' asked Phameas, breaking the silence.

'We'll find one,' said Dexion.

'Really? How can you be certain?' Phameas said.

'Pythia. Her predictions are always right,' the boy replied. He paused before adding, 'And I saw it too.'

'What?' Evan skidded to a stop. He looked at Dexion. 'Why didn't you mention this earlier?'

'I had the vision after you met with Pythia, and as we were coming here anyway, I didn't think it was necessary to tell you.'

'Dexion, you tell me whatever you see, big or small, no matter where the information comes from. Understood?'

Dexion nodded.

Evan squatted. 'You saw something else, didn't you?'

Dexion nodded again, shrank away, and pressed his lips together.

'What was it? Is there something about the cave we should know about?'

'Not the cave.'

'Must be bad if Dexion's reluctant to speak of it,' Phameas said in a grim tone.

'Is he right, Dexion?'

Dexion bit his lip, and when he spoke, his voice trembled. 'A hideous monster lurks in the sea. She is hungry and not happy to be so far from her home.'

Do you know where she lies in wait? Homer asked.

'She's close.'

'Monster? Is she like the soul-eaters we've encountered?' asked Phameas.

'No, she's much bigger and more terrifying,' Dexion said, his face ashen. 'Men will die.'

The three men stared at each other.

'Ferocious beasts, harpies, objects that have magic, and a high priestess with the power to burn a person's limbs off and alter inanimate items. Sheesh, this has the makings of a bad B-grade movie, if it wasn't real,' Evan said.

'Huh? What are you talking about?' asked Phameas. 'Of course these creatures are real. Wasn't it you who killed two harpies?'

'Yes, but... oh, never mind.' He shook his head and muttered to himself.

'What do we do now?' The Phoenician crossed his arms against his chest.

'We find the cave and recover the relic,' said Evan.

'And what of the monster?'

'We'll tell the others when we return to the beach,' said Evan. 'There's nothing we can do at present, and my interpretation of Dexion's vision is that this creature will attack when we're at sea.'

'Hmmmph.' Phameas' arms fell to his sides. 'Finding the relic to help the gods won't do us much good if we're dead.'

Then we make sure that doesn't happen. Homer scowled in determination.

CHAPTER THIRTY-FOUR

Evan, Phameas, Dexion and Homer trekked across the bleak landscape, the scattering of bushes and shrubs breaking the grim scenery. The starkness and lack of vegetation heightened the sombre mood of the group. Grey-white rocky outcrops dominated, home to wall lizards sunning themselves and scuttling away, disturbed by foreign intruders.

'I cannot get my head around how different this place is to the last time I visited.' Evan pointed with a sweeping gesture. 'All this will be inhabited with houses, farmland, shops, supermarkets, resorts and roads. This is so surreal.'

'No stranger than hearing you speak of unfamiliar things, of which I have no idea what you're saying.' Phameas scratched his temple. 'It is difficult to comprehend, and that flying apparatus you drew in Corinth—' his eyes grew wide and he tapped his head with a finger—'that is hard to imagine and believe.'

'Yes... well, I can appreciate your confusion. It's not easy to understand when you have no knowledge of the concept, or of machines.'

Homer touched Evan's arm. *If the two of you have finished, we should investigate that rock-strewn embankment.*

Evan turned to see what had caught his half-brother's interest. Bramble had taken root in the crevice of the rocky wall and, with the determination and intrepidness prevalent in nature, had spread itself along the wall.

'That is promising,' he said, smiling at Homer.

Homer nodded and, with a crooked grin, indicated for Evan to take the lead. The thick verdant thicket shrouded the wall as its counterpart had hidden the stairwell on the beach. Evan halted by the wall, leaned closer and felt the cool breeze against his warm face. He reached out to grab a handful of the bramble when he was shoved aside, and fell hard to the ground. Dexion and Phameas hurried to his side, both horrified and relieved.

'Master Evandros, you were almost bitten by a snake!'

'Snake? Where?' Evan scrambled to his feet and pulled out his sword.

'You'd be dead if it wasn't for Homer,' said Phameas, jerking a thumb over his shoulder. He stepped aside, giving Evan full view of the two-metre-long black snake with yellow striping, its head no longer attached.

Evan's face went pale. 'Frick!' He reached out and clasped Homer's shoulder. 'Thank you.' He glanced at the foliage. 'I do hope there aren't any more snakes lurking in the bush.' Evan turned at the familiar ringing sound.

Phameas brandished his sword. 'Better a dead serpent than me.' And he began to cut at the bush, keeping an arm's length from the greenery.

When Phameas tired, Homer took over, and then Evan stepped in. Before long, they stood in front of a large opening, the cave dark and uninviting, and the air dank and musty.

'Time to use that device of yours to let the others know we found a cave,' said Phameas.

Evan slid his sword back into the sheath and pulled out the bullroarer. 'We're going to need torches. I don't know if there are any stout limbs in that pile.' He moved away and picked the highest point to stand. He rotated the flat piece of wood, faster and faster, the roar reverberated across the vacant expanse. After five minutes, he stopped, and all was quiet. It was as if the bullroarer had rendered the world into stillness. Evan returned to the mouth of the cave where the others waited.

'How long should we wait for an answer?' asked Phameas.

'Why are you whispering?' Evan asked.

'I don't know,' Phameas said, shrugging, still whispering. 'It's your contraption, it cast a spell.'

Evan scoffed. 'There's nothing magical about the bullroarer.'

'You are wrong, my friend,' Phameas said, pursing his lips.

Evan set out to explain how it worked when he heard the response, a low timbre growing in momentum and into a vibrant roar. Then it was gone, as if someone had flipped the power switch. The earth descended into an uneasy quietness, as if a cloak had been wrapped around the living and thrust into a void.

Phameas crossed his arms, his face smug, and gave a firm nod. 'There you are, just as I said. Not a sound or movement. It's as if we've crossed over to the afterlife.'

'Interesting comparison, Phameas. I guess one day we'll find out what life is like after death,' Evan said, not wanting to offend his friend's beliefs. He didn't believe anything happened once you passed from the land of the living. When you were dead, that was it; no Elysian fields as the Ancient Greeks imagined for a person who shed their mortal coil. An island for the virtuous and heroes who had been granted paradisiacal haven. If it were true, Evan would look forward to spending eternity in such a place. However, he was pragmatic and expected infinite nothingness.

'We need to return to the meeting place to guide the others here,' Evan said, not wanting to dwell any further on his mortality or the possibility of not going home.

I'll go. There's no need for all of us to trek back and forth, Homer said.

'Would you like someone to come along?' Evan asked.

Homer smiled and shook his head. He wiggled two fingers, imitating a person running.

'You think you'll be quicker on your own?' Evan gave him a lopsided grin.

Homer nodded.

'Take this.' Evan thrust the bullroarer at him. 'In case you need to call us.'

Homer quirked his brows at him.

'Just take it.'

Homer rolled his eyes and took the wooden object. He shoved it between his belt and khiton. Homer raised his hand, spun on his heel and took off, leaving small puffs of dust in his wake.

'For a big man, he is quick. I don't think I've ever seen anyone cover such distance so fast,' Phameas commented as Homer disappeared over the crest. 'There's nothing for us to do but wait.'

The three sat in shade of the wall of the cave, and metres away from the dead snake. To pass the time, Phameas asked Evan questions about his world. He described the various communication devices and how people could interact with others from great distances without leaving home. Evan tried to explain how it worked, but their lack of experience with technology made it difficult for them to comprehend.

'This time you are from sounds complicated and scary,' said Phameas.

'It can be, but no scarier than being here,' Evan said. 'Now if we had a car, planes to travel on and mobile phones to call each other at moments like this, our search for the relics would be easier, and over quicker.'

Dexion frowned.

'You don't think so?' Evan asked the boy.

'It may be easier for travelling. As to finding the relics, not so. The people of your time do not believe in the gods or the power of the Mother Goddess. They would not seek them,' said Dexion.

'Ancient artefacts are important and precious during my time but not for the reasons we require them,' Evan said. 'Archaeologists investigate history and search for swords, arrowheads, jewellery, palaces, anything relative to the past in order to learn what happened and how people lived,' he said to Phameas. 'For instance, your people, the Phoenicians, invented the alphabet that is used to this day, and were renowned sailors and ship builders.' He turned to Dexion. 'Sicily, your place of birth, an island off the Italian coast, has an amazing history of occupation: the Greeks, Carthaginians, Romans, Byzantines, Moors, and the Normans.'

He stopped. From their stunned faces, he knew it was too much.

'There's no magic in your world.' Dexion gazed up at him saddened.

'Not in the way you mean,' Evan said.

'No wonder your people have lost connection with Mother and her gifts. It is why they are aimless, feel unworthy and seek purpose with evil people who are intent on destroying everything and everyone they hate.'

'I don't think the loss of magic has anything to do with a person's lack of self-worth. It's more complex and a lot to do with politics, economics and religious fanaticism. It is the rule of man and their corrupted interpretation of holy texts that has created the mess of my world.' Evan's vision fell on the dead snake. 'Let me explain it like this: you know of the beast Hydra?' Dexion nodded and Phameas shook his head. 'It's a snake with five heads; big and lethal. You cut off its head and two grow in its place, and if you keep chopping the heads, they double every time. Then there are so many you can't keep fighting and it becomes too dangerous. That's what it has become with these evil people you refer to.'

'Herakles killed Hydra by burning the stumps before the head could grow back,' Dexion said.

'Yes, but even Herakles would have trouble destroying this version of Hydra.'

'Mother's magic can stop them,' said a confident Dexion.

'Perhaps.' He reached for his bag and pulled out his cloak. 'I am going to have a nap.' He lay back, adjusted the makeshift cushion and closed his eyes, not wanting to talk anymore about his home and era. He focussed on the slight breeze that caressed his warm bare skin and the chirping cicadas, their song reminding him of the hot summers at home. He dozed off to the quiet banter between Phameas and Dexion.

'E-van-dros...'

Evan's ears twitched. He sighed and rolled onto his side.

'E-van-dros...'

His brows furrowed and began to stir.

'E-van-dros... E-van!'

Evan bolted upright. The use of his shortened name, and the one he preferred, he had not heard since being taken from the twenty-first century. He looked around seeing, only the slumbering forms of Phameas and Dexion.

'E-van...'

The hair on the back of his neck stood on end.

'E-van... come...'

'What the hell?' Evan's heart skipped a beat.

'E-van... come...'

He stood, eyes drawn to the yawning mouth of the cave.

'Come...'

With faltering steps, Evan tottered to the opening and paused. He wanted to turn and run, but his legs wouldn't do as told.

'Come...'

His breathing quickened, and the blood in his veins gushed like a sudden downpour. He closed his eyes, straightened, took a long deep breath and walked into the cave. Evan's skin tingled, goosebumps popping along his arms and legs. His gut told him it wasn't the cold air. His nose wrinkled at the musty air and another scent, one he couldn't identify. He opened his eyes and took another step, out from the comfort of the sun's light and into the gloomy space of the cavern. His eyes dilated and adjusted to the dimness.

The stone floor was covered in dirt and desiccated leaves that had not been disturbed by humans or animals in a long time. Evan could touch the ceiling at the entrance, but as he moved a little deeper, it rose out of his reach. He ran a hand over the cold, bumpy stone wall, dirt and grit crumbling to the ground under his touch. His sight followed the walls into the immutable obscurity, where the passage narrowed into an unknown domain, one akin to a woman's womb. Cobwebs covered the darkened voids, a home of fine silken lace for the spider and a trap for the unsuspecting insect.

Evan stood alert, eyes scanning and ears heightened. He got a sense of affection rather than hostility the longer he remained, surrounded by the preternatural aura. The apprehension he had felt earlier, when the voices had called him, faded. It was if the cave had been waiting for him to arrive. He moved further forward until the impenetrable darkness made it difficult for him to see where he was going.

He closed his eyes, allowing himself to be consumed by the peace the cave offered. It was if he was being held in his mother's arms. Evan sensed the cave was ancient and appreciated the reason why it had been frequented by ancient humans who were more in touch with the Earth than the people in a thousand years to come. The question was, what did they use it for?

He cast his mind back to the lectures at university when the sound of murmuring drew his attention. Evan opened his eyes, thinking it was Phameas and Dexion, and swivelled to face the mouth of the cave. No one was there.

'Trick of the wind,' he said to himself in a low voice. He waited, ears attentive as a sonar, but he heard nothing.

Evan re-focussed and tried to recall a lecture on human use of caves other than for painting animals, hunting and shelter. Images of slides flickered through his memory, and as he narrowed his search, the murmur returned, this time louder and with more voices. He swung around but saw he was alone. The resonance continued. Female and male voices reverberated and grew in cadence, resembling the din in a busy restaurant. Evan strained to hear what they were saying; they were talking over each other, the words indecipherable.

'Evandros, what are you doing?'

Evan jumped, and whirled to see the High Priestess standing at the entrance with Leander at her side. The voices continued their barrage.

'Evandros, are you all right?' Leander asked, his eyebrows drawn together.

'Do you hear them?' The white of his eyes were prominent with the darkness behind him.

'Hear what?' asked the High Priestess.

'The voices: women and men, lots of them.'

'I cannot hear any. Are you sure?' she asked, scanning his face and then the gloomy interior of the cave.

'Yes! They are here.'

'What are they saying?' The High Priestess entered the cave.

Evan exhaled, closed his eyes and pressed a fist to his forehead. 'I don't know. They were talking at the same time. Some were singing and others were chanting.'

The High Priestess moved closer to the stone wall and placed a hand against the rough surface. 'The cave may have retained the memory of those who worshipped our Mother, and anyone who enters may receive messages from those who have long since passed.'

'Then why can't you hear them?' Evan asked, raising an eyebrow.

The High Priestess stiffened, her lips pressed into a white slash.

'Perhaps you can as you entered the cave first,' Leander said with haste, and gave Evan an imploring look. He turned to the High Priestess. 'That may be why you and I cannot hear them.'

'It is possible that Evandros—' she emphasised his name—'the first person to enter the cave is the recipient of the cave's gift.' The hard expression on her face did not ease. 'The question is, why did you come alone?'

'They summoned me, and I didn't want to wake Phameas and Dexion.'

'What did they say?' The High Priestess' gaze bored into his.

'They called for me by name and said to come.'

'And you didn't understand what they were saying?'

'Like I said, they were talking over each other and it was difficult to make sense of what they were saying.'

The High Priestess smoothed the front of her sapphire khiton. 'Should they wish to contact you again, be sure to ask them to speak one at a time.'

'Sure, why not? And while I'm at it, I'll ask them as to the whereabouts of the labrys,' Evan muttered to himself.

'What was that?' she asked, her ice-blue eyes glittering.

'If they do call again, I will do as you suggested.' Evan smiled.

The High Priestess stared at him. Evan kept his face neutral.

'We should search the cave while there's still daylight outside,' she said, after a long pause.

'I agree.' Evan nodded. 'Dexion has the torches; we prepared them while we waited for you.'

'Before we do, I would like time alone in the cave to commune with the Mother Goddess,' she said, turning her back, dismissing the two men. Evan looked at Leander; neither spoke and they left the cave.

CHAPTER THIRTY-FIVE

Alexina closed her eyes and calmed her mind, allowing the aeons old cave to imbue her with its powerful energy and strength. She stood there, like many priestesses before her, feeling the power of the Mother Goddess pulsate throughout her body, her heart, a loud throbbing in her ears, the one sound breaking the mystical tranquillity.

She focussed on her breathing, each inhalation deeper than the last and amplified within the womb of the Earth Mother. Alexina reached out to connect with the ancient priestesses and of the secrets they held.

A murmur of sighing filled the cavern, and then came the soft whispers, the resonance sibilant as they became numerous and more distorted. The voices of the priestesses of the past revealed themselves, from the very first, who had taken on the role of protector of the Mother Goddess, to the last, who had died during the devastation that consumed the island.

Alexina bowed her head in reverence, and listened to each as they imparted their knowledge, empowering her with gifts no mortal had possessed since the unfortunate death of the last High Priestess. The gifts were many: healing, regressions, divination, fertility and the power of life and death. Each attribute ensured the continuation of birth and renewal, and nurtured the harmonious relationship between nature and humankind.

When the shadow of the ancient priestess finished delivering her secrets, Alexina collapsed. She felt weak, like a newborn babe, brought into the world full of life, yet unable to walk and talk. As she lay on the cold, unyielding ground, her mind swirled with images of dances and songs. Many of the rituals of life, such as bull jumping and boxing, honoured the gods. She had thought she had understood everything about the virtues of the sacred rites and the wisdom her people had inherited and dutifully continued.

But she had been wrong.

After listening to the ancient priestesses, she realised there was so much more to these facets of life. Everything was so much clearer to her now, and she could not believe how much had been lost. Alexina now understood why the Olympian gods were concerned by the actions and behaviours of the ancients—the Atlanteans were destined to become the new younger gods.

'You have learnt the true destiny of your ancestors,' said a voice as old as the earth.

Alexina knelt straightaway and bowed her head. 'Mother.'

'My esteemed daughter, a great revelation has been bestowed upon you,' the Mother Goddess said. 'What will you do with this newfound information?'

'It is not my place to make such decisions,' Alexina replied, her tone respectful and moderate.

The Mother Goddess smiled. 'You are the greatest priestess that has ever served me, and now you have been given an extraordinary gift that has been lost for thousands of years. You have it in your power to reject the plight of the gods. Do you not want to see your people restored to supremacy?'

'It would be hubris to challenge the gods.'

'But you do want to see the Atlanteans take their rightful place in the world?' the Mother Goddess pressed.

The desire to claim absolute rule, to take back what had been stolen, was strong. It was their birthright. Alexina thought back to the places they had visited, their imprisonment, of the fear and anger when people had discovered who they were. She looked up at the glorious face of the ancient deity.

'I would like our people to return as leaders of academic discipline, where everyone is given the opportunity to learn from thousands of years of mastery.'

'You will not share what you have acquired today with your fellow Atlanteans. They may not agree with your decision; they may prefer to seek dominance.' The Mother Goddess clasped her hands, her eyes darkening.

Alexina blinked and sucked in a breath. She had seen that same trait in Evandros. 'I believe they will support the idea of communicating our collective expertise with those who have not yet discovered applications and knowledge we've been fortunate to attain.'

'Then is it your contention you will not use the objects against the Olympian gods, my child?' the Mother Goddess asked, gaze penetrating.

'We will not. When we find the sacred relics we will depart for Atlantis and set them in their rightful location,' Alexina said, her stomach tightening.

The Mother Goddess nodded. Her face revealed nothing, yet her eyes were hard as black ice. 'The Dark Master cannot, must not get hold of the icons, even if it means losing those closest to you. However, Atlantis is not your final destination; on the island of Krete, not far from the palace of King Minos, there is a sacred tree. This is where you must place the objects.'

Alexina's mouth fell open. She stared at the Mother Goddess, her mind recoiling. Alexina began to sway on her knees, and her skin chilled. She flopped back on her haunches with a heavy heart and trembled. This would change the plans the elders had envisioned, the future of a restored Atlantis now ruined in light of this new revelation. They had been certain the ancients' writings meant the new location of their home was where the descendants of Atlantis would ascend to sovereignty and once again be revered throughout the world.

'Daughter.'

Alexina's head tilted upwards. Her eyes widened, seeing the Mother Goddess in her true form. She straightened on her knees, unable to take her gaze off the magnificence of the ancient goddess.

'The icons will be returned to the isle of Minos, for only then can the Dark Master be destroyed and the rightful heirs of Minos restore the worship of Gaia. You'—she pointed—'are endowed with the knowledge and power of the priestesses of the past, and it is now up to you to ensure it is never forgotten. You must recover two items concealed within this chamber: one is the relic you seek, and the other is a gift for Evandros. Do not leave until you have found his gift, for without it, the final object cannot be retrieved.'

'What is it we need to find?' Alexina asked, her mind spinning.

'It is a labrys the people used for the offerings of blood, and it is the only weapon that can be used against the bull of Minos.'

'Do you know where we can find it?' Alexina fought hard to stop the multitude of thoughts and protests she wanted to voice.

'It is hidden within the cave. The Dark Master also seeks it, and you must find the labrys before he does.' The Mother Goddess paused. 'Tell Homer not to slay any more of my serpents; the fire will encourage them to retreat.'

The goddess left. Blackness descended and enveloped the cavern, leaving Alexina alone. She remained kneeling, oblivious to the hard, uneven surface. Her mood mirrored the gloominess of the chamber, with the hope of restoring Atlantis to its former glory extinguished like the flame on a burner. She could not and would not defy the Mother Goddess. Yet the knowledge of her predecessors had been handed to her for a reason. Or was it a double-edged sword, like the gift Divine Zeus gave Pandora on her marriage to Epimetheos? Once Pandora had opened the pithos, pandemonium had showered the world, pernicious raindrops that had infected the race of humans.

Alexina stood, ignoring the pain in her knees and legs after staying in one position for so long. It was something she'd need to contemplate at length, and heed the Mother Goddess' warning. She stepped to the mouth of the cave, her gaze falling on Evandros. She watched as he interacted with Dexion, his affection for the boy evident on his face. The Mother Goddess and Evandros were connected, but how? That was another mystery she needed to solve.

CHAPTER THIRTY-SIX

Evan saw the High Priestess emerge from the cave. He frowned, noting her strained expression and pale complexion. Leander was walking over to her, with Hektor not far behind.

'Something has happened,' he said and went to join them. Evan saw Leander take her hand, which she did not rebuff. She was trembling. The hair on his arms stood on end. 'What is it?'

Her hand clutched Leander's tighter, seeking strength from him. She pressed a finger to her lips, closed her eyes and began to invoke the white-light.

She then opened her eyes, her voice as flat as a dull key on a piano. 'After I had finished communing with the high priestesses of the past, the Mother Goddess visited and revealed startling information. She said there are two objects we must recover from inside the cave.'

'What in the name of the gods!' Hektor said.

'Moloch! I knew this was too easy,' Phameas said, crossing his arms against his chest.

'First they tell us there are two objects to find, then Pythia says they won't work without the original statue. Now we need to retrieve another lost item? What else haven't they told us?' said Evan, angry.

'I understand your frustration. What the Mother Goddess revealed is essential, and if we don't locate the object, a weapon, we cannot succeed,' she said.

'This is ridiculous!' Evan gritted his teeth.

'A fool's errand!' Phameas glowered.

'Let Kronos have them!' Evan spat.

When they fell silent, the High Priestess added, 'Mother said you'll need this weapon to face the Minotaur.'

'Great, more validation that the stories of Theseus killing the Minotaur are fabricated. Great.' Evan kicked at a loose stone. Then he stilled as the revelation hit him. He turned to Dexion. 'You meant the actual labrys and not the one that goes with the icon.'

Dexion nodded.

Evan slapped his forehead. 'What an idiot I am. You told me, and I didn't even realise what you meant.'

'We all misunderstood Dexion's meaning,' said the High Priestess, 'and this is not the time for recriminations.'

Evan nodded, annoyed at missing Dexion's clue. 'Let's get on with it, then.'

'Wait a moment, who's Theseus?' asked Phameas.

'He was an Athenian hero and king,' said Evan. 'The story is rather long, and I'll do my best to give the short version. King Minos' son journeyed to Athens and entered sporting competitions, of which he won. While he and some friends were out travelling the countryside, a group of disgruntled young Athenians attacked and killed them. As you can imagine, King Minos was not happy and demanded retribution. The king of Athens, Aegeos, sought the counsel of Pythia, who instructed him that, in order to avoid war, he must appease Minos and send nine youths and nine young women to Krete for a nine-year period. The eighteen young Athenians were led to the Minotaur's lair and never seen again.'

'How does Theseus fit in?' asked Leander.

'Theseus was the illegitimate son of King Aegeos, living in another region of Attika. When he learns he is a prince, he heads off to Athens, asks to see the king and explains who he is. Theseus learns about the treaty between Minos and his father, which he doesn't like, and offers himself as one of the youths to be sent. When he arrives on Krete, Princess Ariadne sees him and falls in love. She offers to help him escape the labyrinth and tell him of a way to kill the Minotaur, if Theseus takes her with him when he flees. He agrees. Ariadne gives him a ball of twine, so he can find his way out, and a sword imbued with magic. He succeeds, and the two run away with the other young Athenians and sail away. Theseus returns to Athens a hero and becomes their king.'

'So it is assumed Theseus slew the Minotaur,' Leander said.

Evan nodded. 'Yes, and herein lies the problem. We cannot know as no one was there to see him fight the Minotaur.'

'What of Ariadne? Couldn't she confirm his story?' asked Hektor.

'She didn't see the fight, and Theseus left her behind on Naxos, after stopping there for the night.'

'That was not honourable. She risked her position to help him.' Hektor frowned.

'Can't disagree with you there,' said Evan.

'What we can assume from the tale is that the Minotaur is vicious and difficult to kill,' Phameas said, not happy.

'It would seem so.' Evan felt the dread spiral up his spine and bury deep into his core. *Maybe I won't return home.*

'There is more,' the High Priestess murmured. 'The relics will not be returning to Atlantis.'

'What? Does that mean we cannot go back home?' Hektor was alarmed.

'Divine Poseidon said that is where they must be restored!' Leander said.

'Mother said the sacred objects belong on Krete and we are to search for the hallowed tree near the palace of Minos. This is where they must remain.' The High Priestess' voice was flat and without expression. 'After we have completed our task and the Dark Master is thwarted, we can return home.'

Homer scribbled on his tablet and thrust it at the High Priestess. She gave him a tiny smile and laid a hand on his arm.

'Homer has reminded me we have been chosen by the gods for this important task, and it doesn't matter where the relics are situated. We are here to defeat the Dark Master and to save our home and people.'

The big man wrote while the High Priestess spoke and then showed her his tablet again when she finished.

'You are right. Time we locate these items and sail for Krete,' she said.

CHAPTER THIRTY-SEVEN

Evan entered the cave, torch held aloft, the flickering flame casting a yellow glow. The others filed in after him. With the cavern awash in a brilliant radiance, the craggy walls, which still held their secrets, were revealed for the first time in a thousand years. Evan moved deeper into the cave, away from the entrance and the security of daylight.

'Apart from the labrys, do we know what the other object is we're looking for?' Leander asked.

'Pythia said it's a double-headed tool,' said Evan.

'Double-headed? Isn't that your labrys?' said Phameas. 'Are we searching for one or two items?'

'Two,' said the High Priestess, confident. 'The one Pythia mentioned belongs to the statue of the Mother Goddess and is smaller. The weapon Mother spoke of is bigger, the same size as Hektor's axe, or perhaps larger.'

'I hope it's not too big. It'd be too heavy and cumbersome to carry,' Evan said.

'Remember not to touch the sacred object,' the High Priestess warned.

'You can count on that!' said Phameas.

They traversed further into the womb of the cave, the pitch-black surroundings oppressive and stifling. No one spoke, making the cave eerily quiet except for the sound of their collective breathing. Evan inspected the walls for hidden crevices in case the item was recessed inside a cavity. The tunnel came to a bend and continued onwards. He slowed and stopped, hearing a faint brushing noise.

'What is it?' Leander asked in a whisper.

'Not sure. Something ahead.' Evan resumed walking, the others falling into step. His nose twitched, and the blood flurried in his veins, the sound growing louder.

'Can you smell that?' asked Dexion as he edged closer to Evan.

'What is that stench?' The High Priestess covered her nose with a hand.

'Animal excrement,' said Leander.

A pungent emanation swept towards them, a malodorous wind that grew stronger.

'Bats.' Evan closed his eyes. 'Of course there are. How could I be so stupid?'

As he uttered the last word, the cave rang like a bell with a high-pitched screeching, sonorous and deafening. A surge of shrieking bats swarmed, and bringing with them the hideous and foul stench stirred by their panicked flight.

'Get down!' Evan shouted, shielding Dexion and the High Priestess with his body.

The cacophony was remorseless, and then it was over. One by one they stood, staring in the direction the bats had flown, wary they might return. Evan tapped his ears, the ringing akin to being at an AC/DC concert. He heard the familiar buzz of wings and crouched, pulling Dexion and the High Priestess with him. The others didn't ask questions and echoed his lead. They watched a solitary bat fly haphazardly overhead and disappear into the dark tunnel, following the throng that had passed before.

'That was different,' said Phameas. When he saw the others give him a vacant look, he repeated it louder.

'I hope they don't come back,' shouted Leander.

'Duck if they do!' Phameas grinned.

Leander chuckled and Homer beamed, giving the shorter man a little shove. Evan clasped the High Priestess' elbow and helped her stand upright. He checked on Dexion and saw he was fine. The levity of the situation eased the tension everyone felt. They continued their journey, with Leander giving a lesson on various bats he'd seen and of their unique behaviours. He stopped on seeing a fixture.

'Is that an altar?' he asked stepping closer.

The stone ledge, carved from the rock, had a smooth surface that reflected the light of the flames. Behind it, in the wall, were niches containing figurines—animal and human—as well as rhyton cups and horns from bulls. In the centre of the table, the surface was darker and had a slight depression. The High Priestess ran her hand over the ancient altar.

'This is where the high priestesses would have made sacrifices to the Mother Goddess.' She began to sing, her voice soft and melodic.

"From the womb of the earth may life breathe,

"From the womb of the earth may life be renewed,

"From the womb of the earth death will be received,

"From the womb of the earth the cycle of restoration is complete."

Evan spun one way, then the other. Homer put his hand on the hilt of his sword. Leander pulled out his bow, and Hektor moved into a fighter's stance. Phameas, the whites of his eyes wide and luminous, had a dagger in hand, while Dexion appeared unperturbed. Other voices, joined the High Priestess, those of ancient singers, and created an eerie echo as the lyrical tones dispersed throughout the cave.

When the last note faded, the heralds stopped, and the cave plummeted into reverent silence. Evan stared at the High Priestess, whose eyes shone, her body radiating a blue aura.

'The sacred relic is here,' she said.

'How can you be cer…?' The last word died on Evan's lips. The High Priestess smiled, both serene and exultant.

'It is here,' she repeated.

Leander helped the High Priestess search the immediate surrounds of the altar while the rest explored the walls, niches and crevices. They were careful not to break any of the votive icons and vessels, moving them out of the way and placing them back when they found nothing.

'Not so different from the temple where we found the coins,' said Leander as he knelt at the base of the altar.

'This is nothing like the temple,' Evan retorted. 'First off, there were no bats and two—'

'I think I have found something,' Leander said, scooping the dirt to the side.

They crowded around him, casting extra light over where he was digging. He shifted more dirt, and there appeared a small square hole, the length and width of his hand. He scraped out more dirt, then stopped and looked up at the High Priestess.

'I can feel something solid beneath this layer of sand.'

He stood to the side to allow the High Priestess to take his place. She removed the dirt, and the outline of the object emerged. The handle was made from gold, and the double-headed axe blade made from obsidian. The High Priestess picked it up and held it out to them. It was no bigger than the golden serpent.

The gold was embossed with tiny images Evan recognised from various books he read and websites he'd viewed, but on the verso was something very different and not familiar. On one side, the Snake Goddess held writhing snakes in each hand and was surrounded by priestesses; on the other side, there was a tree in the centre with priestesses circling it, while a group of females shook the tree.

'Now to find its bigger counterpart,' said the High Priestess. She wrapped the object in a scarf and stored it in her bag.

They ventured farther into the fathomless cave, the tunnel veering away from the hewn-rock altar. Ten minutes had passed when Evan felt a slight breeze.

'Wait,' he said and inched his way forward. He stopped. 'A dead end.'

The others sidled alongside and stared at the fissure. Leander lowered his torch and peered into the subterranean ravine.

'Now what?' Phameas asked.

'We could jump over it,' Hektor said with a shrug. 'It's not far.'

'You may be able to, but there's no way I can,' said Phameas, backing away from the ledge.

'Not all of us need to leap over the pit,' Leander said.

'No,' Evan agreed. To Phameas, he said, 'You and Dexion remain here with the High Priestess.' He then looked from Homer to Leander to Hektor. 'Who'd like to go first?'

'I'll go,' said Leander. He backed up a few steps and, with a little burst of speed, leapt over the chasm with ease, his torch casting its light in an arc. Hektor didn't waste time and went next, followed by Evan, then Homer. Evan froze. Something cold and scaly slithered over his foot.

'What is it?' Leander asked.

'We're not the only ones here,' Evan said and swallowed. His hands were clammy. He swept his torch over the ground. 'Cripes!'

The others lowered their torches. Evan stared at the mass of writhing serpents. A snake hissed, tongue flickering, and reared when a torch got too close. The torchlight fluttered as Evan recoiled and stepped back from the heaving mound.

'Moloch! I've never seen so many serpents!'

'They are covering something,' the High Priestess said and pointed.

'The problem is, how do we get from here to there without getting bitten?' Evan gulped.

Homer pulled out his sword and lifted it over his head.

'*No*, Homer!'

The flight of the blade came within inches of the nearest clutch of snakes. Homer glanced over his shoulder at her.

'You must not kill any of the serpents. They are sacred to the Snake Goddess,' she said, her hands outstretched.

Homer grunted and lifted his weapon away to return it to the sheath strapped across his back.

'What are we supposed to do? If we move closer, they will strike,' said Hektor, eyeing the cluster.

'The flame from the torches will ward them off,' Leander said. He lowered his torch and the snakes nearest him slithered away. Homer and Evan followed Leander's lead and cleared a small path. Hektor watched for a few minutes and joined them, seeing the reaction of the snakes. They swept their torches back and forth, edging their way forward until the serpents vacated the area.

A rectangular wooden box, five feet long and two feet wide, the patina darkened with age, was covered with pictograms and script. Evan traced the etchings with his fingers. He recognised the unique symbols as those of the language of the Minoans. He ran his hand over the lip of the lid, searching for a way to open the box. In the meantime, the other three kept the serpents away.

Evan pulled out his knife and slipped the blade between the lid and base. He shifted the dirt and grit that had gathered over the countless years. He then levered the lid with the knife, the wood creaking as he exerted more force. The lid gave way and Evan opened the box. Inside lay the labrys. The outer edge of the double-headed axe was engraved with swirls, and the flat head was inlaid with a golden image of a butterfly—the symbol of the soul. Evan closed the lid and stood.

'Time to leave,' he said.

CHAPTER THIRTY-EIGHT

'There they are!'

'Captain, they have returned!'

Jason jumped from the bow of his ship and hurried to greet Evan and the others as they trudged across the beach. Evan closed his eyes for a minute to drink in the cool breeze that swept in from the sea. All he wanted to do was take a dip in the water to revive his senses. He opened his eyes and raised a hand to acknowledge Jason.

'We were going to start searching the island for you,' Jason said as they came within hearing distance.

'The exploration took longer than we expected,' Evan said. He and Homer carried the box between them.

'It appears you were successful.'

'You have no idea what we had to do to retrieve it,' Evan said with a shake of his head.

'I look forward to hearing the story.'

'I hope you have food prepared,' said Leander with an expectant look. 'I am starving.'

Jason grinned and clapped him on the shoulder. 'My friend, you are in luck. My men have caught a large haul of fish, for which we are grateful to the god Poseidon, and are busy roasting them.'

Leander sighed and smiled at Jason. 'That is very good news.'

Later that night they sat around the dying embers of a fire, conversations subdued as the evening wore on. The cool night breeze caressed Evan's skin, and he began to nod off, his eyelids shuttering.

'Evandros, we should tell Jason of the vision Dexion had.' Phameas' voice sounded as if it had been amplified.

Evan started and his eyelids jettisoned open. 'Wha…?'

Phameas gave him a bemused look. 'Remember what Dexion told us while we were waiting by the cave for the others?'

Evan sat up. 'Oh, yes, the sea monster.'

Jason leaned forward. 'What's this about?'

'Dexion'—Evan glanced over at the slumbering form of the boy—'had foreseen the ship being attacked by a very hungry and angry monster.'

'Did he mention what it looked like?' asked Jason.

Evan shook his head. 'He said it was large and hideous.'

'And ferocious,' added Phameas.

Jason dragged a hand over his cheeks. 'There is always danger sailing the seas. It is unpredictable, and who knows what lurks beneath? As sailors, risking our lives is a daily adventure.'

'Adventure!' Hektor blurted. 'There is nothing noble about sailing.' He stood and stormed off.

'What was that about?' Jason said with raised eyebrows.

'Our ship and crew were attacked by the Kraken. We were the only survivors,' said Leander. He got to his feet. 'I'll go and check on him.'

'I am sorry, I did not know,' said Jason.

'How could you? You weren't told what had happened,' Evan said. He stared at the glowing coal, remembering the scene Zeus had made him watch, and then, without warning, he was floating in the midst of the debris. He clenched his jaw, and his stomach roiled.

'I am sorry if I have angered you. I didn't mean to bring forth terrible memories,' Jason said, noticing the scowl on Evan's face.

'You haven't, someone else did.' He rose to his feet. 'I'm going to turn in.' Evan picked up his bag and moved away from the group to a quieter spot on the beach. He dropped the bag and sat. He gazed over the inky water, the toing and froing of the tide soothing. He lay back and stared up at the sky, the position of the constellations different to what he was accustomed to and foreign. The Southern Cross, far away in the southern hemisphere and a symbol of his country, seemed beyond his reach from this distant location and time.

'Home is where the heart is,' he murmured, his eyes drinking in the sparkling gems in the sea of the night sky. His eyelids drooped. 'Home... is where I belong. When can I go home?' He yawned, and the last image he saw before falling asleep was of the twinkling stars.

He was holding the sacrificial labrys, veiled in utter darkness. He could not see anything, not even his hand until he held it within millimetres of his face.

What was that?

He turned to his right but was blinded by the obscurity. He heard a scraping noise to his left, and then it was behind him. Evan pivoted one way and then the other, clutching the labrys, knuckles turning white.

A hand reached out...

Evan bolted upright and grabbed the hand whose light touch rested on his shoulder. He shivered and his teeth chattered as the cool sea air licked his sweat-drenched skin.

'Be still,' said the soothing voice. 'You are safe. You were dreaming.'

Evan twisted away, keeping a hold on the hand. He gaped.

'What are you doing here? The last time I saw you was in Delphi.'

'I am here to help,' said Melaina.

Evan thrust her hand away. 'Really? Your offers of help don't equate to much, in particular when it is needed. Where were you when the earthquake happened and I fell into the crevice?'

The goddess' brows lowered and her eyes narrowed. 'As I said, I cannot reveal myself to the other gods. To do so would escalate what is a complicated situation.'

'Yes, I wondered about that, how the gods must not know of your existence. Why is that? Why the secrecy? Are you working for Kronos?'

Melaina went still and remained quiet for a few minutes.

'I am his daughter.'

'What the frick!' Evan felt the blood drain from his face. 'You've been playing me the whole time! You were giving me hints to lead your father to the objects. What a bitch! Shit, Hektor was right! I don't know which infuriates me more, that he was right or that you were conning me.' The veins in his neck stuck out like thick cords and his eyes dilated. Quick as lightning, he closed the gap between them and had his hand around her neck. 'You have made a fool out of me,' he said through clenched teeth. 'I do not appreciate being duped.' His fingers tightened and the irises of his eyes disappeared.

Melaina's mouth opened and her eyes were as wide as baseballs. 'Wait...' Her voice came out in a croak.

Evan's vice-like grip squeezed harder. 'There is no mercy for deception.'

'*Stop*! Let her go!'

Evan turned his head but did not relinquish his hold on the goddess' neck. He took in the glowing blue form. He blinked when the figure materialised. 'You are not who I expected. What brings you here?'

'I believe you already know the answer to your question.'

'I do, yet I'd like you to explain your reason for showing up, Apollo.' Evan's tourmaline eyes glinted.

'We have known of Melaina's existence from the time when she was conceived,' Apollo said. 'We've been watching to see what she would do, ever since Kronos escaped Tartaros.' He walked closer. 'We know Prometheus is her guardian, or as close as an immortal can have.' Apollo centred his attention on the goddess. 'Where is the old man? He should be wary; Father Zeus is keen to know of his whereabouts.'

Melaina closed her eyes and opened them, trying to speak.

'You know you cannot kill an immortal,' Apollo said, hands behind his back.

'Maybe not. Yet you kill and harm people when the mood suits and without provocation, like when you attacked me in Delphi. Why?' Evan did not shift his attention from the goddess in his grasp. 'Why did you?' he persisted when Apollo did not answer.

'I do not need to explain myself to you,' the god of prophecy and medicine said, jaw tightening.

A slow smile crept across Evan's face. 'I find it interesting how Melaina hasn't retaliated in some way. A goddess should be able to use her powers to strike back, yet either she is unwilling to act or she cannot.' The smile disappeared. Melaina recoiled at the interminable blackness of Evan's eyes. 'Which is it?' He leaned towards her. Her breath quickened. 'Why did you save me from falling to my death?'

'Because she is in love with you,' answered Apollo.

Evan stared at her. Melaina avoided his penetrating gaze and met Apollo's. 'And you are in love with her,' Evan said. 'That's why you attacked me.'

Apollo gaped at him. 'How... what...?'

'You came to protect her,' said Evan. 'Here, take her.' He thrust Melaina at Apollo.

'How do you know I am not here at Father Zeus' instruction?' asked Apollo.

Evan raised a brow at the protective embrace in which the God of Healing held Melaina. 'I hope you do a better job watching her. I am guessing she hasn't told Kronos of the extra little things she has done or of the clues she has given me.'

'You wouldn't have known to come here if I hadn't told you to see Pythia,' Melaina said, eyes flashing.

'Perhaps not,' Evan acknowledged with a nod. 'And for that, I thank you. Yet, it is possible Kronos orchestrated this, redirecting our ship away from Krete and to Pylos, where you happened to appear. Coincidence... I don't believe so. Although you did make the secretive meetings a pleasant experience. Not often I get the opportunity to spend time with a beautiful goddess, in spite of your deceitful intentions. Kronos' devious plan to...' Evan stopped and slapped his forehead as the realisation hit him like a bowling ball. He looked from Apollo to Melaina. 'Now I understand.' He spun on his heel, picked up his bag and sprinted to the ship, leaving the two immortals staring after him.

CHAPTER THIRTY-NINE

'How can we sure that is what Kronos is planning?' Leander asked. The man looked as if he had been run down by a bull. The misery and pain that emanated from his face and body was reflected by the High Priestess.

'I'm as sure as I am that the sun rises in the east,' said Evan. They were standing in a small circle, shoulder to shoulder, by the prow of the beached ship.

The High Priestess raised a trembling hand to her brow, the only outward sign that she was worried. 'I don't understand why.'

'It makes perfect sense. You are the human embodiment of the Mother Goddess, the giver of life, and the one person besides Her who can handle the objects without being killed. If you conceive His child, then your innate ability will be passed on to the baby, and he'll be able to use the relics,' Evan said.

'The time you speak of is many centuries away. It is not possible for the High Priestess to be still be alive then, let alone give birth to a baby,' said Phameas.

'Our blood is infused with that those of the gods,' said Hektor.

'What does that mean?' Phameas was puzzled.

'We are born with immortal blood.' Leander's voice was scarcely above a whisper.

'What? You can't die? Well, I got the rotten end of a pointy stick.' Phameas crossed his arms against his chest and brooded.

Homer tapped Evan on the shoulder and held out his tablet for him to read.

'Why is Kronos doing this now?' Evan read out loud. 'Good question, Homer. I don't know. The most logical answer is that this wasn't meant to happen and the original plan got disrupted.'

The High Priestess said in an abrupt tone, 'Not meant to happen? Disrupted? What do you mean?'

'If we weren't sent to search for the relics, life as we know it would remain the same. We would not know about the gods losing their power and eventual demise,' Evan said.

'But we were tasked to find the sacred objects and it changed the path,' Leander said, clenching and unclenching his hands.

Evan nodded. 'And to restore the true course, Kronos amended his plan to ensure his offspring will still become the new god of the world.'

'This doesn't make sense,' said Phameas. 'How was Kronos going to impregnate the High Priestess if you hadn't embarked on the mission for your gods? You'd be home and not here.'

'Quite right,' said Evan. 'I'm sure he had a scheme for that and changed it when Zeus and the Family interfered.'

'We will not allow him to take the High Priestess,' said Leander, his jaw tightening.

'We won't. We do need to be extra vigilant and make sure the High Priestess is not left alone.' Evan looked at her. 'Otherwise you will become the mother of a new god and birth a world religion.' He blinked as he stared at her. His heart almost stopped.

'What is it? You look as if you've swallowed a mouthful of seawater,' said Phameas.

Evan swallowed, unable to take his eyes off the High Priestess in her blue khiton and silvery-white head scarf. 'Ah… it's nothing, nothing important. Let's get ready for departure.'

A few hours later, Jason was piloting the *Argo* towards the mouth of the caldera. Evan, Phameas and Dexion stood with Jason, watching the horizon beyond the centre island.

'It should take a day, two at most, to sail to Krete,' said Jason as he adjusted the rudder. They neared the scorched, desolate and inhabitable isle, which reminded Evan of the time he'd visited Mt Etna in Sicily, not long after it had erupted. Around the volcanic mountain, the land was burnt to a crisp. Not a tree or shrub had survived. *And that was a minor eruption,* he thought to himself.

'While you and the others were searching for whatever you needed to find, my men and I were discussing our next adventure. They made a suggestion that I thought was good.' Jason made another minor adjustment, and the ship responded veering away from the black landmass.

'And that was?' asked Evan.

'After you've completed your business on Krete, we'd like to take you back home,' Jason said.

'Home?' Evan repeated.

'Back to Atlantis.' Jason gave him a funny look.

'Oh... Atlantis. That is very generous of you and your crew.' *I plan to go home, to the twenty-first century when this is over, and Zeus had better fulfil his promise to send me back.* Evan ran his hand over his stubbled hair, the prickly edges tickling his palm.

'Ah, Evandros, Homer wants your attention,' Phameas said. 'I don't like the look on his face.'

Evan glanced at Homer's frenetic beckoning to the starboard side.

'Dear Mother Goddess!' the High Priestess cried out.

Evan flew across the deck. Leander and Hektor reached the High Priestess first. Leander put an arm around her and drew her away from the prow.

'In the water...' she said to Leander.

Homer and Hektor scanned the waters and were soon joined by Evan, Phameas, and Dexion.

'By the gods!' A sailor stumbled backwards, his arms propelling in his haste to get away. He collided into one of his mates and both crashed onto the deck. Entangled limbs floundered in the air until one man managed to get loose, scrambled to the middle of the ship and cowered by the mast. He pointed leeward side. They turned to look.

'Poseidon's beard, what is that?' Hektor's eyes widened.

Edging close to the ship was whirlpool and a dark mass.

'Gods, that had not better be that monster that attacked our ship,' said Hektor in a hoarse tone.

Six heads on long snaking necks and six yawning mouths filled with sharp-edged teeth erupted from the water. The air whistled as it moved.

'Moloch!'

Evan stood immobilised and watched as the heads slithered from one side to the other, a macabre dance, and then disappeared down the side of the ship. His heart hammered against his ribcage.

'What are we going to do?' Leander asked, holding a very pale High Priestess in a protective embrace.

'Kill it,' she said in a strangled voice.

'I can weaken it with my arrows,' said Leander, standing straighter.

'It has six heads. I have a feeling it's going to take more than arrows to impair this monster,' Phameas said. He reached for his sword.

'The arrows may slow it down enough for us to get close and cut the heads off,' Hektor said. He had pulled out his labrys and held it with both hands.

Evan looked to Homer, who gave him a grim nod while grasping his weapon. Evan pulled his sword out from its sheath, the blade glinting under the sunlight. He slipped his hand through the straps of the shield and hoped it provided some protection.

'Argonauts! Arm yourselves!' Jason shouted, bounding forward with his sword held overhead.

The six-headed monster reared over the prow and a head darted at Evan, mouth open wide, displaying its three rows of razor-sharp teeth. Evan flung his shield out. The head butted against the aegis, and he tumbled onto his back. He rolled to the side, staggered to his feet and slashed at its face. He gagged at the scent of decaying meat as the leviathan pulled away. Homer and Phameas ran forwards, swords brandished, and attacked.

The monstrosity yelped at the barrage of missiles, the hail of Leander's arrows and rocks projected from the crew's slings, but it kept attacking. Its unusual barking was deafening, each yelp sent shivers up Evan's spine. The heads writhed forwards, backwards and sideways, mouths snapping open and shut, as it tried to snare a victim.

A few of the slingers dared to get closer. The monster's heads darted at them and took two. Their screams were cut short after they were tossed back and swallowed in one gulp.

Jason cursed and yelled for the remainder of his crew to step back.

'This is not working!' he shouted.

Homer and Hektor swung their weapons with grim determination and fended off heads as they drew near. Leander continued to release arrow after arrow, his aim precise. Evan fought alongside Phameas as they worked hard to deflect the ceaseless attacking heads.

'He's right!' Phameas said between strokes. 'We are not having any effect!'

'What else can we do?' Evan shouted back.

The ship listed.

Evan slipped, arms flinging into the air.

The creature raised itself out of the water and tried to latch on to the ship. Its twelve dangling legs crushed the wooden rail as it tried to hang on, but it slithered back into the water. Bodies collided and smashed against each other. Shouting and curses filled the air. The ship rocked from side to side, water spraying the deck and dousing everyone on board.

The sea monster launched itself at the ship and clung on, the vessel lurching. Evan slid across the deck, skated through the broken gap and fell into the churning water. On resurfacing, he saw Homer and Hektor fall into the water, not too far from him. Evan watched as those on board defended the ship from the monster.

'Holy cow, it is huge!'

The bulk of its girth remained underwater by at least ten kilometres, and its legs and feet, while helpless out of the water, moved with power and surprising agility.

'We need to divert its attention from the ship,' he said, raising his voice, 'and make it follow us.'

'What if it doesn't?' Hektor asked.

'We harass it from beneath.'

'The odds are not in our favour,' Hektor said.

'What do you suggest, then?' Evan asked.

Hektor didn't respond. Evan swam away from the ship and monster, not bothering to check if they followed. Swimming with the sword made it difficult to move fast, and as to the whereabouts of his shield, it could be sinking to the bottom of the sea. He dove beneath the waves and held his sword as he would a harpoon. Evan swam as far as he could before surfacing for air. He saw the distance he'd swum was less than a kilometre and hoped it would be far enough to attract the monster.

'*Hey!* You oversized buffoon! Over here!' Evan waved his arms and shouted. 'Oi! Turn around, you brainless six-headed twat!'

Homer splashed water and thrust his sword in the air, waving it about, and Hektor yelled. The three men bobbed up and down, hollering and slapping at the water, trying to draw its attention.

'This is not working,' said Hektor, dropping his arms. 'The noise from the ship is louder, and if we don't do something soon, the creature will sink it.'

'The only other thing we can do is swim back and try to attack it from underneath,' said Evan. 'That is, if we can get close enough to it...' Evan stopped and stared. 'Do that again, Homer.'

Homer gave him a puzzled look.

'When the blade of your sword caught the sunlight, the refraction hit one of the heads, and the monster reacted.'

Homer's eyes lit up, and after a few attempts, he managed to redirect the glint from his blade into the monster's face. It yelped and the head jerked back.

'We need to get closer,' said Evan. 'And with the three of us shining light at it, we may be able to get it to retreat.'

They stopped on the fringe of the choppy water, lifted their weapons to the sun and deflected the rays. The creature reacted with a high-pitched mewling, the three heads lurching away. The men aimed the streams of light to the other three heads. The crew saw what they were doing and raced to do the same. The monster squealed, the heads reeling to avoid the rays of sunlight. They continued their assault until it backed away and submerged.

Everyone on board cheered and embraced each other.

'Watch out!' Evan shouted.

The incensed creature rammed the ship. The people fell and scattered across the deck like marbles.

'Damn it!' Evan struck out towards the ship.

CHAPTER FORTY

'If we do not stop this onslaught, Skylla will kill your precious son and everyone on board that ship!' Poseidon glared at the King of the Gods. Not getting a response from his brother, he whirled on his heel to face the pantheon of gods, who had gathered in the throne room on Mount Olympos. 'If we do not put an end to Skylla's actions, Kronos wins, and we will be left with nothing and no one to attend to our needs.'

Poseidon twisted back to Zeus and thrust his finger at him. 'Mother said that we were to help our children when required. This is such a time, or are you comfortable'—the Sea God swung back to his immortal siblings—'and are you willing to be replaced by Kronos, whom we banished aeons ago, and who intends to be the sole immortal to be worshipped by our mortals, whom we brought into existence?'

'No!' Ares roared. 'I will not allow my reputation as the god of war to be one of cowardice. No longer will I stand aside and wait for our children to be annihilated before they recover the sacred relics. It is time we assist and ensure they survive to continue our bequest.'

'I agree.' Athene faced her father. 'If we do not intervene, all will be lost.'

'If memory serves, we did come to an understanding to provide support where warranted,' Hestia said, brushing down the front of her lime-coloured khiton. 'This is one of those times when it would be expedient to intervene.'

Zeus drummed his fingers on the armrest of his throne and pondered the arguments. He considered first the words of his warrior daughter, whose wisdom and countenance served her well, and under her guidance the city-state that carried her name was flourishing beyond expectation. Whereas, Ares, renowned for his temper and irascible behaviour, was detestable; yet, if not for his combatant expertise, their mortal fledglings would not have learnt the craft of warfare and repelled the barbarian hordes. While the hearth and home drove Hestia's words, she signified the importance of family and unity.

He also knew Mother would not be happy if he failed to aid his son and his companions. He often thought about what she had said about the Atlanteans not being ready to be thrust back into the world. What did she mean? Did she have a plan for their re-emergence? What if he hadn't learnt of their fate? Then Kronos' scheme would have gone ahead and a new youthful god been born. No, that would not and could not happen.

He stood and said to his brother, 'You and Ares will aid the Atlanteans, but do not harm Skylla, for she was tricked by Eris. Ares, you will replenish any lost or damaged weapons.' Zeus turned to Hermes. 'Find Eris and learn what you can of her plans. We need to know how she intends to impede the Atlanteans. Now go.'

CHAPTER FORTY-ONE

Each time Evan neared the ship, a large wave induced by the sea monster pushed him away. His limbs ached and grew heavier with every stroke. He could hear the voice of the swimming instructor in his head, yelling at him to stop splashing so much and make each stroke clean and smooth. He drew in a ragged breath and lifted his leaden arms to have another go when a gigantic silver trident burst from the depths of the sea. Evan shielded his face from the sudden burst of rain. He gaped at the towering figure that thrust the three-pronged weapon at the sea monster.

'Skylla, you will desist!' Poseidon's voice boomed. The creature recoiled. 'The Goddess Eris has used trickery to lure you away from your home with promises of bounty. Go back to your nest and nurse your wounds. I assure you she will not go unpunished.'

Skylla barked and moved away from the ship, and then submerged, disappearing into the deep blue Mediterranean water. Evan sighed in relief and allowed the tension to flow from his body. Exhausted, he doubted he could swim the distance to the ship when he was plucked out of the sea and found himself standing with Homer and Hektor. He blinked, swaying. Dexion and Phameas rushed to his side to support him.

'The creature you battled is known as Skylla. Do not be angry with her, as she had been deceived by the Goddess of Discord,' Poseidon said. He was standing on the deck with another god, who was dressed in shiny black armour, wearing a helmet with black plumes and carrying a sword and shield.

'She is doing her utmost to either hinder or harm us,' said Hektor. 'This was not the first attack we've fended off from the goddess.'

'She seeks revenge against us and those who are in alliance with us.' Poseidon's eyes bored into Evan's. 'She will continue to cause havoc.'

'That's really helpful,' Evan said, unable to keep the sarcasm from his voice. 'How do you propose we stop these monsters the next time she sends one? We weren't able to kill or even stop this one.'

'We will provide aid in the event your lives are endangered,' said Ares. 'Father Zeus sent us to stop Skylla and inform you of our intentions.'

Evan retorted. 'I am glad our lives are so important to you, considering we're the ones who are risking them on a daily basis for you.'

Ares' eyes darkened and his jaw tightened. He put a hand on the hilt of his sword when the High Priestess intervened and shot Evan a warning shake of her head.

'Evandros is upset. We've endured much since leaving Atlantis,' she said, stepping into the space between the gods and her companions. 'You must understand, after a millennium of isolation, we are challenged with readjusting to interaction with fellow mortals and provocations over their fears of our presence. There is the constant threat of the Dark Master and the Goddess of Discord, who wish to impede our quest for the relics.' She paused and glanced at Leander, who gave her an encouraging smile. 'We are grateful for whatever support you can give us.'

'We do recognise your plight, High Priestess, which is why we are here,' said Poseidon. 'We are pleased you have found the first relic. One more to retrieve and normalcy will be restored.' The Sea God squinted at her. 'You *do* have at least one object in your possession?'

'Two, though the second one is a weapon to use against the Minotaur,' Evan said and gestured at the ornamental crate nestled in the prow of the ship. 'I have a request.'

Poseidon lifted an eyebrow.

'Would you be able to repair Jason's ship? Skylla did a bit of damage in her attack.'

Poseidon studied Jason and the Argonauts, who stared, stupefied by the presence of the gods. 'It is done.'

Everyone turned. The damaged section of the ship was restored. Evan was about to say thank you, but the gods had gone.

'Why didn't you tell…?' Leander stopped as Evan put a finger against his lips.

'Not without the protective shield.'

'While you lot chat, we'll get underway,' said Jason.

'Why didn't you tell Divine Poseidon we found the second relic?' asked Leander. They had gathered under the white shield of the High Priestess.

'We don't want Kronos or Eris to know we've got it. And there was something else. Neither Poseidon nor Ares knew we had the second object. If they don't know, then it means the other gods aren't aware. The question is, why don't they?' Evan said.

'The gods must be told we have them,' said Hektor. 'It is the purpose for our being here.'

'I realise that, and they will be informed.' Evan rubbed his brow. 'I think it's safer if we keep the knowledge to ourselves until we work out why they haven't found out about the second item. This situation could also work in our favour.'

'How so?' asked Leander.

'The element of surprise,' Evan answered. 'Since the outset of this expedition, we've encountered trouble, and I'm sure there's more to come. The fact Kronos and Eris are still trying to stop us from recovering the objects is good.'

'Hmmph. I don't see how,' Hektor said, crossing his arms against his chest.

'I do,' said Phameas, piping in. 'Their continual need to disrupt what we're doing will distract them from finding out that we have two of the items.'

Evan beamed at Phameas. 'That's right. By fuelling their desire to thwart us, their focus is diverted and this will give us time to complete the task.'

'That may be the case, but there is another aspect to consider,' said the High Priestess. 'You are presuming that they won't find out we have the sacred relics.'

Evan shook his head, still smiling. 'Oh no, I'm sure they will learn we have the objects, but by the time they do, it may be too late for either of them to do anything.'

'They may find out sooner,' Hektor said.

'Then we keep our mouths shut and discuss everything about the search and objects under the shield.' Evan looked at each of them. 'Agreed?'

'I concur,' said the High Priestess. 'We need to be diligent and careful of what we say. Even the most innocent comment could alert the Dark Master and the vengeful goddess.'

'Why did you tell Divine Poseidon about the sacrificial labrys?' asked Hektor.

'A bit of truthful information is a way to allay misgivings. And as Pythia is Apollo's intermediary, the gods may not be privy to all the information she revealed. They'd know she instructed us to visit Thira, but not that we now must find the statue of the Mother Goddess.'

'Another distraction?' Leander said, lifting a brow.

'In a sense. We don't want to show all our cards at once,' Evan said.

'Cards?' The High Priestess' brow furrowed.

Homer shook his head at Evan and sent him a warning look.

Shit! Evan bit his lip, thinking fast. 'Like the pieces on a Senet board; you don't want to reveal all your moves to your opponent.'

'Ah… the act of stealth,' said Leander whose face cleared with understanding. 'Yes, a clever ruse to outwit our foe.'

'You got it,' said Evan, sighing with relief. He needed to be more careful with what he said, or he'd be in a right mess with no easy way to explain himself.

CHAPTER FORTY-TWO

*E*ris stormed across the black marble floor. She was furious with Skylla, who had failed to maim any of the Atlanteans, but she was more infuriated with Poseidon and Ares, who had intervened. She drew to a stop and stomped back, her hair writhing in the wake of the abrupt change in direction.

In addition, she would not be told what to do or treated as a slave, and nor would she be reduced to the lowly status of being an immortal's mouthpiece. The Dark Master's plan of creating a Messiah for the pathetic mortals was laughable, for no individual—immortal or mortal—could dominate the world. How dare he think he can replace me with this puny mortal who will be a god to everyone?

'I do not think so,' she said out loud.

When the Dark Master had conquered the Olympian Gods, she would cajole him into revealing the Messiah's name, and she'd be the one to stop this nonsense.

Somewhat mollified by her new plan, Eris turned her thoughts back to the troublesome Atlanteans. They were proving to be stout adversaries. They had managed to kill two of her precious harpies and now, with the assistance of the gods of the sea and war, fended off the terrible Skylla, whose appetite for mortal flesh was formidable. She needed to think of something that would hinder the Atlanteans from finding the relics. The Dark Master was searching for the remaining item himself, not trusting her or her pets to assist. She would allow him to locate it, and when the right time presented itself, she would take it from him. But first, the Atlanteans must be dealt with.

She paced the length of the throne room, dismissing one idea after the next, when she recalled how Circe had held Odysseus on her island for a number of years. She had lured his crew to her palace and then turned them into animals—lions, pigs, monkeys—and when Odysseus had learnt of their fate, he had confronted Circe. The goddess, enamoured by Odysseus, had given him a potion, making him forget about his home, Ithaka and his wife, Penelope. This had worked until the meddlesome Hermes told Odysseus about an antidote, which helped restore his memory. The more Eris thought about it, the more she liked the idea.

A wicked smile crept across her attractive face; she needed to find a worthwhile accomplice who would be willing to entice not only the male Atlanteans, but the entire crew of the Argo as well as the Phoenician. The smile on her face faded as her thoughts turned to the High Priestess and the boy. Though she had promised the Dark Master she would not kill the High Priestess or her brother, he had not said she could not impair them. The boy, on the other hand, was negligible and expendable.

The Island of Hephaistos came to mind. Eris clapped her hands, and did a little twirl. Hephaistos' mother, Hera, had cast him onto the island when he was a baby because she had found him ugly and he was injured, causing him to become lame. But that was not why she remembered it. The island was now ruled by women, and no man lived there for fear of death.

This was where the last descendants of the Amazon Queen Hippolyte had gone, fleeing from Herakles, who had been sent to kill them in their homeland in the Pontus. Very few knew that the women who resided on the island were of Amazonian descent. Eris needed to think of a plan to ensure the Atlanteans and the crew of the Argo would somehow find themselves on the island. The problem was, the Isle of Hephaistos lay in the northern region of the Aegean Sea, and the Argo was far south. Which of her pets could create chaos and confuse the orientation of the ship?

Eris' eyes lit up and she clicked her fingers.

'Of course! Why didn't I think of them earlier?' She called for her last harpy. 'Find the three orb-eyed giants and tell them I want to see them straight away.'

The harpy blinked, lifted its wings from which a foul stench was emanated, and with a hop it soared out of the room.

Eris then disappeared, leaving the throne room empty.

CHAPTER FORTY-THREE

Evan stirred and woke to the rosy glimmer of dawn. Jason had anchored in the bay of one of the numerous islands, that dotted the Aegean Sea, each as unique as the last. Evan stepped over the slumbering forms of Dexion and Phameas. The island appeared too small for any inhabitants, except for wildlife. He knew that of the three thousand islands, many weren't inhabitable. He took in the crystal-blue water and smiled, yanked off his khiton and dove in. A little while later, the *Argo* left the cove.

To keep distracted from the ponderous technique of sailing from one island to the next, Evan and Dexion played Senet. Phameas wanted to learn how to play and sat watching, Evan describing the various moves. Evan then taught Phameas to play against Dexion. Their game was disrupted when a crew member shouted an alarm. They joined the others at the prow of the ship. The glare of the sun on the water made it difficult to see at first.

'What is that?' said Evan, shielding his eyes.

'I have a bad feeling about this,' Phameas said in a low voice, 'a real bad feeling.'

'Are they... do they look like giants?' Evan said, his stomach pressing into the rail as he leaned forward as far as possible.

Three distinct and gigantic figures appeared on the horizon, their movements ponderous yet deliberate in the direction they travelled.

Evan felt the hairs on the back of his neck stand on end. 'They can't be...'

'The Cyclops,' the High Priestess said, going rigid. 'Dear Mother.'

The giants continued to lumber towards them, and the sea began to surge, rocking the ship. The swells increased and the momentum pushed the ship backwards. The waves expanded with the goliaths' movement and forced the *Argo* back with faster impetus.

Jason ran to the steering oars and shouted, 'Man the oars! We must turn the ship or it will be ripped apart by the waves!'

Fine sprays of seawater showered the deck. Evan clutched the railing, his stomach lurching with the rise and fall of the ship.

'You need to move faster!' Evan bellowed over his shoulder. 'They're getting closer!'

'Rowers on the starboard, raise oars! Rowers on the port side, oars in and let us get this ship turned!' Jason clutched the steering oars, the muscles on his arms tightening and the veins sticking out.

The oarsmen dipped the oars into the choppy sea and rowed, the force of the currents resisting their efforts to manoeuvre the ship. They struggled against the heaving sea and the ever-approaching figures, water spraying across the deck like rainfall.

'Starboard rowers, oars in!'

There was a sudden shift and the ship started to pull away, moving with ease and smoothness. Evan kept watching the three giants until they receded into the distance. Jason then instructed the crew to stop. Many slumped over their oars, their heavy breathing filling the sombre air. Evan, Phameas and Dexion offered the men cups of water. Jason went to each of his crew and conveyed words of solace and commendation on their efforts.

'What are the one-eyed giants doing here?' said Hektor. 'They had sided with the gods in the war against the Titans after Divine Zeus freed them from Tartaros. Why would they rise against the Olympians after all this time?'

They may have been offered a prize of extraordinary worth, one they could not resist regardless of their affiliation with Divine Zeus, Homer scrawled.

'And we know who can offer such rewards,' Leander said, eyes narrowed.

'The question is not if the Cyclops will attack again but when,' said Evan.

'What can we do to stop them?' asked Phameas.

'I don't think we can,' Evan replied. 'Our other problem is how far the ship strayed off course in that assault.'

'The Dark Master and the Goddess of Discord are trying to divert our journey to Krete,' the High Priestess said in a matter-of-fact voice.

Evan nodded. 'Or prevent us from arriving there.'

'The Cyclops didn't seek to sink the ship,' said Phameas, 'which they could have done with ease.'

'That is a good point,' said Evan. 'So they don't mean to kill us, just get us out of the way.'

A sound strategy to delay or subvert our attempts in locating the sacred relics, wrote Homer. *It's what I'd do, if I had the power.*

'Divine Poseidon and Ares said they would help us in such situations,' Hektor said.

'If our lives are in danger, they will come to our aid,' Evan said with a shake of his head. 'The Cyclops' did not pose such a threat, as yet.'

'Do you doubt the word of the gods?' Hektor's nostrils flared.

Evan felt the familiar rush of hot blood surge through his veins. It was akin to having an electric shock, but still being conscious.

'Master Evandros, should you ask Jason how far we've travelled?' asked Dexion.

Evan blinked, the fire in his blood dwindling. 'Yes, Dexion, we do need to know where we are.' Without another word, he turned on his heel and marched over to Jason.

'Stormy weather brewing,' said Jason, gesturing at the heavy and leaden sky.

'That's all we need now,' said Evan, glancing skyward. 'By the way, great job on piloting the ship through the confusion and thanks to your crew in getting away from the Cyclops.'

'I didn't think we'd make it. I thought the rudders would break in the strong currents.' Jason's face was lined and greyed with fatigue.

'A sailor's life is one of adventure and peril,' said Phameas. 'That is why we enjoy it so.'

Jason barked out a laugh. 'Spoken like a true salty. It is exciting and I would never give it up.'

'How far are we from Krete?' asked Evan.

'We are three days' sail from Krete,' Jason answered.

'Not as bad as I thought.' Evan clasped the back of his neck with a hand. 'Where are we now?'

'We're nearing the islands of Naxos and Ikaria. With the storm heading in our direction, it's best we land at the Port of Naxos and let the weather pass,' Jason said, 'then continue to Krete.'

'Okay.' Evan let his arm fall to his side and sighed.

'Don't worry, Evandros, I will get you to Krete,' said Jason, with a smile.

'That's the least of my concerns, Jason. It's what will happen in the meantime,' said Evan.

'That is in the hands of the gods.'

'And therein lies the nub of the problem,' Evan muttered.

After two days on Naxos, they were back on the water, sailing for Krete. Around midday, the crew set up the mast, and the canvas billowed in the strong wind from the dying remnants of the storm. Evan's attention was drawn to the decorative wooden box. He squatted to scan the images when Jason shouted for the crew to furl the mast and ready their oars. Evan glanced over to what had captured Jason's interest. He stood and stared, and his skin went cold.

'Shit! Not again.'

Three familiar figures powered their way through the water. With a roar, the Cyclops lifted their arms and pounded the surface of the sea.

'Double shit!'

He ran over to the High Priestess and grabbed her hand.

'Dexion! Over here, now!'

He secured them against the mast and then ran to help Jason. The tumultuous rumble of the sea speeding towards them was immense.

'What?' Evan pointed to his ear. 'I can't hear you!'

Jason shouted, the words lost in the deafening noise of the roaring waves. Evan didn't have the opportunity to ask again when the ship rode the largest wave he'd seen before slamming onto the next immense swell.

'Argonauts! Unless you wish to spend an eternity with the hounds of Hades, row like you never have before!' Jason's scream pierced through the momentary lull.

Evan didn't know if it was the threat of meeting the God of Death or some other force, but the crew rowed as if pursued by Hades' hounds. At times the oars did not even touch the water, but the men kept rowing. One of the men lost his grip on his oar, which jerked back like a whip and smacked him in the head, knocking him out. Evan watched as Phameas slipped and skidded his way to the fallen man, moved him to the side and took his place.

Evan tightened his grip on the steering oar, ignoring the quiver in his muscles and the pain in his shoulders. Another man lost control of his oar and collapsed, the oar disappearing into the raging water. Homer and Leander moved to take over from a few men who appeared to be flagging. Hektor followed, dragging his feet in the process. Torrents of water doused the deck, drenching everyone many times over.

Wave after wave crashed against the ship. The ferocity of the sea and the relentless pursuit of the Cyclops pushed the ship further and further away from its original position. A few more oarsmen lost their battle to keep going, unable to hold on to their oars. Evan and Jason fought to keep the ship from capsizing. Water continued to rain on them. Evan thought he'd end up overboard, battling with the relentless agitation of the rudder.

Then it was over.

The water dropped back and the turbulence subsided. The sea was flat and clear for as far as the eye could see, the sky blue and cloudless. Evan's legs gave way under him and he thudded onto the deck in a collapsed heap. Jason sat with a thump next to him.

'I guess we should be grateful we are alive,' Evan said, flopping onto his back and closing his eyes. 'I wonder where we are?'

'I'd say we are many, many days away from Krete,' said Jason, exhaustion lacing his words.

'Many, many, huh?' Evan began to laugh. Jason looked at him, startled. 'Not just a few days, but lots.' Evan guffawed. Jason's mouth twitched and he started laughing. Their laughter drew concerned looks from the others. Phameas and Homer approached the two men, who clutched their stomachs, tears rolling down their faces.

'Perhaps they drank some seawater and it has made them delirious,' Phameas to Homer.

The comment made Evan and Jason laugh more. Phameas rolled his eyes and shook his head.

'They'll be fine, let's leave them.'

CHAPTER FORTY-FOUR

Queen Antioche stood on the ramparts of her palace to watch the merchant ship leave the port of Hephaestia. It was filled with high-quality goods from the island, including the precious purple cloth desired by rulers and wealthy patrons from nearby city-states. She instructed the captain first to go east, to the lands of Persia, as the king had promised to buy a large quantity of the material.

On board were her fiercest warriors, to protect the merchandise and to ensure the captain got the best price on all items. It was not that she did not trust the captain, but she knew how fallible men could be when given an offer difficult to refuse. She did not allow such weakness, not in her people nor herself. If she showed such flaws, it would undermine her authority as a leader and provide an opportunity for outsiders to dominate.

When her ancestors had come to this island looking for a safe haven, they had vowed that no man would rule them, nor fool them ever again by their chicanery. Men were a commodity, and their usefulness limited to the continuation of her people. If it wasn't for that one essential element, she would sacrifice each man to the goddess Artemis. She watched as the ship sailed past the northernmost tip of the island and disappear from sight. The queen turned away and walked back into the palace.

As soon as she stepped into the tower, her hand-maidens surrounded her, chatting and voicing their concern over the same topic: the need for fresh, virile males. Exasperated, she sent them away to leave her alone in the megaron. The embers of the previous night's fire smouldered, the whispers of the smoke curling, drawn into the opening in the roof.

She stared at the fire pit, pondering where they could acquire more men. Her administrators had warned that if they did not procure males for procreation, their people would, in time, cease to exist. It was getting more difficult to overpower their neighbours and steal the men, as had many have migrated elsewhere, and there were no suitable males available in those territories.

'I believe I have the answer to your dilemma,' said a voice, and a violet mist appeared. The miasma cleared and the Goddess of Discord stepped around the hearth to face the queen.

Queen Antioche leapt to her feet and shouted for her guards.

'There is no need for alarm,' said Eris in a cool tone. 'If I wanted to harm you, I would have done so, and no amount of warriors could have helped.'

'Who are you and how did you get in here?' Queen Antioche's guards formed a protective circle about her while another group surrounded the intruder.

'I am Eris, Goddess of Discord.'

The queen drew in a sharp breath, her heart quickening. The goddess' reputation was less than savoury, and those who tried their wits against her lost a great deal. Those more unfortunate, or perhaps fortunate, lost their lives.

'Why are you here?' the queen asked in a hostile tone.

'You require male stock, and I can offer you a host of men. Not only are they robust, but there are those who come from an ancient bloodline, one that has ties to the gods.' Eris glanced at the armed warriors. 'And they will boost the strength of your soldiers.'

'What is it you want in return?' The queen was suspicious, and eyeballed the goddess.

'Nothing untoward,' Eris said with an innocent look. 'All you need to do is hold the men captive for a while, the longer the better. In return for your collaboration, you will be rewarded with the ongoing engenderment of your race.'

'Is that all you require, for us to detain some men?' Queen Antioche repeated, her eyebrows squishing together.

Eris nodded and took a step. The warriors gathered closer, but she smiled at them and lifted a hand. The women came to a halt, unable to move. She approached the queen until the two stood toe to toe.

'Yes, that is all. You get what you need and you'll have done me a great service while you delay the men.'

Queen Antioche swallowed, unable to breathe, but stood tall as she gazed into the goddess' ice-blue eyes. There was no way to determine what the goddess would do to her and her people if she did not accept the offer. But the promise of healthy men was tempting.

'Where are these men you speak of?'

'They are not too far. As it happens, they are on their way and should arrive any day now. I do suggest you send someone to watch the small western cove, for that is where they will land.' She paused, her eyes hardening. 'I have one request of you, and if you fail to follow my instructions, you will no longer acquire the use of these men.'

The queen's heart almost stopped. The goddess' fathomless eyes drew the queen into a vortex of confusion and chaos.

'You have an herb that makes people forget who they are and what they were doing. Make sure you have enough ready to drug each man, and plentiful supplies to keep them oblivious,' the goddess said.

The queen quavered.

Eris wheeled away, flicked a hand and forced the warriors to jump back.

'Oh... there is one other thing,' the goddess said, looking over her shoulder, her eyes returning to their normal shade. 'There is a woman travelling with the men. Lock her away and do not allow her to make any contact with the men. She will try and steal them away. There is also a boy with them. Do as you wish with him.' The goddess beamed, exultant and charming, disarming the queen's efforts to remain composed. 'You do this and you will live out your lives in peace.'

'Where do these men come from?' the queen asked, trying to keep her voice from trembling.

The goddess whirled to face her. 'A majority are Greeks and come from Thessaly, and four men are from Atlantis.' She smirked at the reaction of the queen and her guards.

'Atlantis? Weren't they destroyed?'

'It appears they survived. You can learn all you wish of how they managed to escape death when they arrive,' the goddess said. 'Are we agreed on the terms of this arrangement, Queen Antioche?'

The queen nodded, her mind reeling from the news. She thought how fortuitous the union would be and how much stronger her people would become. No one would be able to resist the dominance and bloodline of the Amazons mixed with that of the Atlanteans.

'Very good. I wish you every success in this new endeavour.' The goddess smiled, and then laughed.

A smoky violet vapour shrouded her body and spiralled into the opening of the roof, leaving an empty space where the goddess had stood. Queen Antioche reflected on the unusual discussion, annoyed by the strongarm tactics the goddess had used to trick her in front of her warriors. But the offer of Atlantean men was too tantalising to refuse.

'Go and bring my administrators. I want them assembled here within ten minutes,' she said.

Two of her guards remained and stood on either side of the throne. The others dispersed in various directions, in search of the women the queen wanted. She then smiled and began to look forward to meeting these Atlanteans. Her loins stirred at the anticipation of taking one as her lover, or perhaps she should have all of them.

CHAPTER FORTY-FIVE

'Is it possible to plot a different course to Krete so we avoid being swept away by the Cyclops again?' the High Priestess asked Jason.

'We were considering that as an option,' said Evan.

'And?' she prompted.

'I can navigate another course, but as I was telling Evandros, it will take longer,' Jason said.

'We have already lost days running away from the giants. What are a few more?' said Leander.

'It is more important we arrive on Krete, and if we must take a circuitous route then that's how it must be,' said the High Priestess.

'What if the Dark Master learns of our new plans?' said Hektor.

'What alternatives do we have? We have to get to Krete,' said Evan. He looked at Jason. 'If you chart alternating courses and make the changes straight away, we may be able to stay ahead of Kronos and Eris. We should stop at ports along the way as a decoy, and with luck, we'll make them wonder what we're doing.'

'They are gods, trickery will not fool them,' Hektor said.

'No, it may not, but we must try, Hektor, or we have lost,' said the High Priestess jutting out her chin.

Evan was stunned. He had not expected the High Priestess to speak to Hektor in such a manner. Not given previous encounters. Perhaps the alleged threat of Kronos' role for her had affected her more than she realised.

Over the next few days, Jason made subtle changes as he charted the waters to their final destination. Homer and Phameas sat and watched Dexion and Evan play Senet. They were laughing at Evan, who had made a strategic error in placing one of his pieces and allowing Dexion to make a clean sweep of the board. Evan shook his head, grinning, and they reset the board.

'Evandros!'

'What is it, High Priestess?' Evan asked, still smiling and eyes on the board.

'I think we have been found out,' came the choked response.

Evan stood and knocked the Egyptian board game with his foot, the pieces scattering. He looked at where she pointed. There was a large flock of birds swarming towards them and the three lumbering figures not far behind.

'Jason!'

'I see them!'

'Arm yourselves! I don't think those birds are here to eat fish!' Evan said. He picked up his sword and shield and faced the fast-approaching flock.

Jason yanked on the steering oars, sending the ship veering away from the unusual assailants. A few birds broke away from the flock and flew over the ship, screeching. Evan winced. The large birds had long, elegant necks, their bodies and wings in different colours and patterns, the tips of the wings dark.

The bulk of the flock fanned into a V formation and swooped in perfect synchronicity. Evan pushed Dexion to the deck and threw himself over him. His clothes fluttered as the birds flew over.

Horrendous screams pierced the air. Evan whipped his head from side to side, heart thudding.

'Not good, not good at all.' He sat back on his haunches and said to Dexion, 'Are you all right?'

'Yes, master.'

'Stay here and don't get up. I have a feeling the birds will be back.'

A handful of the crew had been speared by feathers. He scrambled over to one of the men, his upper arm pinned to the railing with a feather. Evan grasped the feather and pulled.

'What the blazes!' He glanced at his hand, blood seeping from where he had grabbed the feather.

Evan glanced up and saw the birds were returning. He grabbed the edge of his khiton and yanked out the feather. The man screamed.

'Here, hold your hand over the wound to stem the blood flow.' He then darted back to where Dexion lay face down, arms covering his head. Evan picked up the shield and ran towards the incoming birds using the shield as a battering ram. A bird fell out of the sky and landed at his feet with a thud.

Evan leapt over it and saw Leander shooting arrows. Birds dropped into the sea as each arrow found its target. In unison, the birds swerved towards Leander and released a volley of lethal feathers.

Evan dashed out in front of Leander and held out his shield. The feathers bit deep into the bronze and leather layers, his fingers tingling and arm vibrating from the impact. Leander acknowledged him with a quick nod and kept firing. Though their numbers were reduced, the birds returned for another attack, and again Leander's accurate aim cut through the flock. Everybody cheered, seeing the birds fly away.

'It's not over!' Evan pointed to the giants, who kept moving towards them.

'Argonauts, to your oars!' Jason roared.

Evan dropped his weapons, jumped into one of the vacated seats and grasped the oar. He matched the other oarsmen with their strokes, Jason shouting at them to row faster. His frantic yells urged the men to pick up the pace. Evan's chest heaved, his shoulders stretched and pulled with every movement. He heard someone scream and peered over, the rumble of water getting louder as it drew closer.

'Shiiiiite!'

The wall of water screened the sky and stretched for kilometres in breadth and height. Streams of water were dumped on the ship like a torrential storm. Evan rowed as if the demons from hell were chasing.

The sea receded into the wave, dragging the ship with it. Then the ship shot out from the shadow of the wall of water. The wave crashed behind the vessel. A huge surge elevated the ship to a massive height and the force propelled the vessel at great velocity. The oar was ripped out of Evan's hands. He tried to get up but fell onto his backside with a hard whack. He twisted to see how the others fared. Phameas had Dexion and Homer held the High Priestess in a vice-like grip, the pairs pinned against the mast. Leander and Hektor were crouched by the bow. Jason clung to the steering oars, his hair and clothes whipping about his body. The crew were pinned in their seats and those who hadn't lost their oars were fighting to hold on to them.

Evan watched as Jason lost his footing and was tossed back and forth like a ragdoll. If he didn't get help, Evan knew Jason would either have every bone broken or be thrown overboard. He placed his arms on the sodden deck and slithered out from his seat like a serpent. The ship pitched and rolled; Evan rotated to one side of the ship. The vessel lurched the other way and Evan plunged headfirst towards his original position.

He slid as the ship pitched and was propelled headlong towards the starboard side. The oarsmen watched wide-eyed as he catapulted towards them. Part of the sail had broken away from the mast and with it the rope that had fastened it to the post. Evan gritted his teeth and flung a hand out to the flailing rope. He grabbed it after a few missed attempts and hauled himself towards the mast.

To Evan it seemed to take forever to reach the mast. When he did, he anchored himself against it. He pulled the rope free from the sail and tied it around his waist. He then began to crawl across the deck towards Jason.

The continuous rolling and precarious angle of the ship slowed Evan's progress. The rope saved him many times from nosediving into the churning sea. The bow speared upright into the air and Evan slid across the deck to where Jason clung on to the oars, the sea lapping at his feet. The ship slammed onto the sea's surface, the force of the impact causing Jason to let go. Evan flung himself at Jason and grabbed his arms.

Waves and wind buffeted the ship, the water jettisoning across the deck with remorselessness. To Evan it seemed the maelstrom would never stop. Jason grunted and, with Evan's body as an anchor, shimmied closer to the steering oars.

'If we get out of this alive, I am going to find the nearest tavern and drink until I cannot stand!' Jason yelled.

Evan gave him a wry smile. 'I will join you!'

Hours later it fell silent. Evan loosened his grip on Jason's arms and surveyed the now-calm sea. He let go of Jason, untangled the rope and sat up. Jason got to his feet.

'Gods,' Jason muttered and then voiced expletives.

The ship was strewn with remnants of the sail, rope and broken timber. Half the mast was missing. Many oars were lost and the rest damaged, some beyond repair.

'At least we didn't lose anyone in the mayhem,' Evan said after Jason finished his tirade.

'No, must be grateful to gods for that at least. The problem now is getting this hunk of wood to a port for repairs. We're at the mercy of the currents, and let's hope they don't take us to hostile shores.' Jason shook his head and went to check on his men.

Evan picked his way through the debris to Phameas and Dexion.

'Are you all right?' he asked. Evan squatted.

'We're fine,' said Phameas. He looked about the ship. 'Though the *Argo* appears to have taken the brunt of the attack. At least she still floats.'

'Thank goodness for small mercies,' said Evan, glancing around. He frowned, seeing Leander hovering over Homer and the High Priestess. 'That doesn't look positive.' He stood and walked over.

Leander looked up at him, his face pale and grim. 'She was knocked unconscious and we can't wake her.'

Evan turned to Homer. 'May I take a look to determine whether she has a bump on her head?'

Homer bit his lip and nodded.

Evan knelt by the two and ran the tips of his fingers over her head. 'She has a good size lump on her head, a few centimetres from her hairline.' He then checked her pulse. It was slow but steady. 'There's not much we can do until we land and find a physician. Until then, keep her comfortable and put a damp cloth against the bump to help reduce it.'

'I'll do that,' Leander said.

'Thought you might volunteer,' said Evan. 'Make sure you keep the compress as cool as possible.'

'I'll help too,' said Dexion.

'Let me know if you notice any changes,' said Evan.

'What do we watch for?' asked Leander.

'If her eyes start flickering under the eyelids, her breathing increases or the colour on her face improves, to start with.'

Leander swapped places with Homer.

'We need to help clear the deck and try to restore order,' said Evan.

An hour later, the debris was sorted; what could be salvaged was kept, and the rest tossed into the sea. Evan joined Jason and a few of his men, who were leaning over the rail and peering at the hull of the ship.

'Is it damaged?' he asked, taking a look.

'Considering what we went through, the *Argo* is in sound condition,' Jason said, straightening. He moved along the length of the ship and examined the timber. 'We need to land, and soon. It will take weeks if not months to repair the damage.' He eyeballed Evan, his expression grave. 'You have very serious enemies who do not want you to find whatever you are seeking.' His attention strayed to where Leander nursed the High Priestess. 'How serious is she?'

'Not good,' Evan said. 'There could be complications we're not aware of after her being struck on the head that hard. If she wakes up soon, that's good. If not...'

'The gods may come to her aid,' Jason said.

'We can only wait and see. Without the High Priestess, we cannot finish what we've been tasked to do,' said Evan. 'I don't want to put you, your men and your ship in any further danger. Once we arrive at a port, we'll scout for another crew and ship to sail to Krete.'

'Not a chance, Evandros. My ship and crew have seen and encountered plenty of strange occurrences sailing the Bosporus and Black Sea. By Poseidon, we survived the clashing rocks! We will not allow these disruptions stop us from taking you to Krete and back to Atlantis,' said Jason clapping Evan on the shoulder.

'You and your crew are good men, Jason. I will make sure you are paid well,' Evan said.

Jason laughed. 'My friend, we are happy to have the opportunity to search for the gold of King Minos and take what is there.'

'It's yours as far as I'm concerned,' said Evan. He looked across the now-calm blue sea. 'Do you know where we are?'

Jason nodded. 'You won't like it. We are close to the Hellespont. Traders like myself use this route to enter the Isthmus to explore the wealth of the eastern regions.'

'We are that far north?' Evan said, and then rubbed hard his stubbled cheek. 'The Cyclops really did push us way off course. How long will it take to get to Krete after the *Argo* is seaworthy?'

'It is at least a four-week journey,' Jason said, scratching his head. 'We may be two to three months away from Krete, depending on available supplies to fix the *Argo*.'

'Dammit!' Evan wanted to scream.

'I am sorry, Evandros.'

'It's not your fault, Jason. It has happened and now it's time to adjust and work with it. Where do you hope we land?'

'If we drift into the north-eastern current, then we have a good chance at landing close to Ilios. Our other, lesser options are one of the many islands.'

'I'd like to see Ilios,' said Evan. The unfortunate diversion might turn out to be fortuitous after all, and offer a chance to see the legendary city of Troy. 'I've heard a lot about Priam's city.'

'You may be disappointed, as the city is not as grand as it was when King Priam ruled. The majesty of the place can still be seen, though you do need to look past the run-down buildings,' said Jason.

'The war would have destroyed much of the palace and city,' Evan said, somewhat disheartened.

'The survivors tried to rebuild, but in the wake of Priam's death and his family, looters ravaged the capital. Not that there was much left after King Agamemnon and his army had plundered the city.' Jason sighed.

'What is it?' Evan asked.

'I was thinking of the last time we stopped at Ilios, and meeting King Priam to negotiate a pass through the Hellespont. A ruthless man but fair.'

Evan stared at him. 'You met King Priam? That was, what? Over six hundred years ago! How is that even possible? How old are you?'

Jason laughed and tapped the side of his nose. 'Nothing is impossible, son of Zeus.'

Evan's jaw fell open. 'What...? Are...?' He rubbed his brow. 'Did...? This is way too much. The chance meeting at the gulf of Corinth, and then at Piraeus—were they orchestrated? By Zeus?'

Jason grinned. 'The possibility of our paths crossing may have been difficult if Divine Zeus hadn't explained what he wanted.'

'And you agreed to do it?' Evan was incredulous.

'One cannot refuse the King of the Gods when he demands your assistance,' Jason admitted.

'That sounds about right,' Evan said, his stomach hardening. 'Jeez, did you land in a pile of hot sticky manure. What did he offer you?'

'Immortality and riches,' said Jason with frankness.

'Nice carrot he offered you,' said Evan, shaking his head.

'What's a carrot got do with it?' Jason asked with a quizzical frown.

Evan ignored the question. 'How much did Zeus tell you about this expedition and of me?'

'He said his son and companions were on an important errand of the gods and needed the best captain, crew and ship to provide passage across the Corinthian Gulf.'

'That's it?'

Jason nodded. 'Not long after we dropped you off on the northern shores, Divine Zeus came to me and instructed we head for Piraeus and await your arrival. We were to take you wherever you must go and then home to Atlantis.'

'He knew all along what was going to happen.' Evan pursed his lips and his nostrils flared. 'The slimy bastard planned it all along.'

Jason recoiled. 'You should not curse the gods, in particular one as powerful as your father.'

'I don't care, and he knows what I think of him,' said Evan arms straight, hands locked into fists. 'He should have told me! Instead, we floundered around, I was stabbed in a sword fight, and almost got killed in an earthquake, nearly bitten by snakes, attacked by a friggin' sea monster, and now the giants. If we were prepared, we could have avoided these incidents.'

Jason regarded him in silence for a few minutes and said, 'If the gods were to give us everything on a gold platter, then we would not learn or fight to survive. It is our intelligence that allows us to strive and adapt to circumstance, both the mundane and harrowing. The fact my crew and I are here, is proof Divine Zeus is giving you the best chance to stay alive and complete your quest.'

'You may believe that, but I don't. I wouldn't even be here if it wasn't for my useless counterpart, whose ineptitude had Zeus replace him with me. I can't wait until this is over and I get to go home.' Evan glanced across the deck and watched Dexion help Leander with the High Priestess while Phameas, Homer and Hektor sat nearby. 'I am glad you and your men are here, Jason. I do not mean to offend you with my anger and frustration. This journey has been a difficult adjustment for me, and one that I plan to rectify soon.'

CHAPTER FORTY-SIX

'How is she?' Evan asked Leander as he knelt next to him. He took in the pallor of her face and her slow breathing.

'No change,' said Leander.

'Have you checked the bag of medical supplies the physician in Kyrene gave the High Priestess?' Evan asked.

'I would not dare touch anything that belonged to the High Priestess,' Leander said horrified.

'In this circumstance, I don't think she would mind.' Evan stood. 'Are those her bags by the prow?'

Leander nodded. Evan strode over to the bags and grabbed the larger one. He returned with the bag and flipped the lid. He pulled out various small vials and pouches and read the labels.

'See anything that may help?' Leander asked.

'Not so far,' said Evan.

'What are you looking for?' asked Phameas.

'Something with a pungent smell that may revive the High Priestess,' Evan answered.

'We should ask the Mother Goddess to heal the High Priestess,' said Hektor.

'You go do that.' Evan pawed through the bag, ignoring Hektor.

'Phew! That would wake up the dead,' Phameas said, pulling a face. He handed the noxious pouch to Evan.

'Yuck, that is awful.' Evan waved the small bag under the High Priestess' nose. Leander moved his head, scrunching his nose. Evan moved the bag away and they waited for a reaction.

'What else is in here?' said Evan when there was no response. He and Phameas resumed their search. They looked at each other, the bag empty.

'There have to be some herbs or medication that will wake her,' said Leander in a strangled voice. 'I will not let her die; not here and not like this.'

'We went through every item, and I'm reluctant to give her any medication if I don't know what it is for. The best we can do for now is keep her comfortable and give her water,' said Evan, sitting back on his heels. 'As soon as we land, we'll ask after a doctor. I am sorry, Leander.'

'You talk to the Mother Goddess. She healed you when you were injured,' Leander said.

'I...'

'Please, Evandros.' Leander gazed at him, eyes watering.

'All right, I'll give it a go, but I can't promise she will listen to me,' said Evan. 'I'll go over there.' He got to his feet and moved away. He stood facing the sea. 'How am I supposed to do this?' He glanced over his shoulder and saw them watching with expectation. 'Sheesh… just what I need, an audience.'

'Mother will answer whether you speak to her out loud or through your mind,' said Dexion.

Evan jumped. 'You scared the living daylights out of me!'

'Sorry.'

'You're the best person to contact the Mother Goddess,' said Evan, 'after all, you have a connection with her.'

'I have reached out to Mother and explained what happened,' said Dexion.

'Oh good, then I don't have to,' said Evan, relieved. 'What did she say she was going to do?'

'Nothing.'

'What? Why not? The High Priestess is her representative.'

'Mother won't let her die and said help is near,' Dexion said.

'I guess that is good news, but she can heal the High Priestess here and now,' said Evan.

'Mother says we're about to land and it's important we stop here for a while.'

'Is that all she said?' Dexion nodded. 'That's a tad cryptic.' Evan pondered him for a moment. 'Have you had any visions?'

Dexion shook his head. 'The gods are quiet. I'm not getting any information from them.'

'I don't like the sound of that,' said Evan. 'Has this happened before?'

'No.'

'Either they've decided to remain silent to prevent Kronos and Eris from listening in, or...'

'Or the Dark Master has found a way to stop them from channelling to people with my ability,' finished Dexion.

'And Zeus hasn't worked it out,' Evan concluded. 'Looks as if we can't rely on using your visions to obtain information, not for the time being.'

'I am sure Divine Zeus and Mother will soon learn of the problem,' said Dexion with certainty.

'No doubt, but until they do, we'll keep it to ourselves.' Evan turned to where the others sat with Leander, keeping vigil over the High Priestess. 'They don't need to know your prophecy radar isn't operating.'

CHAPTER FORTY-SEVEN

'Land larboard side, Captain!'

'Thank the gods.' Jason exhaled, the relief evident on his face. He adjusted the steering oars to match the currents and headed for the small speck on the horizon. 'We are fortunate. Our freshwater stores are almost non-existent, and the huge waves of salt water ruined the fresh food we had. It appears the gods have been watching over us.'

'If that's what helps you sleep at night,' Evan said under his breath.

'What's that?' Jason asked.

'I'm looking forward to drinking fresh water and having solid ground under my feet.' Evan didn't want to upset Jason by saying it was the undercurrents and dumb luck that land was sighted. With a handful of oars in working order and the mast broken during the Cyclops' storm, progress was as slow as a snail's pace. 'We should arrive early morning, yes?'

'Judging by the strength of the currents, and by the will of the gods, we should reach land sometime during the night,' Jason said.

'It may be risky to go too close to the land while it's dark.'

'Indeed, there's no way of knowing what dangers lay ashore. If we do come within sight of land at night, we'll anchor until morning.'

'A wise precaution. In the meantime, what would you like us to do to prepare the ship for landing?' Evan asked.

'Tie anything down we didn't lose in the storm,' Jason said. 'Any improvement on the High Priestess?'

'Not yet.' Evan wiped a hand across his mouth. 'It appears the bump on her head is more extensive than we first thought.'

'Let's hope there is an able physician on the island who can help her regain consciousness,' Jason said.

Evan nodded. 'If there isn't, then we're in trouble. We can't finish our mission without her.'

It did not take long to secure loosened objects as much of the equipment had been swept away by the massive waves. Evan and Phameas checked on the High Priestess, over whom the ever-vigilant and devoted Leander sat watch. With the exception of attending to his ablutions, he remained with her at all times.

'Land has been sighted,' Leander said, glancing up at them.

'Yes. We're a day or less away from landing.' Evan gazed at the High Priestess' serene, flawless face. He couldn't understand why the Mother Goddess hadn't healed her priestess as she had cured him.

'That is great news,' said Leander. 'The sooner we arrive, the better, and gods willing, I hope there is someone who can help the High Priestess.'

'As soon as the ship is secured, we'll search the island for a village,' said Evan.

'How long we will be on the island before setting off for Krete?' asked Hektor.

'Hektor, the most important things we should concentrate on are getting aid for the High Priestess and fixing the ship,' said Leander, his brows drawn in angry line. 'Without either, we won't be going to Krete.'

Evan could feel the corners of his mouth twitching and worked hard not to smile.

'Of course, I'm sorry, Leander, I didn't mean to offend,' Hektor said, his words stilted.

'It may be prudent you think first before speaking,' said Leander, words clipped and tone terse. 'We are in an unfortunate situation, and your insensitive remarks are best left unspoken.'

Hektor's face turned a blotchy red, and his jawline tightened.

'Homer, why don't you and Hektor go and give a few of the rowers a break?' said Evan. 'Phameas and I will come and relieve you in an hour.'

Homer nodded and, with a hand on Hektor's shoulder, ushered him away.

'I'll apologise to Hektor later,' said Leander, his tone still heated. 'I know he is loyal, and a good man in a fight, but he doesn't stop and think first before speaking. The conversations we've had on when not to talk have not penetrated his thick head.'

'No arguments from me,' said Evan.

'You haven't helped either with the way you goad him,' Leander snapped.

'Whoa there, Leander,' Evan said, eyes narrowing. 'You are anxious and I will give you latitude as you are worried about the woman you love. But I will not be blamed for Hektor's behaviour and inability to be a decent person. His actions and words are the result of his failings, not mine.'

'I am sorry, Evandros. It's difficult to see her like this. I don't understand why Mother hasn't healed her as she did you,' said Leander in a worried tone.

'I wonder at that too,' said Evan, sighing.

Jason decided to continue sailing at nightfall rather than setting anchor and had his men light torches at the prow. Four members of the crew kept a keen eye on the water and rotated with four other men on the hour. With the gradual movement of the ship, it was easier to maintain watch for anomalies. One man had whispered that the God of the Sea was vengeful, and if he became aware of Jason violating the law of the sea, they would be doomed for eternity, as no mortal should ever try to outsmart a god.

Evan began to nod off. The silence on the deck and the gentle lull of the ship had a soothing effect. He was startled into wakefulness by Phameas' vigorous shaking.

'What is it?' he said in a grumpy voice.

'Listen.' Phameas put a cupped hand to his ear. 'We're no longer on the open sea.'

Evan sat up, wide awake. He stood and peered over the black sea and smiled. He recognised the sound of waves crashing against the shoreline.

'Thank goodness.' He clapped Phameas on the shoulder. 'What a relief, we've made it.' He sat back down and Phameas joined him.

'Never in my years as a sailor have I seen monsters or encountered such calamity,' said the Phoenician.

'I've seen a few monsters, but they were the human kind,' said Evan, yawning. 'Dexion did warn you that your beliefs would be challenged if you came along, not to mention the danger we'd be facing.'

'Aye, he did, and I don't regret my decision,' said Phameas in a cheerful voice. 'The stories I'd have to tell when this is over would entertain people for generations.'

Evan chuckled and yawned again. 'That they would, my friend.'

The last thing he heard was Jason yelling out orders for anchors to be dropped. They'd wait until sunrise to determine whether it was safe to sail into the cove.

CHAPTER FORTY-EIGHT

'We must get the High Priestess off the ship.' Leander stood over Evan and Phameas. 'Perhaps being on land will help her recovery.'

Evan blinked, shook his head and raised his hand to shield his eyes. 'That would be difficult, as we're nowhere near the shore.'

'Not so, we're about to land,' said Leander. 'Jason resumed sailing as soon as the sun rose.'

Evan rubbed his face and got to his feet. 'Why didn't someone wake me?'

'There was no need, until now.' Leander rocked back and forth on his feet. 'How are we going to get the High Priestess off the boat?'

'Geez, Leander, give me time to clear my head.' Evan pinched the bridge of his nose and stifled a yawn. 'We've got to beach the ship first before we can do anything.' He glanced down and saw Phameas was still asleep. He stooped and shook his shoulder. 'Hey, Phameas, wake up! We're landing soon.'

Phameas swatted at Evan's hand and mumbled.

'Come on, Phameas. Time to get up.'

'You have disrupted a very pleasant dream. I was surrounded by a bounty of beautiful women vying for my attention.' Phameas raised himself on an elbow and glared up at them. 'It is rude to wake a man from a gratifying experience such as the one I was having.'

Evan laughed. 'You can return to your exotic dream tonight.'

Phameas grunted and stood. 'One does not have the same dream twice.'

'Perhaps you'll have a better and more enjoyable one,' said Evan, eyes twinkling.

'I'd have more luck at winning Senet,' Phameas said. 'Now, what is the problem?'

'We need a way to get the High Priestess from the ship and onto land,' said Leander.

'Easy,' said Phameas with a shrug. 'With Jason's permission, we use the mast as a sling to lower the High Priestess.'

'Why didn't I think of that?' said Leander, slapping his forehead.

'Your mind is too full of the High Priestess and has no room to consider anything else,' Phameas said with frankness.

Evan bit his lip and avoided looking at Leander's astonished face. Phameas looked at the tall men.

'Well, it's true, is it not? A man's mind can be addled by thoughts of a woman.'

Evan cleared his throat and fought to keep a straight face. 'It's more complex, the feelings a man has for a woman, and they do have a way of consuming a man's mind and physical urges.'

'Very true.' Phameas sighed.

'My relationship with the High Priestess is nothing like you are suggesting,' Leander said, face reddening.

'We know that, Leander, it's a little more complicated,' said Evan in an even tone. 'For one, she is my sister.'

Leander's face turned a few shades lighter than his golden tan. 'Gods! I had forgotten. My apologies, Evandros. I didn't mean to offend.'

'Lucky for you, I am a tolerant brother and I believe you are an honourable man. She could do worse.'

Leander gaped at him, then the colour returned to his face and his brows drew together. 'I have every...' He stopped and his expression lightened. 'You had me believing that you did not approve of my affections and intentions for your sister.'

'I know, and it was priceless to see you squirm and get indignant.' Evan grinned. 'And you don't need my permission or approval, you need hers, which I don't think will be an issue.'

'You don't know how relieved I am to hear you say that.' Leander's shoulders sagged.

The men were quick to transfer the High Priestess to the shore as soon as the ship was beached. They used the mast to make a temporary shelter for her and made her as comfortable as possible. Jason organised his crew to scavenge the beach and nearby trees and shrubs for driftwood while he and a few others assessed the vessel's damage.

Evan gazed at the pristine blue water, the gentle lapping summoning him. He reached the water's edge and the tide swept over his feet and receded. The soft white wet sand sank beneath his feet, both soothing and calming. Soon his feet were covered. Evan closed his eyes and relished the refreshing water as it lapped over his feet and splashed against his legs. He pulled off his khiton, threw it behind him, waded in and dove into the water.

The rush of water filled his ears, and he swam until his lungs urged him to surface for air. He took in a deep breath and treaded water enjoying the solitude. He lay back, arms and legs spreadeagle, and closed his eyes. Nothing but the gentle waves cushioning his body and the ripple of waves created a peaceful haven. He always felt at home by the sea. If he was from this era, as Zeus insisted, Evan understood why he had learnt to swim at an early age, and the solace he felt whenever he was near the ocean. Evan opened his eyes and treaded water again. That was a big if. He still believed there was a logical explanation for what he was experiencing. He saw Phameas, Dexion and Homer in the water and swam over to join them, not wanting to dwell on the why or how he had gotten there.

Sometime later, they went ashore and joined Leander and Hektor, who were sitting under the shelter with the High Priestess.

'We'll explore the island for a town and hope it is occupied by people and that there's a doctor amongst them. If not, I don't know what else we can do,' Evan said.

'I don't believe that is necessary.' Leander's attention was fixed eastwards.

'What is it?' Evan asked.

Leander stood. 'It appears as if we have been discovered.'

Evan ducked out from under the shelter, the others following.

'That can't be good,' he said.

They stared at the strange procession that marched towards them. Armed warriors sat astride horses four abreast, the column stretching at least three kilometres, and at the rear was a horse-drawn cart. The leader, flanked by two warriors, headed the column. Evan shielded his eyes, the sun reflecting off the bronze armour and black-plumed helmets.

Jason and his men joined them as the newcomers neared. The leader pulled back on the reins and raised a hand, halting the army stopping a short distance from their position. The commander dismounted with practised ease, and two warriors were quick to follow. The warrior took off the helmet and shook their head.

'It's a woman!'

Her two guards removed their helmets, garnering more responses of disbelief. They signalled, and the rest of the mounted warriors dismounted. The honey-blonde-haired woman tucked the helmet under her arm and surveyed the dishevelled men.

'Who's in charge?' she asked.

Homer pushed Evan forward.

'I guess that would be me,' said Evan, with a glower at his brother.

'What brings you here?' The warrior turned her piercing gaze on him.

'We were caught in a storm and blown off course.' He swung his hand out to the *Argo*. 'As you can see, the ship was damaged, and the currents brought us here. We'll be on our way as soon as we have repaired the ship. More pressing is that we need a doctor for our High Priestess, who was injured in the storm.'

'I am sorry to hear your High Priestess is unwell,' the woman lamented. 'I will have my royal physician attend to her. Where is she?'

'Here, under the shelter,' Leander said, stepping forward.

She beckoned one of her guards. 'Return to the palace and bring the physician.'

The guard gave a quick nod, spun on her heel and, with extraordinary agility, leapt on the back of her horse, and thrust her helmet on. She was galloping away before Evan and the others could blink. A warrior from the front row stepped into her position by the leader. Evan watched the swift precision and discipline of the warriors as they moved to fill the vacated stations.

'I am Queen Antioche. Welcome to the Island of Hephaistos.'

Homer elbowed Evan. 'Quit doing that,' he said in a whisper, and addressed the queen with a slight nod. 'Good morning, Queen Antioche. I am Evan...dros. My companions: Homer, Phameas, the boy Dexion, Leander, Hektor, and this is Jason, captain of the *Argo*, and his crew, the Argonauts.'

The queen scrutinised each man as Evan introduced them. 'We have brought food,' she said when he finished speaking. She signalled for the cart.

'Hearing of your arduous journey, I assume you haven't eaten or had much water to drink.'

'Our food and freshwater stores were contaminated during the storm,' said Jason. 'We ate and drank what we could salvage.'

'I hope you brought enough.' Phameas gave her a lopsided grin.

She smiled, the transformation highlighting her grey eyes and beauty. 'There is enough food, water and wine for everyone.'

The driver of the cart stopped alongside the queen and her guards. The crew gasped and gawked. *Some things never change*, Evan thought, bemused. Food was not the only load on the cart; scantily clad young women alighted from the rear, their hair coiffed and faces made up. Their faces were painted white, which contrasted against their kohl eyeliner and eyeshadow. The rouge on their cheeks was stark, with bright circles and dots to resemble the sun. The women carried baskets of bread and fruit and mingled with the men as they handed out the food. Evan took a piece of leavened bread and an orange and smiled his thanks at the pretty girl. She gave him a bashful smile and moved on.

'Is there anything else I can help you with?' the queen asked, watching the interaction and distribution of the food and beverages.

'Yes,' Jason answered, and swallowed a morsel of bread he'd bitten into. 'To repair our ship, we require timber, rope, dowels and hammers. Do you have such supplies we could purchase?'

'The island doesn't have a great forest, not enough for your needs. We have very good trade relations with many Ionian cities, and I could arrange for an exchange of goods for the timber and rope for you. However, my merchant ships are abroad, but as soon as they return, I will send them to those cities,' the queen replied.

'My thanks,' Jason said, bowing. 'Would it be possible in the meantime for me to have my men search for wood to begin repairs?'

She shrugged. 'Of course, if you are able to find what you need, but as I've said, there aren't a lot of trees on the island.'

'How long will it take for your ships to return?' Evan asked.

'It will depend on whether they sell everything.' She turned her grey eyes on him. 'They could be away for three months.'

Evan felt his gut tie in knots. More time lost, time that delayed him going home.

'Is there something wrong?' the queen asked, tilting her head to the side, concerned.

'I was hoping we'd be back sailing sooner, is all,' Evan said.

'I will do what I can to expedite the help,' she said. Her attention was drawn to the scattering of her attendants and the men who followed them like puppies, keen for their attention. 'To appease your concerns, I'd like to invite you to come to the palace and join me for a meal this evening.'

'That is very generous, Your Highness but we cannot impose on your hospitality any more than what you have already offered,' said Evan.

Phameas and Jason stared at him as if he'd lost his mind.

'Nonsense,' the queen said. 'I will send a retinue of my royal guard to escort you when the hour arrives.' A warrior approached her and spoke to her in a low voice. 'I've been informed my physician has arrived. We will depart after her assessment on your High Priestess.'

She moved away and approached an older woman who carried a heavy-looking black bag. They spoke amongst themselves and then the queen pointed to the shelter. The woman nodded and, escorted by the warrior who was sent to collect her, she entered the makeshift tent. She shooed out Leander and Hektor. Leander exited, arms crossed and wearing a dour look.

'Why don't we sit and wait by the water?' said Evan. 'I'm sure the doctor will tell us what to do following her examination of the High Priestess.'

'In all my travels, I have never seen female warriors,' said Phameas, unable to take his eyes from the unspeaking, watchful and well-armed soldiers. 'They are impressive, if not a little intimidating.'

'I believe that is the point,' said Evan. He thrust his chin at Jason's crew, who were still peacocking. 'Your men may want to be careful in their actions regarding the women; I don't think the queen will be generous or forgiving if they get carried away.'

'There is no harm in a little fun,' said Jason, grinning. 'Besides, after what we've been through, they deserve some raucous diversions.'

'Not if it offends and takes a woman's liberty without her consent.' Evan glowered.

'What is wrong with you? A man has needs, and the woman must do as he demands,' said Jason. 'Women do not have a say in what we men require; they follow our commands.'

Evan shook his head. 'Rubbish. You treat women with respect. It's what they deserve. You will be surprised by what they offer in return.'

'Women are treated the way we mandate and are answerable to men,' Jason said, crossing his arms against his chest.

'I'd like to see you say that to Queen Antioche,' said Evan. 'I bet she has a different opinion.'

'The healer has finished,' said Leander, standing.

She walked straight to the queen, who listened as the older woman talked. The queen looked at them with a grave expression. They spoke a little longer and then the queen walked over. Evan stood, brushing the sand from his hands, and he and Leander moved to meet the queen.

'My healer informs me your High Priestess' heart has a strong and steady beat. She is, however, concerned with the lack of response to the tests she did,' the queen said. 'She would like to bring the High Priestess to the palace, where she can treat her.'

'Why can't she administer to the High Priestess here?' Leander asked, brow wrinkled.

'My physician has exceptional facilities in the royal palace and remedies at her immediate disposal. She can observe the High Priestess while in her care and make modifications to the tonics.'

'We appreciate your hospitality, Queen Antioche, but we'd feel more comfortable if your doctor treated the High Priestess here,' said Evan.

'In the case of healing, I defer to my skilled and knowledgeable physician. I agree with her assessment and believe it is best for the High Priestess to be taken to the palace. I understand your concerns, and to allay any fears, I will show you where she'll be nursed when you come this evening,' the queen said.

Evan turned to Leander. Though not happy with the arrangement, they agreed to the queen's proposal.

'Very good,' Queen Antioche said, smiling. 'The High Priestess will be my special royal guest while she is in my home.'

CHAPTER FORTY-NINE

Jason's men dispersed the minute the queen and her entourage left. Evan and his companion watched as the procession wound its way over the sandy hill and disappeared down the other side. With the High Priestess gone, a sombre mood descended on them like a leaden rain cloud. Even though Evan knew his relationship with the High Priestess wasn't easy, her absence made him anxious. He rubbed his brow. He sensed something was off but couldn't work out what.

'We need to keep occupied,' Evan said. 'That way we don't dwell on what we cannot control. I'm sure Jason will have a job for us until the queen sends for us.'

Homer, Hektor and Leander assisted Jason and his men with lifting and moving the *Argo* while Evan, Phameas and Dexion were sent to purchase rope. They set off and followed the path the queen and her entourage had taken earlier.

'Which way do we go?' asked Phameas, looking left and then right.

They came to a forked trail: one branch went north, towards mountain ranges and the other went east.

'Let's go that way.' Evan pointed to the path that led away from the mountains.

'Quite barren, this island. The queen wasn't lying about the lack of trees,' said Phameas, after they had travelled a few kilometres.

'Don't you think it's odd how the queen turned up soon after we landed? Or am I being too suspicious?' Evan asked.

'Most monarchs keep watch of their coastlines. It's the best way to keep out thieves and invaders,' Phameas replied. 'What other reason could she have?'

'I don't know. With everything that has happened, I am wary.' He turned to Dexion. 'Have you had any signs or messages?'

Dexion shook his head.

'That worries me too.' Evan took in the rocky landscape, broken by a scattering of spindly trees and scrub.

'Maybe the dream I had is fortuitous,' said Phameas with a wide and easy grin. 'My dream of being surrounded by attentive women came true! Could the gods have gifted me with Dexion's ability, seeking another vessel for their message?'

Evan stopped and stared at him. *Would they do that? Why would they do that?* He toyed with the possibility for a few seconds. 'I don't think it works that way.'

'No matter. Tonight we spend time with a coterie of beautiful women,' said Phameas, rubbing his hands together. 'Come on, let's get what we need. I want to get back to take a swim and fix my curls.'

Evan almost laughed out loud, thinking his friend was jesting until he saw the look on his face. It was one of anticipation and eagerness. 'Lead on.'

They continued along the path. Phameas and Dexion chatted between themselves, oblivious to Evan's lack of interaction. He couldn't shake the feeling that something wasn't right about their landing. Why this island? And then there was the battalion of female warriors. The only race of women he had read about were the Amazons who lived in the region around the Black Sea, or so some historical sources stated. The existence of a race of warrior women could never be confirmed, yet their feats, unique lifestyle and fearlessness were the stuff of an enduring legend.

'What is that noise?' said Phameas, looking up at the sky.

Evan stopped and waited. When he didn't hear anything, he shrugged and resumed walking.

'There!' Phameas said. 'You had to hear that! It sounds like a squawk and a hoot combined. I've never heard such a strange sound.' He whipped his head from one side to the other. 'It's coming from over there.'

He took off, forcing Evan and Dexion to follow. The cacophony grew louder and more raucous as they drew closer.

'Whatever the animal, it's as if they are travelling with us,' Phameas said, his pace quickening.

They came to a pink lake teeming with birds. They were tall, standing on one spindly leg, with long curved necks and black-tipped beaks that had a downward bend. Disturbed by their presence, the flock squawked louder and took flight, their wingspan casting a shadow on the ground. The three watched as they soared into the sky, a vermillion hue against the brilliant blue vista.

'Flamingos,' said Evan. 'This must be their home.'

'I have never seen such graceful birds,' said Phameas.

'That is surprising with the travelling you have done. Odder still is what they are doing this far north,' said Evan.

An hour later they came to a town, the buildings and layout similar to the Greek settlements. Women emerged from the houses in ones and twos as they entered through the gate. Before long, they were surrounded by a bevy of females. The beaming women were eager to help and offered them refreshments, many carrying jugs filled with wine and platters of food.

'Where are the men?' Phameas asked in a low voice.

'Perhaps they are working in the fields,' Evan said.

Dexion shied away from the persistent women, moving closer to Evan and clasping his hand.

Evan cleared his throat. 'Excuse me, would you have any rope to sell? We require a substantial amount to fix our ship.'

'The stock we have will not be adequate for your purpose,' said one woman. 'Our supplies are just enough for our horses and to hang carcasses.'

'Oh. Is there another town where we can buy rope?' he asked.

Another woman shook her head. 'Items such as rope, we obtain from buying and selling with other cities. I am sure Queen Antioche can assist with your request.'

'Yes, she told us she would when the ships come back from trading,' said Evan. 'Thank you for your time and the food and water. We must return to our ship and friends.'

The women parted and allowed them to pass. Dexion clung to Evan's side and averted his face when a young girl ran up to him and held out a piece of bread.

Evan smiled at the girl and took the bread. 'I will give it to him on your behalf.'

The girl nodded and skipped away, her plait bouncing against her shoulders. Dexion stuck to Evan as they walked back to the entrance. They remained quiet until there was a fair distance between them and the town. Only then did Dexion peel himself away from Evan.

'Here you go,' he said, handing the bread to the boy.

'I've seen many peculiar places, but this has to be the most unusual,' said Phameas. 'There weren't any old men that you usually see in a market or in the streets.'

'There weren't any boys either,' said Dexion, holding the bread in his hand and away from his body as if it were a poisonous object.

'I may be wrong, but my gut is saying otherwise. I think we have stumbled into a colony of Amazons,' said Evan.

'Amazons? I thought they were eliminated hundreds of years ago,' said Phameas. He looked over his shoulder at the diminishing view of the town. 'We didn't believe they existed. How could a race of women be warriors? And fight like men?'

'Would you fight one of them in combat?' said Evan, jerking his thumb back at the population of women. 'What I learnt from my studies is that they were fierce, aggressive and expert horse riders, capable of shooting arrows and hitting their targets while riding.'

'I remember a story my father told me about how Herakles, as one of his tasks, was to bring back Queen Hippolyte's girdle,' said Dexion.

'That's right,' said Evan. 'The belt was given to her by the god Ares as she was the most fearless of fighters. There was a battle, with many of the Amazons killed. I recall reading an article about the origins of these women. It is possible they are Scythians and the women fought alongside the men.'

'There are no men here,' said Phameas.

'Yes, their absence is telling. The fact the Amazons have settled here is peculiar; they were nomads and moved a lot. They were either forced from a nomadic lifestyle because of the expansion of settlements or they came here to protect themselves,' said Evan.

'My father said the Amazons didn't live with men and mated with them when they wanted,' said Dexion.

'That's how they'd propagate their race. In my time in the future, archaeologists found evidence of burial sites with tall, tattooed women who had high status in their communities. They were buried with weapons, just like the men, and when they examined the bodies, they found signs of their being in battles.'

Phameas scratched his head. 'My head aches when you use words I am not familiar with.'

'Sorry, mate.' Evan grinned. 'I do get a little carried away, and besides, you two and Homer are the only ones I can be my true self with.'

'I know.' Phameas paused and asked, 'What is "mate"?'

'It means "friend". It is a common word people use where I am from.'

'Ah... I like it,' said Phameas with a small shrug.

'You need to be careful not to use the word with the others,' Dexion said as he nibbled on the bread.

Evan sighed. 'It slipped out.' Dexion glared at him. 'I'll take more care, I promise.'

Back at the beach, they came to an abrupt stop and stared. Phameas whooped and started running, pulling off his clothes and plunging into the sea to join the Argonauts. Evan and Dexion picked up his discarded apparel and joined Homer, Leander and Hektor. Jason stood in the shade of the ship, hands on hips, and watched on, disgusted.

'What are they doing?'

'They are preparing for dinner,' Jason said, words dripping with scorn. 'They stopped working early so they could spend time washing and sprucing up for an evening with the ladies.' He snorted. 'From the way they are behaving, you'd think they haven't seen a woman in months.'

Evan could not help but laugh.

'Stop that!' Jason admonished. 'Can you believe this? We still have many hours of sunlight to work before the queen sends her warriors, yet here are the fearless and stoic crew of the *Argo*, busy preening themselves *hours* before we need to depart!'

'Perhaps we should consider bathing ourselves,' Hektor said. 'We do not want to offend the queen by being the odorous ones in the group.'

'Everyone has gone mad!' Jason threw his arms in the air and clambered aboard his ship.

Homer chuckled and Leander wore the faintest of smiles.

'How about it? Shall we join them?' Evan said.

CHAPTER FIFTY

The mood on the beach was festive; the men chatted and laughed, clustered in small groups, while they waited for their escort. Jason had succumbed and joined the others in bathing, realising no amount of cajoling his crew would change their minds about going back to work on the *Argo*.

The men went mute at the vision of the advancing female warriors. They marched in unison and with precision, a formidable display giving the impression of armed readiness and skilled fighters. Each was dressed in a short black khiton trimmed with purple, the right shoulder exposed, as was their right breast. Strapped to their backs were crescent-shaped shields, and each carried a bow. Slung over their shoulders were quivers full of arrows, and at their waists were short swords sheathed in a leather halters. The retinue came to a standstill and stood at silent attention. The only sound was the lapping of the water on the shore.

The warrior leading the escort stepped forward. 'Which of you is Evandros?'

Evan raised his hand.

'You and your companions will go first, followed by the captain and his crew,' she said.

Evan bit his tongue. This might not be the right moment to say something glib, given the well-armed troops. Instead he nodded. With a quick glance at the others, he moved towards the escort. The warrior spun on her heels and strode into the gap the cohort had made. With the men flanked on both sides by the warriors, the leader gave a clipped order and the cohort began to march, forcing the men to keep up with them.

They were guided into a valley surrounded by mountains, the slopes sheer and rocky with the occasional tree breaking the stark grey landscape. The mountain pass gave way to pastoral land that rose and fell in gradual waves. Further along was the palace, a line of beacons flickering from the high walls.

The palace was built on a high flat tableau with a wide circuitous ramp, and sheltered below was a village.

A large contingent of women had gathered in the main square to watch the group be led through the streets of the village. Many stood on their toes to get a better look. Dexion wedged himself between Evan and Phameas.

'This must be what it feels like to be a caged animal on view for the public,' he mumbled. He looked closer at the crowd. 'See anything unusual about the women that are here?'

Phameas scanned the faces on one side of the road and then the other. 'They are older, perhaps past their child-bearing years. Much older than our escort.'

'That is interesting, weird and concerning,' said Evan.

As they left the village, the sound of excited voices and boisterous laughter washed over them.

'I wonder what they are laughing at,' said Leander, glancing back with a baffled expression.

Evan's nagging feeling that something was off wouldn't go away. It wasn't that the queen and her legions of women had done anything; they had been most courteous and hospitable. And that was what had set Evan's antenna on high alert. He pushed aside the niggling thoughts for the moment, his architectural side taking over on seeing they had reached the foot of the akropolis.

They began the climb up a steep ramp. On their right was a wall ten kilometres high, and to their left a sheer drop. Their escort had them moving at a brisk pace, and soon they entered a gate with a wide plinth that bridged the span of the wall and covered the gateway. Sentries guarded an open entrance, standing on either side of two large wooden doors lined with bronze. They cleared the entrance and turned a corner to enter another gate that gave way to a smaller entry. They filed into a courtyard, where on the left of which was a stoa with twelve columns and six doorways. They turned right and entered a propylon with a large door.

Evan caught a glimpse of the colourful friezes that depicted female warriors fighting and wanted to stop to study the art on the walls in the propylon, but their escort kept them moving. They came to another, larger courtyard and the leader stopped, forcing Evan to skid to a halt to avoid a collision.

'Inform Queen Antioche her guests have arrived,' she said to a guard standing outside.

The warrior gave a curt nod, turned on her heel and marched between the painted wooden columns, disappearing from sight. While they waited, Evan studied the design of the palace. It was similar in structure to the palace in Pylos, though there were distinct features that emphasised the difference in the styles of painting.

The frescoes showed the partisan relationship between humans and nature, not just hunting and the triumph of capture that was a dominant theme in the palace at Pylos. The images, painted in bright, festive colours denoted joy and love of life and kinship with the goddess of hunting. Her relationship with wilderness and animals as well as childbirth featured in many of the friezes. There were also scenes of war, tales of conquest. Most revealing were those of men conquered by a race of female warriors.

The qualms Evan felt deepened.

CHAPTER FIFTY-ONE

They were ushered through the propylon and emerged onto a smaller, interior courtyard. Guided into an outer hall, they passed columns and scaled stone steps covered in plaster that were adorned in square ornamental motifs.

A wide band of decorated alabaster slabs were fixed to the lower parts of the wall. A pattern of alternating stylised palm leaves and lotus flower tiles were linked by scrolls and rosettes. Embedded within each section were round pieces of blue glass that signified the beginning and end of the design. They stopped at three floor-to-ceiling wooden doors, embossed in bronze with acanthus leaves etched into the metal. The middle door opened and the leader entered the room.

'Queen Antioche, presenting Evandros, his companions, and captain of the *Argo* and the Argonauts,' she said and stepped aside so the men could enter the megaron.

The room was set out like the one in Pylos. A hearth in the centre, with four pillars that supported the beams of a flat roof and a square opening allowing the smoke to escape. Against the east wall was the throne on which sat the queen. The difference between this megaron and that of Pylos was that this one was filled with women.

Evan felt the atmosphere tingle with heightened expectation and something else; it was tangible but elusive at the same time. A whisper of excitement filled the room as they filed in. Evan kept Dexion close and scanned the room. He sensed no danger, but instinct told him this was not an ordinary gathering.

The women were dressed in a colourful array of khitons, some more revealing than others. Each woman had spent time styling their hair: some had it coiffed, while others left their tresses long and curled, with ribbon woven through. The queen stood and the chamber became silent. The men were mesmerised. She wore a sheer white khiton with a bronze shoulder exposed, the elegant folds sculpted to her statuesque body.

Homer nudged Evan forward. He cleared his throat and bowed. 'Queen Antioche, thank you for your invitation. We are honoured to be here.'

'I am pleased you have accepted my offer to dine with us, Evandros of Atlantis,' she replied. There was a collective gasp from her constituents and a quiet excited chatter started. The women stopped when the queen resumed speaking. 'We have a great feast prepared.' She pointed. 'There are cushions, seats and tables for you to sit in comfort, and plenty to eat and drink.'

Evan could feel the heat of the men's enthusiasm as they murmured to each other, eager to move and sit with the waiting women. Leander leaned forward and whispered in his ear. Evan nodded.

'We are grateful for such a warm welcome,' he said, 'but may I ask if it is possible to see how our High Priestess is faring? We are worried about her and would like to visit her.'

Her face became serious. 'Of course, Evandros. I gave you my word that you could see your High Priestess on your arrival. There has been no change, and she will continue to receive the best treatment my healer can provide. I will take you to her now.' She turned to Jason. 'Captain, you and your men may eat. The ladies will attend to your every need.'

The Argonauts did not need further encouragement and fanned out without hesitation. Two to three women sat with each man, offering food and wine. Jason beamed at Evan as he was guided by two women to a corner. Evan shook his head and gave a wry smile.

The queen, and four of her royal guard, shepherded Evan and his companions back into the small courtyard and turned right. They entered a stoa and zigzagged through a maze of corridors, went down a set of stairs, entered a doorway and came to a small enclosed garden. The queen indicated for them to wait and walked through a door. There was a murmur of voices, and the queen reappeared with the physician.

'It's too early to tell whether the High Priestess will respond to the treatment I've started, and I have many more remedies to try,' the older woman said.

'May we see her?' Leander asked.

The physician looked askance at the queen, who gave a brief nod, and she then acquiesced. Leander, eager to see the High Priestess, went first, followed by the others. Besides her pale complexion, the High Priestess looked as if she would wake at any moment. Leander knelt by the bed and took her hand.

'Alexina, I know you can hear me. We are all here. We need you to waken. You are important to us and we cannot go on without you.' Leander swallowed. 'Mother Goddess, please bring her back to us.' He kissed the palm of her hand, laid it back with loving care and stood. His eyes shone bright with unshed tears.

'Have you tried contacting your father?' Evan asked. 'He is the god of healing.'

'I have. He hasn't responded to my requests,' said Leander, chin dropping to his breastbone.

Evan put a hand on his shoulder and gave a reassuring squeeze. 'Keep trying. It's a matter of time. We'll give you a few minutes alone.'

He patted Leander's shoulder, and he and the others left the room. Evan noted with interest the heated discussion between the queen and her physician. A warrior approached them, and they ceased their conversation. Queen Antioche was quick to react and strode towards them, a broad smile dispelling any of the anger she had displayed earlier.

'Let us return to the feast, and you can tell me about your homeland and how the people of Atlantis survived the Deukalion,' she said.

The queen gave her healer a meaningful look before leaving. Evan saw the worried expression on the physician's face as she turned away to check on her patient. Evan frowned. Something was wrong. Somehow he needed to speak to the healer. Alone.

They returned to the megaron, and from the cheerful sounds emanating, it appeared Jason and his men were enjoying themselves. The sentries pushed the door open for the queen to enter. The revelry mellowed. Queen Antioche headed straight to her throne.

Colourful, cushioned seats were arranged on either side of the stone chair. She sat and with a sweeping gesture indicated for them to do the same. Within minutes, three-legged tables were brought out and placed by their sides followed by platters of steaming and aromatic food. Young girls appeared at their sides and poured red wine into black painted cups.

The queen raised hers. 'May the gods watch over us, grant us wisdom and prosperity. To the great Huntress, for bestowing us with the gift of life.' She poured a little wine on the floor and then took a sip. 'Enjoy the feast!'

The room erupted into loud cheers, the megaron swamped with laughter and chatter. The din reminded Evan of an overcrowded and popular pub. The queen picked up a tender morsel of stewed meat and popped it into her mouth. She sat back and watched the banquet, her exquisite face not giving anything away. Evan grabbed a piece of bread and dipped it into the stew.

'Tell me, Evandros, how did your people survive the destruction? Legends say the gods destroyed your home and everyone in it,' the queen said.

Evan swallowed and washed the remnants of food down with a little wine. 'A handful of ships managed to escape the island before the volcano erupted and imploded on itself. One ship was beached on the shores of Egypt, and the others made it beyond the Straits of… um… er… the Pillars of Herakles.'

'You have come from the other side of the Pillars?' she asked, eyes wide. 'What is it like? What is your population? Are there any other peoples?'

Evan had to smile at the barrage of questions. 'It's an island in the middle of an ocean. As to how many people live on the island, I'd say around twenty thousand, and there are other lands with different cultures. I have a question for you.' Evan took a bite of his makeshift roll of meat and vegetables. The queen raised a brow at him. 'How did you know some of us are from Atlantis?'

'You mentioned it in your introductions,' she said, tensing.

Evan sipped at his wine, shook his head and placed the cup on the floor. 'Nope. I think someone told you about us before we arrived.'

'Why do you think that?' she asked in a tight tone.

'One, you were too well prepared when you met us on the beach; two, you knew we were coming; and three…' Evan checked off each point on a finger. 'Well, I can't think of a third reason, and while all this is nice, it's a ruse of sorts.'

'If someone did tell me of your impending arrival, what would I gain from misleading you?' The queen gave him a cool stare.

'To answer the first part of your question: whoever or whatever spoke to you did it to prevent us from reaching our destination. As to why you would trick us, that I haven't worked out,' he replied, tapping the side of his head with a finger, 'but I will.'

She smiled, though it was not a smile of humour. 'Could it be possible that whoever told me who you were thought I might be able to aid you? Your ship needs extensive repairs, and I have the means to help.'

'Granted, that is plausible,' said Evan, 'though considering what we just went through, and previous obstacles, I'm not convinced this encounter is a coincidence.'

The queen leaned towards him revealing the curve of her breasts. 'Then let me assure you…' She paused, her sweet perfume of jasmine wafting over Evan, clouding his concentration. She added in a whisper, 'We will assist you in any way imaginable.'

Evan wasn't sure if it was the warmth from the hearth or the potent wine that addled his brain. The temperature, her proximity and the alluring scent radiating from her body were heady.

He cleared his throat and averted his eyes from the generous view of her cleavage. 'After this evening, I daresay the crew won't need much persuasion.'

Her eyes were twinkling as she surveyed the room. 'They do seem to be enjoying themselves.'

Evan tossed back the remainder of his wine and skimmed the room. He swayed on his seat and clutched the sides. He wiped the sweat from his brow. Opposite sat Homer and Hektor, who were responding to the attentiveness of the beautiful young women, while Leander looked uncomfortable and embarrassed. Phameas was laughing and regaling his trio with stories from his seafaring days. Jason's earlier rant that day was forgotten as he returned the affection given by his group of women, and many Argonauts had retreated to the darker recesses of the megaron to engage in amorous unions.

Evan closed his eyes and felt the room spin. He opened them and the room stopped spinning. 'Whoa, that wine has some juice.' He stood. 'Dexion, get me out of here.'

'Master Evandros, what is wrong?' Dexion held Evan upright.

'I think I'm going to be sick.' Evan swallowed back the rising bile.

Evan staggered out with Dexion's help, and managed to make it outside before throwing up. He wiped his face with a shaky hand. His skin was clammy, hair damp, and his body felt as if it were running a fever. He sat on the cool marble bench and clasped his pounding head in his hands. The queen emerged from the hall with her royal guard. Homer, Leander and Hektor were right behind them.

'The queen is here,' Dexion whispered into his ear.

Evan raised his heavy head and blinked bleary-eyed at the newcomers. Queen Antioche sat next to him and touched his face, her expression marked with concern.

'Shall I call for my healer?' she asked. 'You are very hot.'

'I'll be fine, the fresh air is helping,' he said, dragging a hand over his mouth and chin. 'I don't mean to be rude, but I think it is time for me to leave.'

She frowned. 'Perhaps you should stay. You may need the services of the healer.'

Evan stood and swayed. The queen jumped up and grabbed his arm.

'I think the sea air is what I need right now. Thank you for your kind offer.'

Queen Antioche removed her hand. 'Very well.'

They bid her goodnight, and with Homer and Leander's assistance, Evan tottered back to the beach, collapsed under the makeshift shelter and fell asleep.

CHAPTER FIFTY-TWO

Evan's head pounded and his mouth was as arid as the Egyptian desert the following morning. He cracked open an eye and shut it straight away. The bright sun dazzled and blinded him. He tried again, the vista swimming for a second or two and then stilling. The blueness of the water glistened under the sunlight. Evan sat up with a groan and held his head. The constant ringing grew louder, and his head felt as if it had been jammed in a vice and squeezed until it would explode.

'Oh, good, you are awake,' said Phameas in a cheerful voice.

'Not too loud, please,' said Evan, clasping his head tighter.

'The queen came earlier. She wanted to see you, but you were still sleeping and snoring with enthusiasm,' he added. Evan could hear the laughter in his tone. 'She brought a tonic her healer prepared for you. It will get rid of the pain and nausea.' Phameas held out the cup.

Evan grasped it with a palsied hand and raised it to his mouth. 'Good God! That is horrible!' He spat and spilled some of the muddy liquid over himself.

'She guaranteed it will make you feel better after you drink it,' Phameas said with a deadpan expression.

'You drink it!' Evan thrust the cup back at Phameas, who raised his hands and took a step back.

'I'm not the one with the sore head.'

Evan grimaced and drank a mouthful. The bitter liquid made his mouth water, leaving a thick film on his tongue and greasy residue over his teeth.

'I am not drinking the rest of that! I'd rather have the hangover.' He dropped the cup onto the sand, the murky contents sloshing over the rim. He lay back and closed his eyes.

'The queen has invited us this evening for another feast at the palace,' Phameas said sitting under the shade next to Evan.

Evan opened an eye and looked up at his friend. 'Really?' Phameas nodded. 'I'll pass. I don't think I could stomach any more of that wine.'

'The queen intends to make amends for your unfortunate experience and insisted we attend the banquet.'

'Insisted, huh?'

Phameas nodded. 'She was most adamant. And I agree you should refrain from drinking the wine.'

'That I will.' Evan raised himself on an elbow. 'Did you find last night's gathering unusual?'

'What do you mean?'

'The women; they seemed too attentive.'

'Nothing wrong with a man appreciating the affections of women,' said Phameas, 'and there were more of them than us, so I guess they were vying for our attention.'

There wasn't any competition between the women as they fawned over the men, and he thought the women's consensual sharing was deliberate. Evan didn't verbalise any of this; the way to convince his friend and the others was to observe tonight's gathering.

An hour later, feeling better, Evan got up, the headache gone and the nausea dissipated. The lure of the sea beckoned. He stripped and waded into the cool, soothing water. When the water reached his waist, he dove in, the sound of the outside world and his troubling thoughts floated away. He let himself be carried by the currents, content to drift and enjoy the solitude. He relished in the luxury of peace, glad to be on his own and not surrounded by the others. It wasn't that he minded their company, but he was used to being on his own.

A face came to his mind unbidden. The queen was withholding information, but what? And how was he going to extract that from her? Seduction was a ploy he could use. He grimaced at the idea. It was a form of coercion, and he didn't like to take advantage of a woman in that way, no matter what era she was from. He needed to think of something else before her warriors arrived.

Queen Antioche sat atop her horse, hidden from view, on a crest not far from the activities on the beach. She watched Evandros take off his clothes, and her breath caught as his muscles rippled with movement. She admired the ease with which he strolled to the water and dove. The power behind the strokes as he struck out for the deeper parts of the sea confirmed her decision. He had surprised her during their conversation, revealing he was much more intelligent and astute than she had anticipated. She would have to act, and sooner than she planned.

Her reassessment of their scheme satisfied her it was the right thing to do as she watched him emerge from the water. Nothing would stop her from making him hers. She continued to observe as he wiped himself, appreciating his athletic body and what it promised. She needed to progress with care given the previous evening's disastrous results. The potion must be further diluted. The Atlantean's tolerance for the concoction was much lower than the others', which she thought unusual.

She wheeled her horse about, contemplating what could be done, for she did not want him to become ill again. He was no use to her if he could not function. It was time she and the physician found a more effective method of issuing the right amount of dosage, one that could dull the man's memory but not affect his ardour.

✶✶

Evan had just donned his khiton when Jason returned with less than half of his men later that morning. He gave Evan a slow, easy grin.

'Where are the rest of the crew?' he asked.

'They decided to remain at the palace and enjoy the queen's hospitality,' Jason said.

'What about the repairs to the ship?'

Jason waved his hand with a careless attitude. 'We can't do anything until the supplies arrive.' He put an arm about Evan's shoulder. 'I had the best night in the company of three women. Charming and ever so accommodating.' Jason resumed walking, forcing Evan to move with him. 'How did you fare with the queen?'

'The wine didn't sit well and I left early,' replied Evan. Jason roared with laughter.

'I am sure this evening will prove to be a better night,' he said, eyes gleaming.

'For one, I won't be drinking the wine, and I have a few questions to ask the queen.'

'You worry too much, Evandros. Enjoy the queen's company and don't bore her with chatter. Pay her compliments, for I have a feeling you have more than piqued the queen's interest.' Jason winked at Evan.

'What? Don't be ridiculous. The queen's only offer is to help.'

They stopped by the hull of the beached ship. 'Help indeed. You, my friend, are in for a remarkable evening.' He chortled as he scaled up the side of the *Argo*.

Evan could hear Jason still chuckling as he walked away from the ship.

'There's no way I missed the signals,' he told himself. He thought back to the previous night and tried to recall what the queen had said and his responses. There was a part in their conversation where he supposed there was an allusion to flirting before he'd started to feel unwell. But he dismissed it. There wasn't much to what she or he had said. He did find her attractive, for she was stunning and she had a quick, inquiring mind he found appealing.

'That's all it was and nothing more.'

'What's nothing more?' asked Phameas.

Evan hadn't noticed his approach.

'Something that Jason said that didn't make sense.'

'Oh... okay.' Phameas paused.

'What is it?' asked Evan.

'We were hoping you might answer a question for us as you have a good memory,' said Phameas.

'Do you remember why we are here?' Leander asked.

Evan was stumped by the question. 'Don't any of you recall how we got here?' He turned to Homer, Hektor and Phameas, who shook their heads. 'What about you, Dexion?'

'I do,' the boy said.

'Moloch! We didn't even think to ask Dexion,' said Phameas, slapping his forehead.

'We were forced here by the Cyclops,' said Evan.

'Cyclops? Ah… yes… the great walls of waves crashing and damaging our ship. Perhaps you can answer another question. Why are we so far from home?' said Leander.

Evan frowned at the blank looks on the men's faces. 'We are here to recover relics of the Mother Goddess to stop Kronos and the birth of a new god.'

Their faces brightened.

'Of course!'

'How could we forget!'

'What is wrong with you? How could you forget why Zeus and the other gods put us here? After all what we have been through,' said Evan, his hands on his hips.

'I don't know,' said Leander, shrugging. 'It's as if my mind was veiled and now it has been lifted. I remember everything now.'

'What about the rest of you?' Evan asked.

Homer nodded. *It is as Leander's says. It was like having a part of our minds imprisoned, and you've released our consciousness.*

'This is a concern. We have no way to work out how you lost your memories,' said Evan. 'You were fine yesterday. What caused the change from yesterday to today?'

'We worked on the ship, had a swim and then spent a glorious evening at the palace,' said Phameas.

A worm of suspicion crawled into Evan's mind. 'No one drink the wine tonight.'

'Do you think they poisoned us with the wine?' said Hektor.

'I had a severe reaction to the wine.'

'Perhaps you had too much,' Hektor said.

'Evandros had less than I did,' said Leander.

Homer rubbed his stomach.

'No, it wasn't the food. Dexion still remembers everything,' said Evan, glancing at Dexion, who nodded. 'Right, no wine. Better if we didn't go tonight.'

'That may be problematic. The queen will be sending her guards to collect us,' said Hektor.

'Then avoid drinking the wine,' Evan reaffirmed.

CHAPTER FIFTY-THREE

The sun was setting and cast a rosy hue on the horizon when the queen's soldiers arrived. Jason and his remaining crew were first to greet the armed entourage and did not hesitate to move into formation. From their excited chatter in sharing their experiences with the women, they were eager to reunite and rekindle what had been started.

The men's pace quickened as the palace came into view. Evan's gut gnawed and twisted with each step, compelling him to turn and run back to the beach, but the momentum of the march and the unsmiling warriors prevented him. He looked up and his stomach plummeted.

They had arrived.

The group entered the main gate, passing the watchful sentries, and continued along the same path as the previous evening until they arrived at the doors of the megaron. Jason's men nudged each other, jostling to get in front.

'Stop it!'

'Move out of my way!'

'Ouch! That was my toe!'

'Quit it!' Jason said in a hiss. 'You are not making a good impression.' He nodded at the lead guard, who was watching with growing disapproval.

'Right, sorry.'

'Sorry,' echoed the others, staring down at the floor and shuffling their feet.

The central door was pushed open and the assembly of men ushered into the room. Jason and his men were quick to disperse and disappeared into the throng of women while Evan and his companions were guided to the queen and her handmaidens.

'Good evening, Queen Antioche.' Evan bowed.

'I see you have recovered well, Evandros. My healer's remedy worked,' she said with a smile.

'The medication was effective,' Evan said.

'Good, good. Please sit down. This evening the ladies have prepared dance and music for our entertainment while we eat.'

'I look forward to it,' said Evan, sitting. 'You'll have to excuse me for not drinking any of your wine this evening. I don't want to repeat last night's experience.'

The queen leaned across and laid a hand on his knee. 'The wine was much too strong. I have instructed my attendant to add extra water to your cup.' She sat back, the warmth of her light touch leaving a tingling sensation.

'Thank you for your thoughtfulness, but I'll stick with water,' said Evan.

'As you wish,' she acknowledged. 'Are you hungry?'

'I wasn't earlier, but the smell of the delicious food has stirred my appetite.'

'Very good.' The queen lifted a hand, and serving maids appeared on cue, moving around and offering various dishes. Squid steeped in olive oil and garlic; swordfish cubed and baked with tomatoes; fish roasted whole; a bowl of aromatic lentils, cabbage and onions; boiled quail eggs; and platters of figs and pomegranates.

Evan split his bread in half and used one as a plate. He picked a small portion from each dish and began to eat. Evan was aware the queen watched him, even though she did not make it obvious. She asked questions about Atlantis: what was it like, who were the leaders, and why hadn't the Atlanteans made contact? Evan answered each question, careful not to give too much information. Their conversation was interrupted by the entrance of musicians, who struck up a jaunty piece, eliciting clapping and toe tapping from the revellers.

The musicians played a number of tunes before the dancers entered. Dressed in sheer costumes, their sculpted bodies undulated and writhed in time with the evocative music. Evan was entranced by the gyrations of the dancers, and it took a number of proddings from Dexion to get a reaction.

'What?'

'Queen Antioche wishes for your attention.'

'Oh... my apologies, Queen Antioche. Your dancers are very skilled,' he said with a cough.

'We are taught from childhood how to dance and continue to practise until adulthood.' She stood. 'Would you accompany me outside? I'd like to show you the history of our ancestors.'

'Of course.' Evan placed his cup on the floor and stood. Phameas, Dexion, Homer, Leander and Hektor were ready to follow.

'Just Evandros. Stay and enjoy the company of my handmaidens.'

Phameas and Dexion glanced at Evan. He mouthed for them to stay and followed the queen. In spite of his misgivings, Evan was curious as to why the queen had only invited him. The silence and coolness of the night was a stark contrast to the frivolities gaining momentum in the megaron. The courtyard was well lit with torches, the smoke disappearing into the night sky. Here, in this time, Evan could imagine the Goddess Nyx casting her net across the sky and plunging the world into darkness.

The queen crossed over to the propylon and through to the larger courtyard. She veered right to a columned area where floor-to-ceiling plastered walls were decorated in dynamic scenes. The images of people and animals were lifelike and appeared to be breathing, ready to burst from their two-dimensional existence. The queen walked along the length of the wall frieze. Her royal guard did not accompany them, instead they melted into the dark corners of the quad.

'This is the story of my ancestors and where they came from,' she said.

The frescoes varied from female warriors hunting in verdant forests, to graphic settings of fighting, men and magical creatures, to young girls being taught how to use a bow and arrow.

'Thousands of years ago, my people were subjected to many horrors and debased by men, who treated women worse than animals. Their suffering was great and extreme. Women in the tribes killed themselves rather than continue living. There was one who rallied the women, encouraged them to seize their husbands' weapons and slaughter every man. They collected what possessions they could carry and left town to follow the woman who initiated their freedom. She became Queen Antianira, and under her guidance, the women learnt to become formidable warriors.'

The queen moved on to the next panel. 'They roamed the lands, seeking food and shelter until one day they came to a valley brimming with wild horses. From that day, fighting was on horseback and the women trained to use the bow and arrow. To procreate, our ancestors stole men from nearby villages, and mated with them. The men, after their usefulness was no longer required, were killed.'

Evan blanched. He had read the legend of the Amazons' cutthroat approach to sex, but to hear the story and to see the images made his blood freeze. Amused by his reaction, Queen Antioche continued.

'This race of women became renowned warriors throughout many civilisations. Men did not like the idea of female soldiers and attempted to destroy them through war and rape. I am sure you have heard of Herakles, who stole the belt from Queen Hippolyte.' Evan nodded. She went on. 'With him came Theseus, king of Athens, who kidnapped the queen's sister, Princess Antiope, which led to a war with his city.' She continued to the next panel. 'This was the war with the city of Athens; this one is of the Trojan War, allies of my people; and this'—she pointed—'is the war against the Atlanteans.'

As Evan stared at the chaotic and bloody scene, passages of writing flooded into his vision. 'Queen Myrine led the Amazons and invaded Atlantis. It was the first time Atlantis was defeated in a war.' He reached out and touched the scene with his fingertips, the sound of swords clashing and screams of dying warriors seeming to emanate.

'You know who we are?' The queen was surprised.

'I suspected you were Amazons.' He turned to her. 'Why did you show and tell me your history?'

'To explain who and what we are.' She studied Evan's face as he took a step back to examine the panel.

'How did you come to this island?'

'Our lands were invaded and many Amazons slaughtered, forcing the survivors to flee. Divine Artemis guided our ancestors to this island and told us that here, we would no longer be threatened. We've lived in isolation ever since, much like your people have done.'

'How have you managed to keep your race growing?'

'We have strong trading relationships with other cities along the coast of Anatolia.'

'Ah... and they haven't attempted to take control?'

'There's no need. We provide goods they require, and in turn they supply us with stock we do not have.'

Evan nodded. 'A happy economic balance in which men visiting would think they've come to paradise.' His expression changed. 'You don't still kill men, do you?'

She laughed. 'No, that would be counterproductive to our purpose of keeping strong alliances with our trading cities.'

'I'm guessing the warm reception we received isn't only about helping us.' He jerked a thumb at the megaron. 'You are hoping a few intimate liaisons may, and pardon the word, arise from the celebrations? Somehow, I don't think Jason's men will be averse to the meeting those demands.'

She smiled. 'If there are, as you say, intimate associations between your men and my women, then I am grateful. And if Artemis allows fruit from the unions, I and my people will rejoice in the gifts we have been granted.'

'What of you? Would you be seeking to perpetuate your royal bloodline?' Evan asked.

Queen Antioche's pupils dilated. 'As queen, the suitor must have superior qualities that would match my own.'

A heavy stillness descended. Evan's skin warmed at the intensity of her expression.

'Right.' He looked away and concentrated on the wall frieze, trying to ignore the weight of her words. He cleared his throat. 'Ahem… there are quite a few good men in the megaron. Homer, Leander, Hektor, Phameas and Jason are honourable and intelligent men.'

'Indeed they are, but I have made my choice.'

'Really?' Evan said, wiping his brow. 'I hope you've made a wise choice and that he's a decent chap.'

'I do not doubt he is the right man to fulfil what is required of him.' The queen moved closer, her bare arm brushing against his. He bit his lip. Her proximity sent waves throughout his body. 'You seem a little tense. Is there something I can do to put you at ease?'

Evan gave a short, nervous laugh. 'A jump in the sea would help.'

She ran a finger down his arm. Evan closed his eyes. 'A swim does sound like a nice idea, but I have a better one.'

Evan opened his eyes and stared down at the queen. She grabbed the front of his khiton and pulled him to her. Evan stumbled and wrapped his arms around her to keep from falling. Her hands were trapped against his chest, and her grey eyes darkened as she gazed up at him. Evan's heart beat faster as her hands crept up and her arms encircled his neck. Her nipples pressed against his chest. His gaze dropped to her full red lips, and he lowered his head, their breaths mingling. His mouth covered hers. Evan grasped her backside to hold her closer.

She dragged her mouth away and whispered against his. 'My chambers.' She clutched his hand and with quick steps led him through a series of passages until they came to an entryway with a wooden door. She threw it open, and Evan kicked it shut. He swept her into his arms and in a few swift strides set her down on the bed.

CHAPTER FIFTY-FOUR

*E*ris clapped her hands, twirled and did a little dance. 'This is wonderful, just wonderful. The queen is playing her part with perfection. I could not have planned it any better.'

'What have you done?' asked Kronos, striding across the marble floor.

He stared at the Goddess of Discord and not for the first time doubted whether he had made the right decision in freeing her and allowing her to participate in his plan. Her inability to follow orders and provocative sense of dress made her unsuitable for the role he had assigned to her. When her usefulness was no longer needed, he would send her back to Tartaros with Zeus and his disgraceful siblings.

Kronos smirked. Imprisoning the loathsome and selfish immortals had been his plan for so long, and now it was within his grasp. He knew if he organised well and was patient, it would happen. As to the Mother Goddess, she would pay over and over for her transgressions, just as Zeus had punished Prometheus. The smile disappeared. He must find the Titan, to learn the whereabouts of his miscreant daughter, who had vanished.

Eris gave him a smug look, brimming with unrepressed mirth. 'I have done you a great service, for I have found a way to stop the Atlanteans from finding the final relic.'

'You have not harmed them?' he said with a growl, hands clenched.

She sneered at him, unable to understand his obsession with the siblings. 'No, I haven't hurt your precious toys. I have given them a pleasurable distraction, more so for Evandros than the High Priestess. She was in an accident and at present is unconscious.'

Eris outlined what she had orchestrated, the role of the Cyclops combined with the attack from the Stymphalian birds. She went on, explaining the agreement she had struck with the queen of the Amazons.

'Setting the Argo off course was ingenious, and with Evandros being preoccupied for what will be a long time, you can perform a thorough search for the remaining relic.' Eris crossed her arms against her chest and beamed like a cat that had caught the proverbial mouse.

Kronos was reticent as he observed the activities occurring in the queen's chamber. 'Let us hope the High Priestess does not wake and learn what is happening.'

Eris smiled again. 'The queen has instructed her healer to keep the High Priestess unconscious. This will give you the time you need to thwart the Olympian Gods.'

'My dear Goddess, you have outdone yourself,' said Kronos. Eris' face shone with smugness. 'You applied that limited intellect of yours and came up with a practical strategy.' He then glared at her. 'It is your responsibility to keep watch on what is happening. I do not take well to surprises.'

He left as quick as he had arrived, leaving Eris seething.

'Limited intellect! I will show you what "limited intelligence" can do!' she said, spitting with hatred.

CHAPTER FIFTY-FIVE

'There, there my dear,' said a soothing voice. 'You have a nasty bump on the head.'

'Where am I?' the High Priestess asked, eyeing her surroundings. She did not recognise the woman or the room.

'You are safe, that is all you need to be concerned with,' the woman said with a warm smile. 'That and getting better, of course, which is why you are here.' She reached over to the table and picked up a cup. 'Drink this, it will help you recover.'

'Evandros? Where is my brother? What of Leander? Where are my companions? I want to speak to them,' said the High Priestess, her heart fluttering. She tried to sit up but was unable to move. 'What have you done to me?'

'It is all right, my dear, nothing to be alarmed about,' the healer said, patting her hand. 'The knock on your head has affected your ability to move, but it is temporary. You will regain control of your limbs when you have rested and healed.'

'I want to see my brother!'

'I will send for him. In the meantime, I want you to drink this. I cannot have a guest of the queen, in particular one of such esteemed heritage, not well enough to greet Her Majesty.' The healer gave a benign smile and lifted the cup.

The High Priestess stared at the woman, her mind racing. She remembered being on the *Argo* and how they had been trying to outrun the savage storm the Cyclops had summoned, and the vicious attack by birds. The last thing she recalled was crouching by the mast with Dexion.

'Dexion? Where is Dexion?' she blurted, dread filling her heart.

'The boy?' The High Priestess nodded, the whites of her eyes as luminous as the moon in the night sky. 'He is with your companions. Do not worry, they are safe.' The healer lifted the High Priestess' head. 'Drink this and all will be well. You will see.'

'They are all here? Even Jason and the Argonauts?'

The healer nodded. 'Everyone is here.' She placed the cup against the High Priestess' lips and tipped it, forcing her to swallow the bitter-tasting liquid. The High Priestess searched for the one person she thought who might hear her desperate plea. The healer laid the High Priestess' head back on the pillow. Her breathing slowed, and she struggled to keep her eyes open. A ghost of a smile remained on her face as she fell into a deep sleep, relieved she had managed to be heard.

The healer left the room and called a sentry over.

'Tell the queen we have a problem and I must see her at once.'

The warrior nodded and set off at a quick pace, her shining armour swallowed by the dark recesses of the corbelled passage.

THE END

REFERENCE

"TO DEATH [THANATOS] The Fumigation from Manna." ORPHIC HYMNS 41-86 - Theoi Classical Texts Library, n.d. Web. 30 July 2017. Theoi Project © Copyright 2000 - 2017 Aaron J. Atsma, New Zealand.

LIST OF MAIN CHARACTERS

ATLANTEANS

Evan/Evandros—Twenty-First Century Architect/Master scribe and scholar

Zeus—God of Gods and Father of Gods

Alexina—High Priestess to the Mother Goddess

Leander—Water Master

Homer—Master of Husbandry

Hektor—Master Engineer

Phameas—Phoenician sailor on the ship that rescued Evan/Evandros

Dexion—Sicilian slave boy, capture by the Carthaginians

LIST OF MINOR CHARACTERS
IN ORDER OF APPEARANCE

Ares—God of War

Hephaistos—God of Fire and Forge, divine smith

Hera—Goddess of Marriage and Women

Hades—God of the Underworld

Apollo—Sun God; god of oracles, music and diseases.

Hestia—Goddess of the Hearth

King Mentor—king of Pylos

Messenian warrior

Neleos—councilman of Messene

Kallimachos—elderly Messenian philosopher

Kronos—Dark Master

Jengo—Neleos' house slave

Chara—Neleos' daughter

Hekabe—Neleos' wife

Theodoros—juvenile from Messene

Hermes—Messenger of the Gods

Mother Goddess—also known as Gaia; Serpent Goddess

Princess Adrasteia—of Mykenae

King of Mykenae and warriors

Kleitos—proprietor of 'Theagaia' in Korinthos
Jason—Captain of the 'Argo'
Melaina—Goddess; daughter of Kronos
Prometheus—Titan; giver of fire
Pythia—Prophetess of Delphi
Eris—Goddess of Discord
Athene—Goddess of Wisdom
Aphrodite—Goddess of Love
Plato—Athenian philosopher and teacher
Aristagoras—Athenian politician and orator
Phoinix—Athenian youth and student of Plato's
Jelani—Plato's house slave
Skylla—sea monster
Poseidon—God of the Sea
Cyclops/Kyklôps—one-eyed giants
Stymphalian birds—man-eating birds
Queen Antioche—Amazon
Queen's Physician—Amazon

GLOSSARY

Aegis	A layered bronze shield
Agora	The main centre in an ancient Greek city-state. Usually where athletic, artistic, spiritual and political gatherings occurred
Andron	Usually reserved for men only, where the host holds social events such as a symposium and where food and wine was served
Caldera	Is a crater that is formed after a volcano erupts and collapses into itself
Cavea	Where the spectators sat in the theatre according to their place in the social hierarchy
Cella	Inner sanctum of the temple
Doric	One of five classical orders of architecture; a column with no base, a heavy fluted shaft, and a capital with an ovolo moulding under a square abacus
Exedrae	Semi-circular benches
Friezes	A wide central section of a horizontal beam and may be plain or decorated with bas-reliefs
Gigantomachy	The war between the Olympian gods and the giants
Megaron	Large hall or main room; the room supported by columns, the doors providing an opening for light to fill the room, a smoke-hole and apertures under the roof line
Metopes	A square space between triglyphs in a Doric frieze
Metretes	Measurement of liquid. One Metrete is equivalent to 34 litres
Pediment	A triangular shaped gable that sits on a horizontal beam
Peripatos	A covered walkway
Propylaeum	Entrance to a temple
Propylon	See Propylaeum

Stade	The stadion was the oldest event in the ancient Olympic Games. Runners sprinted for 1 stade (192 m.), the length of the stadium
Stoa	A covered walk way or colonnade, usually having columns on one side and a wall on the other
Temenos	A piece of land used as a sanctuary
Triglyphs	A stone block in a Doric frieze, having three vertical channels
Tympanum	Recessed space enclosed by the cornices of a triangular pediment and usually decorated with relief sculptures

AUTHOR'S NOTE

The various locations mentioned in the story were real places and the ruins can be visited today. However, I have taken creative licence on the time-frame by a few centuries. The layout of the city-states travelled to, the type of buildings, usage and description are as accurate as the research collated from print and non-print resources.

Chapter Three

The plight of the Messenians and their servitude to the Spartans did happen, and those who rebelled were killed to quell any further plans of uprising. Why did the Spartans do this? The lands of Messene were considered fertile, with a mild climate and less mountainous terrain that made them suitable for farming. The Spartans wanted this land primarily to increase viable lots for their citizens. To do this, they needed to conquer the Messenians. There were two Messenian Wars, the first in the late eighth century BCE and the second in the middle of the seventh century BCE. As a result, after their conquest, the Messenians were reduced to helots, serfs who worked the land and had to pay their lords—the Spartans—one-half of the produce.

In the second Messenian War was the evolution of the Spartan warrior, male born citizens who were taken from their mothers at the age of seven and taught how to be skilled fighters. It was this warrior caste who fought the Persians at Thermopylae, 300 men, who gave rise to the legend of the battle. In the middle of the fourth century BCE, the Messenians revolted and, with the aid of the Athenian army, settled in Naupactus. Around 400 BCE, the Spartans forced the Messenians from Naupactus; they then resettled in the region of Messene in 396 BCE.

The group of youths mentioned in this chapter were part of a troop called the Krypteia, or the secret police. They were formed to deal with helot revolts, and young Spartans (aged between 18 and 20), served for two years at the discretion of Ephors, leaders and elders of Sparta. They were sent to kill every helot considered to be suspicious or to threaten the Spartan way of life.

Chapter Five

When Neleos leads Evan and the others to his home, there's a scene describing the family's piety and shrines. Household altars were common throughout Greece. Generally, there were two: one devoted to Zeus and the other was to Hestia. It was Homer who first provided details of altars, their importance and their uses. Sacrifices and libations were offered to Zeus, the king of gods and men. Libation was undiluted wine and poured at the altar. Hestia was a domestic goddess, the protector and nurturer of the hearth. The hearth was important to the Ancient Greeks as it provided heat in the winter and fire for cooking. Before a meal, the Greeks offered a bit of food on a plate and placed it near or on the altar, and then they poured a few drops of unmixed wine on the floor.

Slaves like Jengo, an Afrikkan, were a common feature in the wealthier Greek households. They played a large role in Ancient Greek society, as domestic servants, factory workers, shopkeepers, mineworkers, farm workers and as ship's crewmembers. Slaves were, for the most part, prisoners of war, but there were instances in which very poor families sold their children as slaves. The conditions for a domestic slave were better than for those who worked in the mines, or on a ship, though this depended on the attitude of the owner.

The status of women in Ancient Greece wasn't high, and a female slave was at even more of a disadvantage due to her status in the social hierarchy. Female slaves performed a variety of domestic duties, such as shopping, fetching water, cooking, serving food, cleaning, providing child-care and wool working. They were also vulnerable, and often subjected to sexual and physical abuse. Children from such liaisons were disposed of, as female slaves were forbidden from having their own children.

Slaves—men and women—were also prohibited from marrying, as it was only citizens who had that privilege.

Hekabe and the High Priestess would never have been invited to eat with the men, especially in the Classical Greek period. Higher-class women had their own rooms and sometimes buildings separate from the men, who were prohibited from entering them. The "middle-class" had a separate room, and the poorer classes had no extra rooms, with the women either sharing the room or eating their meals outside.

The character Kallimachos mentions Plato and his two commentaries *Critias* and *Timaeus*, which can be found on the Internet in their entirety. It is in these discourses that Plato mentions Atlantis, the political and social structure, hot and cold running water, and the sophistication of the race. With the excavation of Knossos on Crete by Sir Arthur Evans in 1900, and the excavation of Akrotiri on Santorini by the late Professor Spiro Marinatos in 1967, it seems Plato's "story" was more than a moral fable. The descriptions of Plato's Altantis and the archaeological evidence found on Santorini (Ancient Thira) have many similarities; the strongest evidence came when piping for hot and cold water was found at the Palace of Knossos and at the city of Akrotiri.

Chapter Ten

Corinth was a thriving metropolis that rivalled Athens, and was renowned for its signature product and export—the painted black-figure pottery. The location of Corinth enabled it to be a major sea port and trading centre, having access to Italy and the West through the Gulf of Corinth, and access to Crete and the Greek Islands, and to the East via the Aegean Sea.

The city-state was also famous for its prostitutes. The Akrocorinth, a flat-top hill, was the site of the Temple of Aphrodite, supposedly housing one thousand women for the pleasure of men. It was more likely, the women were slaves, captives from wars or purchased by wealthy Greek men and dedicated to the temple as religious offerings. It might be true the sandals they wore did indeed have etchings on the sole saying "follow me", and even if it isn't, the quote has endured for thousands of years.

Chapter Seventeen

Pythia was a name given to the women who served as the Oracle at Delphi. According to various accounts, she was an older woman, though there are vases with images of a young woman holding the position. Where the Temple of Apollo is situated, archaeologists, with the aid of geologists have found a fissure in the ground. After a number of tests, they concluded there were noxious gases that when inhaled caused a person to hallucinate. The room in which the Oracle sat, was built over this fissure, and historians and archaeologists have concluded this gas was inhaled by Pythia, and when she gave predictions, they came out garbled and then were interpreted by the priests. It was the interpretation that was relayed to petitioners.

The site at Delphi pre dates the religion of the Olympian gods and was the sacred site of Gaia/Earth Mother/Mother Goddess. She was revered at the site for thousands of years before, and according to the myth, Apollo fought Python, Gaia's son, and killed him. Thereafter, the site of Delphi came under the realm and worship of Apollo.

Chapter Twenty-Two

Eleusis and the Eleusinian Mysteries did arise from Demeter's search for her daughter Persephone. To make sense of the changing seasons, the Ancient Greeks developed a religious event that both men and women could participate in. The Eleusinian Mysteries began in 1600 BCE and continued until 392 CE, rivalling Christianity. The initiates participated in various rituals, which were secret and still remain a mystery today. The rites were a celebration of Demeter and Persephone's story, how Persephone was taken by Hades to the underworld and then returned to the land of the living. Participants were not allowed to explain what happened, on the penalty of death. However, those who did take part in the mysteries were apparently changed, having a better understanding of life and no longer fearing death.

Chapter Twenty-Three

In Athens, where the concept of democracy was born, the term was not as we understand or know it today. Women, non-Athenians and slaves were not allowed to vote or have a say in the political life of the city-state. The term "democracy" in ancient Athens, was one of privilege, reserved only for the citizens. As such, this entitlement did give the men the ability to voice their opinions. However, if a man was seen to garner too much "power" in the eyes of the citizens, a vote to ostracise them and freeze their assets would be executed. This meant the man in question, and his family, had to leave Athens for ten years and could not access his belongings. In some instances, those who inspired treason or corruption were sentenced to death, as in the case of Socrates.

Chapter Twenty-Eight

Plato, the founder of the Academy in Athens, lived in the fifth century BCE. His teacher was Socrates, who is featured his dialogues, and Aristotle was a pupil of his. His inclusion in the story was essential in establishing the link between his story of Atlantis and that of the Minoan culture, which might have given rise to his writings of *Critias* and *Timaeus*.

Chapter Thirty-Six

The Minoans worshipped the Mother Goddess, and her priestesses were highly revered in their culture. The Minoan women were treated much more equally in society than their latter Greek cousins. They held positions of esteem and were regarded as important citizens, who were closely aligned to the Mother Goddess, as an embodiment of the giving of life. The symbols of the Mother Goddess—the snake and the labrys—were objects used in Minoan religious ceremonies. The snake represented life and death, the renewal of life, just as a snake sheds its skin; and the labrys, the shape much like a butterfly, was a symbol of resurrection. The Minoans were very much in tune with the forces of nature, and did not have temples as the Ancient Greeks did. Trees and caves were used as sites for worshipping the Mother Goddess. The frescos on the walls of the palaces also gives evidence of their love for the sea and nature, which has enabled historians and archaeologists to learn about their religious, communal and funereal practices.

Chapter Forty-Seven

The Amazons were considered mythical, but recent evidence from burial sites in and around the Black Sea have found skeletal remains of women interred with bows, arrows and swords. A nomadic race called the Scythians by the Greeks are more than likely to be the Amazons. Archaeologists have been excavating Scythian burial mounds and found many of them to contain the bodies of women, buried with weapons and horses. DNA testing of the bodies has proven that the women had war injuries just like the men.

Luciana Cavallaro
Perth, September 2017

Mythos|Publications

www.luccav.com

For more information, visit our website.
Be sure to sign up to our e-newsletter to keep up to
date with our latest releases, news and upcoming events.

ABOUT THE AUTHOR

Historical fiction novelist and a secondary teacher, Luciana Cavallaro, likes to meander between contemporary life to the realms of mythology and history. Luciana has always been interested in Mythology and Ancient History but her passion wasn't realised until seeing the Colosseum and the Roman Forum. From then on, she was inspired to write Historical Fantasy. She has spent many lessons promoting literature and the merits of ancient history. Today, you will still find Luciana in the classroom, teaching and promoting literature. To keep up-to-date with her ramblings, ahem, that is meanderings, subscribe to her mailing list at http://www.luccav.com.